HE NEEDED MORE THAN COURAGE TO SAVE HIM NOW

Nathaniel Gill did not want to believe his ears when he heard the verdict of the military court: "You are guilty of desertion—and sentenced to death by firing squad."

How could his own fellow soldiers kill him after he had fought so bravely and well at Lexington and Concord, at Bunker Hill, at Valley Forge, in victory and defeat? How could his superiors not take his word that he'd had permission to visit the woman he loved for a few nights of well-earned peace and pleasure?

But now he had to believe what was happening, as he saw the muskets leveled at him, and heard the officer's voice loud and clear in the still air:

"Ready. Aim. FIRE . . ."

Great Reading from SIGNET

FORGED IN BLOOD

(Americans at War #2)

by

Robert Leckie

A SIGNET BOOK

NEW AMERICAN LIBRARY

TIMES MIRROR

Publisher's Note

This novel is a work of fiction. Names, characters, places, and incidents are either the product of the author's imagination or, if real, are used fictitiously.

NAL BOOKS ARE AVAILABLE AT QUANTITY DISCOUNTS WHEN USED TO PROMOTE PRODUCTS OR SERVICES. FOR INFORMATION PLEASE WRITE TO PREMIUM MARKETING DIVISION, THE NEW AMERICAN LIBRARY, INC., 1633 BROADWAY, NEW YORK, NEW YORK 10019.

SIGNET TRADEMARK REG. U.S. PAT. OFF. AND FOREIGN COUNTRIES
REGISTERED TRADEMARK—MARCA REGISTRADA
HECHO EN CHICAGO, U.S.A.

SIGNET, SIGNET CLASSICS, MENTOR, PLUME, MERIDIAN AND NAL BOOKS are published by The New American Library, Inc., 1633 Broadway, New York, New York 10019

First Printing, February, 1982

1 2 3 4 5 6 7 8 9

PRINTED IN THE UNITED STATES OF AMERICA

To my dear friends
Tom and Laura Benton
with belated thanks
from "Mr. Guilfoyle"

Author's Note

This novel contains numerous historical personages lesser known than, say, George Washington or Sir William Howe. To identify them for the reader, an alphabetical listing of all real characters has been provided at the end of the book.

THE BLOODBORN

(Americans at War #1)

When King William's War began in 1689, it was the opening round in the Anglo-French struggle for worldwide colonial supremacy, a conflict that was to rage for seven decades on battlefields from India to the shores of North America. In the colonies it became a series of savage border clashes between the French and the English. In 1690 a French and Indian raiding party massacres the inhabitants of Schenectady, New York, among them Lieutenant Benjamin Gill and his pregnant wife, Abigail. In her death throes, Abigail gives birth to a baby boy who was christened Jedediah by Magistrate Jonathan Clarke, who has found the child in the smoking ruins of the village.

Vowing vengeance, Clarke takes Jeddy Gill to Boston to live with his sister and brother-in-law, Tom and Agatha Cowlett. While Jed grows up, Clarke joins his old sailing friend, Sir William Phips, in the capture of Port Royal and an illfated expedition to Quebec. Through Phips, Jonathan meets Martha St. John, Phips's ward, on whom Jonathan has his own designs. Jonathan and Martha marry, incurring the powerful Sir William's wrath. He sees to it that Clarke finds no employment in Boston, and the couple is forced to move to the frontier settlement of Deerfield in Massachusetts, along with the Cowletts, who have adopted Jedediah Gill. Martha gives birth to a daughter, Rachel, who becomes Jed's childhood playmate.

On the night of Rachel's thirteenth birthday, she is seduced by Jed, who is now fifteen. On that same night, Deerfield is destroyed by the French and the Indians. The Clarkes and the Cowletts are killed, but Rachel escapes, while Jed is taken captive by an Indian named Half Moon. Jed is taken to the village of Caughnawaga near Montreal, where he is adopted into the tribe as Half Moon's brother.

During his three years of captivity, Jed befriends Father Rale, a Jesuit missionary, and falls in love with Half Moon's beautiful sister, Redbud. He also makes an enemy of the powerful warrior Howling Wolf, who vows to kill him. Redbud, who is pregnant, tells Jed of Howling Wolf's plot and helps him to escape in time to warn the rebuilt village of Deerfield of another French and Indian raid against it.

Jed is overjoyed to find Rachel still alive; they marry and go to the island of Nantucket for their honeymoon. On their return to Boston they decide to live there and open a tavern. The tavern prospers and becomes one of the city's social centers, attracting patrons such as Samuel Vetch, one of the leaders of the second expedition against Port Royal, in which Jed plays an outstanding part.

Jed is also with Vetch on a second ill-fated expedition to Quebec. Before he sails, he witnesses the flogging of a British soldier, which fills him with hatred for British oppression. It also arouses the fierce spirit of independence implanted in him by Jonathan Clarke, the foster uncle whom he idolized. Jed helps Daniel Quinn, an Irish soldier in the British army, to escape from the cruel British captain who ordered his brother flogged. Jed sends Daniel to a tavern in Springfield, Massachusetts. In Quebec, Jed boldly denounces the timid British admiral and general in command of the invasion force and exposes Jared Ankers, a boyhood enemy, as a French spy. Nevertheless, the expedition withdraws in disgrace.

There ensues a period of tranquility in which Rachel gives birth to four children: Malachi, Micah, Mordecai, and Martha. But fighting erupts again in the war against the Abenaki, brought about by attacks on Massachusetts settlers by Indians encouraged by Father Sebastien Rale, Jed's friend during his captivity in Caughnawaga. Jed seizes his musket again, unaware that Redbud has gone with their son, Red Deer, to the village of Norridgewock, which is Father Rale's headquarters. Half Moon goes there, too, and leads the raids against the settlers. Redbud is brutally killed by Massachusetts soldiers; her dying words to Jed are to take care of Red Deer. In the attack on Norridgewock, Jed is unable to prevent the murder of Father Rale. But he saves Red Deer's life. Half Moon escapes.

By 1740, when King George's War breaks out, Jedediah Gill is one of the most prosperous men in the colony. In addition to the tavern, he owns lumber forests, a shipyard, and a fishing fleet. But he is still motivated by an unquench-able hatred of the French and the Indians, so that in 1745 he accompanies his son, Captain Micah Gill, on an expedition to Louisbourg. While Jed fights, Micah is captured by Indians and condemned to death by the French. He is saved by an Indian who turns out to be his half-brother, Red Deer. Red Deer also helps the colonists capture the Grand Battery, the key to the defense of Louisbourg, which surrenders after its loss.

Red Deer has married Kathleen Quinn, the daughter of the Irish deserter, Daniel Quinn. They have a son whom they name Daniel Quinn Red Deer Gill. In 1753, as the cataclys-mic Anglo-French struggle nears its climax, Daniel Gill sets out to make his fortune in the Ohio country claimed by the British. There he meets George Washington, a young major of Virginia militia, and saves his life. Daniel joins Washing-ton in a mission against the French in the Ohio country; both narrowly escape death.

The two are together when Washington attacks the French in the skirmish that triggers the French and Indian War, the climactic conflict in the long struggle for colonial dominion. They are also at the Monongahela under Braddock, where Colonel Washington's leadership saves the British army from annihilation.

By 1759, when Britain mounts the third expedition against Quebec under General James Wolfe, Jedediah Gill is sixty-nine. But he still burns with hatred of the French and their Indians, still thirsts to avenge the murders of the Clarkes and the Cowletts and of the parents he never knew. Over Rachel's objections, he joins the invasion force that sails up the St. Lawrence. His sons, Micah and Dr. Malachi Gill (who is Wolfe's personal physician), are also there.

In Quebec, the Marquis de Montcalm confidently prepares the city's defenses, aware that if Quebec falls, so also does Canada. But Montcalm's problems are aggravated by the cor-ruption of the colony. A crowd of crooks and grafters led by Intendant Joseph Bigot have been bleeding Canada white. Bigot is notorious for his love of gambling and beautiful women, chief among them his mistress, Madame de Pean. However, he and his accomplices are suspect in Versailles, and a commission to investigate their conduct is being formed. Obviously, Bigot desires the destruction of the colony to cover up his crimes. And he is the friend of Governor Vaudreuil, who detests Montcalm.

After the British land, they are defeated in a series of battles unwisely ordered by the impatient Wolfe. As September begins with the danger of the river freezing, it appears that the third attempt on Quebec has also failed. Wolfe becomes ill, but is nursed back to health by Dr. Malachi Gill.

Intendant Bigot is distraught to hear of his impending arrest. He prevails upon Madame de Peán to allow herself to be captured so that she may use her charms to get into the presence of General Wolfe. There she is to offer to show him the secret path from the Anse du Foulon leading up to the Plains of Abraham inside Montcalm's ring of steel. In exchange for this, Wolfe is to take them back to Britain with him. Madame de Peán is captured. She seduces Micah Gill, who takes her to Wolfe. The deal is made, but Wolfe refuses to make it in writing.

In a climactic battle on the clifftop, Micah Gill leads his picked force in routing the French guarding the Plains. In the ensuing battle, the French are defeated, and Wolfe and Montcalm are mortally wounded. So is Half Moon, who entered the battle thirsting to kill his renegade brother. Instead, he dies in Jed's arms, forgiving him with his last breath.

Now Jedediah Gill goes with his sons to the cliff overlooking the St. Lawrence. They pass a tearful Madame de Pean, who brings Bigot the terrible news that Wolfe is dead and that his verbal promise of protection is now useless. In a rage, Bigot strikes her and rushes for sanctuary in Vaudreuil's home.

Reaching the cliff above the Basin, Jedediah Gill is exalted. At long last, he has lived to see the French driven from the continent and his parents avenged. With Micah and Malachi at his side, the first valiant offspring of the fighting family he has founded, Jedediah Gill sinks to his knees and dies.

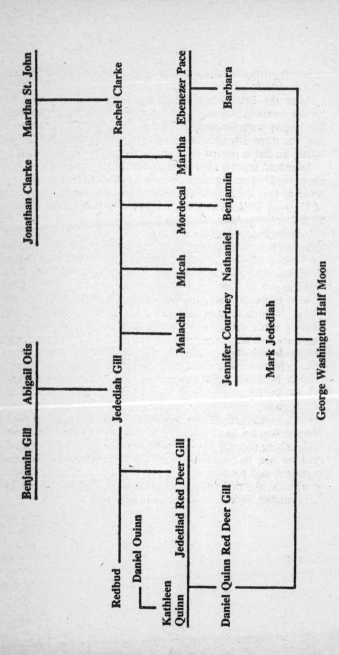

Chapter One

Daniel Quinn Red Deer Gill sat in the splendid coach which his relatives had sent to the Boston docks to carry him to the home of Rachel Gill, the widow of his grandfather. Daniel had been home in Virginia after the adjournment of the first session of the Continental Congress when he had received a post informing him that she was dying. At once, he had taken ship for Boston, and now, riding through the city's streets, he was surprised to see what a great metropolis it was.

Daniel was also impressed by the air of tension he sensed in Boston. Red-coated British regulars patrolled the streets. People hurried about their business with set, guarded faces. Every street corner seemed inhabited by an angry speaker haranguing a sullen mob. Again and again he could hear the words "liberty" . . . "tyranny" . . . The words reminded him of Patrick Henry's magnificent speech in the Virginia House of Burgesses. Leaning forward on the silver-headed blackthorn stick which his grandfather had given him, Daniel Gill recalled the words of Henry's splendid peroration.

"There is no retreat but in submission and slavery!" he had thundered. "Our chains are forged. Their clanking may be heard on the plains of Boston! The war is inevitable—and let it come! I repeat it, sir, let it come!

"It is in vain, sir, to extenuate the matter. Gentlemen may cry, 'Peace! Peace!'—but there is no peace. The war is actually begun! The next gale that sweeps down from the north will bring to our ears the clash of resounding arms! Our brethren are already in the field! Why stand we here idle? What is it that gentlemen wish? What would they have? Is life so dear, or peace so sweet, as to be purchased at the price of chains and slavery? Forbid it, Almighty God! I know not what course others may take: but as for me, give me liberty or give me death!"

1

Daniel remembered how the House had been seized by a shocked silence. But it was the silence of a long ocean roller making for the shore only to break with a thunderous crash. So also was that stunned silence broken, in wave after wave of thunderous applause. And Daniel had joined the other burgesses on their feet, shouting again and again:

"Liberty! Liberty! Liberty!"

Daniel felt the coach he was riding in slowing, and his grip on his cane relaxed. He looked out the window and saw it had stopped outside what appeared to be the finest brick mansion on a street of many such fine mansions. The black crepe on the door told him he had come too late. Rachel Gill was dead.

A footman in the sea-green livery of the Gill family jumped down from the box and opened the door. Daniel Gill alighted and strode up the front steps through an open door and into the hall, where he handed his stick and hat to a black servant.

Barbara Pace was standing in the drawing room where her grandmother's body lay in a big black-lacquered coffin. It reminded her of the time when she was a girl of eleven and there were two coffins in the drawing room. Barbara's mother and father had drowned in a storm off the Jersey capes. Their bodies had been recovered and brought home for burial. How Grandma had mourned for her daughter! She sat alone by the coffin each night, groaning: "Martha! Martha!" She had grieved for her even more than when Grandpa died up in Quebec four years later.

Barbara was surprised that so many of the leading people of Boston and the colony as well had come to pay their last respects to her. Of course, Grandma was the widow of the legendary Jedediah Gill, she thought, but even so—with the city so divided and so many hatreds raging unchecked . . . She had been genuinely surprised to see the Courtneys there. Of course, Joel Courtney had worked with her uncles against the Sugar Act; but of late, he had begun to emerge as one of the city's leading Tories.

A tall bronzed man with high cheekbones dressed in a dark-green coat with tan breeches came into the room. He walked straight toward her, bowing.

"Miss Pace?"

Barbara nodded graciously.

"Daniel Gill, at your service."

"Cousin Daniel!" Barbara exclaimed, embracing and kissing him. "How good of you to come so fast. How did you do it? Never mind, here—I want you to meet the family." Holding his hand in hers, she led him toward Dr. Malachi and Micah Gill, who were talking to Micah's son, Nathaniel. "These are your uncles and your cousin, Natey, Daniel," she said in a proud voice. Amid exclamations of pleasure, they shook hands.

"You look just like your father, Dan," Micah said. "I would have known you anywhere. I served with Red Deer at Louisbourg, you know. He saved my life."

"I know. He used to talk about it."

"Are you hungry?" Malachi asked. "There's plenty of food and drink over there," he said, pointing to a sideboard.

Daniel shook his head, glancing with interest at a blond woman in a light-blue velvet gown standing there beside a heavy man in a silver satin coat. Barbara followed the movement of his eyes, and saw Amanda Courtney gazing at her expectantly. Excusing herself, Barbara went to her side.

"So good of you to come, Mrs. Courtney," Barbara said.

"We are so sorry for your troubles, Joel and I," Amanda replied, moving away from the sideboard. "Of course, your grandmother was always known as the Widow Gill. But she was a great lady in her own right." Amanda declined a glass of punch offered her by a black servant carrying drinks on a silver tray. She ran a hand over her silken blond hair, her full breasts straining against the high-cut bodice of her gown. Amanda turned to stare momentarily at her husband, Joel, who stood by the sideboard greedily devouring food, downing glass after glass of port while dabbing repeatedly at his mouth with a huge white linen napkin. Good Lord, Amanda thought, he had that silver satin coat and scarlet waistcoat made for him six months ago, and they're already too tight! He's digging his grave with his teeth! Well, she thought with a mental shrug, maybe that can't come too soon, either.

"The funeral is on the nineteenth," Barbara was saying.

"Oh goodness, what a pity," Amanda said. "Joel has business in Salem on the nineteenth and he wants me to go with him."

"Quite all right, Mrs. Courtney. We know that your heart will be with us. And it was so good of you to come today."

"I only just found out yesterday. I hope you don't mind my not wearing black. I don't own any mourning clothes, and there was no time to have a gown made."

"What you are wearing is entirely appropriate. After all, my grandmother was eighty-three and there is really no need for an outpouring of grief. She lived a full life."

"Indeed she did. And it was so wise of you to prolong the mourning period. With Boston practically cut off from the rest of the colony the way it is, news doesn't travel too fast."

"Yes. That was why Micah and I decided to wait a week before we buried her." Barbara pointed to Daniel talking eagerly to Malachi and Micah. "That's my cousin, Daniel Gill. The southern branch of our family. He has extensive holdings in Virginia. He was a delegate to the Continental Congress last fall. We sent him a post that Grandma was dying. A pity she died before he could get here. But we're all delighted he came. None of us northern Gills had ever seen him before."

"So thoughtful and kind of him to hurry up here like that," Amanda said, studying Daniel with interest. "He is a handsome man," she murmured. "And those cheekbones. He looks as though he were carved out of marble." She paused. "He ... he doesn't have Indian blood by any chance?"

"He does indeed," Barbara said proudly.

"But ... ?"

"My grandfather was a prisoner of the Caughnawagas for four years," Barbara said succinctly.

"Oh, I see," Amanda murmured, turning to study Daniel again with a startled look in her blue eyes. "Well, Miss Pace, I really am so sorry for your troubles. Oh, my goodness, there's your cousin, Benjamin, just coming in. I must speak to him." Daintily lifting her skirts, Amanda hurried toward a tall, dark man in a coat of laced, blue broadcloth who was speaking to her husband at the sideboard.

Barbara watched her go with unveiled contempt and amusement in her dark eyes, thinking: I wonder if Amanda Courtney really believes that no one in Boston knows of her relationship with Dr. Benjamin Gill? Actually, the only one in town who doesn't is Joel Courtney. Money, food and drink—that's all he thinks of. And judging from the size of his household and his stomach, he's got a lot more than he needs. Why did he bother to take a beautiful young flirt like Amanda to wife if he didn't plan to take her to bed, too? He didn't need a wife. No one expected Amanda even to try to be a mother to Jennifer Courtney whose own mother had died. Barbara had heard that Jennifer hated her stepmother openly, living only for the day when she would come of age. Maybe Jennifer would marry Nathaniel. No, that didn't really seem possible. Not anymore. Not after Joel Courtney had emerged as one of Boston's leading Loyalists, and the Gills had stuck by the cause of freedom. Barbara was still surprised that Amanda and Joel had even bothered to pay their last respects to her grandmother. Maybe it was the buffet that attracted Joel, she thought wryly.

Barbara also smiled to herself when she saw her cousin Dr. Benjamin Gill, talking to Mrs. Courtney. Where did Benjamin get the money to buy Amanda the jewelry that seemed to be the price of her boudoir? Those pearls she's wearing must be worth a few hundred pounds. And Paul Revere was in the tavern a week ago describing the silver pendant set with opals that he was making for Ben. But wasn't Ben broke? Didn't he gamble away the fortune Uncle Mordecai left him? But he did have such beautiful manners. Benjamin Gill was so polished and urbane it was hard to believe that he was an American.

Barbara was surprised to see her young cousin Nathaniel arguing heatedly with Joel Courtney. On such an occasion as this! She wondered what it could possibly be, and tried to sidle closer.

"It is with great regret, Nathaniel," Mr. Courtney was saying, "and especially under these circumstances, that I must tell you that you are not to call on my daughter Jennifer anymore."

Nathaniel was stunned. He swallowed and stared at Courtney as though he had announced Jennifer's death. "But, why?" he blurted out. "What have I done to Jenny? What have I done to you? I always thought our families were on good terms."

"They have been, yes. But I cannot condone your association with those rioters and vandals who call themselves the Sons of Liberty."

"What's wrong with them?"

"This is not the occasion to detail their crimes. You must be perfectly aware of their transgressions. Against the Crown

. . . against private property . . . against the persons of their neighbors who do not share their pernicious notions . . ."

"What of the transgressions of the Ministry?" Nathaniel burst out angrily. "Against liberty . . . against our right to govern ourselves . . . against our property and our privacy with a bunch of ruffians in uniform rammed down our throats. We were born free, weren't we, Mr. Courtney? All men were born free, and they are everywhere in chains."

"Please, Nathaniel," Courtney said in a tired voice. "Please do not quote Rousseau to me. I heard you quoting him to Jennifer the night before your grandmother died. And the pernicious bilge of that troublemaker Locke. And John Stuart Mill. All of those rabble-rousers. They seem to have gone to your head, young man. I don't believe Harvard has been very good for you." Nathaniel's mouth flew open and his dark eyes blazed. "Please, Nathaniel, I do not wish to create a scene," Courtney continued, lowering his voice. "Not here. But I have heard from my own daughter's lips those inflammatory phrases of yours. Ministers of murder . . . enemies of liberty . . . military executioners . . ."

"That's because she happens to agree with me!"

"That is not yet exactly the case, thank God. But I admit, young man, that your powers of persuasion are bringing my daughter dangerously close to them. That is why I am forbidding you to see her or to come to my home." Joel Courtney turned to return to the sideboard. "If you do, Nathaniel, I am afraid I will have to have you arrested."

Barbara Pace watched the color draining from her cousin's face. He closed his eyes, clenching his fists and rocking gently on his heels. Momentarily, Barbara thought Nathaniel might faint, but then he recovered himself and went over to speak to Dr. Joseph Warren. Signaling to the black steward to replenish the sideboard, Barbara joined her uncles listening to their newfound nephew describing the Continental Congress.

"Well, Micah," Daniel was saying, "you might have been able to say that the Congress was moderate to conservative last fall. There weren't many radicals like Sam Adams or Patrick Henry. Most of them were moderates like John Jay or James Duane of New York, or your own John Adams. There were a lot of conservatives, too—rich men like the Rutledges of South Carolina or Joseph Galloway of Pennsylvania or Charles Carroll of Maryland. I think Carroll owns more land than any other man in America. More than my friend George Washington. And Carroll told me he had no intention of breaking with Britain. Why, Edward Rutledge went so far as to say the attitude he feared most in America was the low cunning and the leveling principles of New England."

"Oh, he did, did he?" Malachi snorted angrily. "What else could you expect from a man who owns fourteen thousand slaves?"

Daniel smiled. "Well, Uncle Mal, your own John Adams told me the same thing."

"Then what made them so radical?" Barbara asked.

"Your people. When Paul Revere came galloping into town with the news that you defied Gage and set up your own Provincial Congress, it was like lighting a fire under us. Then when the Suffolk Resolves were read out it was so quiet in the hall you could hear a pin drop. What language! Why even Charles Carroll—he's Catholic, you know—agreed with condemnation of the Quebec Act. He said it was one thing for the king to grant recognition to the Catholic church in Canada, but another to recognize French civil law. We agreed that it was a threat to American civil liberties. So we adopted the Resolves without changing a comma. Incendiary language and all. By the way, who wrote them? Sam Adams?"

Micah shook his head grimly. "All of us had a word or two to say. We're fed up."

"Yes," Malachi said quietly. "And I can tell you, Daniel, that we're being realistic about it. We're preparing for war." Daniel Gill's blond eyebrows rose, and Malachi continued. "Before we dissolved ourselves, we voted fifteen thousand pounds for munitions. We organized the militia into 'minutemen' under three generals and we set up a Committee of Public Safety under that gentleman over there," he said, pointing to a slender man in a sky-blue satin coat talking to Nathaniel. "Dr. Joseph Warren."

"What are you doing with the munitions?" Daniel muttered. "I hope they're not in town."

Malachi shook his head. "Oh, no, they're out in the country. General Gage gave us good warning. Last February he sent an expedition out to Salem to recover the guns and powder our people have been taking from British forts. Well, the lobsterbacks didn't find anything—but they came close. So we moved the stuff out to Lexington and Concord."

"Good," Daniel said, and then catching sight of Amanda Courtney talking to Benjamin Gill near the sideboard, "Who's the lady in the blue gown?"

"Amanda Courtney," Barbara said, open disapproval in her eyes. "She's married to the heavy man at the sideboard. Would you like to meet her?"

Daniel nodded, his blue eyes twinkling, and Barbara snorted, "Daniel, there's more of my grandfather in you than I realized."

"Oh, come on Babs," Micah said, "take him over to her. Malachi and I want to speak to Ben, anyway."

Frowning slightly, Barbara led them toward Amanda and Benjamin. Amanda glanced up with interest as they approached, smiling coquettishly when Daniel was introduced. Benjamin barely suppressed a scowl as he moved away to talk to his uncles.

Micah watched his approach warily, and Malachi said softly, "Tarnation, Mike, the way you look you'd think Ben was Judas Iscariot."

"It could be," Micah muttered. "There's something about Ben I don't trust. He's just a little too suave. Mordecai was like that."

"Yes, when he wanted something. Usually your money. It was really providential, Mordy dying like that. It would have been most unpleasant to have pressed charges against our own brother."

Benjamin came up smiling urbanely. "How are my favorite uncles?"

"Except for the fact of your grandmother lying there in that pine box," said Malachi, "I guess we couldn't be better."

Lowering his voice, Benjamin said, "I hear the stores have been moved to Lexington and Concord."

"Where'd you hear that?" Micah asked sharply.

"From General Putnam."

"Oh," Micah said, relieved. "I just thought it might be from someone who shouldn't know. It's true. Sam Adams and John Hancock are out there in charge of hiding it."

"Where?" Dr. Gill asked easily, keeping an eye on Amanda. He did not like the gaiety of her conversation with his cousin.

"Barrett's house."

"You mean the militia colonel?"

"Yes, Jim Barrett."

"He lives in Lexington, doesn't he?"

"No, Concord."

"Oh, yes." Benjamin glanced at Amanda again. She was taking a sip from Daniel's glass! With a gracious bow, he made as though to return to her side, until Micah asked a question.

"Did you hear anything about a royal frigate from England arriving last night, Ben?"

Ben shook his head silently, struggling inwardly to conceal his desire to depart.

"There's a pretty persistent rumor that Gage got new orders. Get-tough orders. The colony is to be crushed. Members of the Provincial Congress are to be arrested and the munitions seized."

Dr. Gill suppressed a yawn with a delicate movement of his lace-cuffed hand to his lips. "Oh, come now, Uncle Mike—that sounds a bit hysterical. After all, you said yourself Sam Adams and Hancock are out of town. So is John Adams. The only one here is Dr. Warren over there—and I doubt that Gage would move against anyone as popular and powerful as Warren. He got a real scare after he tried to seize the stuff over the river. He didn't like to see four thousand armed and angry farmers piling into Cambridge."

"What about us?" Malachi asked.

"Piffle. Gage move against members of the Gill family? He'd be butting his head against the pillars of Boston society. Especially with Grandma lying there in that big box."

Micah and Malachi pondered silently for a moment. Then Micah shrugged and said, "You're probably right. Anyway, Ben, let us know if you hear anything about any new orders."

Dr. Gill nodded and glided to Amanda's side. Daniel and Barbara had just left her and were talking to General Israel Putnam and Dr. Warren.

"So you like Indians?" Benjamin murmured, taking a glass from a servant with a tray.

"How do you mean?" Amanda countered, watching him warily over the edge of her glass.

"You know who I mean. My cousin Danny. You seemed

fond of him. He's part Indian, you know. One part Caughna-waga, one part Irish and two parts English."

Amanda giggled. "Maybe it was the Irish part I liked. They're supposed to be devils with women, you know."

"I'll show you who's a devil with women," Benjamin muttered, setting his glass on the sideboard, watching Joel Courtney approaching with Amanda's fur-trimmed wrap. "Are you going to be alone tonight?"

Amanda nodded. "Joel has a business meeting with General Gage." Benjamin's sardonic eyebrows rose, and Amanda said, "The general has received orders to crack down. Joel thinks he's going to arrest the leaders of the rebellion."

"Rebellion?" Benjamin repeated, momentarily shocked.

"That's what they're calling it in London, now. Anyway, Joel thinks he'll declare the leaders rebels and try them for treason."

"With attainder to follow?"

"Yes."

"Very clever of that scheming hulk of a husband of yours. I swear, Joel can smell out a profit even faster than a petit four. So he wants them declared attainted and forced to forfeit all their possessions which he will then buy from the Crown for a song."

"Yes," Amanda said quickly. "Now, be quiet—here he comes. And don't make any noise coming up the back stairs."

Dr. Benjamin Gill nodded. Turning to greet Joel Courtney with a charming smile, he exclaimed, "Joel, dear friend, you must give me your tailor's name. That waistcoat, really—I've never seen one so handsome before."

When Dr. Benjamin Gill made his weekly reports to Lieutenant General Thomas Gage, he arrived in the uniform of a colonel of light infantry. It was this that he wore—powdered white wig, gold-braided tricorne, ceremonial sword and all—and with pleasure, as he followed a red-coated orderly into the general's chambers.

General Gage did not arise. Spies, he believed, were worthy of no honors: their only reward was money.

"Well, Dr. Gill?" he asked in a curt voice.

"The Committee of Public Safety has moved its store of munitions from Salem."

Interest gleamed in Gage's eye and his voice became more civil. "Where to?"

"Lexington and Concord."

"Any particular place?"

"Yes, most of it is hidden in the home of Colonel James Barrett."

Gage snorted. "Colonel, eh? Yankee Doodle giving himself airs again." He paused. At the back of his brain a tableau formed: the Monongahela . . . Braddock down and dying . . . the Indians howling and screeching . . . himself wounded . . . Colonel George Washington taking command, riding in Indian dress among the broken and fleeing British soldiery, rallying them . . . "General Buckskin" Gage had called Washington derisively . . . God, how Tommy Gage hated colonial officers . . . . "We'll see how Yankee Doodle and his rabble in arms will stand up to British regulars," he said grimly.

"You're going after them, sir?"

"Indeed I am." Gage pointed to a gold-sealed document on his desk. "I've got new orders from the Crown. The colony is to be crushed. Members of the Provincial Congress will be arrested and placed on trial. The munitions are to be seized. Thieving rabble," Gage muttered. "Most of their powder and arms was stolen from the king, anyway." He looked up at Dr. Gill. "Do you know where I can lay hands on the Adamses and Hancock?"

"They're out of town, sir. Sam and Hancock are in the Lexington–Concord area. John is somewhere farther west."

"What about Warren?"

"He's in town, sir. I saw him this afternoon at my grandmother's wake. But, surely, sir—you don't mean to move against Dr. Warren?"

"Why not?" Gage countered irritably.

"Far be it from me to give advice to a general and a governor, but it seems to me that Dr. Joseph Warren is a bit too powerful and popular to be thrown into a Boston jail."

"Are you suggesting that I disobey the king's orders?"

"Not at all, sir," Benjamin Gill replied easily. "I am merely examining the consequences of such a move. It might provoke a mobilization of minutemen two or three times larger than the last one."

"Looks like they all cleared out," Gage grumbled. "I wonder if they were warned." He glared at Dr. Gill. "Did you see anyone else of importance at the wake?"

"Well, there was General Israel Putnam. But he said he was leaving town right away."

"My God," Gage murmured, "now they're calling themselves generals. That old fraud Putnam takes a few Indian scalps and fancies himself another Alexander."

"Now that I think of it, sir," Dr. Gill went on, "there *was* a big fish there. Daniel Gill of Virginia. He was a delegate to the Continental Congress in Philadelphia."

"Related to you, Doctor?"

Benjamin flushed. "Y-yes," he stammered in a rare moment of confusion. "My . . . my cousin."

"Rather thin blood in your veins, eh, Doctor? Well, there's nothing I can do about Daniel Gill. He's a Virginian. My orders are to make Massachusetts howl. Scatter this nest of levelers and sad parliamentarians and the rest of the colonies will fall all over themselves jumping through the king's hoop. Anything else to report?"

Dr. Gill hesitated momentarily, thinking of his uncles. But then it occurred to him that one day soon they might be willing to pay for their safety, and he decided not to mention them.

"Well, Doctor?" Gage repeated impatiently.

"Ah, nothing more sir."

The general lifted his hand in dismissal, but Dr. Gill did not move. "My, ah, honorarium, General?" he inquired in a suave voice.

General Gage grimaced and pulled open a desk drawer. He drew out a small, heavy sack and flipped it across his desk to Dr. Gill. It landed with a rattle. Benjamin picked it up, opened it and calmly poured its golden contents clattering on the desk. He stacked the thick coins in neat piles and began to count them. "Forty guineas, just right," he said coolly, getting to his feet. "Hard cash is so much more satisfying than paper money," he murmured, slipping the sack into a coat pocket. "Don't you agree, General?"

Benjamin Gill pressed a shilling into the palm of the black stablehand who led him to the door opening on the staircase leading to the huge fireplace in Mrs. Courtney's bedroom. Dr. Gill had changed his military attire for the blue broadcloth coat and tan breeches he had worn at the wake. Stooping to remove his shoes, he went softly up the stairs, carefully opening the well-oiled iron door at the rear of the fireplace and emerging into the bedroom. Amanda gave a little start when she saw him. She was sitting upright in bed wearing a gauzy negligee and reading a newspaper by candlelight.

"These Rebels are so tiresome," she said with a yawn, putting aside the newspaper. " 'Liberty, liberty, liberty'—that's all they can say. I wonder General Gage doesn't have done with it and string them all up."

"Come, Amanda, dear," Dr. Gill called, taking off his coat and taking an object from one of its pockets. "I have a little present for you."

With a cry of delight, Amanda threw back the covers and came running to face him. Benjamin held the object behind his back with one hand, while with the other he gently removed her negligee. He stepped back, panting slightly. "My God, what a body!" he murmured, his eyes devouring her full breasts with the pink nipples firming in the cool air, the curve of her hips and the golden curls nestling in the crotch formed by her beautiful white thighs. "It's you that should be hung, Amanda," he said, his breath coming faster. "You're a menace. You make men mad for you. Make them do terrible things."

"Such as what?" she asked, flushing with pleasure and sucking in her ridged belly.

"You know what. I've just come from General Gage. It's mad and bad and sad, what I'm doing—but, I can't keep away from you. Here," he said in a savage voice, bringing his hand around to proffer a silver pendant studded with opals.

Amanda clasped her hands together and gave a squeal of delight.

"Paul Revere made it for me," Benjamin said proudly, swinging it back and forth to sparkle in the candlelight.

"Oh, Benjie—it's beautiful!"

Benjamin put the pendant around Amanda's neck and fastened it. He stepped back to study it and to drink in her wildly intoxicating nakedness again. She went to a mirror and he studied her from the rear. "Oh, Benjie, thank you, thank you!" she cried, and he came up behind her to seize her in his arms and swing her onto her bed where he pressed his hungry mouth on her fragrant lips, on her nipples, on her navel—even plunging his nose into her pungent secret hair before he parted her white legs and entered her.

"Benjie, be careful of the pendant," Amanda gasped. But Dr. Benjamin Gill's sense of hearing had already been engulfed in the flooding ecstasy of his other senses.

"I don't think we can go on like this, Amanda," Benjamin Gill said. He was lying on her bed in the candlelight with his hands behind his head.

"Why not?" Amanda asked, sliding her small hand down his thigh to seize his inert penis. "Ugh," she said, grimacing. "Mashed potatoes."

"Woman, you are insatiable," Benjamin said in a tone of exasperation. "Will you listen to me? I'm trying to tell you that sooner or later Joel will find out."

"Oh, him! He's too busy making money or stuffing his stomach."

"I don't know. I thought his eyes were sort of watchful this afternoon."

"But what could we do?"

"How would you like to live in England or France? France is beautiful. We could buy a chateau in the Loire Valley."

"With what?" Amanda said scornfully, squeezing his penis again. "You said yourself you couldn't expect anything from your grandmother."

"She hated me," Benjamin said gloomily. "Once, when I was a small boy, she caught me stuffing fish with powder and blowing them up. She called me a little monster and barely spoke to me since. No, all her money will go to Malachi and Micah. Which should just about make my uncles the richest men in Boston." Dr. Gill's face darkened. "I hate them!" he burst out with sudden vehemence. "They accused my pa of milking the family business while they were in Quebec with Grandpa. Uncle Malachi said Pa died of a fever, but I think he and Uncle Mike hounded him to death."

Amanda felt Benjamin's penis rising in her hand and she squeezed it again and snuggled closer to him. "You know, Amanda," Benjamin said, turning toward her, "I've been thinking about Joel's plan to buy attainted estates. My uncles, you know, are members of the Provincial Congress. General Gage told me his orders are to arrest them all and try them for treason. I wonder . . ."

Benjamin felt Amanda's soft little hand on his mouth. "No more talk," she whispered, pulling him toward her.

"You are insatiable," he murmured, rolling over and entering her again.

As he rose toward his climax he heard the door open, a creak on the floor and a voice above him simpering, "Very pretty."

He gasped and freed himself. Amanda screamed and drew the covers up to her neck. Both of them gazed up panting into the sneering eyes and twisted thick lips of Joel Courtney. He dug into his pocket and pulled out a shilling and dropped it contemptuously on Benjamin's bare navel. "Take it," he said, still sneering, "take it and go out and get yourself a good piece of tail."

"Joel!" Amanda screamed, her eyes blazing in indignation. "How dare you!"

"Under the circumstances, my dear," Courtney said drily, "I don't believe you have very much call to be outraged." His face reddened and he took a step toward her. "I should very much like to rearrange that pretty face of yours," he muttered, clenching his fist.

"Careful, Mr. Courtney," Benjamin Gill called warningly, getting to his feet.

"My dear Doctor," Courtney said, his lips twisting again, "I find the noble courage with which you defend your little whore quite touching." He ran his eyes mockingly over Benjamin's naked body, stopping to peer with mock admiration at his crotch. "Having seen your member both rampant and now couchant, my dear Doctor," he purred, "I must admit that you are abundantly endowed. You must have been of great service to my, ah, wife."

"Stop it, Joel, stop it!" Amanda wailed, bursting into tears and covering her ears with her hands.

Fully dressed now, Benjamin Gill came around the bed to confront Courtney. "What are you going to do with her?" he asked quietly.

"If I could, I would like to have the parson burn an ugly little *A* into her forehead. Unfortunately, that would only excite the attention of our sanctimonious fellow churchgoers and perhaps provide dear Amanda with a surfeit of lovers."

"Please be civilized, Joel. Haven't you tortured her enough?"

"You are a cool one, Dr. Gill. You dishonor my name and my house and you stand there and talk as though I were the guilty party. But I will tell you what I will do. Amanda can stay here, if she wishes, receiving food and drink—that is all. Her allowance is cut off as of this moment—and I shall sell her wardrobe and her jewelry." Joel Courtney observed Dr. Gill's eyes straying to the pendant around Amanda's neck, and he said, "*All* her jewelry."

Benjamin flushed and Amanda began to sob softly. She barely noticed when her husband left the room. "Oh, Benjie, Benije," she wailed, "what's to become of me? He's going to keep me a prisoner in this old house and let me curl up and die like a worm."

"No, no, I won't let him," Dr. Gill said, patting her shoulder reassuringly. "Remember what I was saying—about going to France or England?"

Amanda glanced up eagerly with tear-filled eyes. "Do you still mean it?"

"Of course I do. But, first, I must speak to General Gage about my uncles."

"As I understand it, Dr. Gill," General Gage said stiffly, "your intention in informing on these three people is to come into their possessions?"

"That is correct," Benjamin Gill said coolly.

"What of their descendants?"

"In the first place, Daniel Gill has no heirs. In the case of my uncles, a writ of attainder attaints their families as well as themselves."

"But then their estates are forfeited to the Crown."

"In this instance," Dr. Gill said calmly, "I would expect the Crown to waive its claims in recognition of my services."

"Very neat," Gage said sarcastically.

"There are precedents," said Benjamin, ignoring the general's caustic eye. "Particularly during the time of Henry the Eighth. I have spent a good part of the day in the Harvard library studying them. I have also prepared a dossier of my charges against Daniel Gill."

"You are thorough," Gage murmured, reaching for a sheet of foolscap and a quill pen. "Where are these people to be found?"

"At the Gill mansion. In another two hours, they will be

closing the coffin preparatory to moving it to the meeting house for tomorrow's funeral. This was my grandmother's wish."

Gage nodded. Finishing the order for the arrest of the three Gills, he rang for an orderly.

The lid was being lowered on the coffin containing the body of Rachel Gill. Her children and grandchildren filed forward for a final glimpse of the woman who had been so much a part of their lives. Some of the women were weeping softly and there was snuffling among the children, some of whom dug their knuckles into their reddened eyes. Nathaniel Gill's eyes were red, too, but as Barbara Pace had noticed, they were red when he came into the room.

Against Joel Courtney's wishes, Nate had been to see Jennifer. He had found her in the stable behind her house, preparing to mount the box of the handsome black gig her father had given her for her seventeenth birthday. How beautiful Jenny looked on the box, Nate thought with a pang, with her luxuriant brown hair and her calm brown eyes. She had a way with horses, too, Jenny did.

"Jenny," he called softly, and she spun quickly around, the skirt of her blue dress flaring. She gasped. "Natey! What are you doing here? You'll be arrested!"

"Why have you been crying, Jenny?" Nate asked, noticing her reddened eyes. "Is it because you still love me? No matter what your father says?"

"Oh, Natey!" Jennifer wailed, bursting into tears. "What will we do? What will we do?"

Nathaniel drew her to him. He could feel her firm breasts pressing against his chest. Momentarily, he thought of putting his hand on her breast, as Jenny had allowed him to do the night before his grandmother died. But he did not, holding her close instead, kissing her tearstained cheeks and inhaling the fragrance of her hair. His heart ached to think that he might not see her again.

"We could run away and get married," he said.

Jennifer shook her head in despair. "No, we couldn't. You're only eighteen and I'm seventeen. There isn't a parson in the colony who would marry us without our parents' consent."

"We could go south," Nate said stubbornly. "Maybe just as far as New York."

"We can't!" she cried, wailing again. "We can't go *any*-where. The world's about to blow up in our faces. Oh! Why did politics have to come between us?"

"It's not politics," Nate said doggedly. "It's liberty against tyranny. Freedom against slavery."

"Oh, Natey," she said wearily, "please don't go on like that anymore. That's why my fa—" The sound of a coach and horses approaching could be heard on the street. Jennifer's hand flew to her mouth and her eyes dilated in terror. "It's my father! Quick, Natey—you must hide. If he finds you here . . ." Her voice trailed off as she glanced wildly around her. Suddenly she pointed to a door at the back of the house. "In there! It's a stairway leading to my stepmother's room. Nobody uses it. Quick, inside!"

Nathaniel ran to the door and opened it, slipping inside just as a magnificent gilded coach drawn by four matched white horses came sweeping into the courtyard. A coachman rushed up to place an iron step beneath the door, opening it to help the ponderous Joel Courtney alight. He glanced sharply at Jennifer.

"You've been crying?" he snapped accusingly. "What for?"

Jennifer put a twisted handkerchief to her lips and said, "I was thinking of Mommy. Today would have been her fortieth birthday."

"Yes, yes," he said, his tone softening. "April eighteenth. Of course. I should have remembered. Come, my child, don't cry. Tonight we shall dine together and talk about your mother."

Through a keyhole, Nathaniel watched Mr. Courtney put his arm around Jenny and lead her to the front of the house. Nathaniel had began to weep softly himself, and now he burst into tears again at the sight of the lid closing on the face of his beloved grandmother.

"Please, no weeping and wailing," Micah Gill called gently. "You know how Grandma felt about that." Turning to Daniel Gill, he said, "Would you please go for the horses, Dan." Nodding, Daniel left the room.

A few minutes later, the measured tramp of marching feet could be heard on the street. Micah rushed to the window.

"My God, it's the regulars!" he called to Malachi. "They've come for us! Hurry!"

Both men rushed for the door leading to the back stairs. But the other door flew open and a British subaltern rushed inside with drawn sword, followed by a squad of redcoats with sloped muskets.

"Stand where you are!" the subaltern cried.

Micah and Malachi halted. Their families gathered around the coffin shrank back against the wall, watching in horrified fascination while the soldiers came to a heel-clicking halt, bringing their muskets to the ground with a concerted crash.

"By what right do you enter my mother's home in this manner?" Micah cried in a trembling voice.

"On the orders of General Gage, commander of His Majesty's forces in North America. By his orders, I am placing you under arrest."

"On what charge?"

"Treason!"

A gasp came from the relatives around the coffin. Micah lifted a calming hand. "May I see the warrant?" he asked the subaltern.

"I have no warrant, only my orders."

"I see. Has General Gage, then, imposed martial law in Boston?"

"I don't know what you're talking about," the young officer said, becoming flustered. "I have my orders," he said, tapping his breast pocket.

"I am sorry, but I cannot go with you without seeing a warrant. I am an attorney, and I can tell you, young man, that in the absence of martial law, General Gage has no authority to place a civilian under arrest."

The subaltern's face reddened. "I don't know anything about that," he said doggedly, "but I do have my orders. And I intend to carry them out." He turned to the soldiers as though to select the strongest of them to seize the Gills bodily.

Malachi laid a hand on Micah's wrist. "It's no use, Mike," he said, "we'd better go with them."

At that, the subaltern relaxed and asked, "You are Malachi and Micah Gill?" The two men bowed, and the young officer asked, "Where is Daniel Gill?"

A second gasp rose from the vicinity of the coffin and Mi-

cah and Malachi exchanged glances. Barbara shot a quick
glance at the back door and said, "He's not here, but I'll get
him for you." Before the astonished subaltern could restrain
her, Barbara lifted her skirts and ran through the back door,
bolting it on the inside. The subaltern ran to the door and
pulled at it in rage.

"Knock it down!" he roared at his men, and two of the
biggest lowered their shoulders and went crashing into the
door. Pointing his sword at the front door, the subaltern
shouted, "After her!" Four of the redcoats went rushing out
of the room, but they only blundered in confusion around the
unfamiliar corridors.

Barbara, meanwhile, had gone clattering down the back
stairs. She found Daniel standing beside the hearse, talking to
the driver.

"Fly!" she shouted to him. "Fly! The regulars have just arrested Malachi and Micah and they're after you, too."

"Where shall I go?" Daniel called, hurriedly unharnessing
one of the horses.

Barbara pondered for a moment. She was sure Gage would
have the Gill tavern watched, and the Gill business offices on
the waterfront as well.

"Luke Sawyer's," Barbara yelled on a sudden inspiration.
"He lives in the garret over his blacksmith shop across the
street from Gage's headquarters. They'll never look for you
there. Wait until I come to you tonight."

Nodding, Daniel Gill swung aboard the bareback horse
and galloped off.

Luke Sawyer closed the shutters on his garret window before lighting the lantern on the table in the center of the
single room that comprised his living quarters. The light flickered on the grave faces of the four people seated there: Barbara, Daniel, Natey and Seahawk, Sam Adams's faithful
Indian.

"They're in a cell in the guardhouse off the barracks
square," Seahawk was saying. "There's a single soldier
guarding the door with a bayoneted musket at port arms."

"By Jesus, we ought to go in there and get them," Luke
Sawyer said, plopping down beside Barbara and running his
big hands through his thick red hair. "There's still a lot of
Sons of Liberty in town. We could—"

Daniel Gill shook his head. "You'd be like lead soldiers storming a hot stove," he said quietly. "You might get into the barracks square, but you'd never get out. There's two full regiments of regulars over there, Luke. We've got to think of a better way." He stared at Seahawk. "How were you able to find them?"

The Indian grinned. "Easy. I go there almost every day. I was Gage's guide at Ticonderoga. They know me." He winked. "The quartermaster sergeant sells me the king's rum cheap."

Daniel Gill smiled. He began to whistle "Yankee Doodle" slowly, thoughtfully. Then he snapped his fingers. "That's it!" he exclaimed. "I'll overpower the guard, take his keys and let them out."

"But how?" Barbara asked, puzzled. "He'd never let you get close to him."

"Simple. I'll be wearing Seahawk's clothes. I'll be Seahawk."

"Good idea!" Luke cried. "But lemme do it. I'm stronger than you are, Mr. Gill."

"Possibly," Daniel said with a dubious smile. "But I don't think you can play the Indian as well as I can." Glancing at Seahawk, he spoke to him in dialect, "Do you agree, brother?"

Seahawk's eyes widened in astonishment, and Daniel chuckled. "I am a Mohawk like yourself, Seahawk," he said. "My grandmother was a full-blooded Caughnawaga. Now, if you don't mind going outside on the landing, Barbara, Seahawk and I will exchange clothes." Blushing, Barbara arose and went outside. Daniel studied Seahawk dubiously. "It is now April, my brother, have you taken your annual spring bath yet?"

Seahawk grinned and shook his head. "Too cold. Wait till May." Still grinning, he took off his greasy, vermin-infested buckskin shirt and leggings and gave them to Daniel, who put them on gingerly. "At least I'll smell right," he muttered. Then Daniel stuffed his blond hair up under a coonskin cap which had a tail suggestive of an Indian's braided hair. Taking soot from Luke's stove, he rubbed it into his exposed neck and face.

"Now all I need is a flask of rum," he murmured, looking at Luke. "Got one handy, Luke?"

"Sure do," Luke said with a grin, tugging a flask from his pocket.

Daniel took it and went to the door, opening it. "You can come back in, Barbara," he called.

Lifting her chin, Barbara returned to the room, starting in surprise at the sight of Daniel, glancing at Seahawk seated proudly at the table in Daniel's fine brown velvet coat. She stared anxiously at Daniel. "You'll be careful?"

"I'll try," Daniel said, and went downstairs to the street.

Outside the blacksmith shop, he tilted the flask to his lips and took a long pull. Swaying drunkenly, he crossed the street to the barracks. He thought momentarily of how his father, Red Deer, used to tell him of how he had pretended to be a drunken Indian when William Vaughn and Uncle Micah captured the Grand Battery at Louisbourg. Staggering up to the two sentries at the gate, he hiccuped loudly. He began to chant an Indian war song.

The sentries chuckled and one of them said, "Tyke any scalps tonight, mate?"

Daniel pretended not to hear, staggering past them into the barracks square. He could hear them laughing behind him. Across the square, Daniel saw a sentry with poised musket. Tilting the flask again, he drank in full view of the soldier. Then he stumbled toward him.

"Here, you greasy old beggar," the sentry called in a low voice. "Give me a swig of that, will yer?"

Daniel nodded and swayed toward him with outstretched flask. The soldier put out his hand to take it, and Daniel flicked the hot burning liquid into his eyes, catching the blinded man's falling musket with one hand and striking him hard on the jaw with the other. The man sank silently to the ground. Daniel bent over him and quickly removed the keys from his belt. Fitting them one by one into the lock, he finally found the right one, swung the creaking door open and dragged the senseless soldier inside.

"Who's there?" someone cried in alarm, and Daniel recognized Micah's voice.

"Shhh!" he whispered. "Don't make any noise. It's me, Daniel Gill."

There were low exclamations in front of him. Stooping, Daniel felt around with his hands and found someone's arm. "Is that you, Micah?" he whispered.

"No, it's me, Malachi," a voice answered.

"I'm over here," Micah called softly.

Daniel screwed his eyes shut, trying to accustom them to the darkness. Opening them, he saw with dismay that each of the brothers was chained to a wall. Peering at the ring bolt to which Malachi's chains were attached, he saw that it was merely screwed into the wall. He tried to turn it with his hands, but could not move it. He thought of the soldier's bayonet, removed it from the musket muzzle, slipped it through the eye of the ring bolt and began turning it. It gave, slowly at first, but then easier and easier. Luke Sawyer probably would have pulled it out, he thought wryly, but this way was quieter. Finally, the bolt came free.

"Here," Daniel whispered to Malachi. "Get the chain up your sleeve as soon as you can. Keep the wrist-iron hidden under your cuff."

Nodding in the dark, Malachi took off his coat and slipped the chain up his sleeve, while Daniel worked swiftly on Micah's bolt. Handing it to Micah, he began divesting himself of Seahawk's buckskin clothes.

"Put them on," he said to Micah. "You're going to be Seahawk, Sam Adams's Indian friend. Take this flask, too. Remember when you and my father were at the Grand Battery in Louisbourg? And he played the drunken Indian? That's what you're going to do. And try to remember that war chant he told me he taught you."

Quickly, Daniel began to strip the unconscious soldier of his uniform. Thank God he's nearly as big as I am, he thought. And thank God Grandpa Quinn was a British soldier. Daniel grinned in the dark, remembering how his grandfather used to march him around the tavern in Springfield. "Left turn . . . right about . . ." Putting on the uniform, he noticed that the soldier was beginning to stir. Seizing Micah's shirt, he tore it into strips, tying one around the soldier's mouth and binding his legs with the other. Then he snapped an open wrist-iron around his wrist, thus chaining him to the wall.

"Why don't you kill him?" Micah whispered. "It'd be safer."

"Ah, he's only a poor private," Daniel murmured. "Besides, a private's life in the British Army is worse than death." He stooped to grasp the soldier's musket. "Now, this is what we'll do. Micah, you go staggering out the gate chanting that war song. Do what you can to make the sentries laugh. I'll be right behind you with Malachi, acting like I'm marching him somewhere under orders. All right?"

Both men nodded, and Daniel slowly opened the door. Micah slipped out. "He-uh, he-uh," he began to chant, stopping to take a drink from the flask before swaying toward the gate. Daniel followed with musket at port arms, Malachi marching in front of him. Micah stumbled between the two sentries, turned to make a mock salute—and sprawled forward on his face. The sentries laughed, until they heard the clank of Micah's chains as he struggled erect.

" 'Ere, 'ere, wot's all this?" one of them cried, stepping toward Micah with lowered musket.

"Look alive, there, you chumps!" Daniel Gill whispered in a hoarse voice as he came up behind them. "Bleedin' corpril o' the guard's right behind me!"

Both men straightened instantly. Their muskets flew to their shoulders, their faces became set and a fixed, faraway look came into their glazed eyes. They hardly noticed as Micah disappeared and Daniel marched Malachi into the engulfing darkness around Luke Sawyer's blacksmith shop. At once, the three men tiptoed up the stairs. They opened the door of Luke's quarters slightly and slipped inside one by one.

"Pa!" Nathaniel Gill yelled, rushing to embrace his father. "Uncle Malachi! They're here, Barbara—they're here!"

Barbara whirled. She had been at the stove with Luke, helping to fry some cornmeal bread. She saw the three men and rushed at them, bursting into tears. Nathaniel was mildly surprised to see his cousin hug Daniel Gill and kiss him full on the mouth before she threw her arms around her uncles.

"Malachi! Micah! I can't believe it. You're free! You're free! Danny, Danny—how did you do it?"

"Like I said I would," Daniel said with a grin. Then he pointed to the chains still fastened to his uncles' wrist-irons. "Think you can knock them off, Luke?"

"Them little doodads?" Luke sniffed. "By Jesus, I kin bite them off. C'mon downstairs, gentlemen." Daniel and his uncles followed Luke down a steep, rickety staircase into the smithy. Luke lighted a stub of a candle and placed it on a workbench. "Here, Mr. Gill, put your arm up here." His chain rattling, Micah laid his wrist on the bench. Luke peered at the wrist-iron, flouncing his thick red hair. "Alls it needs is a hand sledge," he muttered, rummaging among the tools on the bench. He picked up a small sledge hammer and said casually to Micah, "All right, Mr. Gill, you just close your eyes."

Micah did, and Luke swung the hammer.

Wham!

The iron snapped open and Micah cried aloud in pain, rubbing his wrist. Malachi came over and felt it. "It's not broken," he murmured, gazing sourly at Sawyer. "Do you have to hit it that hard, Luke? I mean, you might miss."

"Me? Never!"

Malachi hesitated. "Surely, there must be some other way."

Luke Sawyer shook his head. He was obviously enjoying himself. "Naw. Ain't but only the one way. Bein' you're a doctor, you should know there's only one way o' doctorin' a disease. Me, I'm a blacksmith, an' I know that that there's cast iron and there's only one way you kin bust it open, which is to hit it dead center an' damn hard. So, if you'll just put your arm up here, Doctor . . ."

Reluctantly, his chain rattling, Malachi lifted his arm into position and closed his eyes.

Wham!

Again, the iron snapped open and there was a cry of pain. Now it was his own wrist that Malachi examined gingerly. "It doesn't seem broken," he muttered.

"Course not," Luke crowed. "By Jesus, Doctor, when I'm aimin' a hand sledge, I could bust a iron open if it was around a baby's head."

Daniel chuckled. "All right, men—let's get back upstairs. We haven't much time."

Barbara was seated at the table talking to Nathaniel. She looked at Daniel as the men came back into the room. "How long before they find they're gone?"

"I don't know. They change the guard every four hours. It's three in the morning now. We've got at the most an hour." He looked at Luke. "Can you get horses?" he asked anxiously.

"No, Cousin Dan," Nathaniel broke in. "That won't do. General Gage began fortifying Boston Neck a few days ago.

There's no way my pa and Uncle Malachi can get out of town. Either on foot or on horseback."

Daniel frowned. "What about the harbor?"

"That's worse," Luke said, frowning gloomily. "The fleet's got this town bottled up like a pudding in a bag. A farmer was in here yestiddy told me you don't dare move a bunch of carrots across the water without the fleet pouncing down on you."

Daniel Gill snapped his fingers. "A funeral!" he cried joyfully. "A hearse!"

"My God!" Micah exclaimed, his eyes lighting up. "I'll bet we can get away with it!"

"Uncle Micah!" Barbara wailed. "You're not thinking of taking poor Grandma out of her coffin?"

"I am indeed. And she'd be the first one to suggest it, too. And laugh about it. C'mon everybody, we'd better head for Ma's house."

With reverent hands, Malachi and Micah Gill lifted the frail body of their mother out of the coffin and laid it gently on a sofa. Kneeling, they both kissed her cold forehead. "We're sorry, Ma," Micah murmured, "but I know you'd understand. Barbara will see that you get buried proper." Barbara rubbed her reddened eyes. But she did not cry. At such times, a Gill did not weaken. She watched quietly while the men shouldered the coffin. Then she went up to her uncles and kissed each one fondly on the cheek; after which, again to Daniel's astonishment, she kissed him full on the mouth. Without another word, the men passed out the back door to the stable. Finding the hearse, they put the coffin up on it, while Luke began to harness a team of horses.

"You sure that thing's big enough for both of us?" Malachi asked, eyeing the pine box dubiously.

"Sure," Micah said. "It was built for Pa, you know—but we buried him on the cliff above the St. Lawrence."

"What'll we do for air?"

Daniel grinned. "I thought of drilling holes in the lid, but we don't have time. Instead, I'll just shim it. That'll give you about a half inch of air between the lid and the coffin."

"Doesn't sound like much," Malachi grumbled. "Well, Mike, you might as well get in first."

"After you, my dear brother."

"I'm the oldest, and I get my choice—the top."

"As an attorney, I can say with authority that the law of primogeniture applies only to inheritance. Not to convenience. You first."

"As a doctor, I can say that if I have to lie beneath you in those filthy, stinking, flea-infested buckskins, I will surely die of asphyxiation."

Daniel grinned again. "All right, you two, quit the quarreling. The horses are ready. Here," he said, pulling a shilling from his pocket, "I'll settle it." He flipped the coin.

"Tails," Malachi called, swearing in vexation when it came up heads. With a sour look at his brother, he crawled into the bottom of the coffin. Micah climbed on top of him, and Luke and Daniel swung the lid into place. Daniel mounted the box and seized the whip and reins. Nathaniel clambered up beside him.

"You and Seahawk better go back to the smithy," Daniel said to Luke. "Not finding you there, the British might think it suspicious."

Luke nodded. "Good luck," he said, scratching his red head and watching anxiously while Daniel called to the horses and the hearse swayed slowly out of the stable toward Boston Neck.

Daniel pulled up on the reins when he reached a barricade guarded by a squad of redcoats. Three Tories from town were with them: probably to identify fugitive members of the Provincial Congress, Daniel guessed.

"Where you headed?" one of them called.

"Roxbury Cemetery," Daniel replied, putting a reassuring hand on Nathaniel's knee.

"Who's in the box?"

"The Widow Gill."

"So the old battleaxe finally croaked, eh? By Jesus, what a devil's brood she brought into the world."

"More like rattlesnakes," another of the Tories grunted, and Daniel saw Nathaniel's eyes blaze and elbowed him gently in the ribs.

"Who are you?" the first Tory shouted.

"I'm her nephew. Daniel Gill. From Virginia."

"How come there's just the two of you? Don't none of them Gills care about the old lady?"

"General Gage arrested the Gill brothers last night," Daniel replied. "They told their families to stay home. But the burial couldn't wait. She's been six days dead."

"Who's the lad?"

"My name is Nathaniel Gill, and I'm not afraid to honor my grandmother."

"Cheeky, eh?" the second Tory growled. "Maybe a little tar and feathers and a ride on a rail will teach him some manners."

"Aw, come off it, Ned—the lad's just lost his grandma." The man studied Daniel. "Mind if I take a look at that coffin?"

Daniel shrugged, feeling goose pimples running up his spine. He laid his hand on the whip. "Not at all," he murmured.

The Tory went around to the back of the hearse. Suddenly, Daniel heard him choking. He returned gasping, holding his nose. "Oh, my Jesus, she's every bit of six days dead! The old crone's beginning to stink already." He waved Daniel on. "Get her out of here! Get a move on before we all get sick!"

Wordlessly, mentally thanking God for Seahawk's indifference to dirt, Daniel Gill snapped his whip gently over the horses' heads and the hearse lurched forward and began to roll slowly onto the mainland. A half hour later, it stopped and Daniel and Nate jumped down to run to the back of the hearse and lift the lid of the coffin.

Micah raised his head, looking at them with dazed eyes. He began gulping down lungfuls of fresh air. "I think I must have passed out two or three times," he mumbled, and then, thinking of his brother beneath him, he scrambled quickly out of the box.

"He's unconscious!" he cried, kneeling beside the coffin and trying to pull his brother erect. Daniel jumped up beside him and lifted Malachi free. They laid him beside the road and began rubbing his face and arms. Malachi's eyelids fluttered. He opened his eyes, staring into those of his brother. "It was your feet that smelled the worst," he said, struggling weakly up to a sitting position. Chuckling, Micah slapped him on the back and hauled him erect, while Nathaniel led the hearse to the side of the road and began unharnessing the horses.

"Now, we can make some time," Daniel Gill grunted, swinging aboard a bareback mount.

"Where are we going, Dan?" Malachi asked, still sucking in air by the mouthful.

"Lexington. To the home of Parson Jonas Clark. Sam Adams and John Hancock are staying there."

Chapter Two

General Gage was determined to seize the Rebel stores of arms in Concord, and also to secure the persons of Sam Adams and John Hancock—and perhaps of those accursed escaped Gills as well—at Lexington. On April 18, 1775, he ordered that his best troops—the grenadier and light infantry companies—from six hundred to eight hundred men—be placed "off all duties until further orders." His orders vaguely stated that this was to be done so that these soldiers could learn "new evolutions." Gage also sent mounted officers out to patrol the road to Concord to keep it free of Rebel couriers.

That night, the elite troops were softly wakened in their barracks by their sergeants. They slipped on their full marching packs and stole out of their barracks past their sleeping comrades. Marching to Boston Common, they formed ranks. To their dismay, they saw that their commander was to be fat Lieutenant Colonel Francis Smith. Colonel Smith was famous in the British Army of North America for his indifference to the welfare of his troops, and still more for his callous disregard for horseflesh. His men saw at once that the horse which their obese leader sat with such obvious boredom was already gasping.

Colonel Smith was satisfied that his command had mustered unobserved, even though they had marched in full view to the Common and formed before him with a clatter of clicking heels and musket butts striking the pavement. He was unaware, of course, that Dr. Joseph Warren had already been informed by Paul Revere that General Gage was collecting whaleboats. Obviously, a secret expedition was to be mounted—probably by water.

"If they go out by water," Revere had said, "show two lanterns in the North Church steeple. If by land, one. Either way, that will rouse Charlestown. Meanwhile, Bill Dawes and

I will be riding to warn the countryside." Dr. Warren had agreed, and William Dawes had ridden west while Revere, booted and swathed in a greatcoat, had himself rowed over to Charlestown. At eleven o'clock, he sprang aboard a waiting horse.

Behind him, two lanterns began to glow in the steeple of the old North Church.

Daniel Gill was lying asleep on the first floor of the home of Parson Clark when he was awakened by the staccato beat of hoofbeats hurrying closer. He rolled over to wake his uncles to either side of him, just as a great voice shouted:

"The regulars are out! The regulars are out!"

"Who goes there?" a guard called.

"Paul Revere."

"Stop making such a bloody noise. You'll wake everybody up!"

"Noise! You'll have noise enough before long. The regulars are out!"

Daniel Gill and his uncles rushed outside. "Are they coming this way?"

"Where else?" Revere cried scornfully. "You'd better fly, all of you. Adams and Hancock, too."

Slapping his horse on the withers, Revere galloped off into the dark. At once, the three Gills dashed back into the house to dress. "Run and wake Sam Adams," Micah cried to Nate, and the youth rushed upstairs. Within minutes, the two most sought-after Rebels in North America had come clattering down the stairs. Daniel smiled to himself at the contrast between them: Hancock, jaunty as ever, despite the danger, dapper as always in an elegant silver satin coat with blue waistcoat; Adams, his mismatching clothes in customary disarray, his shirt and waistcoat plastered with food, but his half-mad eyes gleaming in his great shaking head. The two made at once for their horses.

"Where are you going?" Daniel asked.

"Farther west," Adams replied. "And you?"

"We're staying here. There may be a fight."

Adams nodded, smiling gaily. "What a glorious morning this is!" he cried, and when Hancock shot him a puzzled look, he added, "I mean for America." Bowing, the two cantered off across a meadow.

"Those Adamses are all alike," Micah Gill said drily. "Sam or his cousin John, they're both great with the tongue or the pen. But they don't seem to like the smell of gunpowder."

"That's the way with all rabble-rousers," Daniel said, leading the way toward their tethered horses. "All right, propagandists, if you will. They're expert at getting a war started, but they don't seem to like to get mixed up in it. Take Thomas Jefferson of Virginia. You should hear him denounce the Ministry! What eloquence! Sheer artistry, I tell you, but now it looks like war has come, I'll wager you won't find Mr. Jefferson swallowing gunsmoke. No, it'll be the quiet ones like my friend George Washington who'll be risking their flesh. Well, to each his own, I guess," he said, swinging up on his horse. "Now that the Adamses have done their part, it's time for the Gills to do theirs."

"What's that, Cousin Dan?" Nate inquired, reining in beside him.

"Fight."

The whaleboats had put Colonel Smith's elite force ashore at Lechmere Point in knee-deep water. When the men waded ashore, their pipe-clayed white breeches were stained with mud and their red coats were sodden from the waist down. They had to wait two hours in the chilly darkness for their rations to come, after which Colonel Smith blundered into a backwater of the Charles River, forcing them to wade waist deep before they reached dry ground and the road to Concord twenty miles away.

Almost immediately, they heard bells ringing on either side of the road. Shots came from behind stone fences. At once, Major John Pitcairn of the Royal Marines rode up to Colonel Smith.

"I don't think there's going to be much of a surprise," he said grimly. "In fact, it may turn out to be one on us. I would suggest, sir, that you send an express rider back to Boston for reinforcements."

Wheezing almost as loud as his gasping horse, Colonel Smith pondered for a moment. Then he nodded his head slowly and called for a courier. Meanwhile, his disgruntled men plodded on. They had been on their feet for five hours, bent beneath perhaps sixty pounds of equipment, made heavier by their recent soaking. But their muskets were not wet. They had held them high while wading ashore. Their brightly burnished barrels and gleaming socket bayonets were easily visible to the handful of American patriots drawn up on Lexington Green.

When the four Gills trotted into Lexington Green, they found a force of about seventy men there under Captain Jonas Parker. Daniel Gill studied them sourly. They were typical American militia: some wore hunting shirts, others wore homespun or shapeless towcloth smocks. Their weapons were a hodge-podge of firelocks and flintlocks dating back a hundred years. Many of them, however, held the same ten-pound "Brown Bess" musket carried by the enemy regulars, having been given them to keep during service for the Crown against the French and Indians, or having received them from their fathers. There was no semblance of discipline among the minutemen when the Gills arrived. They strolled about the green chatting or swapping jokes, or sat on a rail fence silently chewing straws. At length, Captain Parker formed them on the green inside a triangle formed by three roads. The road to Concord was at its base, and Parker's men were about a hundred yards above it. The four Gills stood in the front rank, watching intently while the sun danced on the points of the enemy bayonets.

Daniel squeezed Nathaniel's arm. "Got any goose pimples yet, Natey?" Nate shook his head and Daniel chuckled and said, "They'll come, but don't let 'em bother you."

Now the advance guard under Major Pitcairn was in full view, a red-and-white mass moving inexorably toward the green.

"There are so few of us," one of the militiamen said, his voice breaking. "It is folly to stand here."

"The first man who offers to run shall be shot down," Parker cried.

Below them, Major Pitcairn shouted: "Form line of battle!" At once, the rear ranks ran forward at the double to line up with the others and form two sections three men deep.

"Hurrah!" the regulars shouted. "God save King George!"

"Stand your ground!" Captain Parker ordered. "Don't fire unless fired upon. But if they want to have a war, let it begin here!"

Some of his men shook their heads and walked away. Nathaniel ran after them begging for spare cartridges. He came back just as Major Pitcairn spurred his horse forward and shouted:

"Lay down your arms, you damned Rebels, and disperse!"

Daniel Gill walked over to Parker. "The situation doesn't look good," he said calmly.

"I agree," Parker said reluctantly. Cupping his hands to his lips, he shouted: "All right, men, disband—but take your weapons with you."

"Lay down your arms!" Pitcairn cried again. "Do you hear me? Lay down your arms, you damned Rebels!"

Shots crashed out. No one seemed to know where they came from. But a stricken British soldier cried out in pain and Pitcairn's horse, grazed by two balls, screamed and reared.

"Fire, by God, fire!" a British officer shouted, and a volley of shots ripped into the Americans. A farmer standing next to Daniel sighed and slumped to the ground, a British ball through his eye.

Below, Major Pitcairn was frantically trying to silence his men. "Soldiers, don't fire! Soldiers, keep your ranks! Form and surround them!" Pitcairn waved his sword downward again and again to emphasize his orders, but his soldiers ignored them. They were like hungry lions released from a cage. Taunted for months by the despicable Yankees, subjected to a brutal discipline, driven to distraction by their frustrating march, their blood was up—and they unleashed still another volley into the minutemen.

A ragged return crashed down from the green above them. But no one was injured.

"God save the king!" the redcoats roared, and lowered their bayonets to charge.

The militia fled. The Gills sought to disengage from the frightened mob, but they were carried off like flotsam on the crest of a flood. Daniel looked behind him, struggling to get clear of a trio of burly farmers running from the green with flailing arms. He saw brave Jonas Parker standing alone on the green. He had fired once and been wounded. He stood wavering like a stricken bull in the arena, trying to reload.

Daniel Gill winced when he saw the flashing British bayonets disappear in his body.

"Not much of a fight," Nathaniel Gill sniffed, riding west to Concord beside his cousin.

"Maybe not, but it was big enough to start a war," Daniel said. Turning on his mount, he called to Micah, "How many men did we lose?"

"I heard eighteen—eight dead and ten wounded. The British just had that wounded soldier."

"We never had a chance," Nathaniel said in a bitter voice. "I hate running the first time I get shot at."

"It wasn't your fault. Don't worry, Natey, you'll get another crack at them. Maybe even today."

They both fell silent, riding slowly westward with the sound of Colonel Smith's triumphantly squealing fifes and rattling drums growing fainter in their ears. As they neared Concord, they could hear bells ringing. Riding into town, they saw minutemen and some old men and boys from an alarm company hurrying west to cross the North Bridge over the Concord River. They followed them, clattering over the bridge and cantering on to Colonel Barrett's house. There they dismounted and went to see Barrett.

"Glad to have you with us, Micah, Malachi," Barrett said, shaking hands. "We were delighted to hear of your escape. A pleasure, indeed, Major Gill," he said to Daniel. "We can use someone with your experience. We're all amateurs here, you know."

Daniel bowed graciously. "War has a way of making veterans pretty quick," he said. He noticed minutemen lugging barrels into the woods and glanced inquisitively at Barrett.

"Powder," the colonel explained. "Most of the stores have been sent farther west, but we've still got a lot to hide. The barrels of flint, ball and cartridges are being hidden in my attic. They're covering them with feathers."

"Think that will fool the lobsterbacks?"

"Maybe not," Barrett said grimly. "But I don't plan to let them get this far, anyway."

"How many men do you have?"

"About four hundred. I'm going to put my main body on a ridge overlooking the North Bridge." He glanced at Micah.

"Captain Briggs is down with the ague. You still think you can command a company?"

"I sure do," Micah said, grinning.

"And you, Dr. Gill—would you be good enough to set up a surgery with Dr. Williams?"

"Be proud to, if he'll let me borrow his instruments."

"I'd like to use your boy as a courier, Micah. What's your name, son?"

"Nate."

"Good. You ride with Major Gill and me, Nate."

The trio rode off toward the ridge, past a minuteman plowing furrows in which muskets and light cannon were laid and then plowed over. As they rode, they could see a column of smoke spiraling into the sky above Concord.

The smoke came from Rebel gun carriages found in the Town House. The grenadiers had quickly set them ablaze inside, and then just as hurriedly doused them for fear of setting the Town House afire. Then the carriages were dragged outside and set afire again.

"Remember, I want no looting or destruction of private property," Colonel Smith had warned Major Pitcairn. "General Gage's orders are very strict on that score. And the soldiers are to be courteous to the townspeople while searching, even if they are Rebels. They must give a receipt for whatever they take, and everything they eat or drink must be paid for." Major Pitcairn saluted, and Colonel Smith waddled inside Wright's Tavern to refresh his enormous paunch.

Pitcairn stood in the street watching the red-coated grenadiers moving from house to house. He burst out laughing when a huge redcoat backed apologetically out of a house, his hands raised to defend himself against an old woman brandishing a mop. He did not smile, however, when another grenadier emerged from a house drinking from a jug of cider crooked over his shoulder.

"You pay for that, soldier?" Pitcairn snapped.

"Ow oi did indeed, sir. Bleedin' arf a bob the old witch wanted."

A young officer strode up to Pitcairn and saluted. "We found a hundred barrels of flour, sir, and sacks of ball weighing about five hundred pounds."

"Good. What did you do with them?"

"Threw them in the pond, sir," the young man said with a smirk of satisfaction.

"You idiot! You didn't stove in the barrels and slash the sacks? The Yankees'll only come back and grub them up. Why, I ought to—"

A courier rode up, crying: "Captain Laurie requests reinforcements, sir."

Frowning, Major Pitcairn whirled and strode into the tavern.

Captain Isaac Davis, the gunsmith from Acton, had formed his company in the foremost place on the ridge when Colonel Barrett arrived with Daniel and Nathaniel Gill. "It's Abner, Abner Hosmer!" Nate cried in delight when he saw the little drummer boy standing beside Captain Davis. "I haven't seen Abner since we went fishing together last summer." He dismounted and ran to the youth's side. "How about a little 'Connecticut Half-time,' Abner," he called. Young Hosmer shook his head. "Got more serious calls to play today, Nate," he said somberly.

"Look, look!" one of Davis's men shouted, pointing to the smoke curling into the sky above Concord. "They've set the town on fire!" Angry cries arose from the militia, and one of them whirled on Colonel Barrett to shout in a fierce voice, "Will you let them burn the town down?"

Barrett shook his head. "Captain Davis, you may proceed to the defense of the town," he said, and then, raising his voice for all the minutemen to hear him, "You are not to fire unless fired upon." By twos, the militia came silently down the ridge, moving to the tap of Abner Hosmer's drum, Captain Davis at their head.

At North Bridge, Captain Laurie watched them approach with uneasy eyes. Laurie had sent four companies of light infantry over the bridge and up the road to Barrett's house. Three other companies remained behind, guarding the bridge. Laurie did not like the look of the column of Rebels coming silently and unhesitatingly down the steep hill above him, and it was then that he sent back for reinforcements.

They were coming, but because the two companies of grenadiers from Concord were led by fat Colonel Smith, they were coming very slowly. Major Pitcairn trudged beside them in an agony of impatience. It was only a half mile to the bridge, he knew, but at Smith's funereal rate of speed it would take a half hour to reach it.

Now Captain Laurie was attempting to re-form his three companies on the Concord side of the bridge. But the men were strangely unruly. They milled about sullenly, seeming to resent the commands of their unfamiliar officers. Why, oh, why, Laurie thought bitterly, did General Gage ever put the light infantry under this crowd of strangers: "volunteers," thrill-seekers and snot-nosed subalterns out for a lark. Why, some of them didn't even come from the elite flank companies. They wore the silly cocked hat of the line.

Assembling the officers, Laurie told them: "I want you to rake the Rebels with a steady fire. Have the front ranks fire, peel off and run to the rear to reload, while the next rank fires, peels off and does the same. Understand?" The officers nodded, and returned to the men.

"Commence firing!" Laurie called.

A volley crashed out, but most of the shots fell short in the river. One of them whistled past the ear of Captain Timothy Brown.

"God damn it, they are firing ball!" Brown yelled.

The second rank fired. This time they had the range. Captain Isaac Davis fell dead, and little Abner Hosmer flopped onto the earth beside him, a ball through his brain.

"Fire, fellow soldiers!" Daniel Gill cried. "Fire, for God's sake!"

The first full American volley of the Revolutionary War crashed out, followed by shrieks and screams among the kneeling redcoats. Three of them slumped to the ground lifeless and nine more were wounded. As though with one mind, King George's finest soldiers rose to their feet and ran. Leaving their dead and one wounded man lying on the road, they rushed back to town in disorder.

"They're pulling foot!" Nate Gill cried in delight, raising his musket to fire at the milling red mass disappearing down the road, but Daniel Gill knocked it up in the air with the warning: "Don't waste ammunition." Now the overjoyed Americans were cheering and capering on the hillside. They could see the fleeing light infantry blundering into the grenadiers under Colonel Smith. Now all was confusion among the British.

"After them!" someone cried, and the jubilant Americans

gave chase. But they pursued for only a few yards before breaking ranks. Nathaniel Gill rode forward with his father to where Captain Davis and Abner Hosmer lay. Nate dismounted and knelt weeping beside his little friend. "I can't believe it, Pa, I can't believe it," Nate sobbed, cradling the drummer boy in his arms and draping his body across his horse. "Why, only last summer he was telling me how glad he was his pa was going to send him to Harvard."

Micah said nothing, grimly hoisting Davis's body onto his own mount. Together, they led their horses slowly back to the road where Colonel Barrett was conferring with Daniel Gill.

"I think we ought to go back up on the ridge," Barrett said. "What do you think, Major?"

"Good idea. The British in the town must have re-formed by now. If we stay here, we might get caught between them and the troops coming back from your house."

Barrett nodded and gave the order to return to the ridge. Forming on its crest again, the Americans stared silently down at the red-and-white figures lying sprawled beneath them. Suddenly a gangly farmer holding an axe strode onto the bridge. One of the crumpled figures stirred. Panicking, the farmer struck him with his axe. The man sank back onto the road while the farmer ran away.

Now the Americans heard the tramp of marching feet. The four companies which Laurie had sent to Barrett's house were returning. They had found nothing. They were startled, then frightened, to see their three dead comrades lying on the bridge.

"He's been scalped!" one of them shrieked, pointing at the soldier whom the farmer had struck. "They've turned their bloody Indians loose!"

The redcoats quickened their step. They began to run. Unaware of the Americans massed on the hill to their left, they went rattling and clattering over the bridge and back into Concord. There, a perspiring and irritable Colonel Francis Smith was preparing to leave. He hired carriages to carry his dead and wounded, and at noon he began the return march to Boston.

Lieutenant General Thomas Gage was not pleased to receive Colonel Smith's request for reinforcements. With great reluctance he had ordered Earl Percy to take one thousand men and two cannon and march at once to assist Smith.

"It will leave me a little weaker than I like to be here in Boston," he said to Dr. Benjamin Gill who had been conferring with him at the time. "But it can't be helped."

"I doubt if the Rebels would make a frontal assault on the city," Dr. Gill murmured, then, his eyes gleaming, "No sign of my uncles, yet?"

"None," Gage said grimly. "The sentry on duty at the time says all he saw was that filthy drunken Indian and then someone blew out his candle. If it's any satisfaction to you, Doctor, he's already been court-martialed and will be flogged tomorrow."

"Most efficient," Dr. Gill replied. His sarcasm was lost on General Gage, who was shaking his head in exasperation while running a hand over his thick, graying sandy hair. "They've just upped and vanished," he muttered. "God knows how. It certainly wasn't by water. The commodore swears to that. And nothing's gone out Boston Neck except a hearse from Tucker's livery stable."

"A hearse?" Dr. Gill repeated, his voice rising in interest.

"Yes. They were going to bury your grandmother in Roxbury Cemetery."

"That's strange. Our family plot is in town." Dr. Gill turned to the courier who had brought Smith's message. "Did you see anything of a hearse on the Concord Road?"

"Yes, sir. I saw it standing empty just below Roxbury on the north side of the road. Coffin was empty, too."

Gage gasped and struck his desk with his fist. "Damn their eyes! That's how they got away. In a God damned hearse!" He leaned behind him to give a savage yank on a bellpull. Instantly, a flustered aide rushed into the room. "Call off the search!" Gage snapped, and then turning to Dr. Gill, "I'm going to get to the bottom of this, Doctor—and I want you to get busy finding out who helped them get away."

"Simple, my dear General. It has to be my cousin, Daniel Gill—the one your men couldn't find. He's part Indian, you know, and it was probably nothing for him to pretend to be that wretched Seahawk." He paused, putting the tips of his fingers together and placing them beneath his chin. "He probably got away with them. Drove the hearse, if I'm not mistaken. But someone must have helped get those chains and wrist-irons off my uncles," he said in a musing voice, rising to walk to the window overlooking the street. "But, of course!" he exclaimed, looking across the street at Luke Sawyer's smithy. "It must have been that big blacksmith!" He whirled on Gage. "Why not have the smithy searched, General?"

Nodding, Gage reached for the bellpull again. The aide returned and Gage snapped out his orders. Five minutes later, the aide was back with a triumphant smirk on his face.

"Here they are, sir," he cried, holding up a rattling pair of heavy chains and two broken wrist-irons.

Dr. Gill smiled from his place at the window. "I think I see Sawyer coming up the street right now," he said to General Gage.

"Nate," said Colonel Barrett, "I want you to ride along the south side of Concord Road. I want you to alert every farmer you can. Ride into all the closest hamlets and villages and rouse the milishy. Tell them all that the regulars are marching back to Boston and it's time for a turkey shoot."

Nate nodded and rode off. Even as he galloped into the fields beyond the stone fence bordering the road he saw dozens of farmers hurrying toward the road, muskets sloped over their shoulders. Guessing that word of the Battle of Concord was out, he decided to skip the farmhouses and ride into the towns instead. Each time he galloped into a village or hamlet he had never before seen or even heard of, he rode straight for the alarm bell, jumped off his horse and began ringing it vigorously.

"The war's begun!" he shouted at the astonished and sometimes frightened men and women who ran up to him. "There's been a big fight at Concord. We beat them, by God, we beat the regulars! Made 'em pull foot! They're marching back to Boston on the Concord Road right now. Colonel Barrett wants your militia to join the fun. It's going to be a turkey shoot!"

At once, the militia captains formed their companies and led them marching off to the Concord Road—some of the units as small as a dozen men, some as large as three hundred. Eventually, as many as four thousand men were gathered on each side of the sixteen-mile gauntlet running back to Boston. The British were already subjected to a withering fire by the time Nate rode back to the road on his exhausted horse. Dismounting, Nate seized his musket and ammunition pouches and sat down behind a tree. He bit a paper cartridge in two, poured the powder down the bore— saving a few grains for his firing pan—rolled up the paper and shoved it down afterward followed by the bullet, all of which he rammed home into the breech. All around him he could hear the banging of muskets and the screams of stricken redcoats. He could barely see through the drifting clouds of black powder smoke when he rolled over behind the tree and searched the ragged red column for a target. Selecting a big sergeant kicking a soldier into line, he took careful aim at the point where his white belts crossed. Sighting a little to the right, he squeezed the trigger.

The sergeant slumped to the ground, his heels drumming on the road.

Now Nathaniel Gill lost himself in the exultation of battle. He was hardly aware of his movements. It was fire and reload . . . fire and reload . . . like those around him, he blazed away from behind stone walls or from trees, moving steadily abreast of the retreating, riddled British. Redcoat after redcoat sank to the ground. Eventually, Colonel Francis Smith's hired carriages were piled high with wounded.

"Light infantry!" Smith bellowed, waving his sword and pointing toward the wall behind which Nate was lying with three middle-aged farmers. "Take them in flank!"

At once, a platoon of redcoats came running toward the wall with outthrust bayonets. Nate and his companions fired. Two of them fell. The rest came on. There was no time to reload. Nate and the farmers rose and fled, the British pursuing them with loud cries. Nate heard them coming closer and dropped his musket, marking the elm tree where he let it fall. He ran faster. He heard a horrible scream behind him and turned around to see one of the farmers sinking to the ground with his hands clutching the bayonet in his belly. With a brutal yank, the redcoat pulled it free and took up the chase again. Nate ran still harder, making for the brook where he had fished last summer with Abner Hosmer. There was a cave there in the bank of the stream behind a big rock. Nate heard another hideous scream and then another and then the mocking laughter of the British and their blood-curdling shouts as they renewed their pursuit of their final victim. Terrified, he sprinted for the brook marked by a line of birches. He hit the water going full speed, bounding for the boulder, and squeezed, panting, through the space between the rock and the bank. Holding his breath, he shrank back inside the darkened cave.

" 'E's gone!" a cockney voice called.

"Gorblimey! Where'd the snot-nosed blighter bugger off to?"

" 'E's the one I wanted, too. I saw 'im shoot Sergeant Howland."

"Good on 'im," the second soldier grunted. "Maybe we should give the bloody snot-nose a medal instead of a bayonet. Bugger old Hidewhip Howland. I'm glad 'e's gone. 'Im and 'is bloody whip."

"Here, here, soldiers," a youthful, cultivated British voice called. "What's all this lallygagging about? Form! We must return to the column."

Nate could hear them grumbling under their breaths as they formed ranks on the other side of the stream. He heard their muffled footsteps hitting the ground in unison as they marched back through the fields. Letting out his breath, Nate waited for them to get out of earshot. He squeezed past the boulder and began wading the stream. A muskrat swimming upstream saw him and submerged. Going to his knees, Nate squirmed up the bank. Far off, he could see the moving red blob. They were heading for a barn beside the road. Nate followed them from afar. When he came to the big elm tree he had marked he recovered his musket and pouches. Suddenly he saw smoke curling upward from the barn and then yellow dancing flames breaking through the roof.

All along the south side of Concord Road, Nate now saw burning buildings. But there also seemed to be more Americans firing at the British column. And the British column was no longer a disciplined body of soldiers but rather a disorderly mob. Soldiers broke ranks to ransack roadside taverns and houses for food, setting them afire when they left.

Nearing Lexington, Colonel Smith halted. He rode up to Major Pitcairn. "Please form a rear guard to hold off the Rebels while I re-form my men," he ordered. Pitcairn nodded and ordered a platoon of redcoats into place across the road. They formed square. On both sides, the Americans crept up to them. Nate was among those who hid behind a pile of rails and began scourging the enemy. He could see Pitcairn riding among them on an elegant horse, a fine pair of horse pistols stuck into his saddle holsters. Nate took aim and fired. The ball grazed the horse. It reared and plunged, throwing Pitcairn to the ground. Then the frightened beast jumped the wall and ran toward Concord. Nate was delighted to see his cousin Dan run after him, seize his bridle and swing himself aboard. Nate reloaded and fired again at the redcoats in their square. One by one, they abandoned their post, running down the road to join Smith's main body. Soon the entire rear guard was driven in, and Smith was compelled to resume the march with ragged ranks.

Now the dreadful pace was killing Smith's men. They had been on their feet for more than twenty hours and were dropping from exhaustion, especially the light infantry given the grueling mission of guarding the flanks. But the Yankee fire continued unabated. Terrified, some soldiers broke into a stumbling run. Officers ran around in front of them to threaten them at swordpoint. "Slow down, or die!" they warned.

Suddenly a weak cheer rose from Smith's tormented men. Down the road in front of them they beheld the black hats and scarlet coats and neat white breeches of Percy's force, formed in a hollow square. They stumbled inside it, and sank to the ground, their tongues lolling out of their mouths like panting dogs.

Daniel Quinn galloped down the road, brandishing one of Pitcairn's pistols. "Be careful, men!" he shouted at a party of Yankees climbing the wall. "Watch those cannon. They're probably loaded with grape."

As though to verify his warning, one of the cannon bucked and roared and half the men on the wall toppled backward. On both sides of the road, the Americans now crouched carefully out of sight. Daniel Gill rode back up the road to confer with Colonel Barrett, who had been joined by Dr. Joseph Warren.

"Now's our chance!" he cried, dismounting and nodding cordially to Warren. "We can cut them off. While they're resting, we can send a force down the road to cut off their retreat. If we can force them into the countryside, they'll break up and we can pick them off like singles in a bird hunt."

Dr. Warren shook his head sadly. "It's a good idea, Major Gill, but I'm afraid it would need a trained body of men to execute it. Unfortunately, this we do not have." He motioned toward the farmers in homespun or towcloth arriving at and departing from the battle at their whim. "This is really only a crowd of armed and angry farmers. If we tried a flank march with them on either side of the British, I fear we would be cut to pieces."

Daniel Gill pondered. "I suppose you're right," he said in a tone of disappointment, and then, eagerly: "But couldn't we send a party of axemen down the road to fell trees across their path? They'd wash up against it like water against a dam, and we could tear them apart from both sides."

Dr. Warren shook his head again. "I am, of course, only an apothecary, and you are an experienced soldier, Major. But, still, I know my people. For the same reasons—together with those cannon of theirs—I don't think it would work."

Biting his lip in vexation, Daniel nodded and shifted his attention to the British. Smith's men had risen and formed ranks and the entire force was moving out again in the strictest order, the cannon bringing up the rear.

Once again, the Americans began scourging them from both sides of the road, and once again redcoats sank to the ground. But the British fought back. Not a roadside house was spared now. All were set afire. Again and again, the light infantry sallied into the flanks with lowered bayonets. Once they cornered a party of Patriots leaving the battle and drove them into a house where they bayoneted a dozen of them to death.

Nate could hear their screams. With perhaps fifty other Americans he charged the British coming out of the house. They closed. A redcoat lunged at Nate with his bayonet. Nate dodged away from him. The soldier turned to lunge again, and Nate stuck his musket barrel between his legs and tripped him. Turning the weapon upside down, he jammed its butt into the soldier's face. Then he pulled the man's musket away from him and bayoneted him in the belly. Shrieking hideously, the man clutched his stomach, blood and intestines oozing between his fingers.

A blow on the shoulder sent Nate to the ground. Steel glinted before his eyes and he felt a flash of pain in his nose. The bayonet that barely grazed his flesh continued on to bury itself in the ground. With one hand, Nate seized the musket barrel and with the other he pushed himself erect. He wrenched the musket free of his assailant and saw to his horror that he confronted only a terrified drummer boy. The boy backed off with hands outstretched beseechingly. Nate began to pity him. He lowered the musket. But then he thought of little Abner Hosmer and drove the slender blade savagely into the youth's heart.

And then his own brain exploded in a blaze of white and he sank into a sea of darkness.

Chapter Three

Nathaniel Gill awoke to dazzling sunlight. He opened his eyes, quickly shutting them against the blinding light before opening them again. He was lying with other wounded Americans in what appeared to be a makeshift infirmary in a converted church. He felt a hand on his shoulder.

"So you've finally come to," his uncle Malachi said. "You've got a hard head, young man. You're also very lucky. If that musket butt had hit you an inch higher, you'd be dead."

Nate looked up at his uncle, who was dressed in a blood-stained white smock, and shook his head. At once, he cried out in pain and his hand shot to his forehead. "My head!" he cried in dismay. "It feels like it's inside an iron cask and someone's hitting it with a hammer."

"You'll be all right," Malachi said. "In two weeks, you'll be like new."

Nathaniel felt the bandage, and asked, "How's Pa and Cousin Dan?"

"Fine. But your crazy pa took a ball through the shin and it looks like he's got a permanent limp." Malachi shook his head ruefully. "It must have been the last shot of the battle. That scrap you were in was at Menotomy, you know. Well, we hung on to them all the way from there to Charlestown Neck. We couldn't get too close, after that, though, them being under the guns of their ships. It was just as the last lobsterback was moving onto the neck that your pa got hit. They brought him to me," Malachi said, grinning in recollection. "I got the ball out by pressing down with my thumbs to either side. Popped out just like a pea from a pod. Tarnation, did he yell!" Glancing around the crowded infirmary, Malachi said, "You're in Cambridge, now, Natey. There's a whole American army encamped out there on the plain. And we've got Boston under siege. The war's on for sure now, Nate. We must have killed about a hundred regulars and wounded twice that many more. We had fifty dead ourselves and just a few less wounded." Nate thought of Abner Hosmer and the British drummer boy he had killed and his eyes saddened. "Don't go getting mushy thoughts, Natey," his uncle said gruffly. "You can't make a revolution with rosewater. It takes blood. Now, get some sleep and I'll be back to see you tomorrow."

Nate sank back against his pillow wondering how many more of his friends and loved ones would die before the war ended. Within a few minutes, he was asleep. When he awoke, he saw his father limping down the aisle formed by the rows of facing beds. Micah smiled when he saw his son sit up.

"How you feeling, boy?"

"Fine and dandy, Pa—but I'm sure sorry to hear about your leg."

"Just a scratch."

"Uncle Mal says you'll be limping for life."

"Don't listen to him," Micah snorted, sitting down on the bed. "Being a doctor, I guess he can't help himself. They all diagnose doom. Recommend decapitation for a hangnail. I'll be all right, Natey. Your Uncle Mal says you should be up and about soon. He thinks you won't miss any school."

"School! I'm not going back to Harvard. There's a war on, Pa, and I'm going to 'list till it's over."

"You're going back to school," Micah said insistently.

"Pa!" Nathaniel objected stubbornly. "I've always done what you told me to do. But this time I think I'm right. I'll be nineteen next October. That's plenty old enough to fight. Wasn't Grandpa Gill only eighteen when he was fighting Indians? Besides, the term's nearly over. I won't miss much. I can make it up next fall when the war's over."

Micah shook his head grimly. "The war won't be over that quick. We're in it for fair, now, Natey. Lord North's so-called peace proposal arrived the day after the battle and it just made everybody madder. He said he wouldn't tax the colonies that voluntarily paid their share of the war with France. Imagine! That's like a highwayman saying he'll go easy on you and let you give him your money rather than take it from you. All right, Natey, you can 'list. But for three months only. I want you back in Harvard come October."

"I promise, Pa," Nathaniel said, and his father patted him on the shoulder and limped away.

Nathaniel's next visitor was Daniel Gill. From the somber expression on his face Nate guessed that something was wrong.

"Luke Sawyer's in jail," Daniel said.

"Oh, no!" Nate cried, sitting erect. "What happened?"

"They found the chains and broken wrist-irons in his smithy. Why that big clodhopper didn't get rid of them I'll never know. Anyway, Gage says he's going to hang him. There'll be a token trial, of course, but it'll be on a drumhead. There's martial law in Boston now."

"But, Dan, we can't just stand by and let Luke die!" Nate cried, struggling with his bedclothes as though to get to his feet. "We've got to go in there and get him."

"Take it easy," Daniel said, putting out a restraining hand. "There's no way we could do it. Gage can't get out of Boston by land, but we can't get in, either. We've thought of everything. Your pa and your uncle even volunteered to give themselves up in exchange for Luke. But Gage wouldn't even read their letter. He said he didn't negotiate with Rebels."

Nathaniel sank back against his pillow in despair. "Good old Luke," he murmured, tears coming to his eyes. One of them ran down his nose and he brushed it away savagely. "He was like a big brother to me. I *can't* let them hang him. I've *got* to do something. Even if it means me getting—"

"Now, don't go doing something foolish," Daniel said, watching Nate narrowly. "There's a lot wiser heads than yours trying to think of some way to get Luke back. Dr. Warren, General Ward, General Putnam—all of them."

"Old Put? Is he in command in Cambridge?"

"No. It's still Artemas Ward, but he's pretty sick of the stone. If it comes to another fight, you can be sure Israel Putnam will be in the middle of it. I gave him Pitcairn's pistols, you know. He was sure tickled. You'd think I'd given him the tablets Moses brought down from Mount Sinai." Turning to leave, Daniel said, "Now, you be careful, Natey. Don't try anything rash. You just let the Committee of Public Safety get Luke back. I'll be in to see you again when I get back."

"Where're you going, Cousin Dan?"

"Philadelphia. The second session of the Continental Congress starts May tenth. I hear my friend George Washington is already there, wearing his old uniform. So I sent word to Virginia to send mine up, too."

For days, Nathaniel lay on his back pondering Luke Sawyer's predicament. He became so preoccupied with the plight of his friend that he seldom thought of Jennifer Courtney anymore. The day his uncle Malachi removed the bandage from his temple and discharged him from the infirmary, he thought he had a solution.

He would do exactly as Cousin Dan had done! He would ride out to Lexington on his cousin's newfound horse and get Seahawk's buckskins from Parson Clark's house. Then he would put them on and ride back to Boston Neck and slip through the British lines pretending to be a friendly Indian, after which he would leave the horse in Grandma Gill's stable and make his way to the barracks and do for Luke just what Cousin Dan had done for his father and uncle. Because Nate was so young and impetuous and so despairing of his friend's life, he did not consider the manifest difficulties and dangers of his plan. To slip through the British lines might be one thing, but to fool a sentry well aware of what had happened to his predecessor when he humored a drunken "Indian" was quite another. Still, Nate galloped out to Lexington, and at dusk he was riding slowly across the neck toward the British. Suddenly, he saw approaching him what seemed at first a fiendish apparition.

It was as though a huge, prehistoric bird was rising from the primordial mud. Black and dripping, the huge creature flailed about with its wings, as though threatening the crowd of men who whirled about him shouting hideously and beating him with sticks. Nate shrank back into a thicket of maples. He sat his horse in horrid fascination, until he realized that the creature's arms were not wings and that the mud was smoking tar. In the light of the fire over which the tar had been boiled Nate saw that the man was being tarred and feathered. The victim was a big man and a brave one, judging from the way he struck back at his tormentors.

But there were too many of them. They whirled around him, howling in glee while they hit him with clubs or poked him with long poles. Their blows dislodged bits of fluff from his body. They drifted upward, pink in the glare of the fire, and went swirling back toward the British lines. Nate saw that they were chicken feathers.

Now the mob thrust a rail fence between the man's legs and swung him up into the air shoulder high. Once again, they beat him or poked him with poles, trying to keep him off balance so that he would have to clutch at the rail and be cut by it. The man tried to keep his balance, but could not. His head jerked and his shoulders twisted each time he bounced on the rail.

"Ride, Rebel, ride!" the mob jeered. "Ride, Rebel, ride!"

"Here's a feather for your cap, you God damned Yankee Doodle," one of them cried, hurling a handful of feathers at his face.

"Hey, Luke—don't worry none about getting rid of the tar. Where you're going it's gonna burn off!"

Nathaniel stiffened in the saddle. It's *Luke Sawyer!* Oh, my God, Nathaniel thought, swaying and putting a hand on his horse's withers to steady himself. What could he do? There were so many of them!

"Say your prayers, big boy," shouted a man, who was swinging a coiled rope over his head. "We've opened you up at the bottom end, and now we're going to close you up at the top."

The mob roared with laughter, hurrying Luke toward an oak tree with a low-hanging limb. Luke was jolted up and down. No longer able to contain his agony, he began grunting in anguish and then screams broke from his lips.

"Wait till his Rebel friends see what he looks like in the morning," shouted the man with the rope. "Maybe they won't be so quick to fire on the king's soldiers."

Luke's screams rose higher, and Nathaniel at once urged his horse into a gallop. He had seen that none of them was armed except for the clubs and poles and he rode down on them yelling wildly himself. Nate could see the whites of their startled eyes as they fell beneath his horse's hooves. With satisfaction, he heard their shrieks. Then the horse began to shake its head, as though trying to rid his nostrils of the strange smell of the tar. But the odor drove him wild, and he began lashing out with his feet in a screaming, neighing frenzy. Nate had trouble keeping his seat, slowly reining the beast in and calming him while the terrified Tories, dropping

Sawyer with a crash, broke and ran for the safety of the British barricade.

"Quick, Luke, get up behind me," Nate called. "Hurry, before they come back with soldiers."

"I cain't, Natey," Luke groaned, walking slowly toward him with his legs wide apart. "They split my behind open. I cain't ride."

Nate jumped down from his horse and pulled off his buckskins to drape them over the beast in front of the saddle. "Then lie up there," he said, and helped Luke to drag himself across the withers of the trembling beast. The horse sniffed and snorted, but Nate held his head and spoke to him soothingly. Remounting carefully, clad only in his underclothes, he turned and rode slowly back to Cambridge.

When he came to the infirmary, he halted and helped Sawyer to slide off the horse and stagger inside. Fortunately, Dr. Malachi Gill was still there and he came rushing up when Luke collapsed on the floor with a loud groan.

"Oh, my Jesus, what have they done to you?" he cried, bending over the stricken man. "What happened, Luke, what happened?"

"Tory slime," Luke gasped. "They talked Gage into letting them try me in a civil court. Gage wants to keep in with the Tories. Wants to form a regiment of them. So he let me go. That filthy fat finagler of a Joel Courtney was behind it, I know. Why, I heard he even wants to command the Tory regiment, the fat-assed fraud. Try me!" Luke grimaced. "With Judge Hemp and a tar-and-feather jury." Suddenly remembering Nathaniel standing above him, Sawyer put out and then withdrew a tarry hand. "Thankee, Natey, thankee for saving my life."

Nate shifted his feet. "Aw, you'd've done the same for me, Luke," he mumbled.

Dr. Gill had reached down gently as though to peel Luke's clothes from his body when he realized that the man was naked. "The scum!" he swore, his face reddening. "They aren't fit to burn in hell. Quick, Natey, get me some lard. Lots and lots of lard. And some towels and scissors."

Nate hurried outside to the spring house, where he knew the lard was kept. He stooped to seize a tub of it, staggering back inside and stopping at the surgery for scissors and towels. His uncle quickly took the scissors from him and began cutting Luke Sawyer's hair, flinging the tarry red locks into an empty barrel. Then he began to crop it close.

"Aw, Doc, do y' have to?" Luke protested. "Y' know I was always kind of taken with my hair. You cut any more off an' the gals won't look at ol' Luke no more."

Malachi laughed and continued clipping until nothing but a furry quarter inch of tar-free hair remained. Then he took a towel, dipped it in lard and gently began rubbing the tar from Luke's face. Gradually, his white skin began to emerge: first the eyes, then the mouth, until Luke looked like one of those black-faced comedians in a Morris dance, and finally the entire face.

"Now you help me clean his body," Malachi said to Nathaniel, and Nate also seized a towel. Together they knelt to either side of Luke, smearing the lard on his hairy chest, carefully plying the towels to remove the tar before it became caked.

"You'd think I was a newborn baby," Luke grumbled. "Bald head and all, you two swabbing me down like you was midwives cleaning off the afterbirth." Malachi and Nathaniel neared Luke's private parts and he shot erect. "Here, I'll do that meself," he said, reaching for a towel. "That's the part that hurt the most when them Tory scum bounced me on the rail." Gingerly, grimacing and wincing, Luke cleansed his genitals. Eventually, his entire body was freed of tar, and Malachi and Nathaniel helped him stagger to a bed.

"Lie down with a pillow under you, Luke," Dr. Gill said. "There's not much we can do about your rectum."

"They done wrecked my rectum," Luke muttered ruefully, chuckling at his own pun.

"All you can do is lie there until it heals. Drink a lot of liquids and don't eat any solid foods. You understand why?"

"I can guess," Luke said, grimacing as he lowered himself gently onto the pillow, then sinking back against the other pillow at his head. "An' since I cain't eat nawthin' solid, Doc, I might as well start the liquids with a bottle of rum."

A few weeks later—May 10, 1775—the Second Continental Congress convened in the State House in Philadelphia. Most of the delegates were veterans of the First Congress, but there were quite a few newcomers such as Benjamin Franklin and John Hancock. For the first time, Georgia sent a dele-

gate. After the election of Hancock as president, it appeared
that the Congress was unanimous in its determination to
break away from the Crown. Gradually, however, disagree-
ments began to appear. Conservatives such as John Dickinson
of Pennsylvania and his colleague James Wilson had deep
misgivings about an independent American. So did James
Duane of New York. As the differences grew deeper, John
Adams became distressed.

"We've got to pull the colonies together," he said to his
cousins Sam and Daniel Gill as the three strolled in the State
House yard a week after Congress convened. "Ben Franklin
says that if we go to war it must be the unanimous will of all
the colonies. But it looks as if our united front is falling
apart."

"I agree," Daniel Gill said. "I think that war is inevitable.
But there's a new spirit of conciliation afoot. People like
Duane and Farmer John Dickinson think we can be recon-
ciled with the Crown."

"Not after Lexington and Concord," said John Adams.
"Not after Ticonderoga. Not without a few heads rolling."

"Like ours and Hancock's?" Daniel asked with a grin.

His head shaking, Sam Adams nodded. John Adams
halted, spreading his legs and putting his hands behind his rotund body. "The petition from the Massachusetts Committee
of Public Safety couldn't have come at a better time," he said
musingly. "If we adopt the New England Army up there in
Cambridge as our own, it will be a marvelous gesture of
unity."

"But who would command it?" Daniel Gill asked.

"It can't be a northerner. Even though it's our army, we
need someone from the middle colonies or the south to keep
them from splitting away from us."

"John Hancock won't like that," Sam Adams said warningly.

"It can't be helped, Sam. We've got to compromise if we're
going to show the Crown a united front."

"Who do you have in mind?"

"George Washington of Virginia."

"Excellent choice!" Daniel Gill cried, beaming. "He has
the most military experience of anyone in the colonies—and
he's a marvelous leader."

Sam Adams stared at Daniel sourly. "There are some delegates from Virginia who say that the gentleman never won a battle."

"That's not true. I was with him at Fort Necessity. The rain soaked our powder and fouled our muskets. The French and Indians had us outnumbered. I think we got off with good terms. I was with him at the Monongahela, too. That was all Braddock's fault, with his European ideas of parade-ground battle. I wouldn't be here if it hadn't been for George Washington! He saved the day!"

Sam Adams shrugged, unimpressed, and his cousin muttered as though thinking aloud. "I've *got* to do it! Yes, yes, I've got to do it. I will put Washington's name in nomination tomorrow."

In the morning, John Adams arose from his place in the Congress, bowing to President John Hancock in the chair, before turning to address the Congress: "Gentlemen, we must act quickly on the petition from Massachusetts. Our colonies are as yet in disarray. The people are uncertain. They have great expectations but they are also anxious. The Army of New England is in great distress. Nay, it is in danger of dissolution. Each day—nay, each hour—that we squander in indecisiveness is but another day or another hour in which the British Army may march out of Boston to spread destruction and fear as far as it can. I therefore, gentlemen, make a motion that the Congress adopt the army at Cambridge and appoint a general to command it."

A murmur of interest ran through the delegates, and Adams paused—noticing how John Hancock brightened and leaned forward eagerly in his seat.

"Who shall this gentleman be?" Adams asked, as an expectant silence returned to the floor. "I have no hesitation to declare that I have but one gentleman in mind. He is a gentleman from Virginia who is among us."

Hancock's jaw dropped. He gaped at Adams in mortified disbelief, then glared at him in resentment. "He is very well known to us as a gentleman whose skill and experience as an officer—" There was a slight commotion at the door. George Washington, in full uniform, had jumped to his feet and bolted into the library. "—whose independent fortune, great talents and excellent universal character would command the approbation of all America, and unite the cordial exertions of the colonies better than any other person in the Union. Gentlemen, I nominate George Washington of Virginia."

A swelling hum of voices arose in the chamber. To John Adams's surprise, and to Hancock's further mortification, Sam Adams arose to second the nomination. Debate continued until the following day, when Washington was finally appointed commander-in-chief. Called upon by John Hancock to accept, Washington replied:

"Mr. President, . . . I . . . declare with the utmost sincerity, I do not think myself equal to the command I am honored with. As to pay, sir, I beg leave to assure Congress that as no pecuniary consideration would have tempted me to have accepted this arduous employment at the expense of my domestic ease and happiness, I do not wish to make any profit from it."

Blushing, Washington sat down with his ears full of the applause of his fellow delegates, many of who rushed up to congratulate him. Among the first to seize his hand was Daniel Gill.

"Congratulations, sir! No one is more deserving of this honor than you. I always thought that some day you would be a great commander, and now you are the leader of the greatest undertaking in the history of mankind."

"Thank you, Major," Washington replied, still blushing. "And would you now consider going to war with me as my aide again?"

"Yes, yes! By all means!"

"Excellent! I shall ask Congress to commission you a colonel. Consider yourself to hold the rank from this day forward. Also, I should like you to go to Cambridge immediately as my liaison officer there. I am particularly interested in the artillery captured at Ticonderoga. Ethan Allen and Benedict Arnold have reported taking some sixty cannon and mortars. Some of the cannon are sizeable. They should be of great help in forcing the British out of Boston. Can you leave now, Colonel?"

"Immediately, General," Colonel Gill replied.

Colonel Daniel Gill left Philadelphia on June 15 and arrived in Cambridge June 25, just as the Committee of Public Safety was convening in a council of war. News of Washington's appointment had preceded him, relieving him of the probably unpleasant duty of informing both Generals Ward and Putnam—who were present at the meeting along with Dr. Warren—that a southerner had been appointed commander of both them and their army. Actually, Israel Putnam had been the soul of joviality when they both rode up to the council together.

"Glad to see you again, Gill," he said, dismounting and clapping Daniel on the back, his owlish face creased in a friendly smile. "We sure can use you with what we've got afoot."

"What's that?" Daniel inquired, noticing how the captured pistols he had given Putnam were sheathed gleaming in his saddle holsters. Seems like they made me a friend, he thought.

"Bunker Hill," General Putnam answered. "We're thinking of beating the British to the high ground there. If we can fortify it and hold it we can command Charlestown and Boston both. We could mount the guns from Ticonderoga there and look right down Gage's throat. He'd have to pull foot."

Nodding, Colonel Gill followed the burly Putnam into the council chamber. Dr. Warren and General Ward were already there, studying a wall map and shaking their heads. Daniel noticed that Ward looked pale and sickly, as though he were in pain.

"What's wrong, gentlemen?" General Putnam barked.

"We don't like it, General," Dr. Warren said. "It looks like a cul-de-sac. I understand the importance of Bunker and Breed's Hills, well enough. But they're both out on the Charlestown Peninsula between the Charles and the Mystic rivers. The British fleet can bombard you there. Worse, if Gage decides to capture Charlestown Neck in your rear, you'll be cut off."

"Nonsense!" Putnam boomed. "Nobody can hold Charlestown Neck. It gets flooded at high tide."

"So much the worse. Your attempt at escape would be limited."

"We're low on ammunition, too, Israel," Artemas Ward argued. "There are only eleven barrels of powder in the entire army."

"Enough for what we need," Putnam growled. "We should be getting more from Ticonderoga soon. I tell you, gentlemen, I can lead twelve hundred men out on the peninsula tonight. They'll have about ten hours to dig. Nobody can dig better than Americans, gentlemen. By the time the British wake up tomorrow morning, they'll be dug in proper. I tell you, no one fights better from behind fortifications than Americans. Americans are not at all afraid of their heads, though they're very much afraid of their legs. If you cover their legs, they'll fight forever." He turned to Daniel. "What do you say, Gill?"

"From what you say, I gather that you're expecting a British frontal attack." Putnam nodded grimly, and Daniel continued: "Then, with all deference, General, I would suggest that you seem to be counting on what you think the British will do, rather than considering what they're capable of doing."

"What d'ya mean?" Putnam snorted.

"That they have the capability of doing what Dr. Warren fears. Cut off your front with their fleet and your rear with their army. You might be unable to fight your way out either way and might have to surrender."

Putnam scowled. "I think they'll come straight at us. They're still smarting from what we did to 'em at Lexington and Concord. They want revenge. They're dying to make Yankee Doodle dance. Besides, to get to the neck they'd have to cross the Charles and march right through Cambridge. You could hit them from here at the bridge or on their flank."

"They wouldn't need to go on foot, General," Colonel Gill murmured. "Their fleet can land them at the neck."

Putnam shook his head doggedly. "No," he insisted, "they won't try it." He wheeled fiercely on Warren and Ward. "We've got to take the high ground before they do," he cried. "And we can't wait much longer. Do you agree?"

Slowly, Ward wearily and Warren reluctantly, the two men nodded their heads in assent.

Chapter Four

At dusk, a force of twelve hundred men was assembled. The citizen-soldiers wore homespun dyed the color of Massachusetts's oak or sumach bark, or smocks of towcloth. Broad-brimmed hats were on their heads and they carried their muskets sloped over their shoulders. Ahead of them as they shuffled along in the lengthening twilight of June 16, 1775, rode General Putnam, flanked by Colonel Daniel Gill and Colonel William Prescott, another veteran of the Colonial Wars like Putnam but a man as practical as Putnam was impetuous. When they reached the forks near Prospect Hill, they turned right for the march to Charlestown Neck. It was now completely dark. Some of the men stumbled. Nathaniel Gill tripped on a stone and tumbled into Luke Sawyer ahead of him, forcing him to drop his musket with a clatter. . .

"Damn it, Natey," Luke began, closing his mouth abruptly when Captain Micah Gill limping alongside his company hissed fiercely: "Quiet, there! No talking in ranks!"

Silently parading across the neck, the Americans came to Bunker Hill. "All right, Prescott," General Putnam growled, "let's get them started digging."

"Not here, General," Prescott replied, turning to peer toward Charlestown. "I think Breed's Hill would be better. It's closer to Boston."

"But this is higher."

"True, but—"

"Please, gentlemen," Colonel Richard Gridley, the engineer, interrupted. "You're wasting time. I don't have a moment to lose in marking out the lines for a redoubt. Please hurry."

"All right," General Putnam said. "We'll put the main body and the main works forward at Breed's and fortify Bunker to cover any retreat."

"Very good, sir," said Colonel Gridley, riding with Prescott and Colonel Gill as they led the main body along a ridge leading east to Breed's Hill. Captain Micah Gill's company was with this force. So was Dr. Malachi Gill, mounted on a horse laden with saddlebags stuffed with towels, rum, bone saws and drugs. At Breed's, Colonel Gridley at once began drawing the lines of the redoubt in the soft earth. Prescott assembled his company commanders and said, "There's only one order for tonight. Dig!" Nodding, they set their men to work. Turning to Daniel Gill, he said, "Would you be good enough to take a patrol into Charlestown to watch the British?"

"A pleasure," Daniel replied, riding slowly off.

Soon the crest of Breed's Hill resounded to the clink of shovels and pickaxes. Sparks flew in the dark when the iron tools struck rocks. Piles of earth clearly marked the lines drawn by Gridley, as the soldiers who heaped them there sank deeper out of sight behind them. Soon, too, grumbling could be heard from some of the men unaccustomed to such work.

"I can't hardly dig anymore, Luke," Nathaniel Gill muttered. "I've got blisters on both hands. They should have issued gloves."

"This ain't no fancy dance, Natey, boy," Luke grunted. In his ham blacksmith's hands the shovel he held looked like a toy. Beside him, young Asa Pollard giggled and said to Nate, "Serves you right for going to Harvard. You college boys cain't tell a chestnut from a chicken's ass. Bet you ain't held nawthin' in your hand heavier than a writin' pen."

"Oh, shut up, Asa," Nate retorted, and they all fell silent when Captain Gill hissed angrily again: "Silence, soldiers!"

Next morning, Lieutenant General Thomas Gage was awakened by the sound of cannonading by the British fleet. Not long after, he received a message from Admiral Samuel Graves informing him that the Rebels had seized the high ground above Charlestown and had miraculously succeeded in throwing up strong fortifications during a single night.

"God rot their Rebel souls," Gage mumbled aloud, yanking his bellpull for an orderly. "Nothing but human moles." An orderly entered his chambers and Gage said: "Please inform Major Generals Henry Clinton and Sir

William Howe that I wish to confer with them at once in a council of war."

Along with Major General "Gentleman Johnny" Burgoyne, the two officers had arrived in Boston the preceding May 25. Before their arrival, Gage had read a London newspaper describing them as "a triumvirate of reputation," which he took to be a slur on his own record. He also suspected that one of them was in possession of secret orders to replace him. The door opened again, and Gage watched sourly while his batman entered bearing a silver tea service on a silver tray. Under his arm was a snowy white tablecloth which he spread on a table near the window overlooking the harbor. Placing the tray on it he went out again to fetch scones in covered silver dishes, butter, jelly and delicate fine china which he set at three places. Then he stood ramrod straight beside the table. The door opened once more and Howe and Clinton came in. Gage motioned them to the table, sitting there himself while the batman began to pour tea and pass the scones around.

"The Rebels have seized the high ground above Charlestown," Gage announced.

A scowl came over Howe's dark, floridly handsome face. "That will make it deuced difficult here in Boston," he said, taking a scone to break it, butter it and add jam. "Very tasty," he grunted, reaching for another one. "Where did these Yankees learn to cook?"

"Or dig," Gage added sourly. "Yes, it is difficult. We must attack them at once, before they can make their position stronger. Admiral Graves says it's surprisingly strong already. Well, gentlemen?" he said inquiringly, arising to walk to a wall map of Boston.

General Howe followed him, munching, a third scone in his hand. Sir William Howe had grown much fleshier since he led Wolfe's light infantry at Quebec twenty-six years before. Howe peered at the map and pointed at Breed's Hill with his scone. "That where they are?" Gage nodded, and Howe said, "We can flank them and get in their rear. Land at Charlestown and march around the Mystic River side of their redoubt and come in their back door. Piece of cake."

"I disagree," General Henry Clinton said in his toneless voice. He came to the map beside them, his pale complexion a sharp contrast to Howe's. "I believe we should attack across

Charlestown Neck. Seal them off, while the fleet wipes their nose. It's much less risky than a flank march. Certainly we should have fewer casualties."

Both Gage and Howe shook their heads. "It will take too long," Gage said. "Give them time to dig in deeper. Besides, what we need is a smashing victory. Plenty of blood. Rebel blood. We can squelch this rebellion with one bayonet charge."

"I quite agree," Howe murmured. "I've seen the Americans under fire. They don't like cold steel."

"Very good," Gage grunted. "And you, my dear Howe, shall take command."

"I am honored," Sir William Howe murmured, returning to the table to discover with dismay that all the scones were gone.

Daniel Gill and William Prescott stood on the parapet of the newly built redoubt studying the surrounding ground. Almost simultaneously, their eyes fell on the lower ground stretching from the redoubt to the Mystic River.

"I don't like it," Colonel Gill said.

"Neither do I," said Colonel Prescott, and he cupped his hands to his lips to yell at Micah Gill. "Captain, get your men over here to build a breastwork."

"Oh, my Jesus," Luke Sawyer groaned. "More digging! And I'm so tuckered I feel like I done shoed a regiment of cavalry."

Even Asa Pollard protested. "Cain't you get us something to eat and drink, Cap'n? We ain't had nawthin' since last night's supper."

Micah shook his head. "There's nothing to be had. What's wrong with you, Natey?" he said to his son. "Where's your shovel?" Misery in his eyes, Nate showed his father his blistered hands. There were four bubbles on each palm and one at the base of each thumb. "All right, you don't have to dig," Micah said grudgingly, "but you can still carry stones."

Silently, sweltering in the oppressive heat, Micah's men began construction of the breastwork. From the redoubt parapet, Colonel Prescott studied the bay through a telescope. He saw the fleet gathered broadside. Then puffs of smoke . . . the sound of explosions . . . Within moments, cannon balls began falling on the hill. One of them tore off the head of

Asa Pollard. He stood momentarily erect, headless, his torso a stump of spouting blood, before toppling over. Some of the soldiers shrieked and dropped their shovels and made for the redoubt.

"Stay where you are!" Prescott shouted. "See," he yelled, striding up and down the parapet amid the raining cannon balls, "they can't hit anything. It was a fluke, a lucky shot." Prescott turned to focus his telescope behind him and saw General Israel Putnam riding towards Charlestown Neck.

It was Putnam's second trip across the shot-swept neck to Cambridge. Once again he requested reinforcements. "Damn it, General," he said to Artemas Ward. "I can see the British massing for the trip across the bay. They must have twice as many men as I do. I need more!"

General Ward shook his head. "You said you could do it with what you have. Besides, the only regiments I could give you—Clark's and Reed's New Hampshire boys—are out of ammunition. They're crack shots but they can't do much without bullets."

Exasperated, Putnam rode back to Bunker Hill. Behind him, Dr. Joseph Warren quietly prevailed upon Ward to send the New Hampshire troops. "We've found some lead in a church organ, General," he said. "They can make their own bullets."

"Send them out, then," Ward replied reluctantly. "Tell Colonel Stark he's in command. Issue 'em two flints apiece, a gill of powder and a pound of lead cut from the organ. They can make balls with their own moulds or hammer 'em out of slugs of lead."

At once, the general's orders were transmitted to Colonel John Stark. He ordered his men to make fifteen bullets apiece, then formed them into ranks and led them—twelve hundred strong—on the four-mile march to the front. Crossing the neck, they came under grapeshot from the British ships. Men began to fall. Some began to run.

"Hold your men!" Stark shouted to his company commanders.

"Oh, sir, don't you think we should go faster?" young Captain Henry Dearborn called anxiously.

"Dearborn," Stark said calmly, "one fresh man in action is worth ten fatigued men."

They marched steadily on, reaching Bunker Hill shortly before one o'clock in the afternoon.

At one o'clock, with raving fifes and rattling drums, the British came ashore at Moulton's Point. It was a stirring sight, the sun dancing on the tips of the serried bayonets, but it gave Nathaniel Gill a queasy feeling in his stomach, watching the tiny red dots massing on Moulton's Hill.

Atop the hill, General Howe studied the American position. An aide stood beside him. Behind him stood his batman holding glasses and a crystal decanter filled with wine. Howe saw at once that he could not turn the enemy left on the Mystic River as easily as he had expected.

"They've built a blasted breastwork there," he grumbled to the aide. Then he focused on Bunker Hill where he saw more troops. "Got a reserve, too." Next he saw Stark's troops marching toward Breed's Hill. "And reinforcements. I'm going to need more men. Signal for reinforcements, Higgins."

Far above Howe, on the parapet of the redoubt, Colonel Prescott watched the enemy anxiously. "They're waiting for something," he said to Daniel Gill. "Probably more troops." Prescott glanced uneasily to his left and started. "Oh, my Jesus," he groaned, "there's a gap there between the end of the breastwork and the river. They could get through it. No, there's a stone-and-rail fence to the left rear. That'll plug our left. Colonel Gill, would you be good enough to take a body of Connecticut troops and two cannon back there?"

Nodding, Colonel Gill rode off to fortify the rail fence, just as Colonel John Stark arrived in the area with his sharpshooters. Stark introduced himself and studied the position. "There's still a gap," he said, pointing to a narrow strip of beach beneath the riverbank where the rail fence ended. "You could get four men abreast through there, and that's enough to turn our flank." Immediately, Stark ordered his best shots to build a stone barricade on the beach and man it. Then he put the rest of his men behind the rail fence.

"Excellent!" Prescott exclaimed when Stark reported to him. "Now we've got about fourteen hundred men in the redoubt, the breastwork, the rail fence and your beach wall. Let them try us now."

Dr. Joseph Warren entered the redoubt, stepping almost daintily in the mud. He was elegant in white satin breeches and pale-blue waistcoat laced with silver. His long blond hair was carefully combed. Prescott stared at Warren in surprise and inner resentment. Aware that Congress had just appointed Warren a major general, he saluted stiffly and said, "Have you come to take command, sir?"

"I shall take no command here," Warren said, lifting his musket significantly. "I came as a volunteer with my musket to serve under you."

Bowing, the young revolutionary mounted the firing platform.

Sir William Howe was ready.

He now had about twenty-five hundred men divided between himself on the right at Moulton's Hill and General Sir Robert Pigot on the left in the town of Charlestown. Howe formed his own force in three ranks.

"I expect you to fight like an Englishman and as becomes a good soldier," he said to them. There were a few suppressed snickers when he said "Englishmen." Howe guessed that they were from the Welsh Fusiliers and the Irish in the King's Own, but he said nothing. "I shall not desire any one of you to go a step farther than where I go myself at your head." Turning, Howe took a glass of wine offered him by his batman. Sipping, he strode toward the park of six-pound cannon aimed at the redoubt.

"Commence firing!" he called.

The guns flamed and roared and then fell silent.

"What the deuce is wrong?" Howe muttered. A young artillery officer hurried toward him and saluted. He was obviously upset. Howe stared at him coldly. "Yes?"

"Beg to report, sir, the guns' side boxes are filled with twelve-pound balls instead of six-pounders. The cannon are useless."

Howe's florid face became mottled. "God damn your eyes!" he swore. "I'll have you court-martialed for this." Glancing at the glass in his hand, Howe hurled it to the ground in a rage.

On the British left, General Sir Robert Pigot's men were being peppered by sniper fire from Yankee sharpshooters in the Charlestown houses. Pigot sent a message to Admiral Graves who gave orders to burn the town down. British ships in the harbor and batteries on Copp's Hill in Boston began bombarding Charlestown with red-hot ball and "carcasses," perforated balls stuffed with burning pitch. Within a few moments, the town caught fire.

Whole streets of houses collapsed against one another in roaring walls of flame. Ships on the stocks blazed. Churches were burning and their high steeples licked the heavens like great flaming spears. Everywhere there was a hiss and crackle of flames and crash of falling timbers audible to Gentleman Johnny Burgoyne and Henry Clinton watching from Copp's Hill.

"Pretty sight, eh, my dear Clinton?"

"Quite. Rather like a Guy Fawkes' Day bonfire, only bigger."

On the British right, Howe stationed about three hundred men of the light infantry along the Mystic beach, ordering them to storm the beach wall with the bayonet. His main body remained opposite the breastwork and the rail fence held by Colonel Gill and his men. Behind these positions, burly Israel Putnam rode back and forth, shouting:

"Don't fire until you see the whites of their eyes! Then, fire low!"

At the beach wall, Colonel Stark suddenly darted forward about forty yards with a stake in his hand. He drove it into the ground and ran back, yelling: "Not a man is to fire until the first regular crosses the stake!"

"Forward!" General Howe cried, and the attack began.

On the British left, Pigot's regulars climbed steadily upward toward the redoubt. Nate Gill watched them come . . . the white cross-belts on the red coats growing larger . . . larger . . . Nate began to sweat profusely. His stomach turned over. Kneeling on the firing platform with his musket resting on the parapet he felt his calves knotting in cramps.

"I'm scared, Luke," he muttered to Sawyer beside him.

"Who ain't? But you just keep a tight ass, boy. You don't feel like yer gonna shit yerself, do you?"

Nate shook his head and Luke gave him a fatherly pat on the shoulder. To either side of them some of the nervous soldiers began firing.

"Cease fire!" Prescott roared. "I'll kill the next man who fires!"

Micah Gill jumped up on the parapet and began kicking

up the leveled muskets. Silence reclaimed the American redoubt. Pigot's men still climbed toward it.

On the right, Howe's men marched down Moulton's Hill, across a lowland and up the slopes of Breed's against the silent breastwork and rail fences. It was hot. Sunlight streamed into the eyes of the grenadiers and troops of the line in their brimless bearskins or cocked hats. It blinded them as they stumbled through tall grass up to their knees. Sweat darkened their red coats and they began to pant under their sixty-pound loads.

Along Mystic beach the light infantry were trotting to the attack with outthrust bayonets, led by the Welsh Fusiliers.

Now all was thunder and flame and flash, Charlestown burning, batteries booming, naval guns crashing, echoing and reverberating over water and earth, while overhead, now exposing, now concealing the battle beginning below, drifted the billowing black clouds of powder smoke.

Now the light infantry were running. The Welsh Fusiliers went slanting past Stark's stake, and the little stone barricade ahead of them flashed and roared.

Down . . . down . . . down went the fusiliers. Most of them didn't get up. Into the breach swept the King's Own Regiment. Again the flash and crash, and again the redcoats swayed and went down.

Aghast, Howe, in the forefront of the battle as he had promised, sent in the picked flank troops of the 10th Regiment. They formed awkwardly. Officers ran among the reluctant, beating them with the flat of their swords. "Form!" they cried. "Form! The Yankees can't possibly have time for a third volley!"

Again the scarlet lines of sun-tipped steel slanted forward, and there *was* a third volley. Terrified, the regulars of the 10th joined the fusiliers and the King's Own in disorderly flight. Behind them were ninety-six lifeless redcoats sprawled on the blood-clotted sands of Mystic beach.

Sir William Howe was appalled. He realized that he could not force the Mystic beach, the pivotal point of his attack; and yet, he resolved to continue. "We must smash them," he muttered, taking another glass of wine proffered by his batman. "We *must* get through. We cannot let this rabble believe they have beaten British regulars." He sipped his wine and stared morosely at the heaps of his dead, their white breeches splotched with blood, their scarlet coats dyed a darker red, their bodies sprawled and lolling in the ungainly sag of the lifeless. "Grenadiers, form front!" Howe called, and sent two more ranks of soldiers charging against the breastwork and rail fence.

"Fire!" Colonel John Stark bellowed.

"Fire!" shouted Colonel Daniel Gill.

Flame and smoke gushed forth from the American position. Daniel Gill peered through the drifting smoke in exultation. The tightly dressed red ranks had been shredded into little bands of stunned and stricken men. "You've got them, men!" he cried.

"Fire! Fire and reload! Fire and reload!" Again and again the American muskets spoke. Rank after rank took its place at the breastwork and rail fence. British soldiers toppled and fell, their dying breaths issuing from their mouths in long trailing death screams. Others staggered from the field streaming blood.

"Pick off the officers, the ones with the gold braid and silver gorgets," cried Daniel Gill. "We want the officers!" Howe's batman fell with a tinkle of broken glass. So did the general's aide. Every man in the general's personal staff was either killed or wounded. Still he stood there among the wailing musket balls, staring in stunned disbelief, until a courier rode up to inform him that General Pigot on the left had withdrawn.

At once, Sir William Howe sounded the recall.

"We beat 'em again, we beat 'em again!" Nathaniel Gill shouted exultingly, grabbing Luke Sawyer around the waist and hugging him. "We made 'em pull foot again!"

With trembling limbs, and the clamor of the battle on his left in his ears, Nate had been watching the steady approach of the enemy—training his musket below the cross-belts of a big grenadier, waiting for the whites of his eyes to materialize—when suddenly the serried red ranks executed a rear-march and withdrew.

"Aw, 'twere only a feint," Luke Sawyer said, disengaging himself from Nate's grasp. "We didn't do nawthin' here. 'Twere the fellows on the left what did it."

Nevertheless there was jubilation in the redoubt. Even the taciturn Colonel Prescott was smiling. He went among the men slapping them on the shoulder. "Stand fast, my brave soldiers!" he cried, jumping on the parapet again. "Stand fast!" To Captain Micah Gill, however, who had scrambled up beside him, Prescott expressed his apprehension. "We're losing men too fast. I don't mean casualties, I mean deserters. They're draining me like a leaking pipe. I don't think I've got above a hundred and fifty men in the redoubt. Would you be good enough to go back to Bunker Hill and ask General Putnam for reinforcements?"

Favoring his bad leg, Micah jumped down into the redoubt and limped off to find his brother's horse. He found Malachi working in a makeshift surgery next to the exit from the redoubt. Dr. Gill's white smock was clotted with blood and bits of human flesh. He was busy removing musket balls with a pincer, sometimes using bone saws. Micah could hear the groans and stifled screams of the suffering. Some of them had bullets in their mouths, grinding their teeth into them so as not to cry out while Malachi and his associates worked on them. Micah shuddered and went out the exit to mount Malachi's horse and ride back to Bunker Hill.

Behind him, Sir William Howe was preparing to attack again. His plan now was to ignore the beach barricade and to send the light infantry against the rail fence while he and Pigot struck with the main body against the redoubt and the breastwork. On the left, Pigot ordered Major John Pitcairn and his Marines to spearhead the assault. They came marching silently up the hill, Pitcairn at their head with poised sword.

Trembling once again, Nathaniel Gill knelt on the firing platform with leveled musket. It was sighted in on Major Pitcairn, just to the right and below his silver gorget. They came on ... Pitcairn's face became clearly visible ... then his nose ... then the sockets of his eyes ... then the whites ... Nate squeezed the trigger. Major Pitcairn staggered and sank to the ground while all around Nate muskets roared and flames and smoke spouted down from the dugout.

Next to the dying Pitcairn, his son was wounded. He staggered to his father and gathered him in his arms. "I have lost my father!" he cried in anguish, and all around him Pitcairn's Marines raised the echoing lament: "We have lost our father!"

On the right, General Howe saw that his finest were once again being cut down and he shouted: "The bayonet! To the breastwork with the bayonet!" Cheering raggedly, the red-coats rallied and charged—straight into a steady stream of musketry that sickled them to the reddening earth. Sickened, Sir William Howe again beat the recall.

Captain Micah Gill rode up to General Israel Putnam on Bunker Hill, saluted and said, "Colonel Prescott requests reinforcements and more powder, sir."

"Who doesn't?" Putnam growled, glaring at him. "Are things really that bad on Breed's?"

"Not really. We took some fairly severe casualties in the second attack. But we're losing more men by desertion than enemy fire."

"I know," Putnam said wearily, pointing to clusters of soldiers lying on the hillsides. "They drift back here and then they drift back across the neck. Every time a man gets hit at Breed's, he's got a dozen shirkers 'volunteering' to help carry him back here. I've near worn myself out, beating them with my sword, trying to make them go back. Cowards and shirkers, that's what they are!" Putnam saw a fat colonel sitting on a stone with his head between his knees. He spurred his horse toward him. "God damn you, Gerrish," he swore, "why haven't you moved your regiment to Breed's as I ordered you to?"

"I'm completely exhausted, General," Samuel Gerrish wheezed plaintively, mopping his perspiring forehead with his sleeve.

"You mean you're completely cowardly!" Putnam snarled, lifiting his sword as though to strike him. Colonel Gerrish cringed in terror, and Captain Gill laid a restraining hand on Putnam's wrist. "Don't, sir," he murmured. Still swearing, Israel Putnam sheathed his sword and rode off, drawing it again when he found two of Gerrish's companies lying on the safe side of Bunker Hill. Jumping down among them he began beating them with the flat of his blade.

"Get in ranks, God damn your lily-livered souls! Form! You there, with the spontoon—get it up in the air where they can see it. Get in ranks! Form! Poise your muskets! God damn it, next time I'll hit you with the edge."

One by one, sheepishly or sullenly, the reluctant soldiers of Samuel Gerrish's regiments formed two companies. General Putnam turned them over to Captain Gill, remarking, "Tell

Prescott that this is all I can give him. And there isn't any powder."

When he returned to the redoubt, Micah was surprised to find his men drawing powder rations.

"I broke open the cannon cartridges," Prescott explained. "We've got enough powder and ball now to beat off another attack."

"Do you think they'll come again?"

"By all means," Prescott said, pointing below him and handing Micah his telescope.

Through the glass Micah could see the British forming again on Moulton Hill. Some of the units seemed parade-ground fresh. They were. Howe had called for reinforcements and Henry Clinton had brought four hundred more regulars across the water. Reporting to Howe, Clinton stared around him with unbelieving eyes.

Howe nodded grimly. "It is not a sight that I should ever wish to see again. I tell you, my dear Clinton, I have served my king since I was a boy, just as you have. I have never known defeat. But when I saw the finest troops in the world going down like ninepins before this wretched rabble in arms, *I felt a moment that I never felt before.*"

"You are going to begin the game again?"

"Yes," Howe said grimly, looking around for his batman and another glass of wine, until he realized that the batman had been killed. He sighed. "Yes. And I want you to join Pigot against the redoubt on the left, while I go again against the breastwork."

Once again, Nathaniel Gill knelt on the firing platform watching the approach of the enemy. This time, the silent, steady march of the redcoats seemed more awesome. For the first time Nate noticed how the strength of the redoubt had dwindled. He plucked at Luke Sawyer's sleeve. "I'm down to five balls, Luke," he whispered. "How about you?"

"Seven," Luke grunted. "I sure wish I had a bayonet."

"So do I," Nate mumbled, just as Colonel Prescott cried "Fire!"

For the third time the silent fort erupted in noise and flame. For the third time, redcoats began to fall. But this

time, British cannon came into play. Flaming balls rained
down upon the redoubt. Men began to fall from the firing
platform, men began to jump down to make for the exits.
Now the British line was only ten yards away from the fort.
They entered the ditch outside of it and began climbing its
walls, leaping down among the Americans with downthrust
steel blades.

Nate fired his last shot at a redcoat hurtling down on him
and felt himself knocked off the platform. He fell sprawling
on the ground, gazing upward in terror as another redcoat
drove his bayonet toward his stomach. Then the soldier sank
to the ground with his head split open. Luke Sawyer had
clubbed his musket and was standing over Nate, roaring like
a bull, swinging his weapon round and around to clear a
circle among the cowering redcoats while Nate scrambled to
his feet.

Nate could hear Colonel Prescott bellowing, "Twitch their
muskets away! Use your guns for clubs!" Nate seized the
fallen regular's musket and joined Luke in battering a way
through the milling mob. He could see Prescott parrying enemy bayonets with his sword, hear the clang of steel on steel.
Again and again, he thought Prescott had been bayoneted,
but the blades merely caught his loose linen coat. Eventually,
it was in tatters—but Prescott survived, to be joined by
Colonel Daniel Gill from the American left, where Howe had
at last prevailed.

Now the redcoats were leaping into the redoubt from three
sides. Even little General Pigot, too small to vault the wall,
climbed a tree and swung himself into the battle. Daniel Gill
struck at him with his sword, but missed. Nate struck at him
with his club, but missed.

"Give way, men!" Prescott called. "Save yourselves!"

A tide of terrified Americans flowed toward the only exit.
It was too small to receive them all and many of the fugitives
washed up against the rear walls like water against a dam.
Screams and supplications rose from the throats of the cornered. But the British were relentless.

"Bugger the bloody beggars!"

"Kill! Kill! Kill!"

"Look it 'im. 'E wants quarter, poor little tyke. Up his ass,
myte! 'Ear 'im screech!"

Borne toward the exit, Nate caught sight of his uncle

Malachi on his left. He was rising from a wounded American he had been attending, pointing down at him, opening his hands beseechingly—when a redcoat bayoneted him in the throat and stomped on the face of the wounded man. Nate felt himself fainting. Pressed in on every side by frantic Americans, he was sinking down among them to the slippery, reddening mud—when he felt someone seize him and pull him towards the exit. It was Luke Sawyer. Still bellowing, Luke yanked Nate outside of the fort and swung him up on his shoulder. Nate felt himself losing consciousness. Before he passed out he saw a figure in muddy white breeches and a bloodstained blue waistcoat lying on the ground. Nate gasped. It was Dr. Joseph Warren. Then Nathaniel Gill did faint.

Beside Dr. Warren was the lifeless body of his father.

Chapter Five

General George Washington arrived in Cambridge on July 2, 1775, and took command the following day. He was delighted to find Colonel Daniel Gill waiting for him and at once began a tour of the camp.

The new American commander-in-chief was dismayed. The camp was a huge, sprawling, filthy, smoking, stinking jungle in which each man cooked his own mess and the latrines ("necessary" houses) were built cheek by jowl with living quarters. Even the tents lacked military regularity. Some were made of boards, others of sailcloth and still others of both. There were huts of stone and turf or of birch and brush, while some were no better than lean-tos.

Passing one of the overflowing necessary houses, Daniel Gill felt a desire to hold his nose. He saw General Washington blanch and gasp when a cloud of greasy smoke swirled out of a colonel's tent.

"By God, what are you doing in there, Colonel?" Washington called angrily.

"Cooking my ration of beef, sir," the colonel replied cheerfully. "I do it myself in my own tent to set my officers a good example."

"*Good* example, indeed! I can think of nothing worse. Are there no camp kitchens for the men to cook their food in?" The colonel shook his head, nonchalantly munching on a chunk of beef, and Washington went on in exasperation, "Do you mean to say that every man in this army cooks his own meals in his own tent?" Bobbing his head cheerfully, the colonel finished eating and wiped his greasy fingers on his breeches. Washington exploded in wrath. "By Jehovah, I've never seen such inefficiency! This is an *army*? By God, sir, do you realize the risks of fire? Just one tent, that's all it would take to burn down the entire encampment. Colonel, where can I find the chief engineer?"

"That's me, General," the colonel said happily, making an awkward bow. "Yours truly, Silas Ripley."

'By God, sir, you won't be tomorrow if you don't get this camp cleaned up! Look at those piles of offal outside every tent! Look at the flies on them! Do you want the army to melt away from smallpox? Do you have a nose, Colonel? Can you smell the necessary houses? By God, sir, I ought to rub your nose in one of them! Do you hear me, Colonel Ripley? I want camp kitchens built and I want the offal cleaned up and burned and the necessaries filled with dirt every day and new ones dug every two weeks." The general glanced around him grimly. "And that, Colonel, is only the beginning. You will report to me first thing in the morning. Do you hear?"

The colonel gave no answer. He had snapped to attention at Washington's first bellow and he still stood transfixed as his commander-in-chief swung angrily away and strode deeper into the encampment.

"I oughtn't to have lost my temper," Washington muttered to Daniel. "It's usually a good idea to give an incompetent a tongue-lashing, but here . . . I feel like a stranger in this army. I'm going to have to pick my way carefully."

They were passing a tent with windows made of woven bush. Outside it a private sat on an empty powder keg while a captain shaved him. Both Washington and Daniel Gill stopped short in disbelief.

"What are you doing, Captain?" Washington asked quietly.

"Shaving him, sir. You stop fidgeting, Sam Dawson."

"But is he not a private soldier and are you not a captain?"

"Don't make no never-mind in this here army, General. Sam Dawson's an old customer of mine. He voted for me for captain, too. Can't forget an old customer or a constituent, General."

With an effort the general controlled himself. He drew in his breath and let it out slowly, walking farther into the camp. Outside another tent a lieutenant was taking a musket apart. He sprang to his feet and saluted when he saw Washington, spilling the parts on the ground.

"Do you carry a musket, Lieutenant?" Washington asked in surprise.

"No, sir—that's Corporal Will Taylor's musket, sir."

"You perform such services for enlisted men? You, an officer?"

The lieuetnant flushed uneasily. "He's an old customer of mine, sir. And he voted for me for lieutenant. You can't forget—"

"Yes, I know," Washington interrupted coldly, "you can't forget an old customer or an old constituent."

Turning, General Washington strode quickly back to his quarters. Once inside, he exploded in wrath again.

"It's just what I was afraid of, Daniel. That leveling spirit. Every man's just as good as the next one and maybe even a little better. By Jehovah, sometimes I wish the Crown had created an aristocracy in this country. How can you fight a war with a democratic army? Where they elect their officers and vote on whether to go on parade or open a campaign. You can't run an army like a town meeting. When you fight for freedom, Daniel, you've got to give up some of your freedom." He sat down behind his desk, opening his blue coat faced with buff and removed his wig, stroking his fading hair. "Discipline! That's the one thing we need. And respect for authority. And liberty is going to give way to regulation, by Jehovah, if I have to wear out a thousand whips doing it."

"You're going to introduce flogging, sir?" Colonel Gill asked in surprise.

"Reintroduce it! It seems to have fallen out of fashion here." The General leafed through a pile of papers on his desk. "Listen to these so-called court martials. Here's a fellow went home without leave because his cow was freshening. Another was asleep on post. A third was drunk on duty. Another tells his sergeant he isn't worth the fluff off a bug-tick's behind. Oh, they convict them well enough. But what sentences! One is fined a shilling, another one shilling sixpence—but no floggings. How can they have them flogged, when—as we just learned—they're most likely old customers and constituents? Well, that's going to change, too." Washington ran a hand over his hair. "The troops are bad enough, but some of these officers. Look at this: one colonel and two captains accused of cowardice at Bunker Hill. Two captains charged with drawing more provisions and pay than they have men in their company. Another captain, for abandoning his post and allowing the enemy to burn down a house beside it. And more . . . Well," he said grimly. "I'm going to break them, break them and cashier them! Would to God that I could hang them!"

"For an example, sir? I don't think it would work. They'd resign their commissions in droves."

"Yes, and the men would follow and the Revolution would fall apart. I'm aware of that, Daniel. This isn't much of an army right now, but as long as its in the field the Revolution is alive. The British have to contend with it. My job is to make them respect it. After discipline comes order. My God, when I see some of these companies drilling I'm reminded of comic opera. I've got a plan here for reorganizing the army, Daniel. At least the foot troops. It's based on a line regiment of seven hundred and twenty men divided into eight companies. This will give us the uniformity we need."

"Are you going to recruit men for the duration of the war, sir, as you said you'd do?"

"Congress won't let me. I have to go along with the short-term enlistments, three months to a year. Which means I may be the first commander in history asked to form an army on the field of battle knowing that it will melt away in six months, leaving me to recruit a new one. Less than six months. The Connecticut troops say their enlistments expire December first and they're going home. By Jehovah, Daniel, I wonder if I would have accepted the chief command if I had even suspected such problems. Do you realize that some of the other colonies are forming armies of their own and paying larger enlistment bounties than the Continental Army? And I have to blush for my sister colonies of the south like South Carolina and Georgia. They don't want to send us any troops at all. And Congress tells me that if I cannot get a new army up to strength by January first, I will have to depend on militia as an interim force. Militia! They make even these fellows in Cambridge look like Caesar's legions."

Washington fell silent, misery in his pale eyes. Daniel Gill studied him sympathetically. Then his own blue eyes clouded with pain as he said softly, "General, I am sorry to say that I have more bad news to report. We are down to only thirty barrels of powder."

"Thirty! By the great Jehovah, I was told that we had at least ninety."

"That was a mistake, sir. There's only enough to issue nine cartridges per man if the British should attack."

"We've got to have powder! And artillery! We need guns and shot. Send that man Knox in here, Daniel, that young fellow Henry Knox who says he's an artillerist."

Daniel left the general and returned with a plump, cherubic young man in his middle twenties. Washington studied him sourly. He disliked and distrusted fat soldiers. Momentarily, he thought of Braddock at the Monongahela, lying on his back mortally wounded like an overturned turtle.

"You are familiar with artillery, Mr. Knox?"

"Yes, sir. I had a bookstore in Boston and I used to read up on ordnance for hours at a time."

"Surely that is not the same as professional training?"

"Perhaps not, sir—but the British artillery officers who came into my shop seemed to think it was."

"Very good, Mr. Knox. I am impressed by your confidence. You shall be commissioned in due time. At the moment, I want you to inquire into the extent of artillery and ammunition in this camp and to take steps to acquire what is needed. I will give you a warrant to the Paymaster General for a thousand dollars to finance your purchases and pay your expenses. I would suggest that you go to New York first, and after that to Ticonderoga."

"I will leave immediately, General," Knox replied.

After he left, General Washington sighed and said, "My first day has not been a very auspicious start, Daniel. Fortunately, there is some good news. Smallpox is breaking out among General Howe's men, and Boston is very low on provisions, especially flesh meat. Please compose an order calling for all cattle and fowl to be moved as far into the countryside from Boston as possible. And tomorrow I think we should see about extending our fortifications around the city."

Chapter Six

"Amanda?"

Amanda Courtney raised her head listlessly. "Yes, Joel?" she replied in a toneless voice.

"I am returning your room to you. Your jewelry and your clothes."

"Please don't toy with me, Joel," Amanda said, sitting erect and smoothing the bodice of her shapeless dress of unbleached homespun.

"I am serious. I have decided that you have suffered enough." An eager look came into Amanda's blue eyes and her husband continued, "The fact is, General Sir William Howe is coming to dinner tomorrow night. He is replacing General Gage, you know." Joel coughed delicately behind his hand. "The fact is, General Howe can be most useful to me. I should like you to be sure that he is thoroughly entertained."

"Thoroughly?" Amanda repeated, getting to her feet and eyeing Joel warily.

"Yes, my dear, thoroughly. Here is the key to your room."

Amanda took the key without a word. She had been on the verge of embracing her husband in gratitude, until she realized what the terms of her liberation were to be. She went at once to her bedroom, took off the detestable dress that she wore and hurled it into the fireplace. As a gesture of open defiance, she dressed herself in the light-blue velvet gown she had worn the day . . . the day . . . Joel Courtney raised his eyebrows when Amanda appeared in that gown for dinner that evening. But he said nothing.

The following evening, Amanda was radiant in a dress of white taffeta and a bolero of red velvet embroidered with seed pearls. Her beautiful blond hair was piled in coils on her head and held in place by a turquoise comb. Around her neck was the pendant Dr. Benjamin Gill had given her. Amanda's blue eyes sparkled coquettishly when General Howe appeared. Sir William was delighted by the beauty and vivacity of his hostess and excited by her open flirting. At one point during dinner he was astounded to feel the pressure of her knee upon his. He responded and felt a rising warmth in his loins when it was not withdrawn. Sir William shot Joel Courtney a covert glance, but his host did not seem to notice. Sliding a tentative hand beneath the table, Sir William squeezed his hostess's knee. Amanda smiled gaily at him. Feeling Courtney's eye on him, Sir William withdrew his hand and patted his mouth with his napkin.

"May I compliment you on your kitchen, Mrs. Courtney," Howe said. "I believe it's the equal of any house in England. And the claret! Where do you get such claret, Mr. Courtney?"

"Direct from Bordeaux. I keep a full cellar, General. There's always danger of war with France again, you know."

"There is indeed. They didn't like losing Canada. And the Comte de Vergennes is only waiting for a chance to come to the side of these wretched Rebels. I shall take good care to see that he doesn't get it."

"I am sure you will, sir. When do you propose to attack them?"

"In the spring. Lord North is sure to send me reinforcements by then, and a fleet. I expect my brother Dick will command it."

"Excellent! I can hardly wait to see the trees of Boston Common decorated with the bodies of these ruffians. Will you hang Washington, General?"

"Indeed. With all his officers. And all the delegates to that nest of rebellion—the Adamses, Hancock, all of them—the so-called Continental Congress."

Joel Courtney beamed, a smile on his thick lips. "Some of them are the richest landowners in America. Why, Charles Carroll of Carrollton must own a tenth of the colony of Maryland." Joel pursed his lips. "Do you know, Sir William, I have always thought that the Crown made a big mistake by not establishing an aristocracy in America." General Howe glanced up with interest, and Courtney continued, "Especially here, in Massachusetts, the home of the leveler. That's what's at the bottom of this rebellion, you know. Every man up here thinks he's just as good as the next man, and maybe even a little better. With an aristocracy to keep them in check—a tug of the forelock for m'lord, that sort of thing—and to serve the interests of the Crown, we might never have landed in this sorry mess."

"Interesting suggestion," Howe murmured thoughtfully. "Quite. I shall mention it in my next letter to Lord North. But most of those fellows at the Congress, they're all men of substance, aren't they?"

"They are indeed. But it was the rabble-rousers like Hancock and Sam Adams that got them there. A rebellion like this could never have started in the south, where there is almost no middle class. But it was the mobs that got the rebellion going, General. Burning, looting, tarring and feathering. Have you ever seen a man tarred and feathered, General?" Howe shook his head, and Courtney went on. "It's hideous." Joel paused, as though distracted. He had remembered his rage when he heard that Luke Sawyer got away. Bunglers! But at least he had gotten Sawyer's smithy for next to nothing and now it was doing a brisk business with General Howe's army. "Hideous, I say. You would not believe one human being could inflict such debasing torture on another." Joel shuddered. "But, as I say, Sir William, once you've smashed the rebellion, it would be an excellent idea for the king to create an American aristocracy. Seize the Rebels' property and parcel it out among those of us who've remained loyal. Incidentally, sir, has there been any resolution on the property of the Gill family?"

"None as yet, Mr. Courtney. I believe that General Gage has promised the bulk of it to Dr. Benjamin Gill, a relative but a loyal servant of the Crown."

"But General Gage is going home. Has Dr. Gill anything in writing?"

"No. But General Gage has made me aware of his . . . ah . . . peculiar services."

Joel Courtney thrust out a thick lower lip. "Hmmnnn. Well, perhaps we can discuss it at another time, Sir William. Amanda, General, will you be good enough to excuse me for a moment?" Grunting and wheezing, he pushed himself back from the table and rose to leave the dining room. Outside the open door, he paused, listening.

"Mrs. Courtney," General Howe was saying. "May I thank

you for a delightful and delicious evening. I can tell you that nowhere in my travels have I met a lady as gracious—and I may say, as beautiful—as you."

"Thank you, Sir William," Amanda said, blushing prettily. "I am indeed flattered. And it was a pleasure having you call."

"May I call again?"

"Indeed. Joel is so busy with his affairs . . . sometimes I feel so lonely . . . I would enjoy it so much . . ."

Outside the door, Joel Courtney thought to himself: The little hussy! I do believe she's going to enjoy it.

Dr. Gill recognized the black man who silently handed him an envelope as the servant at the Courtney home who opened the back door for him. Eagerly digging a shilling from his pocket, Dr. Gill handed it to him and tore the letter open. It was from Amanda! He began to read:

Benjie! Benjie! Benjie!
He let me out of my cage!
My fat friend the jailer gave me back my bedroom, my clothes and my jewels.
He didn't do it because he loves me but because he wants me to become "a companion" to General Howe.
The general is lonely so far away from home and my fat friend wants me to comfort him. As a reward, he expects Sir William to look the other way while he seizes all the Rebel properties he can get and feeds them to his accomplices at rigged auctions.
I have something very important to tell you.
Please come to me tonight.

                                        I love you, Benjie!
                                        Amanda

On fire with desire, Dr. Gill hastened to Amanda's bedroom. He found her, once again, reading in bed by candlelight. She sprang to her feet and came running toward him, her negligee parting as she came. Dr. Gill saw the face and body—the golden curls nestling seductively in her crotch—that had been at the back of his brain since they had parted, and he seized her and carried her back to her bed.

"Benjie, I locked the door this time," Amanda gasped as he slid his slender long hand between her thighs and parted them.

"You're much nicer than Sir William, Benjie," Amanda said, snuggling closer to him. "Sir William is very polite and courtly, but he's also a little portly, too, and fat men just don't have much to work with. I've often wondered why the skinny men are so much bigger."

"My God, woman, are you a connoisseur of masculine equipment?"

Amanda giggled. "I've seen a few."

"So you did not come to the good Joel as a virgin?"

"Oh, him! He's got the tiniest little dauber. I think he just has water rights to it."

Benjamin chuckled. "Come, now, tell me," he murmured, idly stroking her thigh, "who was the first?"

Amanda giggled again. "Parson Williams." Enjoying the expression of horror on Benjamin's face, Amanda said, "He was a widower and I was only fourteen. The first few times I went into his house with him it was to pray together. But then it got to be something else. Every time he did it, he'd jump out of bed and go down on his knees and pray to God for forgiveness. I really didn't like him," Amanda said, pouting, "but he did give me a pony and he always told my parents I was a good Christian child."

Benjamin shook his head wonderingly. "And then?"

"Joel's brother."

"Whaaat?"

"Well, it was some time ago. Joshua was nothing like Joel. He was much, much younger and much better looking. Dark and handsome . . . a lot like you, Benjie . . . dashing . . . He was a sea captain, too. But I didn't want to spend my life watching from a widow's walk. Besides, Joel was already rich. That Joshua! He laughed himself silly when he saw me coming down the aisle wearing white. I was so mad at him, I almost didn't cry when I heard he was drowned at sea."

"Do you know, Amanda," Benjamin said, getting to his feet and beginning to dress, "I'm beginning to feel a certain sympathy for your husband. By the way, what was the important matter you wanted to discuss?"

"Joel is after the Gill estates."

Dr. Gill's face darkened. "He is, is he—with the cooperation of General Howe?" Amanda nodded, and Benjamin struck his fist into his palm. "He can't do that to me! General Howe knows that General Gage promised me my uncles' properties. And now that they're both dead, I've got an even better claim as their nephew."

"What about Nathaniel? He was the one who rescued Luke Sawyer, you know. When Joel heard that Jennifer's fiancé had done that I thought he was going to have apoplexy."

"Nate's a Rebel. He has no standing. If you'll recall, my dear, those properties were going to get us a fine home in France or England."

"I haven't forgotten," Amanda said, yawning and drawing her negligee over her shoulders. "And I mean to speak to Sir Billy about it. This time I think my fat friend made a mistake. He wanted to get close to the general through me, and he did. But, I've gotten a lot closer."

Chapter Seven

The shock of losing both his father and his uncle at the Battle of Bunker Hill had been too much for Nathaniel Gill's young mind. When he awoke in the hospital at Cambridge, he could remember nothing beyond that point. For days he lay in the hospital, staring miserably at the ceiling by day, and by night, wandering through the ward murmuring, over and over: "Who am I? Where did I come from?"

When Barbara Pace and Daniel Gill came to visit him, he gazed at them with no sign of recognition in his blank eyes. Barbara kissed him tenderly on the forehead and Daniel patted him on the shoulder. Barbara put a box on the bedside table.

"Maple-sugar candy, Natey," she said with a smile. "Your favorite."

"It is?"

Barbara shot him a puzzled glance. "Of course it is, silly. You know that."

"Do I?"

"Please don't tease me that way, Natey," Barbara said with a frown. "I . . . I don't like it."

Nate took a piece of the candy and bit into it, chewing slowly. "Ummm. It is good." He stared at Barbara and Daniel inquiringly. "I'd like to thank you, but I don't know who you are."

Barbara gasped. "Please, Natey, don't say things like that. You *must* know who I am. I'm your cousin Barbara Pace and this is your cousin Daniel Gill from Virginia."

Nate shook his head in slow denial. "I . . . I guess you must know who you are and who I am, but I don't." His eyes clouded in misery. "The . . . the doctors say I may never know." Then he looked up eagerly. "Please . . . please tell me who I am."

Her lips trembling and her eyes moist, Barbara said: "You're Nathaniel Gill of Boston. You're a student at Harvard College. Your grandmother died in April—"

"Please," Nate interrupted, "how long ago was that?"

"More than two months ago," Barbara replied, fighting back the tears. "In seventeen seventy-five. You fought at Lexington and Concord a few days after she died. And then at Bunker Hill a week ago. That's when . . . that's when you lost . . ." Barbara could not go on. She put her face in her hands and began to sob. Daniel put his hand on her shoulder.

"Maybe you'd better go," Nate said in a low voice. "I know you mean to help me, but you're hurting yourself more."

Nodding, kissing him again on the forehead, squeezing his hand in hers. Barbara seized Daniel's arm for support and left the room.

Next day, Luke Sawyer came to see Nate.

"Who are you?" Nate asked in a dull voice after Luke wrung his hand warmly.

"Who am I?" Luke repeated in dismay. "Nate, it's me—Luke Sawyer, yer old friend. Here," he said, putting his hand in Nate's, "feel the calluses on my hand. Does that mean anything to you?"

"Only that you do hard work," Nate muttered.

"But I'm a *blacksmith*!" Luke cried in dismay. "You've *gotta* remember that!" Nate shook his head despairingly, and Luke rushed on: "Don't you remember my smithy? The night we rescued your pa and Uncle Mike from the lobsterbacks?"

Again, Nate shook his head, mumbling: "I don't even remember my pa or my uncle."

Stunned, Luke Sawyer took his departure. But he was back the following day with an envelope in his hand. "Nate, Natey," he exclaimed eagerly, "I've got a letter for you."

Nate glanced up in curiosity. "From whom?"

"Jennifer Courtney."

"Jennifer Courtney?" Nate repeated, puzzled. "Jennifer!" Recollection exploded in the mind of Nathaniel Gill. He reeled at the speed of his memory racing back to Bunker Hill. He saw his Uncle Malachi being bayoneted to death and he put his hands over his eyes and sobbed. He saw the body of Dr. Warren and then his father's, and he cried aloud. "No! No! I can't stand it! Say it isn't true, Luke."

At once delighted that the youth had recovered his memory, but sobered by the misery of his first recollections, Luke put a steadying hand on Nate's shoulder. "Try not to think too hard, Natey," he said soothingly.

"It is true, isn't it?" Nate sobbed, lifting a tearstained face. Luke nodded his head slowly, squeezing Nate's shoulder. Stark grief in his eyes, his sobs subsiding, Nathaniel sank back against his pillow. He shut his eyes, and Luke Sawyer tiptoed softly away from him. Eventually, Nate fell asleep. He awoke, shouting, "Jennifer!" and tore open the letter still in his hand. He read:

Dearest Natey,

I have just heard of the death of your pa and your uncle, and I am writing to tell you how sorry I am. It's awful to try to tell a person you love as much as I love you how sorry you are. I know that I can't hope to share your grief, Natey. I only wish I could. I loved your pa and your uncle so much. Especially your pa. He was always so kind to me. You remember how he taught me to ride when I was a little girl and how he laughed and laughed when we both fell in the tub when we were ducking for apples. Oh, Natey! There will be so many good things for you to remember about your pa after you get over losing him.

Natey, I am writing this letter in installments because I don't dare risk having Pa catching me at it. Oh, Natey, life here is becoming almost unbearable! There is nothing but hate all around me. It's terrible to have to listen to my pa and other people you used to know so well saying such terrible things about you and the others with you, and they seem to enjoy doing it. The kindest things they can say is that you are Rebels and traitors. I have to listen to it because I don't dare say anything in your defense. When Pa found out that it was you who took Luke Sawyer away from the mob I thought he would start foaming at the mouth. So I just sit still and do my needlework and try not to cry. You were very brave to have done that, Natey, but then I always knew you were brave since that Easter week at Concord when you dove into the freezing water of the cow pond to save Abner Hosmer's life. Oh! And little Abner is dead, too!

Life is very hard here in Boston. It is very cold and

there is a shortage of firewood because the British cannot get out into the country. There is almost no beef. Of course, we do not suffer in this house. As you can guess, my pa always keeps a well-stocked kitchen and cellar. General Howe has become a great admirer of my stepmother's. He visits her frequently. She tries to send me out on errands before he arrives. But I hide across the street until I see his coach coming and then I do what she wants me to. It's fun spying on her, Natey! She's such a sneak herself.

When will it all be over, Natey, this terrible war that is keeping us apart? When will this madness that is pitting brother against brother and friend against friend come to an end? Oh, Natey—I love you so! I miss you so! I think about you all day long. I pray to God to spare you. Please, Natey, be careful! I know you are strong and brave and impetuous—which is why I love you so—but please be cautious. And then when this dreadful war is over you can come to me and marry me like you promised.

I love you, Natey
Jenny

P.S. Please don't write to me, Natey. The whole atmosphere of my house is so poisoned with suspicion, I'm afraid anything you write might fall into the wrong hands.

Write to her! Nathaniel thought. Of course not! I'll *go* to her!

Nate knew of a rowboat berthed at Lechmere Point, about six miles from Cambridge and less than a mile across the harbor from Boston. If the boat wasn't burned up when the British set fire to Charlestown, he intended to row across the water to Boston and to go to his grandmother's house to get the British soldier's uniform left in the stable by his cousin Dan. If it was still there! If it was, he would put it on and go openly through the streets to Jennifer's house. If it wasn't, he would have to go anyway and hope he wasn't recognized.

Slipping through Charlestown, Nate could smell the charred ruins of the town. The stumps of half-burned shipyard stocks stood gaunt against the sky like giant broken fingers. The rowboat was there! So were the oars clamped underneath it. Nate slid the oars into place and began to row. *Squeek, squeek*. Nate cursed himself for not bringing oil. The oarlocks squeaked. He rowed on, *squeek, squeek,* through the dark water.

Nate paused at the oars. He thought he saw a swinging light and heard a low murmur of voices. Nate waited until he saw or heard nothing, and then rowed on.

Squeek, squeek.

"What's that noise, mate?" a voice called, and Nate quietly shipped his oars.

"Sounds like a squeaky oarlock to me, Bill."

Nate began taking off his clothes. He rolled them into a bundle and slipped softly into the water holding it. He would swim the rest of the way.

" 'Ere, 'ere, wot's that noise?"

Now Nate heard the creak of oars and saw the light of a lantern approaching over the water. He sank quietly beneath the surface. Forced up again for air, he heard the voices again.

"It's a bloody rowboat, Bill. Might as well take it in tow."

" 'Ope it belongs to one of the Yankee scum. But where's the bleddy owner, that's wot I'd like to know."

"Over there! Over there!"

Nate saw the lantern swinging toward him and heard a loud splash as one of the sailors dived into the water and swam toward him.

"It's a Yank!" the sailor yelled, and seized Nate by the shoulder. " 'It 'im with the oar!"

Nate broke away from his assailant. He felt the man reaching for his genitals and brought his own knee up into the sailor's groin. He groaned and clutched his abdomen and Nate clasped his hands around his neck and began to strangle him, pushing him below the surface. The man struggled feebly and Nate pushed his thumbs deeper into his windpipe. He felt a blow on his shoulder and saw the other sailor wielding an oar above him. Feeling the body he held go limp, Nate dodged another blow by the second sailor and dived underneath the boat. He began to swim underwater toward Boston, surfacing every fifteen or twenty seconds farther and farther away.

"Bill!" he could hear the seaman in the boat calling. "Bill! Where are you, mate?"

Gradually, his voice became fainter and Nate began to swim on the surface. It felt good swimming through the cool water naked—then he remembered his clothes. They were gone! He couldn't possibly go through the streets of Boston like this. Nate thought of swimming back to the point, until he realized that he was almost on the Boston shore and was tiring. He could never make it back.

In the light issuing from the window of a building ahead of him Nate could see a British sentry striding back and forth on the waterfront. His musket was sloped. Nate dived again and swam underwater beneath the wharf. Surfacing, he crouched underneath it listening to the steady clumping of the soldier's feet. He walked exactly forty paces, turned and strode off another forty. Nate timed his movements. He swam to the end of the sentry's course, grasped the end of the wharf and pulled himself slightly out of the water. When the sentry reached that point and turned to make his return march, Nate pulled himself completely out of the water, ran silently up behind him with his hands clasped overhead and brought them down with all his strength onto the base of the man's neck. There was a sharp *spat* and the soldier sank soundlessly to the ground.

Nate quickly stripped off the man's uniform and put it on. He seized his bayoneted musket. Looking down at the unconscious soldier he saw that he was young. About his own age . . . his cheeks were rosy . . . Nate felt sorry for him. But then he saw again his uncle being stabbed to death and his own father lying lifeless on the ground and he heard once again his uncle Malachi saying, "You can't make a revolution with rosewater, Natey," and he drove the bayonet into the man's throat and lowered his spouting, dying body into the water.

Nathaniel Gill never again pitied an enemy soldier.

Jennifer Courtney had just driven into the courtyard in her new gig. As she entrusted it to a stablehand she saw a British redcoat approaching with sloped musket. She nodded politely and was about to inquire what he wanted when he leaned his musket against the side of the house, seized her and kissed her full on the mouth. Infuriated, Jennifer freed herself and lifted her hand to slap his face. Instead the hand flew to her mouth in astonished disbelief.

"Nathaniel! It's you. But what . . . what are you doing in a British soldier's uniform? Oh, Lord, if my father catches you! They'll have you hanging by your neck so fast it'll make your head spin."

"To say the least," Nate murmured, smiling broadly, and even Jenny giggled at the incongruity of her remark. "Aren't you going to kiss me?"

At once Jenny sprang into his arms, throwing her own around him to hug him while she pressed her lips fiercely against his. It was a long kiss. Both were panting when they released each other to stare adoringly into each other's eyes. Suddenly, Jennifer glanced around her wildly.

"You can't just stand here, Nate! Someone will see you. Someone will want to know what I'm doing talking to a British soldier." She pointed to the back door where Nate had hidden the last time she saw him. "Quick! In there!" Grasping his hand, with a rustle of her pink taffeta dress she led him hurriedly inside. Nate kissed her again and stepped back.

"You always did look good in pink, Jenny," he said. "I declare you're even prettier in the flesh than when I dream about you. And that's mostly all the time."

Jennifer laughed and stepped into his arms again. She felt his hand go to her breast and squeeze it gently. She let it remain there. Now she felt his embraces become more fervid. She felt warmer. Nate was panting as he whispered, "Where do these stairs lead to?"

"Behind the fireplace in my stepmother's bedroom."

"Is she home?"

"No, she went riding with General Howe."

"Come on," he said, seizing her hand.

"No, Natey—no!"

"Yes!"

She shook her head. "No, Natey, I don't want to."

"Yes, you do! Please? What if something should happen to me? What if I should get killed in battle? You'd never forgive yourself for not letting me. Please, Jenny—please! You may never see me again."

Jennifer lifted her head slowly and fixed him with her soft brown eyes. "I love you, Natey. I'll do anything for you. Even this. But let me go up first," she said, lifting her pink skirts in her hand and running quickly upstairs.

She was in her stepmother's bed with the sheets drawn up

to her chin when he entered. He began to undress. "Hurry, Natey, hurry," she urged him, panting again. "But don't look at me. I don't want you to see me. Just get in next to me. Oh, Natey, Natey," she moaned, squirming underneath him and beginning to fall into the rhythm of the act. "Do it to me, Natey, do it to me. Ohhhh, *Natey*."

"I think you ought to go back with me, Jenny," Nathaniel said, beginning to dress.

"What for?"

"So we can get married, silly. You could stay with my cousin Barbara out at the summer place in Concord."

"But I don't want to get married right now, Natey. I love you more than anyone in the world, but I don't want to get married now. I'd rather wait until the war's over. It wouldn't be much of a marriage, either—you marching off every which way. I couldn't go with you. I'd hate to sit and just wait . . . waiting to hear that maybe you'd . . ."

"How can a girl as pretty as you be so practical?"

"My ma taught me," Jennifer said proudly. "She told me that before I did a thing to think what would happen because I did it. And I honestly think being a private soldier's wife would be anything but romantic. And I sure wouldn't kowtow to the officers' wives, either."

"All right. But you could still stay with Barbara until the war's over. I just hate the thought of you being in Boston with all these damned Tories. You said yourself you hated the life you were leading."

"But I can't just go, silly! I can't swim across the harbor like you can. How would I get out of Boston?" Jennifer stared at Nathaniel in his red coat and white breeches and shook her head. "You can't go on wearing that uniform. Where'd you get it, anyway?" Nate told her and her dark eyes widened in horror. "Now you certainly can't wear it. They've probably found his body by now and they'll be looking for you. Wait here," she said, rushing out the bedroom door. She returned with clothes of her father's. "Put these on," she said, shyly turning her back.

"My God," Nate said in a rueful voice. "I think your pa is bigger around than he is tall." Jenny giggled and turned around. Nate held her father's blue breeches out from his stomach. "You could stick a pillow in there," he muttered.

Jenny giggled again, going out the door once more to return with needle and thread and her mouth full of pins. She quickly gathered up the breeches' loose material, lapped it, skillfully pinned it up and sewed it together. Nate put on a silver satin coat which fell from his shoulders in folds. "It fits me like a tent," he grumbled.

"But it's better than being caught in a British uniform and hung," Jennifer said.

"They'd hang me anyway. Just for being a Rebel."

Jennifer's eyes clouded in pain, and she said, "Please, Natey, please, please be careful."

Colonel Daniel Gill was in high spirits as he rode from headquarters in Cambridge toward Concord to visit his cousin, Barbara. It was mid-October in 1775. Because General Washington doubted that General Howe would attempt to break out of beseiged Boston before winter set in, he had given Daniel a two-day leave. The day was glorious, one of those peculiar to the northeast when the air is bright with the golden light of autumn and exhilaratingly cool. The fields were a bright gold, too, plotted and pieced among the lines of trees or the copses riotous with the colors of the season: yellowing maples mingling with the reds and browns of the oaks and birches. Daniel leaned forward to pat Major Pitcairn's horse on the withers. "Beautiful day, eh, Liberty?" he called, and the horse pricked up its ears. Daniel began to whistle "Yankee Doodle." To his surprise, Liberty began to caper to the tune. "That a boy," Daniel cried, chuckling. "Poor Pitcairn would be proud of you. I guess he must've trained you to dance like that."

Suddenly Daniel remembered another glorious day in Massachusetts more than twenty years ago when he had left home to seek his fortune in the Ohio country. How lucky he had been to run into George Washington who was just setting out for the Ohio to warn the French to withdraw from British soil. Befriending Washington had made his fortune. George himself had become one of the wealthiest men in the colonies after he married Martha Custis. What a wedding that had been. By God, Danny boy, he told himself, and maybe it's time you got hitched yourself. You're getting pretty close to forty and it's time the Gill family opened up a southern branch.

Rounding a bend in the road, he saw the Gill farmhouse across the field and cantered up a path leading to it. Barbara Pace saw him coming from the porch and she ran down the steps to greet him. Daniel dismounted and kissed her, holding her in his arms just a moment longer than usual.

"It's such a wonderful day, Barbara—how about a picnic?"

Barbara's blue eyes sparked in delight. "Great! You harness up the buckboard while I pack a lunch."

Within ten minutes they were riding back out the path. "Turn left here," Barbara said.

"Where are we gong?"

"One of my favorite places. It's just the other side of Lexington."

They rode on in silence. Daniel noticed that Barbara was embroidering a green wool cloth with gold thread. "What are you doing?" he asked.

"Making you a saddlecloth," Barbara said, blushing slightly. She held it up. The green cloth was trimmed in gold. On either side was a gold circle enclosing a beer tankard imposed on a dripping tomahawk. Around this device was a band bearing the inscription: "Taken at the Flood."

"Very interesting," Daniel murmured. "I saw that insignia in stained glass over the door of your grandmother's home and I meant to ask about it."

"It's the Gill family's crest. Grandpa designed it. He always said it was the tomahawk that gave him life and the tavern that put him on the road to riches."

" 'Taken at the Flood'?"

"That was his favorite quotation. 'There is a tide in the affairs of men which, taken at the flood, leads on to fortune.' It's from William Shakespeare."

"How apt," Daniel mused. "That's exactly what we're doing now. If we hadn't taken the tide of fortune at the flood at Concord and Bunker Hill, we might have allowed it to ebb and missed our revolution."

Barbara nodded, pointing to a farm on their right with a stone gristmill and a millrace and waterfall emptying into a millpond. "That's it," Barbara said, and Daniel turned off the road to ride through an open gate. "This is where my great-grandmother used to picnic. Great-grandfather Clarke would follow her out of town to spy on her."

"I never heard that one," Daniel said, lifting the picnic hamper onto the ground.

"Yes. She had a friend who played the violin and she would dance a solo minuet. Great-grandpa would watch her from the woods."

"And so they were married, eh?" Daniel said, laughing. He seized Barbara around the waist and began to dance with her, whistling a minuet from Mozart. He finished with a sweeping bow and then took her into his arms and kissed her.

"I love you, Barbara, and I want you to marry me," he said.

"Oh, Daniel!" Barbara wailed. "I love you, too! And I do want to marry you. You're the man I've been waiting for all my life. But we're *cousins!*"

"That doesn't make that much difference. Lots of people who are cousins get married. Besides our blood lines aren't really that close. You're pure English stock, but I've got Indian and Irish blood in me. It wouldn't be that dangerous at all."

"Do you think the church would approve?"

"Sure it would. The Episcopal Church isn't tough at all on consanguinity."

Barbara frowned. "Episcopal? But I'm a Congregationalist."

Daniel shook his head in mock exasperation. "For a lady who says she loves me and wants to marry me, you sure can think up problems." Barbara smiled and Daniel embraced her again. He kissed her tenderly and she responded with passion, but she gently detached the hand that sought her breast.

"No," she said softly, "I'm like Mary was: 'I know not man.' I have waited this long to give myself to the man I love on my wedding night and I can wait a little longer."

"I think I love you even more for that, Barbara. You will marry me, then?"

"Yes."

"When?"

"Whenever you say."

"Tomorrow!" Daniel Quinn yelled, frightening a flight of migrating starlings from their perch high in an oak tree. "Tomorrow!" he shouted in jubilation, swinging Barbara into the air. "Tomorrow and tomorrow and tomorrow!"

Chapter Eight

As the year 1775 neared its end, Colonel Daniel Gill noticed that General Washington seemed more and more harassed. Although he had strengthened his fortifications around Boston until he had a line fourteen miles long, he seldom went into the field to inspect them. Most of his time was spent writing to Congress, to the various colonies, pleading for more men, more arms, more money.

"The Congress adopted this army and put me in command of it," Washington said to Daniel one day, "and they've done precious little ever since. They don't seem to hear when I tell them we have a shortage of shoes, that some of the men are walking around with rags on their feet, that we need bayonets. They seem to think that they can legislate a revolution. Pass a law declaring the war won or maybe disqualifying the British Army. They don't seem to understand that this little army *is* the Revolution. If it melts away, so does the Revolution. And it is melting away, Daniel—what are today's rolls?"

"Down to less than thirteen thousand men, sir."

Washington sighed. "It'll be down close to ten thousand tomorrow when the Connecticut troops go home." His face darkened. "Dirty, low, mercenary spirit. Base desertion of their country and their cause."

"Couldn't you do anything to stop them?"

"I tried. But they insisted that they had signed on for only eight months and they were going home December first. By Jehovah, there's another thing the Congress doesn't understand. The evil of short-term enlistment, of having to form a new army every six months or so. If I could get long-term enlistments, an army I could form and train for the duration, I would almost guarantee victory. But they won't listen," Washington sighed again. "General Lee wants to speak to them. He says he thinks he can persuade them to stay."

"General Lee, sir?" Daniel asked in surprise. "I never thought he was particularly persuasive. He's a typical British Army officer. He hasn't been in America long enough to understand our citizen-soldiers."

"Well, he wants to try," Washington said, accepting a bundle of letters brought into his chambers by a courier. One of them was from Henry Knox and the general opened it eagerly. He frowned. "He's got the artillery from Ticonderoga, all right, but he's having a devil of a time getting it here. Here," he said, handing Daniel the letter. Daniel read:

I have the honor to report that the ordnance from Ticonderoga is safely enroute to Boston. It is indeed a noble train of artillery, fifty-nine pieces ranging from the big twenty-four–pounders to a handful of small mortars. So far we have encountered no sign of the enemy, but we are meeting with difficulties of terrain and weather. As you may imagine, my dear general, it is no small task to transport them down from the northern lakes in the dead of an American winter. At the outset they were loaded on barges, but the barges sank and the guns had to be grubbed up. After the lakes and rivers froze they were put on sleds, but sometimes the ice broke under the weight of the cannon and the guns sank and we were obliged to recover them once again. Upon the arrival of snow, we had to place the artillery on sledges for the remainder of the ground journey, as we are now doing. It is quite a spectacle, my dear general, the horses and oxen panting and gasping while the column goes toiling up one snow-covered hill, and then the men hauling back on the sledges with ropes on the downgrade and shouting warnings as the cannon gather momentum and threaten to smash into the poor beasts in front of them. Many of these creatures have perished in the traces, but, fortunately, we were able to obtain replacements. Nevertheless, sir, we have surmounted all these obstacles and I am happy to report to you that we should arrive in camp by some time in the middle of January.

Henry Knox

"Good news at last, sir," Daniel said, handing the letter back to Washington. The general nodded, going to the window upon hearing the barking of dogs. "That must be General Lee now," Washington said. Daniel joined him and saw General Charles Lee, a slender man wearing a disheveled uniform, walking down the street followed by a pack of yelping hounds. Lee turned to kneel and pet one of them. Instantly, they were all over him, yapping and tumbling over one another in their eagerness to lick their master's face. Daniel was astonished when he saw the general kissing them back, and then disgusted when he realized some of the dogs were licking the spilled food off the general's shirt and waistcoat.

"He does like dogs," Washington murmured. "I was a dinner guest at his quarters the other night, and I can tell you that I was a bit taken aback when I saw that the other guests were two dogs. One was so big I thought he was a small bear. But they sat on their chairs between us with their plates in front of them just as proper as could be, and damned if the servants didn't serve them their food as though they were the king and queen of England!"

Daniel Gill laughed and shook his head. "I'll bet they didn't get as much food as the general's waistcoat did." He arose. "I think I'll go see how he does with the Connecticut men." Going outside, he followed General Lee to the parade ground where the officers had drawn up the Connecticut volunteers.

"Men, you can't go home, God damn your lily-livered souls," he shouted at them. "You can't desert your country's cause in this cowardly fashion."

Boo! Boooo! Sssssssss!

"We done our share," one of them called out. "Let some others do theirs."

"While I've been wasting my time here," another cried, "a man from Vermont took over my dry-goods business."

"My mother wrote my brother's making calf eyes at my wife."

General Lee stared at the troops in exasperation. "I don't know what to call you," he yelled. "You are the worst of all creatures."

Laughing, the Connecticut men shouldered their muskets and set their faces south, ignoring the groans and curses of the comrades they were abandoning, ducking their heads beneath a shower of stones and exchanging insults with the women of the camp.

General Charles Lee followed them for a few hundred yards, shouting curses. Daniel Gill watched him in dismay. He thought: This is *persuasion?*

The end of 1775 and the beginning of 1776 were almost equally inauspicious for the British Army in Boston. Smallpox was spreading and the food supply was shrinking. General Sir William Howe was so busy struggling to preserve order and discipline that he had little time for anyone but Amanda Courtney. Even Joel Courtney was allowed to sit fidgeting for hours in the general's anteroom, hoping for an interview in which to discuss acquisition of the Gill properties. News that the Rebels had succeeded in moving the guns of Ticonderoga to their lines around Boston came as a distinct shock to General Howe and sank the Tory inhabitants of the city into the deepest gloom. One night in early March Joel Courtney returned to his home for dinner in a foul mood.

"The blasted Rebels have mounted their big guns on Dorchester Heights," he growled to Amanda. "General Howe says he will have to evacuate the city."

Amanda's blue eyes widened in horror. "Leave Boston? Leave everything we own behind? For the Rebels to loot and burn or claim for their own? Oh, Joel—how horrible!"

"Better than staying here to be hung," Joel replied grimly. "Fortunately, because of our friendship with the general, we are among the lucky Loyalists who will be taken with him."

"Where to?"

"Probably Halifax."

"Good Lord! That dreary wet limbo of a place."

Joel threw his napkin down on the table in disgust. "It's outrageous! Imagine! That filthy rabble in arms cooping a British army up for a whole winter and then forcing it to leave. I can't believe it!"

"What of the properties you've been acquiring? When the Rebels come in they'll take them back."

"Fortunately, I have not begun payment on most of them yet. I still stand to lose a few thousand pounds, though."

"But what of our own money?" Amanda wailed. "Our specie! My jewels and clothes!"

"Just what I expected to hear from you, my dear," Joel said maliciously. "Fortunately, the general has given us a generous allocation of space. We will probably be able to take all of our money and valuables." He smiled again with malice. "And I have the honor to inform you that your esteemed friend Dr. Gill is now in jail."

"Benjie!" Amanda cried in horror, her hand flying to her mouth. "Oh, no! What did he *do?* Did you put him there?"

"I had not the pleasure," Joel replied dryly. "General Howe did. Sir William is a clever man. He wants your . . . ah . . . friend to be found in jail when the Rebels arrive, which should serve as his credentials for his loyalty to their cause. In that way, he may resume his invaluable services as a spy. Washington will certainly not suspect a man jailed on a charge of treason. Sir William is aware that that detestable Indian, Seahawk, is actually a Rebel agent. He has planted incorrect information on him in the past. Tonight, he will be allowed to see Dr. Gill being marched off in irons."

"Poor Benjie," Amanda murmured. "He does so love fine things and he hates dirt. He won't like jail. How long do you think he'll be there?"

"Until we evacuate and the Rebel scum come in. Two or three weeks, I should say. Not nearly long enough. However, one must be thankful for even small favors." Joel raised his wine glass to his lips and drank. Some of the liquid ran down his chin and dripped onto his coat. He brushed at the stain angrily with a bunched napkin. "By the way, Amanda," he said, looking up, "have you seen anything of my silver satin coat? I can't seem to find it."

Amanda shook her head. "I haven't seen it. Maybe you took it to the tailor to be let out."

Joel glanced at her sharply. "That will be enough of that!" he snapped. "And what's become of Jennifer? I haven't seen the girl for days."

Amanda Courtney sucked in her breath and stared at her husband. "Jennifer is pregnant," she said.

"Whaaat?" Joel Courtney reared back like a startled steer. "My God, woman, what are you saying? You can't mean that!"

"But I do. I had been noticing that she was getting heavier. I teased her this morning about getting fat and she burst into tears and ran to her room. I followed her and she admitted that she was pregnant." Joel shuddered at the word and

Amanda concluded, "She's been to the doctor and he told her she was."

"By God, this is the end!" Joel Courtney sputtered, slamming his fist down on the table and overturning his wine glass. "The little fly-by-night! The ungrateful little slut to dishonor my good name . . . Isn't it enough that my wife—" Joel paused, glaring at Amanda.

"—should serve your interests?" she inquired sweetly, and Joel glanced away in momentary confusion.

"Send her to me," he muttered. "I'll settle this thing at once."

"Joel," Amanda cried in alarm, "you're not going to turn your back on your own daughter?"

"I am going to get to the bottom of this thing," he answered grimly. "I am not to be made a laughingstock. How far gone is she?"

"Eight months."

Joel grimaced. "Too far gone to take her for a bumpy carriage ride."

"Monster!"

"Shut up! Send her to me as I asked. And leave me alone with her."

Joel saw that his daughter had been crying when she came into the dining room and stood before him. Her eyes were red and there were tearstains on the bodice of her dress of embroidered yellow satin.

"Whose is it?" he snapped.

"I . . . I don't know."

"You lie! You stand there and tell me you don't know whose child you are carrying. Are you telling me that you are nothing but a promiscuous slut who doesn't know whose sperm has made you what you are?"

Jennifer Courtney stepped forward and slapped her father's face. He put his hand to his reddened cheek in astonishment. He let out a bellow of rage and shot erect, lifting his hand as though to strike her. Jennifer stood before him unflinching, with proud and uplifted head.

"I know whose baby it is," she murmured. "I know him and I love him and he loves me. We are going to be married when this dreadful war is over."

"*Gill!*" Joel Courtney roared. "That's who it is. That treacherous little Rebel, Nathaniel *Gill!*"

"Oh, stop!" Jenny sobbed, covering her face with her hands. "Stop it! Stop all this horrible talk about people you once knew and loved. That's all you hear in this house . . . everywhere you go in the city . . . Rebels . . . traitors . . . kill them . . . string them up . . . tar and feather them . . . flog them . . . I . . . I can't stand it, anymore!"

Joel Courtney ignored his weeping daughter. "Yes, that must be it," he said musingly. "There was a British sentry murdered on the waterfront about eight months ago. Had his uniform taken from him." He snapped his fingers. "Yes, and that was when I first noticed my coat was missing." He whirled on Jennifer. "He was here, wasn't he? He came disguised in a British uniform. A spy! He'll hang for that! He came here and you gave him your father's coat to escape in!"

"Yes, he was here and I did go with him!" Jenny replied, straightening with flashing eyes and clenched fists. "It was the first time for both of us, and we love each other! You call me a whore," she cried scornfully. "You of all people—with your little blond doxy charming the general out of his breeches and his better judgment. You hypocrite!"

Joel Courtney's face turned slowly scarlet. It became mottled, and he swayed momentarily, putting a hand to his heart.

"Get out!" he gasped in a choking voice, pointing at the door. "Get out! You are no longer my daughter. I disown you! Get out of my sight, I say, you Rebel's whore!"

Shrieking, Jennifer Courtney turned and ran from the room. She ran out the front door and down the steps and by the time she reached the street she was sobbing again. What will I do? What will I do? she thought despairingly. Where will I go? She thought of asking shelter at the church parsonage, but from a sense of shame she couldn't bring herself to go there. She began running toward the Common. Before she reached it, she heard a horrible whistling noise overhead and then an explosion and saw a house across the street collapse and begin to burn. The whistling noises multiplied. Jenny saw cannon balls go bouncing down the street, sometimes bounding into shops and taverns with a smash of shattered glass. With horror, she realized that the Rebels had begun to bombard Boston.

Natey! she thought, Natey! I'll go to him. But how? Now the cannonade grew heavier. Houses were reeling and shaking. Their inhabitants poured out of them into the streets. A man ran into Jennifer, knocking her against a wall. She clutched fearfully at her stomach. Now she was passing by the British barracks. Soldiers ran out of them. There was a whistle overhead and Jenny was horrified to see a cannonball plow into a cluster of redcoats, striking eight of them to the ground. Some of them had lost their heads. Jennifer staggered past them, covering her eyes so that she wouldn't see the blood gushing from their mangled necks. Alongside her two houses swayed and collapsed with a roar, showering the street with falling timbers and broken glass. Everywhere soldiers and civilians were running with their hands held over ducked heads. They began throwing themselves to the ground. Jenny made as though to hurl herself behind the shelter of a bench, but then, thinking of her baby, stopped herself in time.

Gradually, the bombardment lifted. Jennifer staggered through the debris-filled street, making for Boston Neck. How would she get through British lines? She didn't know, but she stumbled on. There was a rattle of wheels behind her. Jenny turned and saw a horse-drawn cart slowly picking its way toward her. She recognized the driver! It was Seahawk, Natey's Indian friend. She ran up to him. He stopped, lifting his greasy coonskin cap.

"Please, Seahawk, where are you going?"

"Out Boston Neck, ma'am."

"Please, let me go with you. Take me to Natey! He's . . . my . . . husband." She put her hand on her bulging stomach, and Seahawk nodded understandingly.

"Get in the wagon, ma'am. There's some hay you can lie on." He climbed down to help her into the wagon. Jenny noticed that he seemed unsteady on his feet. She thought she smelled rum on his breath. "Maybe you'd better sit up so you won't feel the bumpsh so much," he muttered, clambering back onto the box. "Bumpsh no good for papooshes."

Jennifer sat up. From the box she heard the popping of a cork and a gurgle, then a deep sigh of satisfaction and the smacking of Seahawk's lips. Oh, please, Seahawk, don't get drunk, she prayed. My baby! My baby! Now Jennifer sighed herself. She was exhausted from her ordeal. She became drowsy and fell asleep.

She awoke to the mad swaying of the cart.

"Seahawk! Seahawk!" she cried, staggering erect. To her

horror she saw the Indian standing in the box, swaying drunkenly and flogging the bloody back of his horse.

"Gee-haw!" Seahawk yelled, laughing wildly. "Gee-haw!"

The terrified horse ran faster and faster, screaming hideously. Jennifer was thrown from side to side of the cart, crying out in pain each time. She clasped her stomach protectively. Again and again she scrambled to her feet, clutching at Seahawk's ankles in an effort to topple him and seize the reins. Each time she was thrown back onto the floor of the wagon. Gathering herself for a final lunge, she came to her feet just as a deer sprinted across the road in front of the horse. The maddened beast shied and reared, neighing with its mouth working convulsively over its huge white teeth. The wagon swerved sharply and Seahawk was propelled from the box. Jennifer went flying backward, hitting her head on the wagon floor.

"My baby! My baby!" she moaned in agony before sinking into unconsciousness.

Colonel Daniel Gill was returning from Concord where he had left his wife, Barbara. Although they had been married in October, 1775, they had not been able to go on their honeymoon until March of 1776, when General Washington felt that the mounting of the Ticonderoga guns around Boston was almost a guarantee that Howe would have to evacuate the city.

"Take two weeks, Daniel," he had said with a smile, "and be sure to enjoy yourself."

In the tradition of the Gill family, Daniel and Barbara had gone to Nantucket, even though the weather was still raw and chilly. But the island had been decidedly warmer than the mainland and they had spent ten deliriously happy days there before returning to Concord.

Now, riding along the road to Cambridge with the eastern sky to his left beginning to glow a grayish pink, he was recalling the high points of the idyll that had just ended, when he saw Liberty's ears stand straight up in the air.

"What is it, boy?" he crooned, leaning forward in the saddle. "What do you hear?"

Liberty's answer was a low whinny and a toss of his head. Then Daniel heard what his horse had heard: the clattering of a horse's hooves and the rumble of wagon wheels. Coming down the road toward him he saw a madly galloping horse pulling a wildly slewing wagon. Daniel gasped. The wagon had gone over on one set of wheels, threatening to tumble into the ditch beside the road and pull the horse down on top of him. Then it righted and shot past Daniel so rapidly and with such a racket that Liberty shied momentarily. As it passed, Daniel heard screaming. At first he thought it was the horse, until he realized it was a woman's voice.

Whirling Liberty around, Daniel galloped after the cart. He overtook it within a few minutes, leaning down precariously to grasp the horse's harness. But it was broken. Daniel urged Liberty forward. He came abreast of the foam-covered horse. It rolled its eyes at him and bared its teeth. Without hesitation, Daniel grasped the beast's tender nostrils with his thumb and fingers and squeezed its nostrils shut. The horse fought back, shaking its head viciously, but it could not loosen Daniel's iron grip. Gradually, the choking creature came to a halt. Daniel let go and began talking quietly to it, gently stroking its mane. Shuddering and gasping, the horse finally quieted down. Daniel dismounted and led Liberty in front of it. Turning, he climbed onto the box and saw the form of an unconscious woman lying in the wagon. At once he jumped to the ground and filled his hat with water from a roadside brook. Returning to the woman, he bathed her face gently in the cold liquid. Her eyelids fluttered. She opened them and stared fearfully at Daniel.

"Is my . . . is my baby all right?" she gasped, terror still stark in her eyes.

"I don't know," Daniel said, gently raising Jennifer into a sitting position. "I'll have to get you to a doctor. What happened?"

Jennifer closed her eyes in anguish. "Seahawk," she muttered, "the . . . the Indian . . . He was drunk . . . He spooked his horse . . . It ran out of control . . . Seahawk was thrown out of the wagon . . . I was knocked out . . . My baby . . . Can you tell . . . ?"

"No. But you needn't be afraid anymore. I'm taking you to a doctor in Concord. I'm sure your baby is fine. Where were you going when this happened?"

"I . . . I was looking for my husband." Jennifer's eyes were still squeezed shut, but the tears were leaking out from under them. "He's a soldier in Cambridge," she sobbed.

"What's his name?"

"Gill. Nathaniel Gill."

"Nathaniel *Gill!*" Daniel repeated in astonishment. "He's my cousin! Why, you must be Jenny. Jennifer Courtney. My wife told me about you. I didn't know you and Nate were married."

Jenny opened her eyes. She said nothing, merely bobbing her head up and down in affirmation. Then she clutched her stomach and cried aloud in pain. Alarmed, Colonel Daniel Gill took off his coat, rolled it up for a pillow, and tenderly lowered Jenny backward until her head rested on it.

"You'll be all right, Jenny," he said softly, before jumping down to the road to hitch Liberty to the back of the cart. Then he climbed up on the box and began to drive slowly back to Concord.

Chapter Nine

The barrage into which Jennifer Courtney had blundered was the beginning of the bombardment that forced General Sir William Howe to evacuate Boston on March 17, 1776. With 170 ships stuffed with all the supplies and arms he could take with him, together with hundreds of Tories—including, of course, Joel and Amanda Courtney—he set sail for Nantasket Harbor and thence for Halifax.

Many other Tories were left behind, and it was upon their heads that the wrath of the Rebels descended.

"First thing I'm gonna do, Nate, when I get into town," Luke Sawyer said as Washington's jubilant troops went marching into the city, "is to get me some tar and some feathers and a rail. And then I'm gonna find me a Tory."

Nate said nothing. He was thinking of Jennifer, praying that she had not been one of the fortunate Tories who had sailed with General Howe. It seemed a small chance. Jennifer's stepmother's relationship with General Howe was like a guarantee of special treatment. Nevertheless, the first chance he had, Nate rushed to the Courtney home. He found it empty, as he had expected. On the door was a notice of seizure by the Commonwealth of Massachusetts. Up and down the street, Nate could see the white pieces of paper nailed to the doors of the homes of some of the most prominent families in the city. Momentarily, he felt sad—until he remembered that Jennifer had told him of her father's attempt to acquire the *Gill* properties.

Suddenly, Nathaniel realized that he was rich. He was his father's only living heir, and all of his father's immense fortune, together with what Grandma Gill had left Micah, would come to Nathaniel. Nate was dazzled. For a moment, he thought of rushing to his father's office where all the

family papers were kept in a vault. He would read his father's will, his grandmother's will . . . But the moment of exultation was transitory. Nate thought again of Jennifer sailing
far, far away to Halifax and he despaired of ever seeing her
again. If the Rebels won the war, her father would probably
take her with him to England. If the Rebels lost, then Nate
would be a fugitive pauper. He began walking dejectedly
back to camp.

He hardly heard the clamor around him. On every street
corner, it seemed, bands of Rebels had cornered a Tory. He
could smell the tar boiling over bonfires built with the
wreckage of beautiful furniture dragged from the ruins of
Tory homes. He brushed drifting feathers from his mouth,
flailing his arms against the clouds of down swirling upward
from heaps of stuffing torn from pillows and mattresses. His
ears were full of the screeches and entreaties of Tories being
stripped of their clothing preparatory to tarring and feathering.

He passed Luke Sawyer's old smithy and saw Luke and
other soldiers dragging Ezra Whatley out of the shop. Ezra
was screaming and pleading for mercy, but Luke began stripping off his clothes while the others seized down from a pile
of feathers and grasped the ladles in the hot tar bucket.

"Luke! Luke! What are you doing to Ezra?" Nate pleaded.
"He worked for you. You told me you liked him."

"Dirty Tory, that's what he is!" Luke replied. "He worked
for Joel Courtney, too, after Joel stole my smithy. Anyone
who'd work for Courtney's got to be a Tory hisself. And all
my tools is gone! Hammers, tongs, anvils, nails, shoes—everything! Even the bellows is gone. I know this piece o' shit stole
'em and I'm gonna make 'im dance on a rail, just like they
done to me."

"I'll bring 'em back! I'll bring 'em back!" Ezra Whatley
pleaded, but Luke just snorted and pushed him toward the
men with the dripping, smoking ladles.

"Too late, you God damn Tory slime!" Luke bellowed,
grinning fiendishly when the first splash of burning tar drew a
hideous scream from Whatley's throat.

Shaking his head in dismay, Nate hurried on—anxious to
get the tormented man's outcries out of his ears, but not daring to cover them lest his comrades think him soft on Tories.
Coming to the next corner, Nate found an old man down on

his knees begging for mercy while a crowd of jeering soldiers
pelted him with rotten eggs. Nate started. It was old Lossing,
Mr. Courtney's butler!

"Leave him alone!" Nate shouted at the soldiers. "He's a
friend of mine."

"You a Tory-lover?" one of them sneered, deliberately
picking up an egg and hurling it into the old man's face.

"No," Nate replied quietly, stepping up to the man and
staring him coolly in the eyes, "but I don't see anything brave
or soldierly in torturing an old man who never hurt anybody."

"He's a Tory, ain't he?"

"No, he isn't. He just worked for one. He was Joel Courtney's butler, and if you still think I'm a Tory-lover I can tell
you there's nobody's fat neck I'd like to squeeze better."

"Aw, let 'im go, Jack," another soldier said. "We're plumb
out 'v eggs anyway."

Scowling at Nate, the soldiers turned and ran down the
street yelling toward Luke Sawyer's. Nate walked over to the
old man who was sitting on the pavement weeping and brush-
ing putrid egg from his face and clothes.

"Lossing, it's me—Nate Gill. Tell me, did Jennifer go to
Halifax with her parents?"

The old man looked at him dumbly, then with slowly
dawning recognition. Nate trembled for his reply. Then he
shook his head slowly and Nate's spirits soared.

"No, Mr. Nate—she didn't go. She runned away a couple
weeks ago."

"Ran away?"

"Not exactly. I think Mr. Courtney turned her out."

Nate was thunderstruck. "Turned her *out!* But why should
he do that?"

The old man shook his head again, muttering as he
resumed the cleaning of himself. Nate left him and began
walking back to camp again. She was here! Jennifer had not
gone to Halifax! Maybe she was still in Boston, hiding somewhere. He felt a pang of anxiety, worrying that a gang of
bullies such as the ones he had just dealt with might find her
and brand her as a Tory. Nevertheless, as he walked toward
the encampment his step was brisk and his head was high.
Arriving there, he rushed to see his cousin, Colonel Daniel

Gill, hoping he would give him assistance in locating Jennifer.

"You needn't worry, Natey," Daniel Gill said with a smile. "Jenny's safe and sound. She had quite a time of it after her father threw her out in the middle of our opening bombardment. But she's all right, now." Daniel smiled again at the astonishment in Nathaniel's eyes, turning discreetly away when the youth's face cracked and his body shook with sobs. "And Nate," Daniel said gently, seizing the youth's shoulder.

"Y-yes, C-cousin Dan?" Nate said, pulling a handerchief from his pocket and mopping his eyes.

"You're a father."

"Now you have to marry me, Jenny," Nathaniel Gill said. "You can't wait until the war's over now."

"When?" Jennifer asked, looking up from the carrots she was slicing. They were sitting in the kitchen of the Concord farmhouse. Jennifer blushed at the happy glance bestowed upon her by Barbara Gill at the stove.

"Tomorrow," Nate said. "I've only got three days leave. I've fixed it up with Parson Wells."

"Tomorrow!" Jenny wailed. "I don't even have a wedding dress!"

"Use mine," Barbara put in promptly. "We're about the same size. Land sakes I always thought it was a powerful waste to use an expensive dress just the one time." She glanced sharply at Nathaniel. "You do have a ring, don't you?"

"Doggone it, I forgot," Nate replied flushing. "I didn't have much time anyway. Can't you lend us one for now, or something?"

"I'll take care of it," Barbara said with a wink.

Jennifer glanced down at her baby son sleeping in a white crib beside her. "What'll we do with little Mark?"

"We sure can't take him to the church," Nate said, grinning, and Jennifer turned scarlet.

"You stop that, Nate Gill," she said sharply.

"Mrs. Wilmot will take care of him until we get back," Barbara said. She walked to the crib. Crooning, she passed a hand over the child's face. Mark did not blink. "Still can't see," Barbara said with a sigh, going back to the stove. "It's getting time you had him baptized, Jenny."

Jennifer blushed once more. "But where? I'm not going to . . ." She looked at Barbara, turned perfectly scarlet and left the kitchen. Barbara pretended not to notice.

"Maybe we can wait until the war's over," Nate mumbled. "Tell the parson we forgot. We'd be married some time, then. Nobody'd notice."

"Yes, and supposing something should happen to him before then?" Barbara snapped. "Do you want your child to die a heathen, Nate Gill?"

Daniel Gill had come into the kitchen. "Why not baptize him yourself, Nate?" he said.

"Me? How could I do that? I'm no parson."

"You don't have to be. The church teaches that in case of emergency any Christian can baptize. And I'd say this is an emergency."

"That's the *Catholic* church," Barbara cried scornfully. "Protestants can't do that."

"Of course, they can. Episcopalians do, anyway."

"How come you became an Episcopalian, Cousin Dan?" Nate asked idly. "I thought you were a Catholic."

"I was. I'd probably still be if I could've found a Catholic church or a priest. But down south those animals just don't exist. Why, in Georgia and the Carolinas, I'd say a good third of the population is Irish—mostly from the Catholic south of Ireland. But they're all Protestants. If they hadn't changed, they'd've been lower than the slaves. Look at it this way. If a man migrated and had a family who would his children marry? Each other?"

"I never realized that," Nat drawled, getting up to look down proudly at his newborn son. "He's kind of blond, now, but I think his hair's going to be black like mine. He looks like me, too. Look at those hands of his. I'll bet he'll be able to shoot a musket by the time he's five."

"Guns," Barbara muttered contemptuously. "You men and your guns. That's why we're always having these terrible wars." She glanced at her husband. "Do you really think we can baptize him, Dan?"

"Sure," Daniel said, stooping to lift the crib onto the table. "Want me to do it?" No one answered so he seized a water pitcher, poured a little water into his cupped hand and let it trickle onto the baby's forehead. "Mark Jedediah Gill," he murmured, "I baptize thee in the name of the Father, the Son and the Holy Spirit." The baby wailed as the water ran into his eyes and Daniel gently dried his face with a towel. "Now he's a proper Christian, Nate," he said with a smile. "If you're still squeamish about it, though, have a parson baptize him officially in a couple of years." He put the crib back on the floor, and grinned. "If you find the right parson, he might even backdate the certificate for you."

"You stop that, Daniel Gill," Barbara snapped.

In the morning, all four rode in the buckboard to the church. Jennifer was radiant in a wedding dress of white silk flounced with lace across the breast and a broad-brimmed picture hat of white starched lace. Beside her in the back Barbara was dressed in a gown of pale blue trimmed with white lace and a matching bonnet. Colonel Gill, of course, wore his dress uniform of buff and blue while Nathaniel was in his uniform consisting of a dark-blue coat with white facing and white metal buttons, white breeches, blue stockings and short black leggings and shoes of black leather. His cap was of black leather edged with white with a black cockade and red plume.

It was hot inside the church. Flies buzzed around the heads of the wedding party while Parson Samuel Wells married Nate and Jenny. When the time came for Nathaniel to put the ring on Jennifer's finger, Nate turned expectantly to Daniel, who quietly handed him a band of diamonds flashing in the sunlight streaming into the church. Jennifer gasped when Nate slipped it onto her finger. Then, even though there was no one else in the church, the parson preached a marathon sermon on the text from First Corinthians: ". . . he that giveth his virgin in marriage, does well . . ." Jennifer didn't stop blushing until Parson Wells was halfway through. By the time he had finished, Daniel's and Nate's heavy uniforms were dark with sweat.

"Phew!" Daniel exclaimed, taking out his chronometer and examining it. "Two hours! I think I should have stayed Catholic."

Laughing, the wedding party drove back to the farmhouse where Mrs. Wilmot had prepared a wedding feast of roast beef, Yorkshire pudding with gravy, green beans and baked potatoes. There was apple pie for dessert, and Daniel had provided a bottle of sparkling hock which they drank with the meal. Jennifer wasn't sure she liked the hock. The bubbles got in her nose. But since both Daniel and her new husband thought it was great she said nothing. She didn't really like the French brandy which Daniel opened after dessert, either. She thought it was too strong. She almost clutched her neck when the fiery liquid went down her throat. But Jennifer did like the toast given by Daniel.

"I heard it from my grandfather," he said getting to his feet and extending his glass. "Actually, it's an Irish benediction on a traveler going on his way. And since you two are about to begin the long journey through life together, I think it's appropriate." He lifted his glass solemnly. "May the road rise with you, may the wind be at your back and may God always hold you—in the hollow of his hand."

Everyone drank and even Jennifer joined the hand clapping. Then Barbara came to her shyly and handed her a velvet box. "It's your wedding present, Jenny," she said.

Jennifer opened the box and drew forth a string of chaste white pearls. "They're beautiful!" she exclaimed, her eyes shining.

"They were my grandmother's," Barbara said. "I'm sure she'd want you to have them."

"Oh, Barbara—you're so good to me!" Jenny exclaimed, coming to her cousin-in-law's side to kiss her. She glanced at the wedding ring on her finger in admiration. "This is gorgeous, too," she said, making as though to remove it from her finger. "Whose is it?"

"Yours. Now, Jenny, don't be silly. Put that ring back on your finger. It's yours. It was my grandmother's. She gave it to me, but I'm sure she'd be delighted for you to have it. You see," she said, pointing to the ring, "it was originally just a plain gold band. That's all Grandpa could afford when they were married in Deerfield. But when he got rich he had it set with diamonds. One carat to each side and two carats in the middle. Grandma loved jewelry."

Still dazzled, Jennifer held the ring up to the light, watching the gems catch fire. "So do I," she murmured.

"Here's something for you too, Natey," Barbara said, arising to go to the hall. She came back with a blackthorn stick with a silver handle and handed it to Nate.

"Grandpa's walking stick!" Nate exclaimed, hefting the cane and staring at it fondly. "When I was a little boy and he wanted to tell me something important, he'd hook me with the handle and pull me toward him."

Daniel peered at the stick. "It's just like mine! The one Grandpa Quinn gave me."

"Of course," said Barbara, nodding her head. "Your grandpa gave it to Grandpa Gill on his thirtieth birthday in thanks for saving his life. See? On the handle it says, 'With Gratitude: D.P.Q.'"

"Daniel Patrick Quinn," Daniel breathed reverently. "I'll be damned."

As night approached, Daniel and Barbara discreetly withdrew, leaving Jennifer and Nathaniel to themselves. Jennifer picked up a candle holder and lighted the candle from the silver candelabra on the table. "If you carry Mark upstairs, I'll light the way," she said. Nate nodded and carefully lifted the crib, following Jennifer into the bedroom that had been his grandparents'. Jenny lighted two betty lamps and Nate gazed in nostalgia at the big canopied four-poster with matching canopy and bedspread of green and gold with the family device embroidered on them. He put the crib down and came quickly to Jenny's side, seizing her about the waist and kissing her hungrily.

"Are you going to undress?" he whispered.

She drew back. "Natey, I . . . I . . . can't . . ."

"Whaaat?"

"I . . . I'm still all torn up inside. Mark weighed almost nine pounds. The doctor . . . he says I . . . I can't . . . not for another month . . . That's one reason why I wanted to wait."

Nathaniel Gill was thunderstruck. "You mean . . . on my wedding night . . . I can't . . . ?"

Jenny nodded her head sorrowfully. "I . . . I'm sorry, Natey . . . Honestly, I feel awful. But it would hurt me . . . tear me up again . . ."

Nathaniel gritted his teeth and raised his clenched fists over his head in anguish. Then he slowly lowered them. "All right, I'm no monster," he said between clenched teeth. Jenny began to cry softly and he came to her side. "I'm sorry, Jenny," he said. "I love you. I'll wait." He kissed her gently on the lips. Then he put on the uniform coat he had taken off and turned toward the door.

"Where are you going?" Jenny asked in alarm.

"Downstairs to finish the brandy," said Nathaniel Gill.

Nathaniel Gill awoke to the sound of a baby crying. At first, he did not recognize the noise, but then, realizing that it was the wailing of his son, he shot erect in bed. Across from him in a chair by the window sat Jennifer. She was breast-feeding little Mark. Although she had her knickers on she was bare from the waist up. Nathaniel stared at her firm full breasts in an agony of desire that he knew would pass unrequited. Then he watched fascinated while his son sucked greedily at Jenny's nipple.

"Good morning, dear husband," Jenny said with mock sweetness. "Did you sleep well? And how do you feel?"

"All right, I guess," Nate mumbled. "My tongue's a little thick and I've got a terrific headache."

"Do you realize that you went to bed with your uniform on?"

Aghast, Nate looked down at his rumpled shirt and breeches. "I took my coat off," he muttered.

"Very thoughtful of you." Jenny arose, put Mark back in his crib and began to dress. Nate stared at her imploringly. "I can't . . . ?" Jenny shook her head, and Nate put his coat on in disgust. "Some marriage," he murmured sarcastically.

Hurt, Jennifer came to Nate's side and put her arms around him. "Please don't feel bad, Natey," she said, fixing him with her shining soft brown eyes. "I . . . I love you so much. . . . It was sweet of you to stay away. I'll make it up to you, Natey, honest I will. As soon as I'm better, I'll come to Boston. I'll take a room at the tavern and stay for a week."

"Who'll feed Mark?" he said, pointing to his tiny son.

"Mrs. Wilmot says she knows an excellent wet nurse. Barbara wanted me to have a wet nurse in the beginning. But I preferred to feed him myself."

"All right. But you'd better come as soon as you can. Cousin Dan says General Washington will be moving the army to New York soon."

"You're leaving *Boston?*" Jenny said in a horrified voice. "But who will protect us?"

"You'll be all right. Cousin Dan says the British are probably glad to be out of Boston. It's a trap and it's not that important strategically. New York's the place. If the British can take New York and the Hudson River they can cut the colonies in two. So that's where we're going."

Jenny looked at him proudly. "I always knew you had brains, Natey."

Chuckling, Nate came to her and kissed her fondly. "I'm glad I stayed away, Jenny," he said softly, stroking her hair. "It'll be that much better when you come to me."

Nathaniel rode back to Boston behind Colonel Gill on his horse, Liberty. On reaching the camp, Luke Sawyer rushed up to him.

"Where you been, Natey? I've been looking all over for you. You damn near missed muster."

"Muster? What's going on?"

"We're going to New York."

"When?"

"Tomorrow."

Nathaniel Gill groaned aloud. He thought of Jennifer. Once again he saw her bare breasts and the exciting way they swung when she got to her feet and put Mark in his crib. And once again the war was to deny him the satisfaction of his desire. Nate watched glumly while his cousin walked his horse to General Washington's headquarters, dismounted and went inside. Then, with reluctant steps, he followed Luke to their tent.

Inside headquarters, Colonel Gill found General Washington talking to Major General Charles Lee. With one thin leg draped over the other, his wig slightly askew, discharging a faint odor of dogs, General Lee sat in a chair opposite Washington behind his desk. Colonel Gill sat down and listened.

"For some reason, my dear General," Washington said, "Lord North is under the impression that what he calls 'the loyal people of America' live mainly in the south. British strategy this spring and summer, it appears, will be to try first in the south before making an attempt on New York. Their objective is Charleston."

"Indeed?" Lee said, raising his eyebrows. "But isn't Charleston rather well defended?"

"It is. It has the best defenses of all our ports. But the enemy seems to believe that if they capture Charleston, all they will need to do is raise the Union Jack and all of Georgia and the Carolinas will come flocking to the king's standard. We cannot afford to lose Charleston, General. There are indeed many Tories south of Virginia, but there are more, many, many more, waiting to see which way to jump. If Charleston falls," he said grimly, "they will indeed jump the other way, and I fear the Carolinas and Georgia will be lost to the Revolution." Washington lifted a letter from his desk. "Colonel William Moultrie, who is in charge at Charleston, has described to me the extent of his fortifications. They seem adequate. Still, I would prefer someone with extensive siege experience to command at Charleston. That is why I am sending you there, my dear General."

"I am indeed honored. Who is in command of Lord North's expedition?"

"Admiral Sir Peter Parker for the fleet, and General Clinton for the ground forces."

"Henry, eh? Dear, dear Henry. Thank you, my dear General. It should be most diverting."

The Comte de Vergennes was the foreign minister of France. Perhaps the very soul of his foreign policy, next to serving the interests of King Louis XVI, was the destruction of British power. To that end, he thought he saw in Britain's enforced evacuation of Boston the first faint glimmering of opportunity. In May of 1776, while the British fleet plunged south for Charleston and Major General Charles Lee hurried toward the same city, Vergennes summoned to his chambers Pierre Augustin Caron de Beaumarchais, a famous playwright who was also celebrated for his passionate love of liberty and devotion to the American cause.

"Eh, Monsieur Beaumarchais," Vergennes said, "I have been to see *The Barber of Seville*. Most entertaining."

"Thank you," Beaumarchais said, bowing graciously. "And I have the honor to inform you that I am planning another. I already have the title. *The Marriage of Figaro*."

"Eh, *bien*. You must be making a fortune, Monsieur."

Beaumarchais sighed. "One can never have enough."

"Then, my dear monsieur, I have a proposal that may make you richer." Beaumarchais's attitude of polite disenchantment changed instantly. A glint of avarice gleamed in his eye. "As you know," Vergennes continued, "nothing can make our gracious king happier than a weakening of British power. It is possible that we have our chance in the rebellion of the American colonies. If we can widen the breach between them and King George, we can reduce, by disunion, British power. Understand me, my dear Beaumarchais, I have no love for the colonies. But I hate Britain more. So it will be my policy to aid the colonies. This, however, must be done secretly. To assist them openly would probably provoke a war with Britain that the king does not want. So I propose that you, monsieur, set up a dummy trading company to purchase munitions for the colonies."

"I, monsieur?" Beaumarchais said with feigned innocence. "But where would I get the money?"

"There is a secret fund of one million livres provided by ourselves and Spain. This will be available to you. The firm you will operate is to be known as Hortalez et Cie. Monsieur?"

"I am honored to serve the cause of liberty," Beaumarchais said, getting to his feet. "But . . . but this matter of making me richer . . ."

The Comte de Vergennes smiled as though the playwright had just told a good joke. "Your confusion is charming, Monsieur," Vergennes murmured dryly. "*Très charmant.*"

By the time the British fleet arrived off Charleston—June 4, 1776—the city bristled with a chain of strong fortifications held by about six thousand men, many of them reinforcements from Virginia and North Carolina. General Lee had taken command. He saw at once that the fort of palmetto logs on Sullivan's Island to the north of the harbor was the key to Charleston. Accompanied by Colonel Moultrie, he inspected the island.

"These palmetto logs are soft inside, General," Moultrie explained, rapping one of the logs with his fist. "They'll soak up cannon balls like a sponge. Behind them we've got dirt walls sixteen feet thick. I think she should hold."

"Rather," Lee said. "What's that island over there?" he said, pointing to a small land mass across a narrow strip of water.

"Long Island. It's unoccupied. The strip of water between us is called The Breach."

"They could occupy Long Island and wade across The Breach to here," Lee said musingly.

"I doubt it, General. The Breach is like a moat of shallows and deeps, some of them seven feet down. They'd drown."

"Then let's hope they try it," Lee said, smiling a thin smile.

They did. General Henry Clinton put about two thousand men ashore on Long Island. His plan was to cross The Breach and strike at Sullivan's Island from the north while Sir Peter Parker's bombardment fleet battered the fort from the south. On June 28, while Parker's warships roared a thunderous cannonade, Clinton's grenadiers and light infantry jumped into The Breach. Many of them vanished instantly. Others were trapped in shallower holes, unable to flounder out of them under the weight of their heavy equipment. Clinton ordered boats to the rescue, but the boats were grounded in the shallows. Exasperated, the British general recalled his troops.

Charles Lee watched the failure with satisfaction. "It's now down to a fight between a fleet and a fort," he chortled gleefully to Moultrie. "And there's an old saying that a ship is a fool to fight a fort."

Still smirking, Lee studied the approach of the enemy ships. "Ah, yes, there's the bomb ketch, *Thunder*," he said, focusing his telescope. "I've sailed aboard her. Nine of them all told. Ah, yes, the *Bristol*. That'll be Sir Peter's flagship. *Experiment, Active, Solebay, Actaeon, Syren, Friendship* and what's that little one. Ah, yes—*Sphynx*. Well, Colonel, I think they're about ready to begin the game."

An explosion was heard offshore and a bomb rose into the air from *Thunder*. It fell short, raising a plume of water into the air. More bombs fell, all short, and the men in the fort cheered at the sight of the harmless spouts and geysers rising from the water. *Thunder* fell silent.

General Lee frowned. "I rather fancy they'll be increasing the powder charges in the mortars."

A loud explosion came from *Thunder* but no bomb soared into the air. Lee smiled his thin smile. "Poor fools. I should think they'd have known better. They've probably broken the mortar beds." A few minutes later, *Thunder* drew away. Once again the men in the fort cheered.

Now it was the Americans who were firing with a deliberate and terrible accuracy. *Bristol*'s cable was shot away. She drifted end-on to the fort and was raked horribly. Twice her quarterdeck was cleared of every man except Sir Peter Parker. "Back to your guns, you carrion!" Sir Peter roared, suddenly staggering and clapping a hand to his behind. He glanced behind him in mortification. An American shot had torn off the back of his pants, exposing his singed backside.

Still the American fire continued to batter the British ships. *Experiment* suffered as badly as *Bristol*. Inside the fort, sweating Americans were scorched by the intense southern sun and sometimes scorched by the heat of the muzzle blasts from thirty cannon. "Fire, men, fire!" Colonel Moultrie called to his men. "Keep it up! Keep it up! You're tearing them apart!" The men answered with cheers, sometimes pausing in the battle to take a drink of grog from men racing up and down the fire platforms with fire buckets filled with rum. Even as the American barrage rose in fury, the British continued their own bombardment.

Even General Lee was astonished by the frightful roar that seemed to engulf the island. "I say, Moultrie, I've never seen anything quite so hot before," he murmured.

As though to emphasize his words, a combination of British broadsides struck the walls of the fort with such force that they trembled. Moultrie blanched. "My God, one more like that will shake it down."

Another shot carried away the fort's flag. A cheer rose from the British ships. "They're surrendering!" the sailors yelled.

Inside the redoubt, Sergeant Jasper ran up to Moultrie and said, "Colonel, don't let us fight without our flag!"

"What can you do? The staff is broken."

Jasper's reply was to dash outside the fort while British shot and shell fell around him, seize the flag, and then, fixing it on a sponge staff, set it upright again. Groans now rose from the British while from the Charleston shore, faint on the wind, came the sound of cheering. The blue flag with its white crescent and the word "Liberty" now waved in the breeze again.

And now three of the British ships upped anchor and tried to sail around the western end of the island, intending to pound the fort on its flank and destroy a plank bridge behind the island. All three ships ran aground. *Actaeon* and *Sphynx* collided with one another, *Sphynx* losing her bowsprit. Eventually, two of them worked free—but *Actaeon* was stuck. Throughout the night the jubilant Americans could hear their shots crashing into her until she caught fire and burned. During the night, the remaining British ships slipped their cables and stole away.

Charleston had held.

Chapter Ten

In the summer of 1776 Thomas Jefferson and John Adams were strolling in the courtyard of the State House in Philadelphia.

"The time has come for us to declare ourselves free of England," Jefferson said. "There can be no turning back, now. Not after Boston, not after Charleston, not after that brute of a King George has hired Hessian mercenaries to murder free men of his own blood." He stopped and confronted Adams. "Do you think you could compose a draft declaration of independence?"

"No."

"What can be your reasons?" Jefferson asked, startled.

"Reason first, you are a Virginian and a Virginian ought to be at the head of this business. Reason second, I am obnoxious, suspected and unpopular. You are very much otherwise. Reason third, you can write ten times better than I can."

"Well," Jefferson said, "if you are decided, I will do as well as I can."

Almost immediately, Jefferson went to work on a declaration, after which Congress, much to the author's chagrin, toned down its language and cut about a fourth of its contents. Jefferson's impassioned attack on slavery, which he blamed on the king even though he himself was a large slaveholder, did not get past his southern colleagues. The personal vituperation which he poured upon the king was also deleted. On July 4, 1776, the Declaration of Independence was formally adopted.

As president of the Continental Congress, John Hancock signed first. "There," he said, signing with a big bold flourish, "I guess King George can read that!"

One by one, the other delegates signed—radicals, moderates and conservatives—all united now in the determination to be "Absolved from All Allegiance to the British Crown."

The Adamses signed. "The river is passed and the bridge cut away," John cried jubilantly. Charles Carroll of Carrollton, the wealthy Marylander, signed. He was a Catholic island in a Protestant sea, a fact of which he was aware when he said: "I have in mind not only our independence from England, but the toleration of all sects professing the Christian religion." Next came Benjamin Franklin, his eyes still twinkling over his quip: "We must all hang together, or assuredly we will all hang separately." Then a beaming Thomas Jefferson signed. Among the last to sign was Caesar Rodney of Delaware. No odder-looking man than Caesar Rodney has ever lived. But this bold bantam with a face hardly larger than an oversized grapefruit had ridden eighty miles through a stormy night to put Delaware on the side of the declaration and swing the Congress toward independence.

After him came rotund Benjamin Harrison of Virginia, who also had the gallows on his mind. Staring at the wizened Elbridge Gerry of Massachusetts, a man half his size, he signed with a smile and said to Gerry: "When the hanging scene comes to be exhibited, I shall have the advantage over you. All will be over with me in a minute, but you will be kicking in the air a half hour after I'm gone."

Finally, they had all signed. Some had been solemn, some gay, but all had been defiant—aware as they were that they walked in the shadow of King George's gibbet.

It was done, and four days later the Declaration of Independence was published. A jubilant George Washington had it read to the army, which he had brought from Boston to New York.

Nate Gill was standing in ranks with Luke Sawyer when the declaration was read to them. Nate's eyes filled with tears and his heart swelled when he heard for the first time those noble phrases and ringing phrases that had flowed from Jefferson's pen.

When in the course of human events . . .

. . . .

We hold these truths to be self-evident, that all men are created equal, that they are endowed by their Creator with certain inalienable Rights, that among these are Life, Liberty and the Pursuit of Happiness.

. . . .

And for the support of this Declaration, with a firm reliance on the protection of Divine Providence, we mutually pledge to each other our lives, our fortunes and our sacred honor.

There was a prolonged silence after the reading, broken by a sudden outburst of cheering. Swinging their hats and hurrahing, the men embraced each other.

"Hurrah for the United States of America!"

"July Fourth, that's it! That's our birthday! That's our country's birthday!"

"Down with King George!"

"The filthy fat murderer—hiring those God damn Hessians to fight for him!"

"Let's go get 'im!" Luke Sawyer yelled. "Let's go get King George!"

"Are you crazy, Luke?" Nate shouted. "How can you *get* the king?"

"Down in Bowling Green. His statue! Let's go tear his statue down and melt it down for bullets to kill his God damn Hessians with!"

Howling with glee, the soldiers of the Revolution mingled with the mob streaming toward Bowling Green and the symbol of the hated sovereign they had just renounced.

Chapter Eleven

"Damn it, Luke," Nate Gill complained, dropping his shovel and studying his hands, "I think the calluses on my hands are bigger than the ones on my feet. And here I thought soldiering was all fighting. All we do is march and dig. I haven't fired my musket since Bunker Hill."

Luke nodded and dropped his shovel, too. He sat on the ground next to Nate, morosely chewing on a straw. All around them they could hear the clinking of pickaxes and shovels. It was late August of 1776 and their regiment was at work building fortifications atop Brooklyn Heights, a ridge rising a hundred feet above water at the southern tip of Long Island. It commanded the tiny, mile-square city of New York and was the key to Washington's defense of the city and the vital Hudson River. From the Heights, they could look across the Narrows to Staten Island and the British camp there, or into New York Harbor where the enemy fleet lay at anchor.

An officer wearing the uniform of a captain in the Continental Army rode up the hill towards them. Nate stared at him in surprise.

"Cousin Ben!" he cried, jumping to his feet. "What are you doing in the army? I thought you were in jail."

"I was," Dr. Benjamin Gill said with a smile, dismounting and coming to shake hands with Nate and nod cordially to Luke. "But now I'm out, thanks to you and your friends. I can tell you, Natey, one more week and I would have ended up dangling at the end of a rope. Anyway, General Putnam told me he needed physicians in his division and here I am."

"Have you been out to Concord?" Nate asked eagerly. "Do you have any news of Jenny and Cousin Barbara?"

Dr. Gill shook his head. "No. But I did hear that you and Jenny went and got married."

"Yeah, we did. But I can tell you, Cousin Ben, I haven't had much chance to enjoy it."

"Well, the war will be over soon," Dr. Gill said easily, remounting his horse.

"Not with all them bastards over there," Luke said, gloomily nodding his head in the direction of Staten Island. "I hear tell they got over thirty thousand men. An' God knows how many ships. An' the British fleet from Charleston just sailed in the other day with more men."

"Never fear, men. With soldiers such as you our cause can never fail." Dr. Gill smiled suavely, nodded and cantered off. "Come see me in the infirmary when you can, Nate," he called back toward them.

The two soldiers sat down again. Luke pulled another straw from the hillside and began chewing again. "I know he's your kinfolk, Nate," he grumbled, "but I just don't hold no truck with that man. Did you hear that bullshit? 'Soldiers like you,'" he mimicked in a falsetto voice. "'Our cause can never fail.' *Our* cause. Now that I think on it, Natey, whenever lightnin' hits the outhouse, I ain't never seen Dr. Gill around."

Suddenly Luke sprang to his feet. He had seen a sloop put out from the British camp. He ran to his knapsack and dug out the telescope he had stolen from a Tory home, putting it to his eye and focusing it.

"Damn if they ain't got a white flag flyin'," he muttered. "An' there's an officer all covered with gold braid in the bow."

"Think maybe General Howe's going to surrender?" Nate said, snickering.

Luke did not reply. He followed the sloop as far as he could before lowering it. "I think he went ashore at the Battery," he said, sitting down again.

The officer who did step ashore at the southern tip of the city was Captain John André, a young and handsome man who served as General Howe's aide-de-camp. He carried a message from Howe to George Washington and was taken at once to his headquarters. Washington received him courteously and took the envelope he proffered.

"It is addressed to *Mr.* Washington," the general said coldly. "There is no person by that address in this army. I bid you good day, Captain."

Next day Captain André returned with another envelope.

"What is this nonsense, George Washington, Esquire, et cetera, et cetera?" Washington asked in a tone even frostier than the preceding day's.

"Well, sir," André replied placatingly, "the et cetera actually implies everything."

"Yes, it may—and it can also mean *any*thing. If General Howe wishes to negotiate why does he not address me as he should?"

"Actually, sir, neither of the Howes is empowered to negotiate. They are authorized only to grant pardons."

"Pardon? Since no crime has been committed no pardon is needed. I bid you good day, Captain."

André bowed and departed. Up among the mud forts of Brooklyn Heights, Luke Sawyer watched the passage of his sloop toward the British encampment. A few days later, he had his telescope to his eyes again watching apprehensively as the British fleet began landing Howe's army at Gravesend Bay, just below their position.

"God damn it, Natey, what a sight. If I didn't know they was after our ass I'd be jumping up and down and cheering my head off."

"Come on, Luke," Nate pleaded, "let me have a look."

With a scowl, Luke passed the telescope to Nate, who raised it to his eyes and gasped. Great white sails flooded the bay. Flatboats, galleys and longboats loaded with soldiers rowed away from them to the shore. Kilted Highlanders . . . red-coated grenadiers in their tall bearskin hats . . . green-clad Hessian Jaegers . . . other Hessians in high brass miters and white-and-gold uniforms . . . Then came the artillery, scores of glittering cannon surrounded by their gunners. Faintly on the wind the horrified Americans atop Brooklyn Heights could hear military music . . . the skirl of bagpipes . . . The sun made a million points of light on bayonets and burnished buckles or the gorgets of the officers, on the flashing white oars of the seamen at the oarlocks.

Nate and Luke exchanged glances. They took in each other's worn and muddy uniforms with the rents in the breeches and the buttonless coats, their mismatching muskets lying beside empty packs, their shoes coming apart at the seams—and they sank down beside each other in despair. Three days later, more troops landed beneath them. Luke glumly watched them come ashore, and mumbled, "I wonder what that perfumed son-of-a-bitchin' dandy of a cousin o' yourn has to say now."

Luke Sawyer would have been surprised to learn that Dr. Benjamin Gill at that moment was on a military mission for General Israel Putnam. Putnam had just taken command of the force of five thousand men on Long Island. He had posted his main body to the left under General Sullivan and seventeen hundred men to the right under General Stirling. Unfortunately, Putnam knew nothing about Long Island's terrain.

Putnam was worried about roads that might lead into his rear and ordered them all guarded. But he was still not satisfied and when he rode past the infirmary near his headquarters in the rear and saw Dr. Gill ride up on a horse he called to him and said, "Dr. Gill, would you be good enough to inspect the passes for me? I want to be sure they're all guarded. I wouldn't ask you, except that I seem to be shorthanded at the moment."

"By all means, General," Benjamin Gill said, and turned his horse to ride toward the front of the American position. One by one he checked the passes opening on the vital roads. Each was barricaded and guarded with a courier present to warn Putnam if the enemy were approaching. Dr. Gill was disappointed. He rode on, almost missing a cowpath to his left. He reined his horse in and rode back. He studied the cowpath musingly. Who knows? he thought, and urged his mount into it. Bushes to either side brushed him on the shoulders. Bees buzzed about his head. Suddenly, he noticed that the path was widening. He was delighted. He rode on and came to a road. It was the Jamaica Road leading into Putnam's rear! Humming the popular tune "The World Turned Upside Down," Dr. Benjamin Gill rode his horse into the British lines.

"You are sure, Dr. Gill? Quite sure?"

"Positive, Sir William. There's no one there. And since it was dusk when I left and General Putnam spoke of being shorthanded, I doubt very much if anyone will be there by nightfall."

General Howe clapped his hands together gleefully. "Capital! I shall attack tonight!" He glanced up from his field desk with appreciative eyes. "You have done His Majesty a great service, my dear Doctor. I shall not forget it. Nor will he. Nor have I forgotten your petition."

"I shall be very grateful. And now, with your leave, my dear General, may I take off this detestable uniform?"

General Howe shook his head. "Sorry, no. You have been of such great service in your present capacity I cannot afford to lose you."

Benjamin sighed. "Isn't this all rather endless? I mean, sir, the odds are growing greater that some day someone who has seen me in the British camp may also see me in the Rebel camp."

"Rubbish!" Howe scoffed good-naturedly. "Perhaps your difficulties will end tonight. In the meantime, my dear Doctor, I shall have to place you among the other captured Rebel officers. You will be returned to the American side upon the next exchange of prisoners."

Benjamin sighed again. "As you say, sir," he murmured, and left the tent. Outside, to his surprise, he saw Joel Courtney ride up in the green uniform of a Tory colonel. Benjamin shrank back into a tent alley, watching with amusement as an aide-de-camp dismounted to hurry to Colonel Courtney's side to place an iron footstool beneath him and help him dismount. Good Lord! Benjamin thought, I wonder how many yards of material they needed to make him a uniform. Then he thought: Amanda's back in America! She must be, if Joel is here; and then, she certainly is, with Sir William here. Joel went inside General Howe's tent. Some other officers rode up. Benjamin saw that they were all generals. Clinton . . . Grant . . . the Hessian, Philip de Heister . . . Lord Percy and Lord Cornwallis. They went into the tent and Dr. Gill strode off to surrender himself to the provost general.

Inside, a beaming General Howe welcomed his commanders. "Gentlemen, we are in luck. We have found a chink in the Yankee army. There is an unguarded pass on their left opening on a road leading to their rear. General Grant, I want you to strike the Rebel right. Keep them in place, mind? You, General de Heister will strike the main body on their left. In the meantime, at nine o'clock tonight I shall take our own main body with Generals Clinton, Percy and Cornwallis and make for the pass. You will begin the game, General Grant, at dawn. You, General de Heister will remain in place until you hear two cannon-shot from me signaling that I am in the Yankee rear. Then you will attack. Any questions?"

There were none.

Nate Gill and Luke Sawyer were awakened before daybreak by the sound of artillery fire to their right. With the other soldiers of their company they scrambled erect and ran for the firing platform of their mud fort.

"To arms!" a sergeant shouted. "To arms! The enemy is attacking our right flank. Be prepared to receive them here!"

Nate and Luke busied themselves inspecting their cartridges. They waited nervously. "God damn, I wish I had a bayonet," Luke mumbled.

"Me, too," Nate whispered.

From behind them they heard a cannon fire once, then again.

"What the hell's that?" Luke cried, whirling to face the rear.

From the front came a wild, wailing sound.

"What's *that*?" Nate exclaimed.

Next they heard guttural voices chanting what sounded like religious hymns. Then the rattle of drums and the squeal of fifes joined the wail of the oboes and they saw, swirling out of the mists of dawn toward them, the tall Hessians in the tall brass miters that made them seem like giants.

At first, Nate was terrified. His knees trembled. But then, like the other Americans around him, he remembered that these soldiers were mercenaries hired to destroy their liberty. Cries of anger and derision arose from the fort.

"Let's stuff those miters up their ass!"

"Kill the krauts! Make sausage of 'em!"

"Make shit, you mean!"

"Fire!" shouted Captain Jonah Pepper, their company commander.

Flame and smoke gushed from the American lines. But only a few Hessians fell. They came on steadily, inexorably, their white-powdered heads held high, their white-and-gold legs pumping like pistons.

"Hold your fire, men," Captain Pepper shouted. "Remember Bunker Hill. The whites of their eyes. *Fire!*"

Nate Gill squeezed the trigger of his musket. He thought he saw the soldier he had aimed at crumple and fall. Now the field in front of the fort was littered with writhing Hessians. But then, from the American rear, came the sound of battle. A courier dashed up on a blown horse, shouting wildly. "They're behind us! Howe is in our rear!"

One more volley was fired at the approaching enemy and then the Americans panicked. They jumped down from the firing platforms and tore out of the forts. Cheering, the Hessians gave pursuit.

Nate was knocked down in the uncontrolled scramble for safety. He rose to find a tall Hessian coming at him with outthrust bayonet. Nate parried his thrust on the barrel of his musket. *Clang!* The Hessian swung the butt of his weapon upward towards Nate's genitals. Nate blocked it with a downward jab of his own musket butt. Backing off, the Hessian swung his blade down savagely. Again Nate parried. *Clang!* Pins and needles shot through his hands. The Hessian raised his musket butt outward and jabbed viciously at Nate's face. Nate ducked under it and seized the soldier by the knees, upending him and wrenching his musket from him as he fell. Nate jabbed the bayonet down at him, but the man went sliding and sprawling in the bloody mud. Nate was about to strike again, when a blow on his shoulder from a musket butt spun him around and he caught the flash of a bayonet point coming toward his throat which he knew he would be too late to parry. Instantly, he pulled the trigger of the musket he held, praying it was loaded. It was. The weapon in his hand bucked and his assailant sank to the ground soundlessly clutching his torn throat.

"Nate! Nate!" Luke Sawyer yelled. "For Gawd's sake, let's get out of here!"

Nate whirled and joined Luke, who had once again clubbed his musket and was clearing a path out of the fort. The two men rushed towards a wood in the rear, their ears full of the hideous shrieking and screaming of their comrades. Nate glanced over his shoulder and saw laughing Hessian soldiers slaughtering a party of Americans who had surrendered but were killed on their knees with their empty hands held high. Other Hessians deliberately backed surrendered men toward

trees where they spitted them like roasts of meat. Ahead of
him Nate saw the tall figure of General Sullivan on the edge
of a cornfield, pistols in both hands and waving them at his
terrified troops and trying to halt their flight.

"Stand, I tell you!" he roared. "Stand! Form here in the
cornfield."

Many of them rushed on, unheeding. Others reluctantly
formed ranks, awaiting the onslaught of the regrouping Hessians. They came. A ragged volley flashed out from the Americans. Still the Hessians charged. Once again the Americans
broke, and this time the rout was complete. General Sullivan
was powerless to stop it. Over his shoulder, Nate Gill saw
Sullivan clutch his head in anguish, then draw both his pistols
and go charging alone toward the enemy.

General George Washington had come to Brooklyn
Heights to watch the battle from a central point in the lines.
With him was Colonel Daniel Gill. They, too, heard the first
signs of battle from General Stirling's position on the right,
and then the sputtering crackle signaling a general engagement with small arms. Washington waited patiently for news
of the battle. A courier rode up and saluted.

"The Maryland and Delaware regiments are fighting fiercely, sir," the courier reported.

"They always do," Washington murmured. "They are my
finest troops."

"The enemy tried to take their position four times, but
they drove them off."

"Excellent. And you may tell General Stirling to inform
his men that the commander opposite them is James Grant,
the general who boasted that he would geld every male in
America. Perhaps that will inspire them further."

It did. The Marylanders and Delawares not only repulsed
the enemy but made an unsuccessful attempt to capture a
British-held height. Although Washington was encouraged by
this news, he sank into despair when he saw his left flank
melt away and heard of Sullivan's capture. On his right the
roar of battle rose ominously higher. Howe had sent Lord
Cornwallis into Stirling's rear, ordering Grant to hit him on
the right and the Hessians to strike his front. Attacked on
three sides, Stirling finally ordered his valiant men to retreat.

They tried to escape through the Gowanus marshes, where many of them drowned.

When Washington received word that Stirling had surrendered, he realized that the Battle of Long Island had ended in a disastrous defeat.

When Washington came over to Brooklyn he brought with him reinforcements who were quickly sent into the abandoned positions. Soon, with the return of stragglers who had fled for their lives, the American position was defended again. Howe's officers eagerly urged him to storm it, to sweep the Revolution away right then and there. But those crumpled redcoats on Bunker Hill still lay in heaps at the back of William Howe's brain, and instead he ordered his forces to retire.

"No, gentlemen," he explained to his subordinates, some of whom were trembling with rage. "It would be foolhardy to attack the Yankees behind fixed positions. That is where they fight best. It was only our turning movement that brought them out into the open. We have them, gentlemen, we have them. All we need is patience. We are securely on their front and they are demoralized. My brother's fleet is at the mouth of the East River waiting for a fair wind to cut them off in the rear. Therefore, I intend to conduct the classic maneuver of siege warfare. In the morning, we will begin digging approaches for our artillery. We will batter them from the front while the fleet prevents them from escaping over the river to New York. It will take a little more time, gentlemen, but it cannot fail. And it will save lives."

It was raining in the morning when Washington climbed onto a parapet and saw the British beginning to dig the first of their artillery trenches. Turning, he saw the masts of Admiral Lord Richard Howe's fleet standing at the mouth of the East River where a stiff northeast wind blew rain into their sails. Washington realized at once that he was in a trap. The landward arm of the pincers was already beginning to close and all that was needed for the seaward arm to snap shut was a change in the wind. There was no time to lose, and Washington immediately called a council of war where it was unanimously agreed to evacuate Long Island.

"We will withdraw by stages," Washington explained. "The rear lines first and the forward lines last. Each line will slip into the emptied position of the line behind it. General Mifflin," he said to Thomas Mifflin, "you will provide the forward covering force. You will be the last to leave. And you, Colonel Glover," he said to the stocky, seagoing John Glover of Marblehead, "your Salem Regiment will bring the boats I have collected up to the Brooklyn ferry. Finally, there is to be a rule of absolute silence. The men are not to know what we are doing."

On the night of August 29, 1776, in a howling wind and driving rain, the men of the Salem Regiment, actually sailors in their short blue coats and loose white trousers, brought their boats bobbing up to the ferry landing. Soldiers bent under loads of baggage and equipment silently loaded and boarded them, shielding their faces from the rain with their hats or hunched shoulders. There were no lights, no words except whispered commands. Each time a boat was loaded, it pushed softly out onto the water.

"What's going on?" Nate Gill whispered to Luke Sawyer.

"Quiet there!" a sergeant hissed, and Nate felt Luke squeeze his shoulder warningly. A gust of wind hurled water into Nate's eyes and for a moment he thought he was blinded. He crouched lower into the boat peering back toward the ferry. But he could see nothing.

On the landing, Colonel Glover reported to Washington. "My men are having trouble bucking that northeaster," he said. "They're not making much progress." Washington stiffened. If daylight were to reveal his army out on the water beneath the guns of the British fleet, it would be all over. "General," Glover whispered excitedly, plucking at Washington's boat cloak. "The wind's shifting to the southwest! It's going down! We'll be all right, sir!"

"It is both a blessing and a curse, Colonel," Washington said grimly. "A southwest wind will help us get across to New York, but it will also enable Lord Howe to sail up the East River. We must hurry!" he said to Daniel Gill beside him on Liberty, and spurred his gray horse back toward the lines. Enroute, he encountered General Mifflin leading his troops to the landing.

"Good God, General Mifflin, you have ruined us!" Washington exclaimed. "Why have you withdrawn your troops?"

"On your orders!" Mifflin retorted angrily. "Major Scammel informed me my boats were waiting and I must march at once. I told him I *couldn't* leave! I had sentries and advanced posts out close to the British to watch them, I told Scammel—but he insisted. So I left."

"Those were not my orders!" Washington retorted, still angry.

"By God, General, did Scammel act as an aide-de-camp for the day, or did he not?"

"He did."

"Then I had orders from him!" Mifflin cried, still angry.

Suddenly Washington composed himself. "It is all a dreadful mistake, General," he said in a soothing voice. "Please return to your covering position."

Without a word, General Mifflin turned his horse around and led his troops back to their position. Washington rode back to the ferry with Colonel Gill. A fog came rolling in from the water.

"It is the hand of God," Washington said quietly. "The British fleet will never see us now. The army is saved. Daniel, please ride to General Mifflin and tell him he can withdraw."

Gradually, Mifflin's troops were brought to the ferry and boated. Behind them, the sound of British artillery and musket fire indicated that the enemy had taken note of the strangely silent Yankee trenches and were attacking.

Out on the water, the American soldiers guessed the meaning of the gunfire. Nate Gill whispered softly into Luke Sawyer's ear. "We're pulling foot. We're getting away." Luke nodded, quickly putting a finger over Nate's lips and seizing his head to turn it toward the landing. "Look," he whispered.

Through the swirling mists of the fog Nate saw the last man step down the slippery steps of the landing into the last boat.

"It's Washington," Nate breathed.

Chapter Twelve

Washington's men came ashore on Manhattan Island drenched, demoralized, starving and exhausted. Nathaniel Gill and the soldiers around him had barely the strength to march back to their old encampment where they were dismissed by Captain Pepper. Entering their tents they sank onto their pallets of sodden straw with a single, concerted sigh and fell asleep. Nate Gill and Luke Sawyer slept until reveille the following morning. They awoke somewhat refreshed but still weak from hunger.

"I'm gonna see if there's any food," Luke mumbled, stumbling outside the tent. He returned biting hard on a seabread biscuit. "Harder 'n a musket flint," he grumbled. "But it's still the first food we've had in three days. Here," he pulled a biscuit from his bulging pocket and handed one to Nate. Then he took another and placed it in his pack and gently crushed it into sections with his musket butt. "Only way you can eat the damn things."

"Where'd you get them, Luke?" Nate asked, doing the same with his own biscuit.

"There's a couple of unheaded casks full of them at the foot of Stone Street. You can take all you can carry. Better hurry, though."

Nate hastened out of the tent and joined a band of soldiers around the open kegs who were stuffing their pockets with the biscuits. He filled his own pockets and then the inside of his shirt.

"Better 'n eatin' bullets," one of them growled. "But not by much." He bit hard into a biscuit. "Ow! God damn it to hell! First they break our backs and next they break our teeth. What the hell are these things made of, anyway?"

"Peas-meal and canel, I think," another soldier answered.

"What the hell's canel?"

"A kind of piss-flavored cement," said the other, and Nate joined the general chuckle. Walking back up Stone Street he came upon Luke Sawyer carefully removing the iron grating from a low window in the cellar of a wine shop. It came away with a creak and small shower of rust. Luke took out the window.

"You crawl in, Natey. You're smaller 'n me."

Nate backed nimbly into the aperture and lowered himself to the floor. In the dim light inside the cellar he could see a back door. He opened it and Luke came inside, closing the door. He stumbled against a cask and swore: and then, in a voice of breathless reverence, he said:

"Madeira!"

With cries of delight the two soldiers opened the spigot, cupped their fingers under it and drank draft after draft of the delicious sweet red liquid. Sighing, they turned off the spigot, wiping their hands on their mud-caked breeches.

"There's got to be a better way," Luke said, looking around him. Suddenly, he seized his powder horn and was about to knock the bottom out of it to use for a flask, when Nate pointed to a pile of oil flasks in a corner.

"Just the thing," Luke cried eagerly, seizing two half-gallon flasks and handing one to Nate. They drew the wine again and began to drink in earnest. Then they began to sing:

> At Uncle Joe's I lived at ease,
> Had cider and good bread and cheese,
> But while I stayed at Uncle Sam's
> I'd naught to eat but "faith and clams."

"Yeah," Luke growled morosely, "it sure ain't faith and hams. And it ain't faith and clams, either. It's faith and shams. No pay, no food, no rum, no clothes. God damn it, Natey, when we signed on we was promised six dollars and two thirds a month. So they paid us in Continental currency which ain't worth the powder to blow it to hell. You couldn't buy a good feed with six dollars and two thirds, if you ever git it. I cain't remember when I got paid last, Natey, and I heard tell that the Continental money has gotten so worthless Congress is gonna stop pretendin' and stop payin' us altogether." Luke Sawyer tilted his flask to his lips and took a long swig. He lowered it, wiped his mouth morosely with his hand and belched. "An' the food. We was promised a daily ration of one pound of good fresh or salt beef, or three fourths of a pound of good salt pork, a pound of good flour, soft or hard bread, a quart of salt to every hundred pounds of fresh beef, a quart of vinegar to every hundred rations, a gill of rum, brandy or whiskey a day, soap and candles. And what did we get? Moldy flour . . . bread crawlin' with weevils . . . rancid beef what was half bones and fat . . . That's what we got when we got it. And we was supposed to live for three or four days on it. And what happened to the rum and vinegar and salt?" he muttered fiercely. "You know damn well, Natey, we ain't never seen any of them critters. An' vegetables!" he snorted. "I fergit what a carrot tastes like." He took another drink. "C'mon, Natey, let's try 'The World Turned Upside Down.' " They began to sing:

> What happy golden days were those
> When I was in my prime!
> The lasses took delight in me,
> I was so neat and fine.
> I roved from fair to fair,
> Likewise from town to town,
> Until I married me a wife
> And the world turned upside down.

They finished their song laughing and hugging each other, falling over backwards and knocking over their flasks. "Aw, what the hell's the difference," Luke mumbled, getting two more flasks and half filling them. He held his up to Nate. "Here's to you, Natey—how y' bin enjoyin' your own married life?"

"Aw, cut it out, Luke," Nate murmured, flushing. He thought of Jennifer with a momentary pang.

"Y' know, I ain't been laid since we retook Boston. Remember Ezra Whatley? He sure had a good-lookin' wife."

"Luke Sawyer!"

"Aw, stow it, Natey—you're too wishy-washy. Besides, the lady was willin'. What d'ya say we get laid, Natey, old boy? There's a whorehouse up on the east side. Ain't a whorehouse really. It's a tavern, but there's rooms upstairs and the barmaids is for sale. What d'ya say, Nate?"

Nathaniel shook his head. "I couldn't do that to Jenny."

"Aw, stow it. Don't be a sanctimonious little bug-tick. It ain't like you was a regular two-timer. I know damn well if you was back home in Boston you wouldn't even think of slidin' yer dollywhacker into some other female. But this is different. Jenny's up there and you're down here and a man's got a right to get his wick wet. Besides, whores ain't cheatin'. Kee-rist! After all we bin through?"

Nathaniel thought again of Jennifer. He recalled how she looked feeding Tommy. How her pear-shaped breasts were so firm and seductive. Thinking of her caused a warmth in his loins and he said to Luke: "How . . . how can we, anyway? We don't have any money."

Luke Sawyer scratched his head. "I hadn't thought of that," he mumbled, taking another swig from his flask. He set it down, pondering, flouncing his thick red hair. "I got it!" he said, jumping to his feet. He ran to the cellar door, opening on the street, and flung it open, running back to wheel the pipe of Madeira toward it. In front of the cask he placed a plank over two empty barrels. "Here, Nate, you bring those oil flasks over here. You an' me's starting a wine business." Luke strutted out on the street, beginning to sing "The World Turned Upside Down," in a booming bass voice. A crowd of laughing soldiers gathered around him.

"All right, you mother's mistakes," Luke yelled, "you've lucked into the buy of the century. This here establishment is run by Nathaniel Gill, Esquire, scion of the wealthy Gill family of Boston, Massachusetts. Mr. Gill has just imported him two pipes of the finest Madeiry ever shipped from the Canary Islands. Why, this here Madeiry is said to come from the same grapes that made the wine the Lord drank at the Last Supper. It's delicious! It's mellow! It's guaranteed not to rust, scratch or corrode. It'll slide down yer pipes just as soft and sweet as the nectar of the gods. And now you lucky bastards, you just listen to me. You can buy this here priceless wine for as little as one dollar a gallon, sixty cents a half-gallon. That's right men, queue up! Just belly up to the counter here for the drinking experience of your lifetime!"

Laughing, shoving, the soldiers formed a line in front of the plank counter. Not all of them had enough money, but they pooled what they had to buy the flasks that Nate filled from the pipe and passed over the plank to Luke. News of the "wine shop" spread throughout the Stone Street encampment and within a half hour the pipe was empty. Luke and Nate were considering opening a second one when a tall, thin man with a lumpy face came running down the street shaking his cane at them.

"Out of my shop, you thieving rabble!" he yelled. "Here, give me that money. That's *my* money! You got it selling *my* wine!" The man lifted his cane as though to strike Luke with it, but Luke calmly reached up, wrenched it away and broke it in two. "Thash no way to treat soldiersh who guard you while you shleep," Luke wheezed, swaying slightly—and the soldiers who were watching roared with laughter.

"I'll have General Putnam on you, you drunken swine!" the man shouted, turning to hurry down the street toward headquarters.

"Lesh get the hell out of here, Natey," Luke muttered, "before Old Put puts ush in the guardhouse."

Nate put an arm around his tipsy friend's broad shoulders. "How much money did we make?" he asked eagerly, swaying slightly himself.

"Seventy-eight dollars and sixty cents."

"Wow! That's enough for a good meal *and* the barmaids. And we can *ride* up to the tavern. Maybe we can sleep it off while we're riding. Come on, Luke, there's a livery stable over on Whitehall."

The two soldiers were sound asleep by the time their carriage reached the tavern overlooking the East River on a side street midway up the island. The driver had to shake them awake. They paid him and walked gingerly inside the taproom.

The taproom had white plaster ceilings crisscrossed by smoke-blackened oak beams. There was a fireplace with a brass fence in front of it. Tables and chairs stood on the red tile floor. Half of them were occupied, mostly by sea captains and noncommissioned officers who glanced up in mild surprise when the two bedraggled privates came into the taproom.

Nate and Luke turned their eyes toward the bar, a massive, curved length of shining lacquered wood. When they saw the two barmaids behind the bar they exchanged glances. One was in her early thirties, blond and buxom with a hard face and a loud laugh, the other was smaller, black-haired and vivacious, with a waist so tiny it gave her a classic hourglass figure. Nate and Luke sat down and the bigger one came over to their table.

"Hello there, big boy," she said to Luke, winking, "what'll you have?"

"What's that I smell cooking in the kitchen?"

"Roast pork."

"Tarnation! That's for me!"

"Me too!"

"You got vegetables? *Real* vegetables?"

"Yep. Pig greens . . . carrots . . . mashed potatoes . . ."

"Tarnation! I'll take all three!"

"Me too!"

The barmaid flounced her hair and studied the two soldiers suspiciously. "Got any money?"

"Well, I'll be go to hell," Luke Sawyer exclaimed in dismay. "What kind of talk is that—'got any money?' What d'ya take us for, a couple of Hessian ragpickers?"

"Well you sure don't look like General Washington," the barmaid said, putting her hands on her hips belligerently. Her manner changed, however, after Luke dug into his pocket and spread his money on the table. "My, oh, my," she murmured, her eyes gleaming, "are we gonna have fun tonight, big boy! I like redheads," she said, pausing to stroke Luke's red locks. "And my name's Maggie."

"All right, Maggie," Luke said, "and how about two nice foaming tankards of cool beer."

Maggie nodded and went back to the bar and then to the kitchen. The smaller girl drew the beer and brought it to their table. She smiled at them and Nate saw that she had pretty white teeth and eyes of cornflower blue. He felt the warmth rising in his loins again.

"What's your name, honey?" Luke asked, and she smiled again and said, "Molly." Luke took a long pull at his tankard, setting it down with a sigh. He looked at Molly and winked. "When's the fun begin, Molly?"

She laughed and said, "Any time you say, soldier-boy," and went back to the bar.

"God damn it, Luke," Nate growled, "stop getting me all riled up when we got a meal like that coming."

Maggie returned with two heaping, steaming platters of food, coming back with two more tankards of beer. Playfully toying with Luke's hair again, she said, "Enjoy your dinner, gents," and left. The two soldiers ate greedily and in silence, repeatedly calling for more beer. As they ate, the taproom emptied out. Soon they were alone in it. They finished their meal and pushed their plates away with deep grunts of satisfaction.

Maggie came to clear the table and Luke jumped up and seized her around the waist. "How's about a kiss, baby?" he asked, leering at her and bending her backward.

"How much, big boy?"

"Don't you worry none, you'll get paid," Luke said, kissing her full on the mouth. He released her and she giggled and seized his hand as though to lead him upstairs, when suddenly from the street outside came the sound of marching feet.

"Oh, my God, it's the watch!" Maggie cried, and turned to seize Nate by the hand, too. "Here, both of you, come with me," she said, and hurried them up the stairs into a bedroom with two beds. "They'll want their usual free drink, and I may be a little while," she said with a wink, "but I'll be back."

Both men undressed and slipped into bed. Nate lay on his panting with desire. Gradually, however, he was overtaken by drowsiness. All the food and drink the two of them had consumed that day was more than a match for their passion and both of them fell asleep. Nate awakened a few hours later to feel a soft little hand playing with his genitals and a soft little mouth going over his body.

"For shame, going to sleep like that," Molly whispered pretending to pout. "I don't know if I even want to let you kiss me."

Nate did kiss her and then it was his mouth that went over her body. He knelt back suddenly and said, "Let me look at you," and swept back the covers. By the light of the betty lamp Nate saw for the first time the naked body of a beautiful woman. He knelt there, his eyes gleaming, trembling with lust, and Molly gave a little giggle and leaned forward to seize his throbbing penis and guide him into her.

Nate Gill awoke with a hideous headache. His entire body ached and his eyes burned. His mouth was dry. He felt hot. Nate turned his head listlessly to see that Luke was in the other bed with Maggie. He felt Molly roll toward him and he pushed her gently away. "I . . . I can't," he groaned. Molly got out of bed in indignation.

"What's wrong with me?" she asked angrily. "I thought you liked me."

"I . . . I do . . . It's just that . . . something's wrong with me. . . . Can I have a glass of water?"

Concerned, Molly hurried to a pitcher of water standing on a bureau. She poured out a glass and hastened back to Nate's bed. "Here," she said, gently propping up his head, "I'll hold you." Nate drank greedily, sinking back against his pillow with a sigh. "I . . . I think I'm sick. . . ."

Gently, Molly placed her little hand on Nate's forehead. "Sick? You're on fire!" She knit her brows thoughtfully. "Where'd you two get your uniforms so dirty?"

"Br . . . Brooklyn Heights. . . ."

"Malaria! You've got malaria. That's where General Green got his. That Gowanus Canal is nothing but a malarial marsh." Molly heard Luke Sawyer uttering low groans and she hurried over to wake Maggie and put her hand on Luke's forehead. "He's got it, too!"

"Got what?" Maggie mumbled, rubbing her eyes and pulling on a worn dressing gown.

"Malaria! Our two soldier-boys are coming down with malaria."

"Oh, my God—what are we going to do with them?"

Molly lifted her hands helplessly, gazing fondly at Nate, who had lost consciousness. "There isn't very much we *can* do. They can't be moved. I know that much. I was born in Martinique, and I know the only thing you can do is to try to keep their bodies cool and make them drink lots of water."

"But we can't let them stay here, Molly! Supposing they die?"

Molly stared at the two soldiers and shook her head grimly. "They won't die. Not after what they've been through. General Greene got well, didn't he? And he's twice as old as they are. No, Maggie, I'm afraid we're going to have to take care of them."

Daniel Gill always believed that George Washington's evacuation of Long Island was the most brilliant feat of his military career. Daniel knew enough of military history to know that to conduct a successful withdrawal in the face of a victorious foe was the most difficult of all maneuvers, especially to elude pursuit and lose no men as Washington had done. Nevertheless, Daniel was worried about the habit of procrastination that had seized the general after his army's safe arrival in New York. In contrast to the calm confidence which had so reassured his officers during the retreat, he was now in an agony of indecision. Daniel wondered how a man of Washington's graceful courage under the stress of battle could turn so vacillating once the crisis was past.

For almost three weeks Washington could not make up his mind whether or not to defend New York. He held repeated councils of war, another trait which disturbed Daniel. He could remember his father quoting Grandfather Gill: "Councils of war usually counsel caution. The will of the timid usually prevails over the bold."

Strangely enough, it was Washington who seemed timid during the councils. He could not accept General Nathaniel Greene's advice to burn New York. "Burn it down," said Greene. "It's two-thirds Tory, anyway." General Putnam also urged abandonment of the city. "If we stay here we'll be cooped up in a box, just like the British were in Boston."

"But, gentlemen, Congress is insisting that I stay here," Washington replied. "President Hancock says that to lose New York will demoralize the country."

"Better to give them a burnt city than a broken army," said Greene. "The place is indefensible. Rivers on both sides and a pass up north at Kingsbridge where ships can trap an army. Coves and inlets everywhere. Now that they have Brooklyn Heights they can bombard us here. Without a fleet of our own, we're powerless to stop them."

After agonizing for almost three weeks, Washington finally decided to accept the advice of his generals.

"The army is more important," he said to Daniel after a secret meeting with his officers. "I cannot risk the army in any decisive engagement with a superior foe. The army is the Revolution. It is more important than any city—even Philadelphia. I know that my decision will be misconstrued in some high places—either by misunderstanding of the nature of war or by malice—but I must withdraw once more to the Heights of Harlem. We will begin Sunday evening."

Sunday morning—the sixteenth of September, 1776—

Washington was awakened by a thunderous cannonade. The British were attacking! Warships in the East River were battering American fortifications at Kip's Bay, about a third of the way up the island. Flatboats packed with British and Hessian soldiers began crossing the river. Almost at first sight of them, the Americans defending the position turned and fled.

Washington rode to Kip's Bay in a fury. Followed by Daniel on Liberty, the General rode straight among his panicking soldiers. "Take the walls!" he shouted. "Take the cornfield!" Only a few obeyed. Washington dashed his hat to the ground in a paroxysm of rage. "Are these the men I am to defend America with?" he cried. Shouting curses, he urged his horse among them, striking at them with his cane. But they paid him no heed. Privates, officers, even a colonel and a brigadier general, they ran from an enemy they had not even seen, throwing away their muskets, their knapsacks, bullet pouches, anything to lighten their load and speed their flight.

Washington sat his horse in despair. He did not move. Daniel watched him carefully, fearing that he might consciously be hoping to be killed rather than face the ignominy of another defeat. A party of soldiers in white-and-gold uniforms approached, cheering, waving their bayoneted muskets. Hessians! At once, Colonel Daniel Gill seized the bridle of his general's horse and led him back to safety.

Nate Gill's body burned in the fires of malarial fever. He felt as though he were living in an oven. He thought that his horribly aching bones were in a vise and that someone was twisting it. He drifted in and out of consciousness just as the boat that had taken him to New York had glided in and out of the fog. Sometimes he was aware of Molly bathing his burning body in cool water, sometimes he was not. At times, he threw up the water Molly got him to drink, his spleen was so badly distended.

Neither Nate nor Luke heard the bombardment signaling the landing at Kip's Bay. But Molly and Maggie did. They rushed into the street to find the American encampment in confusion.

"To arms!" the sergeants were crying. "To arms! The British are landing above us."

"We're trapped!" a private screamed. "Just like Brooklyn Heights. They're behind us!"

A sergeant knocked him down with a single blow to the jaw and began bellowing for his company to fall in. Gradually, General Israel Putnam calmed his panicking army of four thousand men and led them north into the woods, along Indian paths winding through a tangle of trees and underbrush. Molly and Maggie watched them pass their tavern in horror. The barmaids were at their window when the British marched triumphantly into town. They saw the enemy troops engulfed in a throng of weeping, shouting Tories. Women as well as men carried British officers on their shoulders. Girls kissed redcoats and Hessians alike, dancing with them in the street. Everywhere the American flags were torn down and the king's hoisted in their place. Then the two terrified women watched the roundup of suspected Rebels or Rebel sympathizers. They were torn from their homes and marched off to jail through lines of jeering Tories who struck at them with their fists and spit at them.

"Hang them!" they cried. "Kill the dirty traitors!"

The two women looked at each other with stark terror in their eyes. "What will we do?" Maggie wailed. "What will we do?" Molly said nothing. She had heard Nate beginning to babble again and she rushed to his side.

Sometimes in his incoherence Nate would recite snatches of the Declaration of Independence, which he had memorized, or quote the family motto: "There is a tide in the affairs of men . . ." Or he would sing "The World Turned Upside Down." Molly would look down at him fondly when he would mutter, "God damn your royal, rotten soul, King George of England, we'll get rid of you . . . you and your filthy murdering mercenaries . . ." But she would frown when he would sit up and cry out, "Jenny! Jenny! Oh, Jenny, I love you so!" Molly had become very fond of Nate Gill.

She burst into tears of joy one day when she saw Nate struggle to sit erect and hunch his shoulders and hug himself as though it were very cold in the room. His body was shaking.

"I . . . I'm c-c-cold," he said with chattering teeth. "I'm fr-fr-freezing!"

"Thank God!" Molly exclaimed, rushing to his side to pull

a blanket over him. "That means the fever's broken. You're over it, Natey, you're over it! You're going to get well."

"I'm sw-sw-sweating like a blown horse," Nate said, his teeth still chattering. "And I'm c-c-cold. It's c-c-crazy, but oh, Molly, it f-feels so good."

Molly laughed, piling blanket after blanket on top of him. Every half hour, she cleared them off and rolled him over to remove the sweat-drenched sheet and replace it with a fresh one. In another hour, Nate was sleeping peacefully..

Next day, Luke Sawyer's fever broke. But both men were still as weak as newborn kittens. For the first few days, they could only take milk for nourishmment. As soon as they were able to take solid food, Molly told them that the British had captured New York.

"Jesus jumpin' Christ!" Luke groaned, holding his head in his hands. He waited until Molly had gone downstairs in answer to the jangling of the doorbell, before he turned to Nate and said, "Now we are in a fix! Here I'd been worrying about what to tell Cap'n Pepper when we got back. We cain't tell him the truth! That we come down with malary in a whorehouse and a couple o' whores nursed us back to health. He'd just laugh hisself silly and tack on ten more lashes. But now," he said gloomily, "I'd say a whip's better 'n a rope."

Nate winced when he heard Luke describe Molly as a "whore." He couldn't bring himself to think that the angel who had been his nurse was a prostitute. "Maybe we can make a break for it at night," he said.

"In these clothes?" Luke snorted. He went to a window and stood at the side of it peering into the street below. "Nawthin' but lobsterbacks and Heiniekoplotzes as far as you kin see. Oh, my Jesus, if it ain't Joel Courtney! He's a colonel! That fat toad is a colonel! How 'n hell'd they ever get his big fat ass up on a horse? They must have used a winch!"

Nate came hurrying to his side. "*Mr.* Sawyer," he said with mock reproach, "I'll have you know you're talking about my father-in-law." Nate grinned. "That's him all right. Oh, how I'd love to ventilate that belly of his."

That night before retiring Nate and Luke discussed their predicament with Molly and Maggie. "We just don't dare go outside in these clothes," Luke muttered.

Molly's eyes brightened. "How about *our* clothes?"

"'Y' mean masquerade as wimmen?" Luke said musingly. He looked at Nate. "Naw. We're too big. Nate's over six feet hisself an' I'm bigger 'n he is. It won't work."

Molly sighed. "Maybe I'll think of something else in the morning."

In the morning all four of them heard a crackling and roaring noise outside and they leaped from bed and ran to the window.

New York was burning!

Whipped by high winds, flames roared through street after street with a dreadful howl. Hovels in the city's hideous slums went up, fine mansions, Dutch houses dating back to Peter Stuyvesant, wharves, churches, the trees in the parks—all were on fire. Soon they were collapsing with bright showers of sparks. Shrieking women and children dashed from their blazing homes to lie down helplessly on the common, their cries of terror and despair mingling with the curses and shouts of the men and soldiers who spilled onto the street to fight the fire.

"Water! Water! We need water!"

On the flanks and the front of the city, men ran desperately to fetch water from the rivers and the harbor.

"Buckets! We need buckets!"

"They ain't any! They're mostly all burned up!"

At the window the two soldiers and their companions watched aghast while the flames spread.

"Oh, Lord, don't let it get up here," Maggie prayed.

Now the fire had engulfed Trinity Church. Flames ran up its steeple like fiery snakes. Soon the tip of the steeple was alight like the flame of a monster candle. Flames ate away the building's outer shingles, exposing the timbers which quickly caught fire themselves. Finally, with a great hissing roar, and a shower of sparks, the entire structure collapsed.

"Oh, my Jesus, look what they're doin'," Luke Sawyer exclaimed.

Crowds of shouting Tories were converging on the British guardhouses.

"They did it, the dirty Rebels! They set the town on fire."

"Let's get them!"

"String them up!"

Maggie and Molly covered their eyes and Nate and Luke watched in horrid fascination while the Tories dragged their screaming prisoners into the parks and hung them from the limbs of the trees. Others were thrown shrieking into the burning buildings.

"Burn, you bastards, burn!"

"Here's a sample of what's waiting down below!"

At last, the wind changed and the fire was under control. Night fell. In the morning, Nate and Luke went to the window again. They could see squads of British soldiers helping civilians clean up the blackened rubble of the city. Then they saw a squad of carpenters approach in a wagon loaded with lumber. The carpenters jumped down and set to work.

"My God," Nate Gill breathed, "they're building a gallows."

Soon another wagon appeared carrying a young American in civilian dress accompanied by a British officer. The American mounted the gallows.

"It's Captain Hale!" Nate Gill cried in horror. "Captain Nathan Hale from Connecticut."

Nathan Hale appeared to be requesting something but the officer below him shook his head. Nathan Hale squared his shoulders and stared straight ahead. Nate and Luke could see his eyes. They were light blue. Nathan Hale spoke:

"My only regret is that I have but one life to give for my country."

Tears sprang to the eyes of both Nate and Luke when they saw Nathan Hale's footing kicked away and his lifeless body swinging on the rope.

"They'll pay, the filthy scum!" Luke Sawyer muttered.

"He didn't even have a preacher or a Bible," Nate cried, almost sobbing.

Maggie came into the room and the two soldiers led her silently to the window. She saw the gently swinging corpse at the end of the rope and gave a little scream.

"You've got to go, or you'll be there next," she gasped.

"But how?" Nate asked. "In these clothes, they'll catch us in a minute."

"I'll get you some others," Maggie replied, turning to look at Luke. "As you know, big boy, there's one thing I do pretty good."

"You sure do, baby. Best lay this side of the Bahamas."

Maggie giggled and pulled out her bed. "So when I bring my gentleman friend upstairs tonight to entertain him, you be

behind the bed. After he takes off his clothes and goes
beddy-bye with me, you bop him on the head with a kitchen
skillet. Then Nate takes his clothes. Then I bring up another
gentleman and you get your clothes."

Luke Sawyer shook his head admiringly. "I sure am glad
you're on our side, baby," he said, and then, with an impish
grin. "You wanna let 'em finish before I bop 'em?"

"Don't be fresh!" Maggie snapped, before going downstairs.

"Be sure to get the right sizes," Luke called after her.

By midnight, much to the amusement of Nate Gill, the
clothes had been obtained. The two "gentlemen friends" were
stretched unconscious on the beds. Attired in the sober black
coats and hats of Tory merchants, Nate and Luke went
downstairs to say good-bye to Molly and Maggie. They were
waiting for them at the door. Each held a flickering candle.
Otherwise the tavern was dark.

Nate thought he saw tears in Molly's eyes. He squeezed
her hand. He remembered guiltily that neither he nor Luke
had paid for their . . . their "services" . . . But he could not
bring himself to mention it.

Molly seemed to guess what he was thinking. She shook
her head slowly. "It's all right, Natey," she said gently. "I've
. . . I've never been happier. . . . I'll never forget you . . .
never . . ." She stood on tiptoe and kissed him softly on the
mouth.

Luke grabbed Maggie around the waist and gave her a resounding kiss.

"Say, big boy," Maggie said, "you didn't even pay for your
dinner."

Luke gasped and dug a hand into his pocket. "Take it all,"
he said, handing her the money. "It'd've been a bargain at
twice the price." He kissed her again. "You know, baby, after
this war is over I think I'm gonna come back here and marry
you."

"What makes you think I'll wait?"

"Aw, sure you will," Luke said, following Nate out on the
street. "An' while yer waitin', baby—keep yer legs crossed."

Chapter Thirteen

When Nate and Luke arrived safely at the American position on Harlem Heights they were taken immediately to headquarters to report to General Washington. Nate was awed by the imposing presence of the commander-in-chief, even though his cousin Daniel was present. Even the irrepressible Luke Sawyer seemed subdued. Washington studied them with kindly eyes.

"Soldiers, I am proud of your perseverance." He smiled his thin humorless smile. "I have heard the . . . ah . . . details of your confinement. Most singular, I should say. Now please tell me of the burning of New York."

In a trembling voice that grew steadier, Nate Gill described the destruction of the city. Then, with tears in his eyes, he told of the hanging of Nathan Hale. Washington's eyes also filled. "They'll pay," he said with quiet grimness.

"The girls who . . . the people who took us in told us General Howe didn't even try him. He just ordered him hung. He wouldn't let him see a preacher or a Bible."

Washington shuddered. "They'll pay," he said once more. "And our nation will always remember Captain Hale's last words. He is our first martyr." The general looked at the two men with kindly eyes again. "You may go, now, my brave soldiers."

The two men marched proudly from the room. Returning to their tent, Nate found a letter from Jennifer awaiting him. He tore it open in delight and read:

Dearest Natey,

Mark sat up all by himself today!

I was so happy I almost cried. Oh, how I wish you could have been here to see it. He was so proud of himself!

Natey, Mark Jedediah Gill has got the bluest eyes you've

151

ever seen. I don't know where he got them from because both our eyes are brown and yours are almost black. Barbara says it must be from Grandfather Gill, so I guess it was a good idea to give him the middle name of Jedediah.

Oh, how I wish you could come home for a little while! Just think, in another three months Mark will be walking and you won't be here to see that, either. Can't you get away somehow? It's been fifteen months since you went out to Lexington and Concord and you've only had three days off in all that time. I think of you all the time and sometimes my heart aches so much that I cry myself to sleep. I won't say any more about it, though, Natey, because I don't want to upset you.

Natey, Barbara and I are back in Boston. Barbara is so efficient. It's amazing that a woman as beautiful and feminine as she is has such a business head on her shoulders. She said if we didn't do something about the Gill family properties they'd fall apart or burn down or be wrecked by vandals. So we moved into town. Mrs. Wilmot came with us to take care of Mark. I run the tavern, now, and Barbara takes care of the shipyard and the fishing fleet. Most of the shipyard was burned down by Tories and General Howe took three of the ships when he left, but otherwise everything is in fine shape. Barbara is having the shipyard rebuilt. She is selling your pa's house, too. Otherwise, she says, it would fall into disrepair. And she boarded up your Grandma's house. We are nice and cozy living above the tavern and Barbara says to tell you not to worry about your property. It'll all be waiting for you when you come back.

Oh, Natey, dearest, when *will* you come back? I worry so much about you. Please be careful . . . be careful . . . be careful . . . I love you so much!

                                        Your loving wife,
                                        Jenny

Nate read the letter again and again with a feeling of rising excitement. Yes, by damn, he would go to Boston! He would see Jenny again and little Mark, hold Jenny in his arms, finally possess his wife after all these unrequited months. But, how? Cousin Ben! That was it. He'd go to Dr. Gill and have him make a recommendation for a sick furlough. At once, Nate sprang to his feet and ran to the infirmary.

"You see, Cousin Ben, I did have a bad case of malaria. If you could just stretch it a bit. . . . Say that I'm in need of rest and rehabilitation . . . say that I need the sort of loving care that I can only get at home . . . something like that. Could you, Cousin Ben?"

"Why, of course, Nate," Benjamin Gill said smoothly, going to sit at his desk and seizing a pen and paper. "How long?"

"Two weeks?"

"Make it three. Your company commander's name?"

"Pepper. Captain Jonah Pepper."

Nate listened in delight to the scratching of Dr. Gill's pen. He wrung his hand in gratitude when Ben handed him the recommendation.

"Thanks, Cousin Ben, thanks! You don't know what this means to me."

"I can guess. Enjoy yourself, Nate. Say hello to Barbara and Jenny for me."

"I will," Nate cried, turning to sprint back to Captain Pepper's headquarters. He handed the doctor's note to him, watching with trembling apprehension while he sat at his field desk and read it. The captain looked up sharply.

"I thought you'd recovered."

"N-no, sir," Nate lied. "I . . . I still get the chills and the shakes. I feel weak and I'm losing weight again."

"Well, I guess there's nothing wrong with it. You've always been a good soldier, Private Gill, and I guess you do need the rest. But, remember, you be here sharp for reveille three weeks from today."

"I will, sir!" Nate Gill cried, his heart bursting with joy. Sprinting back to his tent, Nate left a hasty note for Luke Sawyer before packing his knapsack, shouldering it and turning his face north for Kingsbridge, where he could cross the river onto the mainland. He calculated that if he walked fifty miles a day, he could reach Boston in five days, maybe sooner if he got a ride or two in a wagon. He could hire a horse for the return trip and get back in three days, maybe sooner. That would give him at least thirteen whole days with Jenny!

Nate Gill began to sing.

A few days after Nate departed, Dr. Benjamin Gill strolled through the avenues formed by the neat rows of tents in Nate's company area. He asked a soldier where he might find company headquarters, and the man pointed out Captain Pepper's tent to him. Humming softly, Benjamin walked up to the tent and peered inside. It was empty. Still humming, he walked around it to be sure. He entered from the back and went to the captain's field desk. Humming again, he leafed through the captain's papers until he found a folder marked *furloughs*. Inside it was his note recommending Nate for convalescence leave. He removed it, stuck it in his pocket and went out the way he had come.

Dr. Gill was smiling broadly that night when he touched the note to a betty lamp and tossed it into the fireplace.

"Hey there, barmaid—how's about a kiss?"

"Why, you dirt—*Nate!* Oh, Natey, it's you! It's you!"

Jenny Gill ran around the bar and threw herself into her husband's arms. He held her close and kissed her again and again until his lips were wet with her tears. They parted and Jenny looked at him adoringly.

"How did you get away?"

"Dr. Ben Gill got me convalescent leave. You see, I had malaria and—"

Jenny gasped. "You had *malaria?* Oh, Natey, you could have died! Was it very painful?"

"Sure was. I wouldn't even wish it on King George." Nate momentarily recalled Molly's cool little hands bathing his burning body and he blushed.

"Natey, you've got a terrible sunburn."

"Guess so," Nate mumbled. "I was five days on the road. And I've got a powerful thirst, too. How about a nice cool tankard of beer?"

Nodding happily, Jenny hurried behind the bar to serve her husband. Nate drank a deep draft and sighed with pleasure. Jenny watched him with shining eyes.

"As soon as you finish, we'll go upstairs and see Mark," she said. Nate finished the beer and Jenny called into the kitchen for the cook to take her place behind the bar. Then, seizing his hand she led him proudly upstairs.

Mrs. Wilmot had just finished dressing Mark when they entered the living room. "Land's sake, it's Mr. Nate!" she exclaimed. She lifted the child and held him out to his father. Nate took him tenderly and kissed him gently on the cheek. But his beard scratched Mark's face and he began to cry. Nate felt miserable. "Don't cry, Mark, don't cry," he crooned. "Your pa won't hurt you." Mark had seldom seen a man before and his father's masculine voice frightened him further. He dug his little fists into his eyes and began to bawl.

Jennifer quickly took the child from Nate and began crooning to him. Her familiar fragrance and voice reassured him and he lay quietly against her breast staring curiously at his father. Gradually, Mark became accustomed to a man and soon allowed himself to be fondled by him.

"He sure has grown," Nate said proudly. "What's he weigh, now?"

"Almost eighteen pounds," Jennifer said, taking Mark into her arms and putting him back in his crib. Turning to Mrs. Wilmot, she said: "Would you be good enough to tell Barbara that Nate is home. Tell her to be sure to be home early because I'm going to roast a goose with all the fixings." Mrs. Wilmot nodded and went out the door.

"Where's Barbara?" Nate asked eagerly.

"At J. Gill and Sons'."

"That means Mrs. Wilmot will be gone at least an hour," Nate said, his eyes gleaming and full of desire.

"I know," Jennifer said softly, coming to him and pressing against him. "That's why I sent her there."

Nathaniel and Jennifer decided to spend their belated honeymoon on Nantucket. It was Barbara's idea. "Of course you have to have a honeymoon," she said that night at dinner. "Mrs. Wilmot and I can take care of Mark."

"But where would we go to get away from the war?" Jennifer asked. "Everywhere you go you see nothing but guns and uniforms. I hate it."

"Nantucket, of course," Barbara had replied. "It's a Gill family tradition to go there on your honeymoon. Great-grandfather Clarke went there with his bride. So did Grandpa

Gill. And your pa, too, Nate—and your uncles and my mother."

So they went to Nantucket. Nate took off his uniform and put on the civilian clothes he had worn at Harvard and Jenny wore the yellow taffeta dress she had worn the night of the bombardment, and they rode in a carriage down to Wood's Hole, where they hired a small sailboat and set out for the island. At first, Jenny was afraid to be on open water in such a frail craft. Gradually, however, she relaxed. It was a beautiful fall day—a time of Indian summer—and Jenny was enchanted to feel a mild sun gently bathing her face or making points of gold upon the glittering surface of the sea. Sometimes a light breeze riffled the water, scattering it with silver. At last they saw the island, and then the rooftops of the weatherbeaten cottages on the landward shore.

Jennifer was delighted with the town, with its wide cobblestone streets and quaint rows of shops. They rode out to the seaward beach, where Jenny was momentarily disappointed to find that the wild roses she had heard so much about were not, of course, in bloom. But she was delighted with the baskets of fuchsia hanging over the doorway of every cottage.

"They're so pretty," Jenny murmured, fondling the delicate little bells of white and pink and purple. "I think I'll take some home with me." Facing the ocean, she stood on tiptoe as though trying to peer over the top of the horizon and spread her arms wide. "It's so peaceful. Wouldn't you like to live here?"

"Nope," Nate said. "I agree with you, it's lovely and peaceful and charming. But it's a backwater. Nobody from Nantucket is ever going to be anybody."

"I don't understand you," Jenny said, taking his hand as they strolled along the beach watching a flight of migrating birds heading south.

"I'm going to be *some*body!" Nate cried fiercely. "This is a new country, Jenny, and I've been lucky enough to be born in time to be somebody in it. When this war's over, I'm going back to Harvard and study law."

"But, Nate—what about your inheritance? Barbara says that when the war is over you'll be a rich man. You'd be too old to go to school and you wouldn't need to."

"The money will help. But I want to be a constitutional lawyer like Pa was. You look down in Philadelphia at the

Continental Congress. Most of the delegates are lawyers. Or else they're political philosophers like Thomas Jefferson, men who have read Locke and John Stuart Mill, Rousseau and Voltaire. Sure, there's some just plain rich men—but it's the lawyers who are the leaders. And I'm going to be a *leader!*" Nate exclaimed, his tone again fierce. "My family's been in on America from the beginning. Great-grandfather Clarke . . . yes, and Great-grandfather Gill, too! Everybody keeps forgetting him because Grandpa Gill never saw his parents. All of them! Pa and Uncle Mal, too—they led the fight to get the French off our backs, and now I'm fighting to get rid of King George. When this war's over, Jenny, we'll be the only truly free country in the world. We'll be like a beacon of hope shining in the darkness for the oppressed people of the world to see. And the American Revolution will spread! You mark my words, Jenny, we're going to strike the spark that will set the world afire with rebellion against the tyranny of kings. And I want to be in the forefront of affairs to fan the flames. That's why I want to go back to school."

"I understand," Jenny said, squeezing his hand and turning to stare at him adoringly. "I was just thinking. Maybe tonight we could eat at the inn. Barbara says they have the most delicious bay scallops."

Nathaniel nodded absentmindedly, his mind still dwelling on the glorious future. Jennifer giggled and poked him with her finger. "Come on, Mr. Philosopher, we'd better be going. The sun's going down and it's getting chilly." Still preoccupied, Nathaniel allowed Jennifer to lead him back to their carriage.

For the remaining days of their honeymoon, they followed the same idyllic routine: strolling through town in the morning, riding out to different sections of the island after lunch to walk hand in hand on the beach and eating each night at a different inn or tavern. At last it was time to depart. Nate realized that they would have to hurry to make Captain Pepper's deadline. To his dismay, a storm blew in from the sea. For three days, Nate and Jenny stayed inside the tavern while high winds lashed the island and heavy rains pelted against the windows. Nate was distraught when they finally took ship for the mainland.

"I won't be able to go back to Boston with you," he said to Jenny. "As soon as we hit the mainland, I'll have to head for camp if I'm going to get back in time. You won't mind going back to Boston by yourself?"

"Of course not, silly. And I'll ship your uniform down to you."

"By all means," Nate said, glancing ruefully at his civilian clothes. "I'd hate to be caught in these."

At Wood's Hole, Nate took another boat across Buzzard's Bay before turning his face south while Jenny hired a carriage and rode north. That night Nate put up at an inn. He gave his name to the innkeeper, who started slightly when he wrote it down. Nate went up to his room. Five minutes later there was a loud knock on his door. Nate opened it. A sergeant and two soldiers stood outside.

"You are Private Nathaniel Gill?" the sergeant asked.

"Yes."

"You're under arrest."

Nate gasped. "*Arrest?* What for?"

"Desertion."

Chapter Fourteen

It was early December in 1776 before Nathaniel Gill was transferred under guard from the Boston detention barracks to General Washington's winter camp in Newtown, Pennsylvania, where he was promptly placed in the guardhouse to await trial. Two days later, Luke Sawyer came to see him.

"Natey, Natey, what happened?" Luke exclaimed, staring sadly through the iron bars at his young comrade. "You said in yer note you was goin' on convalescent leave. What happened?"

"I don't know," Nate replied morosely. "All I know is they arrested me the day I got back from my honeymoon. They said I wasn't on furlough and had deserted in the face of the enemy. They said my company had requested my arrest. But how can that be?" Nate cried out in agony, jumping erect to seize an iron bar. "Captain Pepper knows that isn't true! He *knows* he gave me permission to go and he can testify to it!"

"No, he cain't, Natey," Luke said, sorrowfully shaking his head. "Cap'n Pepper's dead. A cannon ball got him at White Plains."

Nathaniel Gill was aghast. He sank back onto his pallet of straw and lowered his face into his hands. "Oh, no!" he sobbed, over and over, "Oh, no!" He glanced up eagerly. "But Cousin Ben's still alive, isn't he? He can testify that he gave me that recommendation."

Again Luke Sawyer shook his head, this time doubtfully. "I wouldn't count on that cousin o' yourn. You ever stopped to figger if somethin' happened to you who'd be next in line fer yer inheritance?"

Nate's face blanched. "Ben," he muttered in horror. "Cousin Ben. But, no! He'd never do a thing like that! Besides, he couldn't! His recommendation is in the company files. That'll prove I'm innocent, I know it!"

"It ain't," Luke said with brutal frankness. "Cap'n Walker—the officer what took Pepper's place—says he cain't find it anywhere."

Nate sank back against the oozing brick wall of the guardhouse. He lifted a limp hand and let it fall. He looked at Luke uncomprehendingly, his usually bright black eyes now dull dark pools staring out of hollow sockets. For a moment, Luke feared the shock of his disclosures might send Nate's mind retreating into the amnesia that had seized him after the deaths of his father and uncle.

"Nate, Nate, you've got to listen to me," he cried eagerly, shaking the bars to gain his attention. "They ain't gonna shoot you, Natey, boy. The men won't let 'em. The men are so disgusted right now they say they're gonna mutiny if they try to shoot you."

"Mutiny?" Nate asked weakly. "What . . . what for . . . ?"

"The army's fallin' apart," Luke said, rushing on to hold Nate's interest. "We bin through hell. Raw, bloody, hungry hell. Everbody's disgusted with General Washington. 'General Washywish,' they call him, or 'Old Retreat and Defeat' or 'General Pullfoot.' An' that's all we've had since you left Harlem Heights. Retreat and defeat with the limeys lookin' at our ass. First he breaks up the army into three parts. He sends one part to Fort Washington and another to Fort Lee across the river in Jersey and takes the biggest part with him up to White Plains. That's where we was, Natey. So Howe gets in behind us again and has the chance to finish the war there and then but for some reason he doesn't. So Washington gets us away again, this time over the Hudson into Jersey. While we're marchin' south we find out that Fort Washington surrendered and then General Greene hauls ass from Fort Lee with Cornwallis chasin' him all the way and then we begin the retreat to the Delaware." Luke paused to draw breath, warily watching Nate out of the corner of his eye. Relieved to see the youth's eyes on him expectantly, he continued: "Kee-*rist*, did it rain! If Cornwallis'd caught up with us and there'd bin a fight it would've had to be with the bayonet 'cause there wasn't a dry musket in either army. And the mud! It was so gooey that if you was lucky enough to have shoes you'd have to take 'em off to walk or the mud'd suck 'em off. All we did was cross rivers. First, the Hudson, then the Hackensack and then the Passaic. Cornwallis almost caught us at Newark. We was just leavin' when he come into town at the other end. And them stinkin' Tory-lovers in New Jersey. They give us nawthin'. No food, no rum, no nawthin'. They hid all their cattle and their dressed meat an' we could tell from the way they looked right through us that they all had Union Jacks up their sleeves an' was just waitin' to wave 'em at the British."

"Well," Nate said, suddenly speaking up to Luke's immense relief, "at least we're safe, now. General Washington saved the army again. I don't think he's a bad general, Luke. I think General Washington is a great man."

"You're a minority of one in this man's army, Natey, boy. Everyone else is prayin' that General Lee will come down here and take charge. That's all they do is talk about Lee. They call him the Guardian Angel. I tell you, Natey, you wouldn't think so much of Washington if you had been with him on the retreat."

"Would to God that I had!" Nate cried out in passion. "What's going to happen to me? After all that my family has done for our country, are they going to shoot me like a dirty coward?"

"Don't you worry none, Natey. I tell you the troops won't let 'em. They know you've been as good a soldier as there is in the army. They won't let 'em, I tell you, even if they convict you."

"When's the trial?" Nate asked in a dull voice.

"Day after tomrrow."

The "courtroom" in which Nathaniel Gill was tried was a company tent fitted with a rough plank supported by two empty powder kegs behind which sat a stocky major in the uniform of the Delaware Line. His seat was also a powder keg as were those occupied by Dr. Benjamin Gill and Captain Arthur Walker. There were no spectators. Nate was marched in between two soldiers and brought to a halt in front of the major. Nate shot an imploring glance toward his cousin, but Dr. Gill seemed preoccupied with his fingernails.

"Prisoner, tennnn—shun!"

Nate snapped to attention and the trial began.

"You are Private Nathaniel Gill?" the major asked in a bored voice.

"Yes, sir."

"You are charged with desertion in the face of the enemy. What do you have to say for yourself?"

"I never deserted!" Nate cried passionately. "I was on furlough when they arrested me. Captain Pepper granted me a three-week convalescent leave."

The judge-major turned to Captain Walker. "You have taken over Pepper's company, Captain. I understand you have been through his files?"

"I have indeed, sir—twice."

"Did you find anything supporting Private Gill's contention?"

"Nothing."

Nate gasped in despair. Silence fell on the courtroom. The judge-major's eyes hardened as he stared at Nate. "Well?"

"I was on furlough, sir," Nate pleaded. "My cousin, Dr. Gill," he rushed on, pointing at Benjamin, "he wrote me a recommendation for sick leave. You see, sir, I had malaria and nearly died. Even after I got better I still got the chills and the shakes. Cousin Ben recommended that Captain Pepper let me go home where I'd get better care than the army infirmary."

Nate glanced imploringly again at Dr. Gill, but this time Benjamin's preoccupation was with a cockroach that had crawled onto Captain Walker's shoe.

"Well, Doctor?" the judge-major asked.

"As sensitive as I am of my cousin's predicament," Dr. Gill replied quietly, "I must still tell the truth. I made no such recommendation."

"Liar!" Nate Gill yelled. "You lie and you know you lie! You did write it! And it was probably you that stole it from Captain Pepper's files!" Nate whirled on the judge-major with flashing eyes. "He *wants* me to die, sir. He wants me out of the way so that he can claim my inheritance. He's not only a liar, he's a *thief!*"

The judge-major glanced inquiringly at Dr. Gill.

"Nonsense," Benjamin said easily. "The boy's half out of his head with that fever he had. He did come to me, as he said, but I refused to fall in with his scheme. He was obviously fully recovered and needed no nursing at all. Look at how healthy he looks, sir, even after being imprisoned."

The judge-major's sharp eyes ran coolly over Nate's figure and he slowly nodded his head. Nate stared at his cousin in a gaze that was the very distillate of hatred and he raised his hands in front of him as though he would strangle him.

"Careful there," the judge-major warned. "Do you have anything more to say?"

"I tell you I never deserted! I'm no coward. I come from a fighting family. Both my great-grandfathers fought the French and so did my granpa and my pa. My great-grandpa and great-grandma were killed in the Schenectady massacre. My grandpa died at Quebec. I fought at Lexington and Concord myself and so did my pa and my uncle. I fought at Bunker Hill and my pa and my uncle were killed there. I fought at Long Island. I never ran away anywhere! Does that sound like a coward who would desert?"

"No, it does not. But cowardice need not necessarily be the only reason for desertion. You did go home, did you not? The sergeant who arrested you reported that you were in civilian clothes. Why?"

"Yes, I did go home. I hadn't seen my wife since my wedding night. She kept writing me letters begging me to come home. But I didn't. It was only after I got malaria . . . I took off my uniform because . . ." Nathaniel Gill ceased to speak. He could read his fate in the steely glint in the judge-major's eyes. He straightened expectantly.

"Private Nathaniel Gill," the judge-major said quietly, "I find you guilty as charged and I sentence you to be paraded before the soldiers of your company and executed by firing squad."

A sob of anguish burst from Nate's lips. He could not contain it. His heart was not breaking for himself, but for his wife, his baby son—and the honor of his family.

"These desertions are ruining us, Daniel," General Washington said to Colonel Gill. "The army is melting away like powder in the rain. We are down to barely three thousand men. If General Lee ever gets here with the main body, we'll be back up to ten thousand. But that's not nearly enough if Howe chooses to seek a decisive engagement. And most of them will be going home at the end of the year when their enlistments expire. Which means I have to recruit and train another new army," he said bitterly, striking his fist into his palm. "By Jehovah, Daniel, when I die they will find it written on my heart: 'Long-term enlistments.'" The general compressed his lips grimly. "But I must stop these desertions. I've instructed all officers sitting on courts-martial to impose the most severe penalties." He glanced at Daniel thoughtfully. "In fact, I approved a sentence of execution only yesterday. A private soldier from Massachusetts. By Jehovah, Daniel, he had the same name as you. Gill."

"Oh, my God, not Nathaniel?" Daniel exclaimed, bounding to his feet and rushing to the general's desk.

"Yes, that is his name. A relative?"

"My cousin! By God, General, there must be some mistake! Nathaniel Gill is as brave a soldier as you'll ever have! I know! He was with me at Lexington and Concord and Bunker Hill. General Washington, please . . . you've got to . . . you *must* commute his sentence . . ."

Washington hastily seized paper and pen. "Go at once to the gallows, Daniel, and order the execution stopped. Here," he said, signing the stay order and handing it to Daniel, who took it and ran outside to swing himself aboard Liberty and gallop away.

Nathaniel Gill held his head high as he marched toward the gallows between two soldiers. He was not, of course, to be hung, but the gallows was the general place of execution. As he approached he could see a corpse dangling on a rope. A cavalryman had been hung for desertion to the enemy, and Nate could hear jeers and cries of derision from the soldiers drawn up in a square around the gibbet. The men were shouting angrily at the hangman who was trying to strip the body of its clothes, his perquisite for performing his ghoulish task. He began with the boots, tugging on them vigorously. But they would not come off. The yelling soldiers began to pelt him with stones. He continued to pull on the boots, like a dog yanking on a root, pausing to shake his fist at the soldiers. Now a shower of stones struck him and he dropped the boots and ran away howling in pain. Shouts of laughter rose from the soldiers—until they saw their doomed comrade marching proudly toward a square embankment of dirt which had been thrown up inside the square of soldiers to prevent the bullets from striking them. At once, the soldiers' chuckles turned to snarls.

"You're killing an innocent man!" one soldier shouted.

"A brave man—bravest of the brave!"

"If you shoot Nate Gill, we'll mutiny, God damn ye!"

The captain in charge of the firing squad paid no attention to the enraged soldiers. He strode up to Nate.

"Kneel!"

"Not to you or anybody else, you filthy swine!"

The soldiers cheered.

"Kneel, God damn you, so you can be blindfolded."

"Don't touch me!" Nate shouted at the two soldiers approaching him with a blindfold. They backed away.

"Kneel," the captain repeated in a choking voice, "or I'll have you flogged!"

The soldiers howled with laughter.

"If you do, Cap'n," a soldier jeered, "you'll have to do it yerself."

"Ain't no enlisted man's gonna whip Nate Gill!"

Exasperated, the captain approached Nate. "Have you any last words?" he asked through gritted teeth.

"Yes!" Nate burst out in a fury. "I hope you *lose!* I hope King George pardons all the men and makes capons of all you officers and parades you naked through the streets of London on the way to Tyburn to be drawn and quartered! Every one of you, right on up to George Washington! God damn your eyes, you selfish scum! You starve us and rob us and ride your horses in silk and satin while we walk barefoot and in rags, and you tell us to be brave from a hundred and fifty yards behind the lines, and then in the name of what you call discipline you order me to my death because you always shut your ears to honest enlisted men and listen to the lies of your own crooked crew." Now the soldiers were cheering wildly. Pausing to draw breath, Nate cried: "You think I'm afraid to die? Do you think I want to live in a country that makes commanders of biological mistakes like you and that snake of a judge-major who sentenced me? Do you think I want a country like that—that's been sucking on me like a weasel ever since Lexington and Concord, asking me to fight on an empty belly and in rotten clothes—to *win?* Win so that gutless toadies and kiss-asses like yourself can hold high office? *Those* are my last words: I hope you *lose!*"

An awed silence fell upon the square of soldiers. In it, Nathaniel Gill could hear the sound of marching feet approaching. He shuddered. It was the firing squad. The end was approaching. His heart bursting in an agony of grief for Jennifer, he again refused the blindfold.

"Go ahead," he said quietly.

The captain turned toward him. His face was white.

"Ready . . ."

There was a rustle of cloth as the soldiers raised their muskets.

"Aim . . ."

Angry cries of protest rose from the soldiers.

"Fire!"

Nate heard the crash of musketry and then the wild cheering of his comrades. Momentarily stunned, having committed his soul to God, he realized that the firing squad had deliberately fired over his head.

"What's this, what's this?" the enraged captain spluttered. "You God damn rascals, what do you mean with this damn nonsense? Don't tell me you missed! At ten yards? Reload those muskets, God damn you, and prepare to—"

"*Stop!*"

Nathaniel Gill recognized that bellowing voice and his aching heart was buoyed with joy and hope.

"Stop it, I say!" Colonel Daniel Gill cried, reining Liberty to a halt and dismounting. He handed the captain the note from Washington. "The commander-in-chief has ordered this man reprieved."

Wonderment on his face, the captain read the order. He gazed sheepishly at the six grinning soldiers of the firing squad. "Maybe it's just as well you missed," he mumbled, and then, walking into the square of cheering soldiers, he motioned them to silence and cried:

"Private Gill has been reprieved by order of General Washington."

Thunderous applause and wild yells of delight burst from the throats of the soldiers. Luke Sawyer broke ranks and ran to Nate's side to undo the pinions. "Natey! Natey!" he cried, hugging him fondly, tears streaming down his seamed cheeks. Nate smiled weakly at Luke.

"Jennifer!" he mumbled in a breaking voice, before he toppled over in a faint.

Chapter Fifteen

It was snowing as Dr. Benjamin Gill rode toward Boston. Below the city, the snowflakes were wet and heavy, sticking to his cheeks and melting there. Dr. Gill peered good-humoredly through the thickly falling snow. It was the first snowfall of the winter and Benjamin had always enjoyed it as a herald of the approaching Christmas season. As he entered the city the snow turned fine, blowing into his face and stinging his cheeks, forcing him to duck his head into his upturned collar. The wind blew stronger. It came howling down the street like a ghostly white wraith, sending the snow smoking and swirling around the doctor and his horse.

When Benjamin bent into it, he felt the letter in his breast pocket crumple. It was a note from Amanda, smuggled into camp by a so-called deserter whom Howe had deliberately planted on Washington. It was short and unsigned but Benjamin knew from its contents who had written it. It seemed that when Amanda left Boston for Halifax she had forgotten to place the beautiful pendant he had given her in her jewel box. She was heartbroken at the loss and asked Benjamin if he could go up to Boston and search for it in her house. Amanda was certain it was somewhere in her bedroom.

The note had arrived just after the court-martial and Benjamin had immediately placed himself on the sick list and ridden off for Boston. He was confident that no word of his cousin's impending execution could reach the city before his arrival.

Coming to the waterfront, Benjamin felt the wind rising from a howl to a shriek. His horse's breath came from its nostrils in shuddering gasps. The animal slipped repeatedly. Dr. Gill became alarmed. The horse could slip and break its leg, leaving him to go on foot through the blizzard to Amanda's house. But, no, he thought, recognizing his surrounding: Gill's Tavern and Landing was just down the street. There was a livery across the way. Dr. Gill had no compunctions about asking for a night's lodging from the cousin and wife of the man he had sent to his death. In fact, he looked forward to it. The tavern probably still offered the finest food in Boston. Reining his horse in to a walk, Dr. Gill rode slowly to the livery, where he put the beast up for the night. Then he crossed the street, bending into the thickening snowflakes, and opened the tavern door.

Jennifer was behind the bar, talking to the barmaid. She glanced up in surprise when Benjamin came inside.

"My goodness, Dr. Gill, what brings you back to Boston?"

"Nostalgia," Benjamin said, removing his gloves and rubbing his hands together. "Brrr. I'm frozen stiff. That's some storm out there. That's what I came up for. I like the warmth in Pennsylvania, but I like to see a little snow, too."

"A *little?*" Jenny repeated, laughing.

"I didn't bargain for a blizzard," Benjamin said wryly. He stamped his feet, shivering again.

"How about a hot toddy?" Jenny asked.

"Jennifer, you are an angel. Could you make it a hot buttered rum?"

"Of course," Jenny said cheerfully, going to the kitchen to return with a kettle of hot water. She poured the steaming liquid into a mug, stirring in rum, butter and brown sugar. Benjamin sniffed the odor hungrily, his mouth watering.

"Stick of cinnamon?" Jennifer asked.

"By all means," Benjamin said, taking the proffered mug from her hands. He sipped. "Ummmm! Jenny, where on earth did you learn to make drinks like this?"

"Stark necessity," Jenny said with a smile. "When we first reopened the tavern, I couldn't tell Madeira from a bottle of port. But I learned fast." She paused in consternation. "Land's sakes, here I go on gabbing away and I haven't even asked you how Natey is."

"Nate's fine," Benjamin answered easily. "So's his friend, Luke Sawyer."

"And Colonel Gill?"

"Oh, Cousin Dan is the darling of the army. He goes everywhere with General Washington and they say he—"

The door flew open and Barbara Gill came inside, wheeling to slam the door hastily against the wind blowing snow into the taproom. She stopped in astonishment when she saw her cousin seated at the bar, quickly concealing the flicker of displeasure in her eyes.

"Ben! To what do we owe this honor?"

Benjamin smiled disarmingly. Barbara had not been quick enough to mask her dislike, but Ben pretended not to notice. "I just got kind of homesick and decided to come home for a visit."

"Have you seen Dan?" Barbara asked eagerly, coming around the bar to join Jennifer.

"Indeed I have. I was just telling Jenny that Cousin Dan is the darling of the army. Everywhere Washington goes, Colonel Gill goes, too. They say the general hardly makes a move without consulting Dan first."

Barbara flushed proudly. Her dark eyes softened. "I just finished a letter to him. Will you take it back for me?"

"By all means."

Barbara's eyes sharpened, flying to the harbor window and the snow swirling outside it. "We might as well close up, Jenny. Nobody's coming here on a night like this." Jenny nodded and went to the door and bolted it. Barbara's eyes shifted back to her cousin. "You're staying overnight, of course?"

"That's very kind of you, Babs.

"Jenny, now that Ben's back, we might as well celebrate and eat that goose you were going to roast for a special tonight."

"Good idea," Jenny said, and went into the kitchen to light the stove.

Ben sauntered around behind the bar to make another hot buttered rum for himself. He went into the kitchen, where he sipped the drink inquisitively and shook his head. "Funny, I used the same ingredients, but it's not nearly as good as the one you made, Jenny."

Jenny smiled, lifting a plucked goose onto a wooden chopping block and beginning to make punctures in its body with a fork.

"What's that for?" Ben asked.

"Let the grease run out. Geese have a lot of fat in them."

"Not nearly as much as ducks," Barbara said, entering the

kitchen and beginning to take down jars of spice from an overhead shelf.

"I love duck," Ben said, adding in a rueful voice, "but trying to eat it with a knife and fork is like trying to nail a custard pie to the wall."

"There's not much meat on them," Jenny said, cutting the goose open and pulling out the entrails. "We had a man in here last night who ate two whole ducks before he was satisfied. Just picked the halves up in his hands and chewed off the meat. What a mess!"

Benjamin chuckled. He was enjoying himself, seated in the warm kitchen before a bright fire burning in the fireplace, sipping his hot drink and watching the two women prepare what he expected would be a delicious meal. He had absolutely no qualms about the hypocrisy of his position, jesting merrily with Nathaniel Gill's loved ones as though he had not virtually sent him to his death. Dr. Benjamin Gill did not often allow misgivings to intervene between himself and his well-being. He felt his actions no more reprehensible than on the occasion five years ago when, pressed by a creditor to pay his gambling debts, he deliberately insulted the man's wife at a ball, thus provoking the creditor to challenge him to a duel in which Benjamin easily killed him.

"My Lord, Babs," Benjamin said, "what are all those spices for? There must be fifteen of them."

"Thirteen," Barbara said. "Plus the sliced oranges. I'm going to make an orange sauce. Wait until you taste it."

"And my chestnut and fruit stuffing," Jenny said proudly.

Two hours later, Jennifer triumphantly lifted the golden brown goose from the oven. She carried it into the taproom and placed it on a table in front of the fireplace in which Benjamin had started a roaring, crackling fire. Barbara opened a bottle of hock and filled the wine glasses. Then she said grace, and began to carve thin slices of steaming white meat off the breast.

"A slice of the breast and a glass of the best," she murmured, smiling. "That was Granpa's favorite saying when he carved a roast."

Benjamin began to eat. "Ummmm! Delicious! Where'd you ladies learn to cook like this?"

"Barbara taught me," Jenny said proudly.

"Cooking is a Gill family tradition," Barbara said. "When

Grandpa and Grandma opened the tavern back in 1710, they said their breast of pheasant was the finest dish on the whole Atlantic seaboard."

"I can believe it," Benjamin said, tasting the wine. "This is delicious, too. I like white wine cool like that."

"We keep it in the springhouse," Barbara said. She fixed Benjamin with the direct gaze of those astonishing dark eyes of hers and asked, "How is the Revolution coming, Ben?"

"Not too well, Babs. Most of the officers and a lot of the men are disgusted with General Washington. They say he's indecisive and lets Howe outmaneuver him all the time."

Barbara shook her head gravely. "I'm sorry to hear that. You don't think we'll lose, do you?" she asked, frowning in anxiety.

"Not at all," he said with easy reassurance. No sense getting them upset, he thought. "Cousin Dan told me we'll be getting help from France soon. Muskets and powder. Maybe twenty thousand muskets. And bayonets."

Jennifer shuddered at the word "bayonets." She thought of her husband with a chill. "Will that help?" she asked.

"Sure. By the way, Barbara, what's being done with the Gill properties?"

Barbara's eyelids flickered. Her cousin's casual tone didn't fool her. "They're all right," she replied laconically.

"I hear you sold Nate's father's house."

"Yes."

"And boarded up Grandma's?"

"Jenny and I decided it would be better for us to move in here. We still use the Concord farmhouse in the good weather. We hid the valuables in the—" Barbara caught herself. She smiled suddenly with the instant charm she had learned to flash in her days behind the bar, and said, "Well, Ben, now that you've tasted our goose and our wine, it's time to taste our brandy."

Dr. Benjamin Gill was awakened by bright sunlight streaming into the taproom, where he had slept on a makeshift bed of pillows piled on the floor. While he dressed, he could smell the tea and hot cornbread Jennifer was preparing in the kitchen. Breakfasting quickly, he said good-bye to Jenny and Barbara, pecking each of them on the cheek. Barbara handed

him a letter for Daniel and he stuffed it inside his coat and
went out the door.

The snow was deep, but the sun was shining so brightly in
a clear blue sky that it was already beginning to melt. Benjamin crossed the street to the livery to claim his horse. He
swung aboard and rode off toward Amanda's house.

Benjamin was pleased to find that the door opening on the
back stairs leading to Amanda's bedroom was unlocked. He
went up the stairs, shivering in the dead cold of the empty
mansion. It was easy to find Amanda's pendant. Benjamin
thoroughly understood Amanda's childish mind, filled with
the fear of hobgoblins and rapists and robbers. He did not
bother to ransack her bedroom but went straight to the window drapes. He found the pendant sewed into the bottom of
one of them. He smiled, put it in his pocket and went out the
bedroom door down the corridor to Joel's bedroom. Who
knows, he thought, he had the time and he might find something of interest. Perhaps Joel left some of his stationery behind. Possessing an important man's stationery might some
day come in handy.

Benjamin rummaged through Joel's massive walnut desk.
He opened the middle drawer and saw a stack of sheets of
foolscap with Joel's name embossed on it. He seized a sheaf,
folded it and slipped it inside his waistcoat. He opened all the
other drawers. They were all empty except one, which was
locked. Ben tugged on the handle but the drawer wouldn't
budge. He looked around him for an instrument to pry it
open, but found none. Ah! he thought, and knelt down to
slide his hand under the locked drawer. He felt a small box
glued to the underside of the drawer and wrenched it free. It
was a snuff box containing a small key. Smiling, Benjamin
unlocked the drawer and pulled it out. He gaped in astonishment.

The drawer contained letters in a familiar handwriting—
not the handwriting of Joel Courtney but of Sam Adams! He
saw one dated January 15, 1771, and written in Philadelphia.
He began to read:

I am afraid, my dear Joel, that the repeal of the Townshend Acts by Parliament has been more dangerous to the
cause of liberty than the presence of an entire British army

in our midst. The people have sunk into the deepest apathy and take no thought of freeing themselves from the shackles of tyranny. Even the boycott of British goods has fallen into deseuetude. If this spirit of indifference is allowed to deepen and spread, my dear Joel, I fear that . . .

Benjamin had read enough. His hands trembling in excitement he removed Joel's stationery from his pocket, dropping it on the desk to replace it with the letters. This was better than *stationery!* Much, much better! A million times better! He remembered, now, that Joel Courtney had worked with the Patriots against the Stamp and Sugar Acts. But then, after repeal of the Townshend Acts, he had gradually shifted to the Loyalist side. Why? British gold? More important, how could Joel have possibly forgotten those letters? Almost laughing aloud, Benjamin patted his bulging waistcoat in satisfaction. So nice to have something like this on a man as important as Joel Courtney. Still smiling, he left the mansion and mounted his horse. He rode slowly toward the livery stable. He thought of the delicious dinner Barbara and Jennifer had given him and rehearsed the table conversation. Barbara hadn't told him much about the Gill properties. Obviously, she didn't trust him. What was that she had started to say?

"We hid the valuables in the—"

Dr. Gill let out a long, low whistle and his horse pricked up its ears. What an opportunity! The city buried in snow . . . Barbara and Jennifer stuck inside the tavern . . . no one outside to see him ride out to Concord . . . Benjamin Gill knew exactly where Barbara had hidden her valuables: inside the buried old cistern where the Committee of Public Safety had hidden powder and bullets. Happily whistling "The World Turned Upside Down," he rode slowly out of the city.

Near the farmhouse, he swerved into the woods beside the road, dismounted and hitched the horse to a tree. Returning to the roadside, he scooped up handfuls of snow to fill the horse's tracks. Then he remounted and rode through the woods to the stable behind the farmhouse where he quartered the horse, seized a shovel and strode through the snow to the barberry bushes above the cistern. There was a space between them, the mouth of the cistern. Scraping the snow from it, Benjamin began to dig. In ten minutes he had uncovered the round iron slab over the entrance. He dragged it aside and started to descend the stone steps. Realizing that he would need a lantern, he broke a window in the farmhouse kitchen and climbed inside. He remembered that there was always a lantern hanging beside the front door. Going into the front room to get it, he heard a knock on the dooor.

Benjamin froze, glancing around him wildly. Catching sight of the musket over the fireplace he took it down and examined it. It was loaded! Benjamin walked softly to the front door and called out in a loud voice:

"Who's there?"

"Me, Silas Webster. Captain Silas Webster of the Boston quartermaster."

Benjamin relaxed. He knew the man. He could be disposed of easily. It was unfortunate, but necessary. No one must know of my being here, he thought. He opened the door, and said, "Glad to see you, Silas."

"Dr. Gill! How be ye? What brings you out here, Doc?"

Benjamin ignored the question, smiling urbanely. "What can I do for you, Silas?"

"My horse done throwed a shoe. I remembered the Gills had a stable in the back and I thought I might find an old shoe."

"Of course, let's go look at the horse's foot."

"Thanks, Doc. I'm sure glad I found you here."

Captain Webster turned to leave and Dr. Benjamin Gill lifted his musket and shot him through the head. The dying man pitched forward on his face, and Benjamin quickly knelt beside him and calmly went through his pockets. More than five hundred dollars! Evidently, pickings at the Boston quartermaster were good. He arose, stuffing the money into his own pockets, seized the lantern and lighted it with a flint and bits of spunk and strode quickly to the cistern. The rays of the lantern flickered on the oozing wet walls of the stone tank. Benjamin lifted his light higher and saw a black-lacquered teakwood jewel box perched on top of a pile of objects wrapped in burlap. Trembling with excitement he opened it and let the lantern's light fall on the gems inside. They caught fire! Rubies, diamonds and emeralds, lesser jewels of opal, garnet, amethyst and sapphire, set in rings and brooches and clasps and necklaces—sparkling, glittering, gleaming and dancing beneath the unbelieving, almost delirious gaze of Dr. Benjamin Gill. He lifted a string of pearls from the box. It was Jennifer's wedding present from Barbara. Perfectly matched! My God! Benjamin thought, Amanda will sleep with me for a thousand nights on end for baubles like these! He shivered in anticipation. Then he closed the box and looked around him. There was nothing else but the objects wrapped in burlap. Benjamin unwrapped one of them. It was a large sterling silver platter! Benjamin gasped. Grandma Gill's silver! It was worth a small fortune! Benjamin groaned aloud and gnashed his teeth in despair. He had no way of taking it with him! He had no saddlebags on his horse, but even if he had had them he could only have taken a few pieces. There must be fifty covers! Benjamin knew. He had eaten many a Thanksgiving and Christmas dinner at Grandma Gill's table. Benjamin shrugged his shoulders ruefully. It couldn't be helped. He ran a hand through his straight black hair, stooped to grasp the jewel box and climbed out of the cistern. Blowing out the lantern and putting it down, he went immediately to the stable, remounted his horse and rode back toward Boston.

En route, he thought of Barbara's letter to Daniel and decided to open it. A glimpse of the intimate relations between a woman and her husband did not embarrass Benjamin. On the contrary, he thought some of Barbara's expressions of love and endearment were quite hilarious. "My, my, my," he chuckled, "so old Iron-Pants has got herself pregnant. I never thought Barbara would ever crawl into bed with a man." His eyes narrowed when he came to the postscript.

P.S. I'm giving this letter to Cousin Ben. He was here last night. We gave him dinner and let him sleep in the taproom. He was his usual charming self, joking and telling droll stories and telling me and Jenny how beautiful we are. I've always remembered, Daniel dear, that the first charmer was a serpent. That's what I think of Ben. Why don't I trust him? Just because he's a womanizer, a wastrel, a gambler and a duelist who seems to specialize in challenging people he owes money to, that shouldn't make me distrust him, should it? Oh, no.

Momentarily, Benjamin was so annoyed he thought of tearing up the letter. But then, realizing that Daniel would some day find out about it, he carefully resealed it and put it back in his pocket. His good spirits returned as he rode south of Boston, bound for New York and a report to General Howe.

"You have had your ear to the ground, Dr. Gill?"

"Yes, Sir William. As the country people in Massachusetts say: 'Close enough to let a mole lick it.' "

General William Howe chuckled. "Jolly good. Well?"

"The Yankee army is falling apart, sir. They're disgusted with Washington. They say he's indecisive and hasn't won a single battle."

"But he always saves his army," Howe murmured musingly. "Go on."

"There's a conspiracy against him. An intrigue. The Adamses are in on it. The idea is to supersede Washington with Gates."

"Gates, eh? Tommy Gage told me about him. He was with him at the Monongahela. Gage didn't think much of him. Said he fights like an old woman."

"General Lee is in on it, too."

"Charles?" Howe said, chuckling again. "I'm surprised Charles doesn't want to replace Washington with a dog."

Dr. Gill laughed. Then he frowned. "The Yankees may be getting arms soon from France. More than twenty thousand muskets and plenty of powder. They're buying it from a private company in Paris."

"*Buying* it?" Howe scoffed. "They don't have the money to buy anything. I'll wager that scoundrel Vergennes is behind it."

"Vergennes?"

"The French foreign minister. He hates England with a passion. This is interesting news, my dear Doctor. I shall report it to Lord George Germain and suggest that he ask Lord North to complain to the French ambassador about it. Now, if you will, Doctor, please provide me with a written report. The subaltern outside will fetch you pen and paper."

Bowing, Dr. Gill went into the outer office, where he quickly wrote his report. He handed it to the subaltern with the question: "Can you tell me where Mr. Joel Courtney may be found?"

"Certainly, sir," the subaltern said, and gave him an address on Broad Street.

The home was a fine brick mansion which had been untouched by the fire. A servant ushered Benjamin into a waiting room and departed to fetch Amanda. Amanda came rushing into the room, darting toward him crying, "Benjie! Benjie! Benjie!" She had just come in from a walk and she was radiant in a gown of blue silk with an embroidered underskirt in a paler shade, her blond hair crowned by a hat of light gray velvet with a curling blue feather. Hurling the hat on a red velvet love seat she rushed into Benjamin's arms. Benjamin embraced her and kissed her hungrily on the mouth. She pressed her body into his and he felt a warmth rising in his loins. Stepping back he took her missing pendant from his pocket and held it up to her.

"You *found* it! Oh, Benjie, you're wonderful—you found my pendant. Where was it?"

"Where you put it, silly. Sewn into a window drape."

Amanda giggled. "I just couldn't remmber. There was a story in the newspaper about a robber in the neighborhood."

Benjamin shook his head in mock reproach. "Honestly, Amanda, I think your head is full of cotton, hay and rags." Amanda pursed her lips in a pout and held the pendant up to the light streaming through a window. While she studied it in delight, Benjamin quickly drew Jennifer's pearls from his pocket, stepped up behind Amanda and draped them around her neck. Amanda gasped. She looked down at the pearls in incredulous rapture.

"Benjie! They're beautiful! Unbelievably beautiful! Perfect!" she cried, fondling the creamy gleaming beads with her fingers. "Fasten them, please, Benjie, so I can look in the mirror."

"After we go upstairs, my dear," Benjamin said with a suave leer, lifting the pearls over her head. "They'll look much better on you with your clothes off."

Chapter Sixteen

Nathaniel Gill was taken to the infirmary to recuperate from his ordeal. He slept for twenty-four hours and awoke refreshed. He felt ready for duty again, but because he enjoyed being free of the discipline of the camp and the food was good, he stayed in the infirmary for another week. During that time he did some hard thinking about what to do about Dr. Benjamin Gill. Nate still burned with hatred for his cousin. His hands would automatically clench and unclench when he thought of him, as though they longed to close around his throat. But Nate realized that he, a private, dared not touch his cousin, a captain. Nor could he bring charges, if only because he had not a shred of evidence. At last, Nate decided to ask his cousin Dan for advice, and he went back to duty carrying a half loaf of bread he had pilfered from the kitchen. The bread was for Luke Sawyer.

Luke gulped the bread down like a starving dog. Then he handed Nate a letter from Jennifer. Nate tore it open eagerly and read:

Dearest Natey,

I have the most terrible news! A robber broke into the buried cistern at Concord and stole all of our jewels! *All* of them! The beautiful pearls Barbara gave me for a wedding present are gone! I cried for two days when I found out. Barbara cried, too. She was heartbroken to lose all the jewels your grandma left her. I always thought Barbara was too strong a woman to ever cry, but she just broke down and bawled. Thank God the thief didn't take Grandma Gill's silver. That would have been too much.

Oh, and there's something even more terrible. Remember Silas Webster who kept the grocer's shop before the war? Well, he was a captain in the quartermaster here and they found him murdered on our doorstep. Shot through the head with Grandpa's musket! When Silas didn't report for duty they went looking for him and found him at the farmhouse. That's how we found out about the robbery. Barbara thinks that Silas rode up to the farmhouse for some reason and surprised the thief and was shot.

She says that because she's convinced that the thief is your cousin Ben. Ben knew Silas and Barbara says he shot him so that he wouldn't talk about seeing him at the farmhouse. She suspects Ben because he was trying to find out about the Gill properties at dinner and Barbara forgot herself and mentioned our valuables. Ben was here, Natey. We gave him dinner and let him sleep in the taproom overnight. Barbara is positive it was Ben. He was a member of the Committee of Public Safety and knew about the cistern. But neither of us has any proof . . .

Nate Gill sprang to his feet with a fierce yell. "The dirty son of a bitch! The filthy swine! I'll *kill* the thieving snake!"

Luke Sawyer gazed at him in astonishment. "What's got into you, Nate? Who you gonna kill?"

"My God damned cousin! The perfumed Dr. Benjamin Gill you distrust so much. And you were right! First he tries to have me executed, and now he steals my family's jewels!"

Nate thrust the letter into Luke's hands. He read it, slowly shaking his head as though in disbelief. "I'll say he's thorough," he muttered. "As crooked as a bucket o' fishhooks. I always thought he smelled too pretty and bowed too low. Them slick fellers is always skunks under the skin." He handed the letter back. "What're you gonna do about it? You cain't prove nawthin' any more 'n you kin prove he lied to the jedge."

Nate nodded, grinding his teeth in frustration. "I'm going to see my cousin Dan. Maybe he can think of something."

Folding the letter and putting it in his pocket, he left the tent and trotted through the avenues of tents toward Colonel Gill's quarters. He almost ran into Daniel coming out of his tent. He immediately yanked the letter from his pocket, and his cousin smiled and said, "So you've heard the good news about Barbara?"

"What *good* news?"

"She's pregnant."

Momentarily flabbergasted, Nate shook Daniel's extended hand and mumbled, "Congratulations." His anger returning, he waved Jennifer's letter in the air and shouted, "That rotten bastard Ben Gill stole all of our jewels!"

Astounded, Daniel seized the letter and read, his face flushing deeper and deeper with anger as he came to the end. His blue eyes glittering dangerously, he listened while Nathaniel explained to him how Dr. Gill had tried to do away with him to obtain his properties.

"My God!" Daniel breathed, "where did we get a viper like that in the family?"

"From his pa. He was a snake, too. While Grandpa and my pa and Uncle Mal were up fighting in Quebec, Uncle Mordecai was milking the Gill company white. If he hadn't died, Pa and Uncle Mal would have preferred charges."

"That's a skeleton I never knew about. Lucky Ben didn't marry and hatch out more vipers."

"What are we going to do about him?"

"There doesn't seem to be much we *can* do. But at least we can let Cousin Ben know that we know about him. I'm going to confront him with this," he said, shaking the letter in his hand, "and with what you told me."

"I'll go with you," Nate said eagerly.

"No. Not in the state you're in. Besides, you're an enlisted man, and if you did what I think you'd like to do, you'd be back in another court-martial. I'll let you know what happens."

Dr. Benjamin Gill had ridden from New York to the Newtown encampment. He was at his desk in his surgery when Colonel Daniel Gill strode in.

Benjamin glanced up with a charming smile. "Well, my dear Daniel, to what do I owe this honor?"

"This," Daniel snapped, handing him the letter.

Surprised at his cousin's hostility, Benjamin began to read. Daniel watched him closely. Only once, toward the end of the letter when his eyelid flickered, did Benjamin let his composure slip. He glanced up with an urbane shrug.

"Poppycock. Surely, you don't believe it, Daniel?"

"I do. I believe that you are a liar and a thief and a murderer and an attempted fratricide. I believe that you stole the jewels and murdered Captain Webster and attempted the legal murder of your cousin by lying to a judge."

"That's quite an extensive credo, Daniel," Benjamin drawled. "Any proof?"

"None. Nothing, except that I prefer my wife's word and Nate's word to yours."

"Daniel, you can't be serious. You know that Nate had a bad case of malaria and I believe he suffered some brain damage. And those two women living alone above the tavern up there in Boston, they're hysterical with fright."

"My wife is not hysterical. Neither is Jenny. You are a smooth one, Ben, but please don't try to come it over me with that nonsense about Nate. His mind is as clear as yours, although I must say a little less twisted."

"You'd better be careful of what you're saying, Daniel. I've had enough of your insults."

"I repeat, you are a liar, a thief, a murderer and an attempted fratricide," Daniel said in a goading, sneering voice. "And what will you do about that?"

"This," Benjamin said, rising from his chair and slapping Daniel hard across the face.

"I see," Daniel said, stepping back and fingering his reddened cheek. "You are challenging me to a duel?"

"I am."

"Delighted. Choose your weapons."

"Swords," Benjamin said with a confident smile.

Daniel hesitated. He had forgotten about his cousin's prowess as a fencer and had expected him to choose pistols as was customary in most American duels. He groaned inwardly. He should have chosen the weapon himself, which was the right of the insulted party. But his honor was at stake now, and he merely bowed in assent and said, "Very well. I shall meet you at dawn tomorrow in the apple orchard beside the Newton road. Nathaniel will be my second."

Nathaniel was horrified when Daniel announced to him that he was going to duel Dr. Gill with swords.

"Oh, no, Dan, no!" he moaned. "That's murder, legal murder! Ben is the best swordsman in New England. He's already killed two men in duels and wounded I don't know how many others. Can't you change it to pistols?"

"No, I can't," Daniel muttered. "But don't worry, Natey. I know something about swords."

"Aw, Dan, you're a cut-and-swinger. You're too strong to be a swordsman. People as strong as you never need to develop finesse. You're a hacker. If it were sabers or cutlasses, I wouldn't worry. But swords! Swords are for fencers like Ben. For parrying and thrusting. Please, Dan—can't you change the weapons?"

"Not now. After all, I do have my honor."

"To hell with your honor!" Nate cried fiercely, turning away with tears in his eyes.

Dr. Benjamin Gill was waiting in the apple orchard when Daniel and Nate arrived. His second was a young medical lieutenant. He had a pistol stuck inside his belt. Nate carried a loaded musket. There were no greetings. Because it was very warm for early December, Daniel and Benjamin both removed their coats. They walked to a clearing among the apple trees, drew their swords rasping from their scabbards, saluted each other and began the duel.

The orchard echoed to the sound of clashing steel. Nate saw almost immediately that Benjamin was playing with Daniel. He deliberately lowered his blade, inducing Daniel to make vicious thrusts at him. Almost indolently, Benjamin turned Daniel's sword aside with a quick movement of his wrist. Nate watched in helpless horror. Eventually, he knew, Benjamin would tire of the sport, like a cat, and then—

Now, Benjamin had begun to parry and riposte, to block Daniel's attacks and counter with swift short thrusts of his own. The tip of his sword entered the cravat at Daniel's throat and Nate closed his eyes, opening them when he heard Benjamin laugh.

"I see that you are perspiring, dear cousin," Benjamin said, chuckling as he cut the cravat in two. "Perhaps this will cool you off," he added, flicking the cravat into the air.

Next he parried a wild swing by Daniel and sliced the shoulder of Daniel's waistcoat. Then he danced away and feinted at Daniel's genitals. Daniel quickly dropped his sword to parry the thrust, his sagging waistcoat swirling as he moved, and Benjamin cut the other shoulder. The garment fell to the ground.

"Ah, but you are still perspiring, dear cousin," Ben called in a mocking voice. "Perhaps you need more air."

Pirouetting and leaping around Daniel like a dancing master, Benjamin cut the buttons from his cousin's shirt with swift sure flashes of his sword. The shirt fell open, flapping in the wind caused by Daniel's desperate movements to defend himself. Now Benjamin slashed the shirt to ribbons, exposing Daniel's massive, heaving chest.

Benjamin stepped back. He tested his sword's point with his fingertip and smiled mockingly again. Then he sprang at Daniel.

Feinting at Daniel's eyes, with two incredibly swift strokes of his sword—so quick that it was easier to hear the swish of his blade than to see it move—he drew a great blood-red X on Daniel's chest.

"X marks the spot, my dear cousin," Benjamin cried laughingly, easily parrying a counter thrust by Daniel. He presented the tip of his sword opposite the center of the X, just below Daniel's breastbone. "This is where my sword shall enter. I am going to disembowel you, my dear cousin. I have been told that this is the most painful way to die, and I am most anxious to hear you scream."

Daniel's reply was to aim a vicious stroke at Benjamin's neck. Benjamin quickly threw up his sword. With a loud clang, Daniel's blade went flying from his hand to spin end over end through the orchard. Daniel stood helpless before his gloating cousin. Blood dripped from the slashes on his chest, giving the X a spidery effect. Benjamin leveled his blade. With an unearthly cry of cruel delight he drove it straight for Daniel's abdomen.

Daniel screamed. But the sword had not entered his belly. Benjamin had slipped on an apple as he leaped forward and in his attempt to recover his balance his flailing blade had pierced Daniel's shoulder instead. It lodged there, stuck in Daniel's muscle and bone. Benjamin struggled frantically to work it free, causing Daniel to scream again in agony. Benjamin put both hands on the sword hilt, and Daniel brought his knee up into his groin with such force that Benjamin sank groaning to the earth, writhing there with his hands clutching at his genitals.

Daniel put his hand on the sword hilt and yanked. Waves of pain swept over him and he almost fainted. Nathaniel ran up, shouting, "Let me do it! Let me do it!" Daniel nodded, swaying. He closed his eyes, bracing himself. Nathaniel yanked sharply on the sword and pulled it free. Daniel screamed. His knees buckled. Nate seized him around the waist until he slowly straightened. Taking the sword from Nathaniel, Daniel staggered up to Benjamin, whose second had come to his side. Nate aimed his musket at the second.

"Get away from him," Nate warned. "Get away from him, or I'll drop you!"

The frightened second backed off. Daniel stooped over Benjamin to seize his waistcoat in his hands. With a single wrench and a flying of buttons, he tore it from his body. Then he ripped Benjamin's shirt off. Making a mocking bow, he stepped back to test the sword point with his fingertip, just as Benjamin had.

"Two can play at this crisscross game, my dear cousin," Daniel said, gasping. With two quick strokes, he drew a small X over Benjamin's heart. "I do not choose to disembowel you, because I don't think I could stand the stink of your guts. But I will have your heart, Cousin Ben. I will have your slimy murdering heart if, in two minutes, you do not tell me where the jewels are and admit you lied in court." Benjamin licked his lips. His eyes dilated in terror. He stared in horrid dread at the sword point poised over his heart. It came closer.

From the roadside came a calm voice, saying. "All right, gentlemen, I think that will do for today." Turning, Daniel Gill saw General George Washington sitting on his white horse. Daniel hesitated. His eyes swiveled back to his sword point, a few inches from Dr. Gill's throat. He tightened his grip on the hilt and his glittering blue eyes bored into the horrified eyes of his cousin. Then he looked again at Washington. The General was staring straight at him, and his face was full of sad reproach.

Daniel Gill sighed and lowered his sword.

Chapter Seventeen

Colonel Daniel Gill's first visitor in the hospital was General George Washington. "I've brought you some nuts, Daniel," the General said, placing a bag of walnuts on Daniel's bedside table and sitting down beside him. Washington sighed. "You are a magnificent fighter, Daniel. If I had just one regiment of fighters like you, I believe I could lick the world. But I am still terribly disappointed in you."

"I . . . I'm sorry," Daniel mumbled contritely.

"This dueling is a disgrace," the General continued, sliding his hand into the bag of nuts to take one. He cracked it open between his palms and began munching the meat inside. "It's one of the scandals of the army. Fellow soldiers of the Revolution having at each other with swords and pistols over some silly quarrel. Good officers being lost to the cause. All this damned childish nonsense about defending their honor. Honestly, Daniel, I thought you were above that sort of thing. If I had lost you, it would have been like losing my right arm. You're the only one I can confide in with complete trust. You have been absolutely selfless. Almost any other officer would have used your confidential position to serve his ambitions. But you have served only me and the Revolution." He sighed and took another nut. "I couldn't believe it when I heard that you were involved in a duel. And with your own cousin! What happened?"

His eyes moist, Colonel Gill explained the circumstances which provoked the duel.

Washington was astounded. "By Jehovah, what a scoundrel! And he an officer in my army! How could an unscrupulous monster like that be serious about our cause? I think I shall dismiss him from the service." He paused, frowning. "I hate to lose a physician, though. We have so few. And the smallpox is breaking out again."

185

"Would you reconsider, sir?" Daniel asked. "I do want to recover my wife's jewelry. Dismissal might be just what he wants. He could disappear with a fortune under his arm. But if he remains in service, I can keep an eye on him."

"Of course," Washington said, rising to his feet. "I shall stay out of it. And please get well soon, Daniel. I miss you. I have actually gotten writer's cramp from having to write all those letters myself. I don't know what's wrong with General Lee," he muttered, taking another nut from the bag. "I have written him almost every day practically begging him to come down from the north with the main body. And now it's December and there's still no answer."

"I'm sure he'll be here soon, sir," Daniel said. "And thanks for the nuts."

Major General Charles Lee was in no hurry to bring Washington's main body south to the winter camp in Newtown. Actually, General Lee was deliberately dragging his feet. He ignored the stream of letters from his commander-in-chief imploring him to march. He was more interested in his own conspiratorial letters to Generals Horatio Gates and Thomas Conway.

Conway, an Irish soldier trained in the French Army, had flooded Congress with a series of anonymous letters attacking the reputation of George Washington. It was Conway's hope to persuade Congress to demote Washington, who detested him, and replace him with Gates, who was his friend. The defeats and retreats which characterized Washington's operations in 1776 had given Conway the opportunity to intensify his campaign of secret slander, and he was delighted to attract an ally as powerful as General Lee.

At last, on December 2, General Lee began marching toward the Delaware. By December 12 he had reached Basking Ridge, New Jersey, where he stopped at a tavern with his aide, Major James Wilkinson. Next morning, still in slippers and nightshirt, General Lee finished his breakfast and began to write a letter to Horatio Gates. He recited the litany of defeats and retreats that had characterized Washington's 1776 campaign. He was particularly caustic about the surrender of Fort Washington in New York.

"There never was so damned a stroke," he wrote. "*Entre nous,* a certain great man is damnably deficient—"

"General! General!" Wilkinson called from the window, "the British are here!"

"*Where?*" Lee cried in incredulity.

"Around the house!"

Lee rushed to Wilkinson's side and saw a colonel leading about thirty dragoons who neatly opened files to go galloping around the tavern and surround it. Lee recognized the colonel.

"Harcourt! God damn his eyes, William Harcourt!"

Turning to Wilkinson, he shouted, "Where is the guard? Damn the guard, why don't they fire?"

Wilkinson seized his pistols, stuffed Lee's letter in his pocket and ran outside. He was just in time to see the dragoons driving the American guard away from the tavern. He ducked back inside.

A maid came into the taproom. "In there, sir," she said to Lee, pointing to a door. "There's a bed in there, sir. You can hide under it."

Lee's reply was a cold, contemptuous stare. He ground his teeth in despair when he heard Harcourt's voice saying:

"*If the general does not come outside in five minutes, I will set fire to the house.*"

Lee waited, and the voice came again:

"*You now have two minutes, before I set fire to the house.*"

Cursing bitterly, not even pausing to change, General Charles Lee threw a blanket coat over his thin frame and stalked outside.

A cheer rose from the dragoons.

"Here is the general," Colonel Harcourt exclaimed exultantly, making a mocking bow. "He has surrendered."

Lee said nothing. He was not happy to have been captured by his old regiment.

The forces arriving at Newtown from Basking Ridge four days later brought news of General Lee's capture. At first, Washington was dismayed. So was Colonel Gill.

"It's a calamity of the first order," Daniel said.

General Washington sat silently behind his desk, his forehead wrinkled in thought. "It could be a calamity," he said musingly, "or it could be a blessing." Daniel looked at him in surprise and the general asked, "Have you ever heard of the

Conway Cabal?" Daniel shook his head. "It is a conspiracy against me organized by that wretched Thomas Conway. Lee's in it. Gates, of course. In Congress Sam Adams and John Adams. And others. Conway's theme is that I am guilty of what he calls 'Fabian slowness.'" Washington snorted in contempt. "A pretty phrase. It should start popping up in some of Sam Adams's speeches soon. Sam is fond of 'inside' language." Washington reached for a handful of nuts from the bowl that was always on his desk and began cracking them. "If the poor fools understood the greatness of Fabius Maximus, they'd realize they were paying me a compliment. I am deliberately adopting Fabian tactics, Daniel. Like Fabius, I cannot afford decisive battle with a superior foe. As he did against Hannibal, I can only delay and harass Howe until I grow strong enough to challenge him. *Cunctator*, that's what Roman posterity called Fabius. 'The Delayer.' And it was considered an accolade." Washington plucked the meat of a walnut from its opened shell and put it in his mouth, chewing grimly. "So you see, Daniel, I am not exactly unhappy to see Lee captured. That means one less conspirator in the field against me." He cracked another nut and chewed thoughtfully. "I seriously doubt that Congress would remove me. As I've told you before, the only reason that I persist in this miserable command, with an army of reluctant scarecrows who cannot hold even the strongest posts, is my conviction that if I were to leave the service all would be lost. No," he said, shaking his head bitterly, "they won't remove me. They're a little more clever than that. Instead, the plan is to create a Board of War with Gates as chairman. That way, he would be my nominal superior. Gates!" Washington snorted, reaching for another nut. "I am not among his admirers. I saw him at the Monongahela. He's too cautious. But just because he served in the British Army, Congress makes a major general of him. And they pass over a fighter like Benedict Arnold just because of some vague accusations of misusing army funds. Anyway, Daniel, the Conway Cabal is one more cross that I must bear." He sighed deeply, seizing a nut and slowly cracking it inside his powerful fist. "I tell you, the Revolution is hanging by a thread. The army is dissolving. Those ragged wretches of Lee's are no better than mine. Everyone is in despair. Congress is preparing to fly to Baltimore. Cornwallis is on the Delaware waiting for the ice to freeze to cross over to Philadelphia. I tell you, if every nerve is not strained to recruit a new army, I think the game is pretty near up."

Daniel Gill stared at his chief in dismay. He knew that seven months of bitter frustration had deeply discouraged the General. But he had never seen him so utterly despondent before, almost openly defeated. It reminded him of Kip's Bay when Washington had silently sat his horse inviting either death or capture.

"Surely, sir," Daniel said eagerly. "There must be some way of rallying the Revolution. Some bold stroke. Like that Fabius Maximus you talked about. Some daring raid that will shock the British and lift our hearts."

George Washington slowly emptied the contents of his hand into the bowl. He sat still, pondering. Gradually, his eyes lighted up.

"Trenton!" Washington cried, bringing his fist down onto his desk with slow savagery. "Trenton, by Jehovah!" he repeated, hope shining in his eyes again. "They think we're finished. Howe is holding New Jersey with only a chain of posts. They've got three thousand Hessians on a six-mile line from Trenton to Bordentown. Half of them are at Trenton under a Colonel named Rall. I'll try to scoop up Bordentown, too—but Trenton is the prize."

"When, sir?"

"Christmas night. The Hessians are fond of religious holidays and this is the biggest of all. We should catch them by surprise." The General picked up a scrap of paper and scribbled on it. "This will be our password," he said, handing it to Daniel. He read:

"Victory or Death."

Chapter Eighteen

Before George Washington could rally the Revolution, he first had to rally his men. Before Christmas, he had them formed in ranks to have Thomas Paine's first issue of The Crisis read to them. Nathaniel Gill listened intently while the immortal words rang out.

"These are times that try men's souls. The summer soldier and the sunshine patriot will, in this crisis, shrink from the service of their country; but he that stands it now, deserves the love and thanks of man and woman."

Nathaniel studied his feet bound in rags and shivered beneath his ragged coat. Summer soldier! he thought. Sunshine patriot! How true! How many thousands of faint-hearts had fallen by the wayside. How could the ragged few who were left ever hope to accomplish the glorious goal of the Revolution? How could these suffering starving amateurs overcome British professionals amply supplied in every detail? Then, listening to the inspiring words, a thrill of hope buoyed his heart and he thought:

How can such men be defeated?

Nathaniel's feet were bleeding before he had marched halfway to McKonkey's Ferry on the Delaware. So were Luke Sawyer's and those of half the other men in the company. Trudging through the snow, Nate could mark the passage of the troops ahead of him by the bloodstains in it. A howling wind whistled in his ears, blowing sleet mixed with snow into his eyes. Nate turned up the collar of his coat and crooked his left arm around his face to shield himself. When he reached the river, his teeth were chattering and he was half frozen. Peering through the storm, he saw the boats Washington had collected bobbing on the water. They were manned by the same men of John Glover's regiment who had evacuated them from Long Island.

Nate passed by General Washington standing on the landing talking to Colonel Henry Knox. His cousin Daniel stood by, holding both Liberty and Washington's horse. Nate noticed the green-and-gold saddlecloth draped over Liberty's back. The sight of the familiar Gill family insignia made him think of calling out to Daniel, but then, believing such familiarity unseemly in a private soldier, especially in the presence of the commander-in-chief, he changed his mind and trudged silently past him.

"I would like to have all the troops on the Jersey shore by midnight," Washington said to Knox. "Do you think that's possible?"

"I'll try, sir," Knox said, ducking his head as a gust of wind struck them both. "But it won't be easy in this storm. There are ice cakes drifting down the river, sir. That won't help, but I'll try."

Washington turned to mount his horse, when Major James Wilkinson hurried up to present a letter from General Horatio Gates.

"From General Gates?" Washington asked, puzzled. "Where is he?"

"I left him this morning in Philadelphia."

"What was he doing *there*? He is supposed to be commanding in the north."

"I understood that he was on his way to Congress."

"On his way to Congress!" Washington repeated, exchanging glances with Colonel Gill. Nodding to Wilkinson in dismissal, the general handed the letter to Daniel. "The intrigue thickens," Washington muttered. "Without asking my permission, Gates leaves his post to press his cause in Congress. Soon I suppose we shall be hearing the phrase 'Fabian slowness' pretty regularly." Washington urged his horse toward a waiting boat with the words:

"Now, we cannot fail."

Colonel Johann Rall awoke in Trenton on the morning of Christmas Day with a monumental hangover. He shaved with a trembling hand while outside his window shivering Hessian bandsmen serenaded him with German Christmas carols.

Colonel Rall had nothing but contempt for the Americans. It was he who had led the slaughter of the Americans cornered in Fort Washington and he had been disappointed when General Howe prevented his Hessians from bayoneting their prisoners, as they had done on Long Island. Colonel Rall shared General James Grant's conviction that the Yankees were congenital cowards. "There's no need my gelding them, my dear Rall," Grant had assured him with a chuckle. "It seems the good Lord made them that way. You can keep the peace in New Jersey with a corporal's guard."

Because of this conviction, Colonel Rall had built no redoubts around Trenton as Colonel Carl von Donop had ordered him to do. He had only a few pickets stationed along the roads. Besides, Johann Rall believed that when one went into winter quarters one should forget about the fighting and address oneself to women and wine. Having shaved and dressed, he rang for his batman.

"Mine breakfast, Rudl," he said curtly. "Und a carafe of vine."

Because it was Christmas Day, Colonel Rall joined his officers and men in church to sing carols and hymns. After church, he celebrated the Nativity in the hearty German manner, drinking so copiously that his hangover vanished and he felt ready for another evening of revelry. Accompanied by his batman he rode to the home of Abraham Hunt, a wealthy Trenton merchant and a devout Tory. He strode into Hunt's drawing room with the question: "Vere are der ladies?"

"Not tonight, Colonel," the merchant said. "They're tired out from last night. How about a game of cards?"

"Goot!" Johann Rall exclaimed and sat down at a table with Hunt and his other guests. They began to play. Servants brought them wine. Around midnight there was a knock on the door and the batman hastened to answer it. He hurried back to Rall's side.

"It's a farmer from outside der town," he whispered to Rall. "He says der enemy—"

"Shud up!" Rall yelled. "Gan't you see I'm busy?"

The batman returned to the door and came back with a note which he silently handed to Rall. Scowling, preoccupied with his hand of cards, Colonel Johann Rall stuffed the note into his pocket unread.

It was still there when his batman helped him aboard his

horse and he rode swaying through the howling storm to his quarters.

Nathaniel Gill's body was also swaying as he entered a wildly bobbing boat beside Luke Sawyer. No one spoke. The troops had been enjoined to silence upon pain of death. They huddled together in the biting cold, ducking their heads into their collars against the lash of the wind. Thin, jagged cakes of ice came floating downstream. They struck the boats so hard that Glover's men at the oars had difficulty maintaining course. It was not midnight but some time after three o'clock in the morning when Colonel Knox rode up to Washington and announced in a booming voice:

"The crossing is completed, sir."

Nodding, the commander-in-chief conferred with Generals Nathanael Greene and John Sullivan, who had been exchanged. "General Sullivan, I am giving you John Stark's sharpshooters. You will take your division along the river road and hit the bottom of the town. General Greene, you will march with me and the main body along a road two miles farther inland. We will hit Trenton at the top."

Nathaniel's company marched with Sullivan's column. The men lost their balance on the slippery road, flailing the air with their arms and muskets to stay erect. Cruel ice cut through the rags on their feet and drew blood. After a few hours Nate's company was brought to a halt. Captain Walker walked up to each man, peering through the darkness at his face.

"Is your musket dry?" he asked Nate.

"No, sir—it's soaked."

Captain Walker reported to regiment that his men would not be able to fire their muskets. Soon a courier from Sullivan's headquarters went galloping back to General Washington.

"General Sullivan begs to report, sir, that his guns and powder are soaked. Not one small arm is fit for use."

"Tell General Sullivan to use the bayonet," Washington said quietly. "I am determined to take Trenton."

Washington rode on. Suddenly his horse slipped on the frozen icy road, neighing in fright and wildly pawing at the ice. Washington calmly reached over to grab his mane and the mount straightened. Down both roads the two columns

marched, steadily slipping up on the still sleeping Hessians.
Grayish fingers of light poked at the sky. It was nearing
eight o'clock when the two columns reached their destination
almost simultaneously. Nate's heart leaped when he saw a tall
Hessian soldier in brass miter and scarlet coat come crashing
out of the bushes alongside the road and go sprinting back to
Trenton.

"*Der feind! Heraus! Heraus!*" he shouted. "The enemy.
Turn out! Turn out!

Nate wished that he had a dry musket. It would have been
an easy shot and the picket never would have said a word.
From the other side of the town, Nate heard the sound of
musketry. Evidently Washington's men had kept their powder
dry.

Lieutenant Jacob Piel heard the firing, too. He rushed to
Colonel Johann Rall's quarters, pounding wildly at his door.
Rall, still in nightshirt and sleeping cap, poked his head out
of the window.

"Vat's der madder you should make such a racket?"

"The Americans are upon us! They're attacking the town
from two sides!"

Rall popped out of sight. A few minutes later he came
clattering down the stairs fully uniformed. "Form!" he
shouted to Lieutenant Piel. "The Lossberg Regiment on
Queen Street, mine own on King and the Knyphausens in
reserve." Everywhere in Trenton the startled Hessian soldiers
were pouring out of barracks and private homes. Most of
them had hardly slept since the Christmas revelry had ended.
They shook their aching heads and dug their fingers into their
eyes. But they formed. Soon the scarlet-coated Lossbergs
marched off to the right on Queen Street, Rall's blue-coated
soldiers to the left on King and the black-coated Knyphausen
Regiment to the rear.

But at the top of each street stood the American artillery,
two guns to a street. The gunners crouched over the touchholes, blowing on their slow matches. Captain Alexander
Hamilton watched them anxiously. Would the guns fire?

"Fire!" he shouted.

Ba—loom! Ba—loom!

The cannon roared and shook, spitting out charges of
grapeshot. The Hessians screamed in agony and went down in
heaps.

"Reload, and fire again!" Alexander Hamilton cried.

At once soldiers rushed forward to shove their sponge poles down the muzzles, swabbing out the bores. Others rammed the powder charges home while still others stuffed the guns with grapeshot. Again the cannon spoke, and again the screams and toppling Hessians. Now, on Queen Street, the Lossbergs mounted their own artillery and fired back. There were no casualties.

"Follow me, men!" Captain William Washington yelled. "Charge!"

Cheering, the Americans followed William Washington and Lieutenant James Monroe down Queen Street, their bayonets outthrust. The Hessians opened fire with their muskets. Both Washington and Monroe fell wounded. But the wildly yelling Americans came on. At once, the terrified Hessians turned and fled, leaving their guns behind them.

At the bottom of the town, Sullivan's men were attacking from the west. General Greene extended his line to join him, while sending other troops to hold the rear. The Hessians were caught on three sides. If General Ewing could seize the bridge over the Assunpink Creek, they would be in a box.

"General Sullivan!" a breathless courier shouted, above the sound of his horse's hoofbeats. "The Assunpink bridge is open! The Hessians are escaping!"

Wheeling on Captain Walker, Sullivan said, "Go at once to the bridge and close the gap."

"Forward, men—at the double!" Walker cried.

Cheering, his soldiers ran toward the creek. They could see Hessians in their colorful uniforms streaming over the bridge.

"The bayonet!" Walker shouted, waving his sword at the fleeing enemy.

"The bayonet! The bayonet!" his soldiers roared.

"Up their backsides with 'em," Luke Sawyer bellowed.

Screeching horribly now, the packed American troops slammed into the Hessian rear with almost the force of a body of cavalry. Screaming Hessian soldiers went flying into the air. Others were knocked down and trampled. Nate Gill drove his bayonet into the back of a big corporal. *"Mutter!"* the Hessian screamed, sinking to the earth with his bowels oozing out of the hole in his stomach. *"Mutter!"* Nate saw Luke swing his clubbed musket and brain a Hessian in a blue coat. Now the Americans were on the bridge, the wooden planks rattling beneath their feet. The Hessians who had got away were sprinting for safety. The shriek and screech of battle was subsiding and Nate heard Captain Walker shouting: "Turn, men, turn! There's more of them in our rear."

At once the Americans wheeled around and presented leveled bayonets at parties of Hessians making for the bridge. They halted, eyeing the steady American muskets nervously. They had no way of knowing that the weapons could not fire. One by one, they threw their own muskets crashing on the ground and put up their hands. Captain Walker detailed a party of men to take them prisoner, he left most of his company to hold the bridge, and with Nate and Luke Sawyer trotted toward King Street where Colonel Rall was re-forming his riddled regiment. They passed an empty barracks.

"In here, Luke," Nate called, "maybe we can find something to dry our pieces. Or else we can pick the touchholes clear."

They ran inside, delighted to find racks of loaded enemy muskets. Each seizing four or five of them, they rushed to the windows and began sniping at Rall's soldiers below. Nate saw a colonel in a black coat riding a horse and waving his sword. "That's him, Luke," Nate yelled, "that's the big boy." Both soldiers took careful aim and fired. Johann Rall toppled dying from his horse with two bullets in his body. From every quarter of the Trenton battlefield came the voices of the American commanders.

"Cease fire! Cease fire!"

Silence fell upon the battlefield.

At once, General George Washington gave orders to have the mortally wounded Johann Rall taken to his quarters and given every care. Then he sat his horse in silent exultation listening to the Hessian soldiers grounding their arms and watching them being marched off with hands held high. Courier after courier rode up to report enemy losses: 920 Hessians captured . . . 25 killed . . . 90 wounded; American losses: two soldiers killed, frozen to death on the march . . . not one killed in battle . . . two officers, two privates wounded.

General George Washington sat radiant on the field. He even beamed when Major Wilkinson, the coconspirator of Conway, rode up to announce that the last enemy regiment had grounded its arms. He actually extended his hand in thanks.

"Major Wilkinson," Washington said, "this is a glorious day for our country."

Chapter Nineteen

It had been a glorious day. Washington's daring stroke had raised the American people from the depths of despair to the pinnacle of hope. His own reputation, so tarnished by the defeats and retreats of 1776, shone as never before. He was hailed everywhere—even in Europe—as a military genius, while Congress voted him powers making him a military dictator.

The commander-in-chief was at last empowered to recruit soldiers for long-term enlistments, the object of his heart's desire. He also moved quickly to persuade the men whose terms would expire at the end of the year to sign on for six more weeks in exchange for a bounty of ten dollars. Meanwhile, he augmented his forces with the battalions of militia marching to his standards after the victory at Trenton.

Sir William Howe was stunned by the defeat of the Hessians. He immediately summoned Lord Cornwallis to his quarters in New York.

"I cannot believe, Charles," he said, "that three old established regiments of a people who make war a profession should lay down their arms to a ragged and undisciplined militia." He stared sharply at Cornwallis. "You are aware that this means you cannot return to England?"

"I know," Cornwallis said bitterly. "I had been looking forward to a few jolly good hands at Brooks's, but I guess now I'm stuck with a winter campaign."

"You are, indeed. I should like you to hold New Jersey for me. I will give you my best troops. Say six thousand men."

"That should be enough to bag the old fox," Cornwallis said grimly.

"Be careful, Charles. I have come to respect Washington. He has an uncanny knack of getting out of traps. He rather reminds me of Fabius Maximus. You recall his campaigns against Hannibal? Washington seems to be doing the same thing. Whether consciously or not, I cannot say. But he has adopted a strategy of raids and attrition, avoidance of decisive battle, all designed to weaken me while he grows stronger. Which is exactly what the *Cunctator* did to Carthage, until Rome grew strong enough to destroy her."

"True. But I much doubt that the Americans will ever become organized in a military way. They have no professional soldiers. Washington may have improved, but most of his generals are amateurs. The Yankees have no factories to make arms and they don't have a fleet."

"France has."

"But surely you don't think Louis of France would put guns in the hands of republicans? The enemies of royalty?"

"Vergennes would. Vergennes hates us. He would do anything to hurt us. Even that. Vergennes is just waiting for the right moment. A decisive British defeat would be just the thing. Trenton wasn't big enough, it was hardly more than a raid—although the Lord knows that it will give Vergennes encouragement. It's already cut the effectiveness of my German troops in half. The Yankees no longer dread them. So I say be careful, Charles. Not cautious, of course. The chief point to remember is that Washington must be brought to decisive battle. Once his army is destroyed, the war is over. Now, then, where do you propose to locate your headquarters?"

Cornwallis arose and strode to a map table. "Here, at New Brunswick," he said, pointing with his finger. "You'll give me a war chest?"

"Oh, yes," Howe said easily. "Say three hundred and fifty thousand dollars in specie."

"Quite enough," Lord Charles Cornwallis said with a confident smile.

From New Brunswick, General Cornwallis marched to Princeton, and then, hearing that Washington had returned to Trenton with his army, he made rapidly for that city. He took Washington by surprise. The American commander, accustomed to the slowness of Howe, was unprepared for the speed of Cornwallis. In the late afternoon of January 2, 1777, the British came up with the Americans on a ridge and quickly drove in their pickets.

Washington was in deep trouble with his back to the Delaware and his face toward the flower of the British Army. Cornwallis's officers exulted. But they were enraged when the general ordered a cease-fire and prepared to camp for the night.

"We must attack now!" Sir William Erskine cried. "If Washington is the general I take him to be, he will not be found there in the morning."

Cornwallis shook his head. "No. The men are tired from marching all day. I will bag the old fox in the morning."

Above the British camp behind brightly burning campfires, Washington had called a council of war. "Our position is precarious," he said gravely. "We have a good defensive position, but if we should be driven from it our retreat will be blocked by the river."

"But the men are in high spirits," said General Hugh Mercer.

Washington shook his head. "Spiritual power will never overcome firepower," he said soberly. "The British have the batteries, the bayonets and the discipline. I believe we must retire."

"Why not go on the offensive, General?" Colonel Daniel Gill inquired. Washington stared at him in astonishment, and Daniel continued, "I mean, why don't we slip away from Cornwallis's front and attack his rear in Princeton. It would give you a victory to go with Trenton. And the British war chest is only eighteen miles away in New Brunswick."

Washington frowned thoughtfully. Then his face brightened and he exclaimed, "By Jehovah, I'll do it! It will shake Howe up again." As though his spirits had been recharged by the audaciousness of the proposal, Washington whirled on his officers with glittering eyes and rapped out his orders. "General Mercer, you will hold the bridge at Stony Brook. General Sullivan, you will take the road to the right and march straight into Princeton. Send the artillery and baggage on ahead. Wrap the wheels in rags to muffle them. Colonel Gill, see to it that a working party of four hundred men is detailed to work close to the British lines with pick and shovel. Tell them to make as much noise as possible. They may even speak to each other. I want Howe to think we're strengthening our fortifications. And detail a party of axemen to cut plenty of firewood from the fences around here. I want those campfires to burn all night. We will march, gentlemen, at one o'clock in the morning."

Captain Walker's company was one of those chosen to work with pick and shovel above the British lines. Nate Gill and Luke Sawyer trudged glumly down a ridge beside a small stream. The weather had thawed and the ground was muddy. When they reached a bend in the stream their sergeant ordered them to begin digging.

"Dig what?" Luke asked. "What're we digging?"

"Just dig," the sergeant said. "And make a lot of noise."

"Well, I'll be go to hell," Luke muttered.

Nate giggled. "Maybe George wants to keep the lobsterbacks awake."

"Well, by Jesus, he's sure keepin' *us* awake!" Luke complained. "And we've bin marchin' all day. My ass is suckin' wind, Natey. I tell you, if'n I git kilt, you mark on my tombstone: 'Bury me face downwards, boys—my ass is tired.' "

Nate laughed and the two soldiers began to dig, their shovels mingling with the clinking and clanging issuing from the tools of the men around them. Nate straightened to lean panting on his shovel. He saw another soldier approaching with a load of firewood in his arms.

"Where are you going?" Nate called.

"To a wedding," the soldier replied with heavy sarcasm.

"Don't be smart. What've you got there?"

"Wedding presents. Lord Cornwallis is marrying the Pope's daughter in the morning and George asked me to bring them some presents."

"Aw, shaddup," Luke Sawyer growled.

Chuckling to himself, the soldier moved off in the dark. Nate heard him drop his load with a crash. He came back still chuckling.

"The wedding's off," he said.

"How's come?" asked Luke.

"The Pope's daughter found out Cornwallis has only one ball."

A shout of laughter rose from the working soldiers, and then their sergeant yelled: "All right, men, fall in! We're going back to camp."

Shouldering their picks and shovels, Nate and Luke and their comrades marched back up the ridge, where they exchanged their tools for muskets and formed ranks for a route

march. When the order came to move out, Nate slipped on
the muddy road and almost fell. Cursing, he stooped to remove the rags wound around his feet. "It's easier barefoot,"
he muttered. An hour later, the weather turned cold . . .
then freezing. In another hour, the road was frozen. Nate
wound his feet in rags again. Soon, the ice penetrated the
cloth and pierced his feet. Like those of many of the soldiers
marching with him, Nate's feet were bleeding again.

When Lord Cornwallis left Princeton in pursuit of Washington, he left a rear guard of about twelve hundred men under Lieutenant Colonel Charles Mawhood. At daybreak,
Colonel Mawhood led his men toward Trenton. Mounted on
a little brown horse, he clattered over Stony Brook bridge at
the head of his troops. To his left he caught the flash of arms
and saw Americans coming out of a wood.

"Yankees!" he shouted to the officers behind him. "It must
be stragglers from Trenton. Cornwallis has bagged the fox!
After them! Cut them off, while I withdraw the brigade."

With thundering hooves, the British officers galloped
toward the approaching Americans, only to rear to a halt and
rush back over the bridge when they saw that the Yankees
were not beaten fugitives but a sizeable force of soldiers
marching in good order.

Colonel Mawhood pointed his sword toward an orchard on
the other side of the bridge. "In there! On the double!"
Cheering, the British raced for the orchard.

Behind them, General Mercer also waved his sword toward
the orchard. "Go to it, men! We need to get there first!" Yelling wildly, the Americans ran down the road and got to the
orchard first. They took cover behind a hedge and began firing. So did the British. Because both sides were invisible, the
gun duel was harmless.

Suddenly, the British rose up with a cheer and came charging toward the hedge. The Americans poured out a volley.
Nate took careful aim at a young officer and squeezed the
trigger. The officer fell backwards clutching his shoulder.
Others fell, but the British came on. Nate bent to reload.
When he came erect, he found himself almost alone. The
sight of the enemy steel had broken the American ranks. Men
were streaming back down the road. General Mercer tried to
stop them. They pushed him aside and ran on. In horror,

Nate saw a party of redcoats surround Mercer and club him to the ground. Again and again they drove their bayonets into him. Nate counted seven times. He turned to receive the assault of a British regular running at him with leveled bayonet, when suddenly he saw the man stop and gape in astonishment. Nate followed his eyes.

Mounted on a white horse, General George Washington was riding straight down the road toward Mercer's fleeing soldiers. Behind him was his main body. Washington waved his hat and cried, "Come, parade with us, my brave soldiers!" But Mercer's terrified troops merely flowed around him. Washington still galloped forward, and the redcoat opposite Nate lifted his musket to fire at him. Nate raised his own musket and shot him dead. But dozens of other redcoats also fired, getting off a crashing volley. A cloud of gunsmoke swirled around Washington, obscuring him from view on both sides.

Colonel Daniel Gill covered his eyes in dread.

The smoke cleared and Washington still sat his horse, erect and valiant, calling to his men and waving his hat to motion them forward. Mercer's men were still reluctant but other troops came charging to the battle. Then Mercer's men joined them with wild yells. The British were driven down the road toward Trenton. Washington led the pursuit, waving his hat again and yelling, "It's a fine fox chase, my boys!"

But the British got away, behind a covering screen of dragoons. Washington turned and led his army back into Princeton where Sullivan's troops had stormed the town. A party of two hundred British held out in Nassau Hall. Captain Alexander Hamilton unlimbered his artillery.

"Fire!" he yelled.

A single ball crashed into the building, and the British poured outside with hands held high in surrender.

Immediately after his victory at Princeton, General Washington held a council of war on horseback. His officers were divided on whether to leave Princeton immediately and make for the safety of Morristown in the northern part of New Jersey or march on New Brunswick only eighteen miles away.

"Most of Cornwallis's supplies are there," Colonel Daniel

Gill cried eagerly. "And their war chest. We could end the war."

"I agree," Washington said soberly. "If I had six or seven hundred fresh men to spare, I'd lead them there myself. But I don't. The men are exhausted. They've been on their feet thirty-six hours. They would never make it. It's a marvelous opportunity, but it can be taken only at the grave risk of losing the army and the Revolution."

Colonel Gill's eyes traveled reflectively over company after company of weary men squatting on either side of the road with closed eyes. He caught sight of his cousin Nate gnawing on a bone he had taken from a dog, and he nodded his head in agreement. So did the remainder of Washington's commanders, and the Americans, shaken awake by their sergeants, straggled slowly out of town toward Morristown.

Chapter Twenty

In the late summer of 1777 Barbara Gill gave birth to a healthy baby boy. But Barbara herself had a difficult time. Because she was thirty-three, delivery of her first child was not easy. She hemorrhaged constantly and the midwife who was in constant attendance did not leave until the flow of blood finally ceased.

Barbara was overjoyed to receive a letter from Daniel telling her that he hoped to be with her before winter set in.

General Washington is sending me to Saratoga to act as his liaison officer with General Gates. He is upset by conflicting reports about the conduct of General Gates and General Benedict Arnold in the battle against General Burgoyne's army and he wants me to go there to obtain an impartial and unbiased picture of what has happened. General Washington has also graciously granted me a week's leave, once I have completed my mission, in order to see you and the new baby. So pray, my dearest, that the battle will be over soon, that the British will be defeated and that I will once again hold you in my arms and look for the first time on my newborn son.

Colonel Gill did not arrive at Saratoga until two days after General John Burgoyne surrendered his army to General Horatio Gates. Daniel had encountered maddening delays of every description. First, Liberty threw a shoe as Daniel rode toward the Delaware, causing a delay of nearly two days before he could be reshod. Between the Delaware and the Hudson were numerous bridges and ferries which were sometimes held by the British or else had been destroyed by them. Daniel had to make frequent detours, or sit his horse in frustration behind long lines of wagons waiting for his turn to cross the water. Riding over a low floating bridge across the Raritan, Liberty was stung in the ear by a bee. He reared and toppled into the water with Daniel in the saddle. Fortunately, the horse kept his head and swam ashore with Daniel swimming beside him. But it was the shore they had just left and Daniel had to get in line again for his turn to cross the bridge. Finally reaching the Hudson, he took ship—only to have a freak tornado blow the craft ashore. Fortunately, it was the same side of the river as Saratoga, and Daniel remounted a frazzled Liberty and rode the rest of the way to the American camp.

Disheveled and dejected by his ordeal, Daniel was nonetheless delighted when he heard of Burgoyne's defeat. At once, he began interviewing officers who had played prominent parts in the victory. He was astonished by the vehemence—sometimes even bitterness or anger—with which almost all of them gave the credit to Benedict Arnold.

"It was Arnold who beat the British at Freeman's Farm," a colonel named Varick told him. "Gates didn't want to attack. He wanted the British to come to him. But Burgoyne had seen a height on our left commanding our entire position. He was making for it. Arnold was in command on the left. He guessed right away what Burgoyne was up to. He begged Gates to let him attack Burgoyne. Gates still said no. Again and again, Arnold begged him—almost on his knees.

"Finally Gates gave in. He gave him Daniel Morgan's riflemen and Henry Dearborn's sharpshooters and Arnold led them against the British under General Fraser and stopped them cold. Then he began probing for a soft spot. He found it at Freeman's Farm between Fraser and Burgoyne and he began attacking again.

"I tell you he was something to see. He was all over the battlefield on that big brown horse of his, waving his sword and sometimes whacking an officer on the head with it to get him to move. Everywhere he went the men cheered and waved their hats. They fought like tigers! They took the lobsterbacks' guns away from them and even beat them with the bayonet. And I tell you, it was all because of Arnold!

"Pretty soon the British began to back up and Arnold saw his chance. He needed only a few more troops to knock them out of the battle and he rode like a madman back to Gates's tent and asked for them. Gates refused. Arnold stormed and raved, but Gates said he wasn't going to release any more men and weaken his position. Gates changed his mind later on, but he sent the reinforcements to the wrong place—to the left instead of the center where Arnold was. Some of the commanders I know think that he did it on purpose—just to spite Arnold. Anyway, by then it was too late. Because of Gates, Burgoyne had the time to stiffen his center with troops from his right and that was the end at Freeman's Farm. The golden moment was gone. I tell you, Colonel Gill, if Horatio Gates had listened to Benedict Arnold, we would have had a complete victory over Burgoyne!" Colonel Varick stared straight into Daniel's eyes. "I'll tell you something else, Colonel. Gentleman Johnny Burgoyne thinks the same as I do. When he was here he kept talking about Arnold's bravery and ability, and he did it right in front of Gates." Varick smiled with happy malice. "That didn't sit too well with the Old Woman. That's what the troops call Gates, Colonel. The Old Woman. They sing songs about the Old Woman hiding under the sink while Arnold is out leading his army against the enemy."

Daniel chuckled. "Well, he does look a little bit like one. Fat and with that long nose of his. At Boston in the winter, he always wore a woolen cap pulled down over his ears underneath his tricorne. It didn't make him look very warlike. Anyway, Colonel, I'm astonished that so many officers are telling me the same thing you have. And yet, Major Wilkinson insists that Arnold had nothing to do with Freeman's Farm."

"Whaaat? Why the dirty, sniveling little liar. Just what you'd expect from Gates's favorite kiss-ass."

"He told me there were no general officers active in the battle. He insisted on it, even after I quoted all the officers who said they'd *seen* Arnold at the head of his troops."

"Well, Colonel, if I were you, I wouldn't pay much attention to James Wilkinson. Matter of fact, it was him that put the bad blood between Gates and Arnold. As Gates's aide he kept interfering with Arnold's troops and countermanding his orders. I wouldn't talk to Wilkinson anymore, Colonel."

"I don't think I will. What about Bemis Heights, Colonel? Can you tell me about that?"

"Not much. But if you want to know about Bemis Heights, there's only one person to talk to."

"Who's that, Colonel?"

"Benedict Arnold."

General Arnold was lying on a cot when Colonel Gill entered his tent. There was a bloodstained bandage on his left leg. Daniel had known Arnold in Boston when Washington authorized him to make his disastrous invasion of Canada. Arnold immediately recognized Daniel. With a grimace, he swung himself into a sitting position and extended his hand.

"Colonel Gill!" he cried in his high-pitched voice. "What brings you here?"

Daniel shook hands with Arnold, surprised again by the strength of his hand. Although he was well built, Arnold was only of medium height. His shoulders, however, were unusually broad. His piercing eyes were a hard blue.

"General Washington sent me here," Daniel replied, sitting down opposite Arnold. "He's gotten so many conflicting reports of what's happening up here he wants me to ferret out the truth."

"Good," Arnold grunted, a scowl coming over his swarthy face. "That's what I want, too. You've heard about Freeman's Farm, I suppose?"

"Yes. By all accounts, it was you who beat the British."

"Thank you. But Gates didn't think so. The son of a bitch didn't even mention my name in his report. He said the battle was won by 'detachments.' From *his* army. When I saw a copy of it, I got so God damn mad I went to him and challenged him on it. We had an argument. He called me insubordinate and told me it was none of my business. I told the fat-assed old woman what I thought of him and he relieved me of my command. He said he was going to replace me with that fat ass of a Ben Lincoln. My God, what an army of fat asses! Gates, Lincoln, Knox. How does Congress measure military ability? By the breadth of your behind? It sure as hell can't be bravery.

"Anyway, Gates told me he'd give me a pass to go back to General Washington with my suite of officers. I was so God damn mad, I took it. But then my officers talked me into staying. So I just sat stewing here in my tent, waiting for Burgoyne to start something.

"He *had* to attack. He'd been badly mauled at Freeman's Farm and Clinton hadn't been able to get up the Hudson to help him. The whole countryside was rising up against him. New York, Vermont, New Hampshire . . . One of Burgoyne's Indians murdered and scalped a local beauty named Jane McCrae. That set the countryside on fire and helped John Stark beat Burgoyne's Germans at Bennington. Low on food . . . surrounded by a hostile population blocking his supplies . . . Burgoyne couldn't wait for Clinton. Either he had to fight his way out to join him, or he'd have to go back to Canada in defeat and disgrace.

"So I sat in my tent, waiting. And sure enough, Gentleman Johnny came at our left again. This time at Bemis Heights. Simon Fraser was going to turn our flank with twelve hundred men. If he succeeded, Burgoyne would feed in more men. Gates himself commanded our left, with Lincoln on the right. Gates, of course, was commanding from his tent sitting on his big fat ass.

"I heard the battle start, Colonel Gill, and I damn near went crazy watching Fraser working his men around our left. He knew what he was doing. Gates didn't. I couldn't stand it anymore. We were *losing!* Command or no command, I jumped on my horse and rode off to the battle. Gates saw me go and he sent a major named Armstrong riding after me to order me back to my tent. I saw him out of the corner of my eye and just rode away from him. I've got some horse, Colonel! I used to be a horse dealer, you know. It felt good hearing the men cheer and call out my name. Right away, I saw a soft spot. In Fraser's center. We charged it a couple times and a whole German unit fell apart. But that Fraser, he was some commander. He rallied his men.

"That's when I turned to Daniel Morgan and asked him for one of his sharpshooters. He brought me a fellow named Tim Murphy and I pointed Fraser out to him. 'That's General Fraser,' I said. 'He's a very able and brave general and I admire him very much. But he has to die! Bring him down, Tim—and we'll beat the British.' Well, Murphy climbed a tree with his double-barreled rifle. I watched Fraser through my glasses. Tim's first shot creased the crupper of Fraser's horse. The next parted the horse's mane. Fraser's officers rode up to him, swinging their arms and pointing toward Murphy. They wanted Fraser to take cover. He refused, and Tim's next shot killed him.

"With that, the heart went out of the British. They withdrew to their earthworks. It looked like the time for the crusher had arrived. I led a charge against their left. They beat us off. We needed more men. I commandeered a brigade. I don't remember whose it was, but, anyway, I couldn't wait to find out and sent the men smashing into the earthwork. They just swept the British clean away.

"There was another redoubt on the British right. I collected two more regiments and sent them into it. They took it and killed the German commander. Von Breymann, I think. But I got hit, too," Arnold said, pointing to his bandaged leg. "Right in the same spot where I got hit at Quebec. I couldn't move. But even so, we had opened holes in Burgoyne's main position on his right and rear. They were rattled. One more solid blow would have finished them off." Arnold grinned sardonically. "And that was when that major named Armstrong thought it was safe enough to come up to me and tell me that Gates was ordering me back to my quarters before I did anything rash."

Daniel Gill exploded with laughter. *"Rash?* Like winning a great battle? Maybe even a war? Tell me, where was General Gates all this time?"

"He was in his tent discussing the merits of the Revolution with a captured British officer. The poor man was dying but Gates still called him an impudent son of a bitch just because he disagreed with him."

Colonel Gill shook his head in slow wonderment. "What a man to have commanded at what may have been one of the most decisive victories in history."

"You think Saratoga is that important, Colonel?" Arnold asked, his eyes narrowing.

"Of course! It could be the turning point in what may become the world's greatest revolution! It could bring in the French on our side."

A scowl crossed Arnold's dark features. "I don't want the French on our side," he said sourly. "Liberty should free itself of tyranny by itself, not with the help of another tyranny. It'll just be a case of trading kings."

"I don't think so, General. The French don't want America. They learned their lesson in Canada. The cost of keeping the colony damn near bankrupted the French crown. All that Vergennes wants to do is do the British a disservice. If we can benefit from French hatred of Britain, I don't see why we shouldn't take advantage of it."

Arnold shook his head doggedly. "If the French come in, I'll guarantee your children will grow up to be papists." He shuddered. "It will be a sad day for Protestants. A bloody day."

Daniel smiled gently. "Do you know any Catholics, General?"

"Of course not! There aren't any to know where I come from."

"That's funny. I've noticed that people who hate another religion usually have no experience of it. My parents were Catholics, General. So were my grandparents. I spent my summers among Catholic Indians. I never noticed anything especially foul or fiendish about them."

Benedict Arnold stared at Daniel in undisguised horror. "And you're Washington's *aide*?"

Daniel chuckled, leaning forward in his chair to point at his buttocks. "See, General? No tail!" He laughed at Arnold's discomfiture. "But don't worry, General—I'm a good Episcopalian, now. And I want to tell you, General Arnold," he said, rising to his feet, "that your account of the battle conforms in every detail with the reports I've had from other officers. This is the account I'm giving to General Washington."

"Thank you, Colonel," Arnold said gloomily. "I hope it gets me a promotion. I need the money. I'm broke and in debt. Look at me," he said bitterly, "I did as much as Ethan Allen did to capture Ticonderoga, I won the Battle of Valcour Island to save Ticonderoga for a year, with the littlest luck I could have conquered Canada, I won this battle, I've been wounded twice—and I'm still just a brigadier." He shifted his body with a grimace, preparing to lie down on his cot again, muttering angrily, "What does a man have to do to get what he deserves?"

Burgoyne had surrendered on October 17, 1777, and four days later Barbara Gill heard the great news from Jennifer, who had heard it in the tavern from a returning soldier. Barbara was overjoyed. From what Daniel had told her, she realized the importance of the victory, but more than that the end of the battle meant that her husband was coming home. Next morning she awoke with her intuition telling her that

Daniel would arrive that day. Humming happily she went to her wardrobe and selected her favorite dress, a brocade in marigold yellow. Putting it on, she studied herself in the mirror, passing a hand over her belly. Good! she thought, the bulge is completely gone. Barbara glanced at her bare neck ruefully. Damn Cousin Ben! If he hadn't stolen Grandma's jewels, she would have worn the amethyst necklace.

Downstairs, Jennifer greeted her with admiration. "My, you look scrumptious this morning. Anything special for today?"

Barbara colored slightly. She felt a little foolish about her premonition that Daniel was coming. "Well, yes," she said. "I'm meeting Silas Newton today. He thinks he's the sharp one, you know, and he wants to buy Grandma's house."

"The *Gill* house?" Jennifer repeated, aghast. "You're not going to sell the Gill house, Barbara?"

"Of course not! Grandma said in her will that there must always be some member of the family living there. No, I'm going to sell Silas Uncle Malachi's house. He doesn't know it, of course. First, I'll take him to Grandma's and give him some ridiculously high figure, and then I'll show him Uncle Mal's for about a quarter of it."

"Think he'll bite?"

"Of course he will!" Barbara said, laughing. "Silas Newton isn't as smart as he thinks he is."

"You are a marvel."

"Not yet," Barbara said, going out the taproom door, "but I'm getting there."

"Aren't you going to wear a hat?"

"Not today. It's beautiful out. Indian summer."

When Barbara returned later in the day she saw a horse standing at the tavern hitching rail. Recognizing Liberty and the familiar green-and-gold saddlecloth, she cried aloud in joy. "Daniel!" she called, wrenching open the taproom door. "Oh, Dan, Dan, Dan! You've come home!" Daniel was seated at the bar talking to Jennifer. He jumped down and ran to take Barbara into his arms. Jenny darted discreetly into the kitchen, tears in her own eyes, while Daniel kissed his wife again and again—on the lips, the forehead and her tearstained cheeks. Barbara stepped back, a worried expression on her face.

"Daniel, you look so thin. Are you well?"

"Of course. There just wasn't that much food at Saratoga."

He smiled and embraced her again. Barbara took his hand and said, "Come, you have to see the baby."

They climbed the stairs hand in hand. Mrs. Wilmot smiled fondly at Daniel and handed him his son. Daniel took him tenderly. The child made a rosebud mouth and gurgled. Daniel laughed aloud. "He's all Gill," he said proudly. "Gill and Quinn and Caughnawaga, but mostly Gill." The baby opened its eyes and Daniel chuckled. "Look at those Irish eyes," he said. "Put in with a sooty finger. And see, Barbara, see the hint of the high cheekbones. Pure Caughnawaga."

Barbara laughed. "He's got one eighth Indian in him, and you act like he's a full-blooded chief. What shall we name him?"

"After the greatest man in the world," Daniel said proudly. "George Washington. George Washington Half Moon Gill. I was very fond of my great-uncle."

"He's the one who captured Grandpa Gill, isn't he?"

"Yes, and oh how he hated him for running away. The first thing he'd ask me when I came to the village for the summer was how Grandpa was. He was always glad to hear he was well, and he'd say: 'You tell your grandpa to stay healthy, because I don't want him to die before I can kill him.'"

"Those were terrible times," Barbara said. "But at least they were reunited at the end. Half Moon forgave Grandpa just before he died and Grandpa died himself an hour later. Uncle Mike said it was very touching."

"It must have been. Well," Daniel said, handing the baby back to his nurse. "You take good care of little Georgie, Mrs. Wilmot. But I don't think he's going to be little very long," he said, his voice full of paternal pride. "Just look at those hands and feet. If he ever grows into them he's going to be bigger than I am." Daniel turned to Barbara, who was watching him with shining eyes. "It's a beautiful Indian summer day," he said. "Why don't we go on a picnic out at the waterfall."

Barbara's eyes sparkled. "Wonderful! I haven't been outside this stuffy old city since summer. I'd love a little fresh air." She lifted her skirts to run downstairs and pack a hamper while Daniel followed and went outside the tavern to lead his horse around back to the stable and harness him to the gig. Within a half hour they were on their way to Concord.

As they pulled away, Barbara looked thoughtfully at the tavern. "I've been thinking of enlarging the tavern," she said. "Or else pull it down to make room for a big inn. Maybe four stories high. Even with the war, Boston's growing. And after it's over, it'll grow faster."

Daniel glanced admiringly at his wife. "Where'd you get this business head of yours? Jenny was telling me about you. She says there isn't a man in town can hold a candle to you."

"I . . . I guess I just had it. If the war hadn't come along, I probably would have lived my whole life believing that a woman's place is in the home."

"Isn't it?" Daniel countered with some surprise.

"Not necessarily. I'm sure there are lots of women who'd rather be running a business like I am than put up with the drudgery of being a housewife. They just never get the opportunity. And they daren't just set themselves up in competition with men. It wouldn't be ladylike. *Ladylike!*" Barbara exclaimed contemptuously. "That's the word men use when they want to disqualify a woman who's smarter than they are. *So unbecoming in a lady,*" she simpered scornfully. "It isn't a pedestal you men have put us up on, Daniel, it's a prison!"

"Whoa!" Daniel cried laughingly, and the horse slowed. "Not you," Daniel called to his horse, chuckling again, "it's the lady-love of my life I'm asking to slow down." He glanced sideways at Barbara. "Do you really think women can compete with men?"

"Of course they can! I've proved it! Oh, I don't mean all women. And I certainly don't mean poor women loaded down with babies and household chores. But some women of education and breeding and wealth can do it. It's just the tradition of male dominance that keeps them down. But women can have their 'new order of things,' too. Just wait and see. Not all of us will be content with being the ornament of the drawing room and the plaything of the bedroom."

Daniel chuckled. *"Touché!"* His eyes narrowed. They were on the road to Lexington, approaching the point where Liberty had thrown Major Pitcairn and bolted into the Rebel lines. "This is where you changed masters, Liberty," he called softly to the horse. "Remember Major Pitcairn?" The horse pricked up its ears and Daniel wondered if he had remembered.

"The fact is, Barbara," he said, resuming the conversation, "this all began when you mentioned expanding the tavern. Don't you expect Nate to take over when the war's over?"

"Jenny says Nate wants to be a constitutional lawyer."

"He can be both. Wealth is no drawback in politics. Look at the Congress. Except for the Adamses and Hancock, they're all wealthy men. Besides, Barbara, we're going south after the war. Remember? We've already opened the southern branch of the Gill family with little Georgie. Don't you want more?"

"Of course. But, I . . . I . . ."

"You'll love the south. And there'll be plenty to do besides raising a family. I'm planning to build the biggest rice plantation in South Carolina."

"South Carolina! Rice! I thought it was Virginia and tobacco."

"It was. But tobacco exhausts the soil too fast. And rice is more profitable. There's thousands of acres available along the Ashley River near Charleston. Just the thing for rice and you can ship the grain off your own docks. All that needs to be done is to build the dikes and drains. You see, you cover the plants with water to protect them when they're young. Then, as they approach the harvest, you drain it off. It's so much more profitable than tobacco."

"But isn't it awfully hot in South Carolina?" Barbara asked dubiously.

"Well, yes. In the summer. But we can always build a summer home in North Carolina or Virginia."

"Or farther north, like Boston?" Barbara asked teasingly.

"If you like. But I tell you, Barbara, the swamp forests of South Carolina have a kind of ghostly beauty like nowhere else in the world. There's all kinds of ponds and little lakes on this property I'm thinking of. We can landscape it and plant it with flowering shrubs and turn it into a fairyland. It's unearthly. Giant trees everywhere. Pines and palmettos, magnolias, gum trees, cypresses . . . And the live oaks! They're the most beautiful trees in the world. They're not as tall as the northern oaks, but, my God, are they wide. Huge, gnarled limbs stretching to either side and forming an umbrella maybe seventy feet in diameter."

"Sounds like good lumber country," Barbara murmured musingly.

Daniel chuckled indulgently. "Spoken like a true Yankee. Business before beauty. Well, here we are," he said, turning Liberty into the path leading to the barn beside the waterfall. He jumped down and helped Barbara alight. Then he grasped the hamper and placed it under a maple tree. They sat to either side of it among the fallen, yellowed leaves. Barbara opened it and drew forth legs and thighs of cold fried chicken, corn muffins, jellies and cheeses, half an apple pie, a jug of cider and a bottle of hock.

"My God, what a repast!" Daniel breathed. "I'm almost ashamed to eat it."

"Why?" Barbara asked, puzzled, breaking open a muffin and spreading it with jelly.

"The way the poor fellows in Pennsylvania are starving, it's almost a sin," he said, nevertheless taking the muffin to munch it with relish. "They're literally starving to death, and if they die of starvation, so will the Revolution."

"But you were just telling me what a great victory we won at Saratoga. Surely, General Washington must be overjoyed."

"He may be, and he may not be. It will probably bring the French in, which is most important. But Saratoga is also a feather in Horatio Gates's cap, and that's bad for the general. You see, 1777 was another bad year for General Washington. He lost at the Brandywine and Germantown. His stock is low again and Gates's is rising. Congress will probably name him chairman of the Board of War, making him Washington's nominal superior. And that will be bad for the Revolution."

Daniel began gnawing on a chicken leg and sipping from the glass of hock Barbara handed him. "The year began with so much hope," he said dolefully. "We had all those new muskets from France—twenty-two thousand of them—and the general had his long-term enlistments. He thought the time had come to meet Howe in decisive battle. When Howe landed in Maryland to march on Philadelphia, we hit him at Brandywine Creek." Daniel sighed heavily. "It was the same old thing. Howe found an unguarded ford, crossed it and came down on our right rear. Just like Long Island. It looked like the end, until General Greene saved the day. So we got away again with the army intact, but Howe took Philadelphia without firing a shot. Congress is in York, now, Barbara.

"Howe put his army in Germantown. He had about nine thousand men. We had nine thousand regulars and three thousand militia. Washington decided to try Howe again. And, by God, Barbara, we beat him! Yes, we did, we beat up their light infantry—their best unit—so bad that Howe himself came hurrying up to rally them. For the first time in the war I heard British bugles blowing retreat. And then we ran away from victory!" Daniel exclaimed in a voice of anguish. "We were driving them in front of us when we came to a stone mansion called the Chew House. It was filled with a hundred or more British soldiers and it was right in our path. We should have gone around it and maintained the pursuit but that damned bookworm of a Henry Knox said no. He convinced Washington that we should knock it down with artillery before we moved on. 'That is the orthodox maneuver,' he said, as though you can fight any battle by the book. No two of them are alike. We should have detailed a company of riflemen to cover the lower windows and doors while the main body pushed on. But we sat down and waited and the Chew House wouldn't fall down. Finally, Washington ordered us on, but by then the British had time to re-form. And then confusion compounded confusion.

"Greene's division was misled by a treacherous guide and got lost. General Wayne thought the blasting at the Chew House in the rear meant that Sullivan was in trouble there. So he wheeled his division around and ran into Greene. That left Sullivan's left open and the British came roaring into it and Sullivan's men panicked and ran away. Soon the whole army was running away. As usual, General Washington rode among them trying to rally them. He exposed himself to the hottest fire. But they kept on running. Poor devils, who could blame them? They held up their empty cartridge boxes for Washington to see that they were out of ammunition, but they still ran away.

"From victory!" Daniel concluded in a voice of bitter anguish.

Barbara Gill said nothing. She looked at her husband with soft and compassionate dark eyes. She noticed for the first time the lines of care cut deep into his face above and to either side of his mouth. But she saw also the nobility of his forehead and the determined firmness of his jaw, and in his dark blue eyes the unquenchable light of dedication. She came to his side and drew his head into her lap, gently stroking his blond hair.

"Don't be discouraged, Daniel," she murmured in a low voice. "We'll win. It's only the darkness before the dawn. With men like you and General Washington we cannot fail to win." She leaned down to kiss him tenderly on the forehead. "And after the war is over, we'll be going to South Carolina."

"*Aut nunc aut nunquam*," the Comte de Vergennes wrote to the French ambassador to Spain after hearing the news of Saratoga. "Now or never. Events have surprised us . . . They have marched more rapidly than expected . . . There is no time to be lost. You must emphasize to His Most Catholic Majesty that the interests for separating the English colonies from their mother country, and preventing them from ever being reidentified in any manner whatsoever, is so important that even if it had to be purchased at the price of a somewhat disadvantageous war it would be worth it. The Crowns of France and Spain must combine to bring about that separation. We need not fear the rise of America as a world power, which France has no desire to see, because the colonies will be weakened and torn by internal dissensions for years to come."

Having finished his letter, Vergennes hastened to the chambers of King Louis XVI.

"It is now or never, sire," he said, arising from one knee. "The American victory at Saratoga presents us with the opportunity to come openly to the side of the colonies. Even at the risk of war with England."

"What?" Louis exclaimed, looking disdainfully down his long Bourbon nose. "A king make war with rabble against a brother king? I have no love for George, of course, but he is still a king. I have no desire to replace the rule of royalty with a crowd of libertarian lawyers and scribblers who call themselves philosophers."

"But, sire, we have already crossed the Rubicon. We gave them arms, albeit secretly."

"Yes. I hesitated then, and I should do more than hesitate now. Think what will happen to royalty if this libertarian disease were to spread across the Atlantic."

Vergennes bowed and spread his hands. "It has already done that, Sire—from here to there. The ideas of Americans such as Thomas Jefferson are not their own. They come from our own Rousseau and Voltaire."

"Quite true," Louis murmured, scowling. "I shall never know why my father trusted that inkstained wretch Voltaire. Do you know what the scoundrel said to my father when Canada was lost? 'What have we lost, sire—a few acres of snow?' Any man who could sneer at his sovereign's loss of more than half a great continent is surely not to be trusted."

"I agree, sire. But although these men may read Voltaire and Rousseau they are not like them. This is not a bourgeois revolution dreamed up by a pack of courtroom malcontents and Sorbonne idlers hatching out a new system of government every other day. True, their army is a rabble in arms— but what government doesn't recruit its soldiers from the lowest classes? It's the leaders who matter, and the Americans are almost without exception men of substance. Jefferson, Washington, Carroll, the Rutledges of South Carolina—all extremely wealthy men. In your domain, sire, the vastness of their landholdings would qualify them as dukes. No sire, this is not a revolution to topple royalty. They do not hate kings like those Sorbonne rascals Danton and Robespierre and the others. The chief complaint of the Americans is that they are taxed without representation. It would not surprise me, sire, if they were to acclaim their own king. If not one of their own number, then surely they could find a sovereign among the royal houses of Europe."

King Louis pursed his lips. "You have written to Madrid?"

"Yes, sire. I have instructed Montmorin to press the matter at once with King Carlos."

"I will write Uncle Carlos myself."

"Excellent, sire!" Vergennes exclaimed, bowing as though preparing to leave.

"Uncle Carlos is cautious," Louis said musingly. "He likes to look before he leaps. So I shall do the leaping, monsieur. I shall form an alliance with the United States and declare war on England. That will make my uncle jump. And Holland, too, and Catherine of Russia." He smiled maliciously and rubbed his long nose with glee. "It should make George cry in his beer."

Chapter Twenty-One

A wailing wind whipped slanted sheets of cold gray rain through the streets of the American encampment at Valley Forge. It shook the flimsy huts hastily erected by Washington's barefoot, starving and half-naked soldiers after their arrival at the desolate valley in early December 1777.

Inside their hut, Nathaniel Gill and Luke Sawyer huddled in front of a tiny fireplace, beating their hands together for warmth. They heard the wind rise in fury, rattling their hut as though a monster hand were shaking it. Up the street they heard a crash.

"Another one blown down," Luke muttered gloomily. "Poor bastards, if nobody takes 'em in they'll have to sleep in the mud."

Luke tried to coax flame out of the pile of sticks in the fireplace, but succeeded only in fanning smoke from it. It came swirling into the hut, thick, greasy, foul-smelling smoke that soon had the two soldiers gasping and choking. Nate ran to the door and flung it open so savagely that the ramshackle hut trembled.

"Chrissakes, Nate, don't shake the hut down. It's the only thing we got to keep out the cold."

"Keep it in, you mean," Nate said morosely, slowly closing the door. "I told you that green wood wouldn't burn. And it's wet besides. We'll have to wait until the rain stops and the wood dries out before we can have a fire."

"But we need a fire to roast our food."

"*Food?*" Nate stared at Luke anxiously. "You're ... you're all right, Luke? You're just joking?" Luke Sawyer shook his head solemnly, a mischievous twinkle in his eyes. "Damn it, Luke, you know there's no food in camp! We haven't eaten for four whole days! Christ, Luke, there isn't any more firecake. Just water." Nate began choking in the smoke again and he went to the door and opened it carefully. From outside the two men heard a chorus of soldier voices croaking:

"No meat! No bread! No meat, no soldier!"

"Hear that?" Nate cried savagely. "They're right! We haven't seen a piece of beef since we got here. And even then it was so thin you could see through it." Nate scowled and sat down on his straw pallet, hugging his knees for warmth. "And it's been nothing but firecake and water ever since. And now it's just water. Damn it, Luke, you know there isn't a dog or a cat left in camp."

Luke nodded sheepishly. "I sure hated to do that to Cap'n Walker's poodle. Cap'n sure was fond of 'im. But he sure did taste good." Luke rubbed his stomach in reminiscence, and then began scratching his body furiously. "How 'n hell lice can live off'n skeletons like us, I'll never know."

"So if you know there's no food in camp, how can you go ranting about it like a man with a paper ass?"

Luke grinned and pointed at his feet. "We got food, Natey, boy," he insisted, grinning. "We got our shoes."

Nate stared at Luke in incredulity. "But, Luke . . . you can't eat *leather!*"

"Sure can. I was talkin' to a feller bin with Arnold at Quebec. He said they was so hungry on the march up there they et their bullet pouches."

"How?"

"You kin roast 'em or boil 'em, but this feller said roastin' was better."

Nate stood up and glanced at the moccasins he had made three weeks ago from a piece of raw cowhide. "Whose do we start with?" he asked dubiously.

"We'll draw straws," Luke said, stooping to seize a pair of straws from his pallet. He held his hands behind his back. "You pick first, Nate."

Nathaniel tapped Luke's right arm and Luke grinned and brought his hand around palm open. "Kind 'v figgered you'd go for the rightie," he said.

Nate glowered. "You sure you didn't switch them behind your back?"

Luke Sawyer was all innocence. "Who, me?" he protested in pretended horror.

"All right, I lose," Nate grumbled. "But we don't have to eat them both at one time, do we?"

"Nope. And just to show you how fair I am, I'm gonna alternate with you. We'll eat half of one of your shoes for breakfast and t'other half for dinner. Then tomorrow we'll do the same with one of mine. That way we kin eat for four whole days and not go completely barefoot all the time."

"You're a genius, Luke Sawyer," Nate said, standing on one leg to tug the moccasin off his right foot. "To tell the truth, I won't really miss them. They're hard around the edges and damn near chafed my ankles off on the march up here." He handed the moccasin to Luke, glancing around him inquiringly. "How in hell are we going to get that wood to burn?" he muttered.

Luke laughed and seized a bundle of straw from his pallet. "Might as well use it for kindlin'. We cain't sleep on the floor anyway. I heared two more fellers from the regiment was found frozen to death on the floor of their hut." He stuffed the straw under the blackened sticks, and dug into his pocket for a flint. From outside the hut came the creak of wagon wheels.

"The meat wagon!" Luke shouted eagerly. "Chrissakes, Natey, mebbe we won't have to eat our own shoes. Mebbe we can get some off them bodies in the meat wagon."

Both soldiers rushed outside to a cart drawn up outside a hut across the street. It was piled high with the carcasses of dead soldiers, most of them either frozen or starved to death. Half of them were naked. Their skin was blackened and wrinkled and their arms and legs were no bigger than sticks. The men from the graves detail who had loaded the corpses on the cart had been neither gentle nor respectful, heaping them helter-skelter with calloused indifference. Some of them lay on their backs with their sightless eyes upturned, their mouths drawn back from shriveled black gums. Others lay with their faces resting on the bare behinds of others, or with their heads hanging over the side of the cart, their tongues lolling from their mouths.

Neither Nate nor Luke were shocked by the gruesome wagon. Cemetery carts had been rolling through the Valley Forge encampment for weeks and the soldiers had quickly become adjusted to them as a perhaps grislier detail in the broad canvas of their ordeal. With the soldier's immemorial sardonic sense of humor they mocked the specter of death that was their daily shadow by calling the cemetery cart the "meat wagon." Nevertheless, Nate and Luke were dismayed and enraged when they found that none of the corpses had shoes.

"God damn grave robbers!" Luke Sawyer shouted, shaking his fists at two soldiers from the graves detail who had carried a body out of the hut opposite the cart and were methodically stripping it of every usable article of clothing. "Who the hell give you ghouls the right to rob all them corpses?" Luke yelled, walking toward them menacingly. Suddenly, the corpse groaned.

"Oh, my Jesus, he's still alive!" Luke exclaimed. "He ain't dead. Put his clothes back on, you God damn grave robbers."

The grave men stared sullenly at Luke. "Aw, what's the difference?" one of them said sulkily. "He ain't never gonna make it."

The corpse groaned again and began to gasp aloud. "Lemme die, Lord, lemme die. . . . Please lemme die. . . . Sick . . . starving . . . soup full of burnt leaves and dirt . . . cold . . . tired . . . nasty hut . . . nasty clothes . . . nasty food . . . vomit half the time . . . smoked out of my senses . . . the devil's in it . . . Oh, my pretty wife . . . my lovely children . . . why did I leave them to die in hunger and filth? Take me, Lord, please lemme die. . . ." Suddenly the man was seized by a paroxysm of choking and coughing. Bile and blood poured from his mouth. With a loud groan, he rolled over dead.

"See, you nosy bastard!" the sullen soldier sneered. "We tole you he was dyin'."

Luke shrugged and walked back to the cart where Nate had grasped a bundle of rags. "At least I can wrap my feet in these," Nate muttered. Then he gasped and shrank back in revulsion. He was staring into the beady eyes of a pair of huge bloated rats who had been under the rags gnawing on the flesh of a dead soldier.

"Oh, my Jesus," Luke cried eagerly, "mebbe we can eat *them!* Lemme get my bayonet," he said, whirling to run back to the hut. But his voice frightened the rats. They clambered over the pile of corpses to jump to the ground and go scurrying off. Disgusted, Luke and Nate returned to their hut. Luke picked up Nate's moccasin and began cutting it up with his bayonet.

"This here leather's pretty soft, Natey. Mebbe we should save your shoes just fer dessert." He chuckled and sharpened a stick and spitted a piece of leather on it, holding it over the sputtering fire in the fireplace. "Why don't you fetch us some water while I prepare the banquet," he said jokingly to Natey. "Mebbe you kin drop in on George an' invite him to dinner. Evening dress, of course. Tell him he kin bring Martha." Nate laughed and went outside with a camp kettle. When he came back he found that Luke had cut the roasted leather into little smoking pieces and put them on two metal plates. The two soldiers sat on the floor to eat.

"Mighty tasty," Luke said, grinding hard on the leather with one side of his jaw. "Got to get the juices workin', Natey, boy." He took a swig of water from a cup to help soften the morsel. "Oh, my Jesus, how I wish the Lord Himself was here. He could change this here water into wine and then we'd really have a feast."

Slowly, in silence, chewing hard for perhaps a half an hour and washing their meal down with water, the two soldiers consumed half of Nate's moccasin. That night they finished the other half and prepared to sleep. Nate lay down on the remains of his pallet.

"Don't do that, Natey," Luke warned. "You'll be frozen dead in the morning."

"I'm tired, Luke. I can't sleep sitting up like you can. Just give me a poke every now and then to make sure I'm still alive."

Nate closed his eyes. He was shivering, but he soon fell asleep. He awoke in horror. He felt tiny feet on his mouth. There was a horrid stench in his nostrils. Tiny teeth began nibbling on his cheek. A *rat!* Gasping, Nate jumped to his feet.

"Chrissakes, Natey—what's wrong?"

"A rat!" Nate said, drawing a hand across his lips as though to erase the passage of those foul feet. "A God damn stinking rat ran over my mouth. He was biting my cheek."

"Mebbe he thought you was dead. Where'd he go?"

"I don't know. Probably outside."

There was a rasping sound in the dark and Nate guessed that Luke had drawn his bayonet from its scabbard. "He'll be back," Luke whispered. "You just lie down again, Natey, boy, an' when he starts nibblin' again you give out a yell. I'll skewer 'im in a second and we'll have some real meat to eat."

"Not on your life!" Nate protested with a shudder. "Do you know what it feels like to have a rat run over your mouth?"

"All right, if yer so squeamish, I'll do it."

"Oh, all right—but for God's sake be quick."

Nate lay down again, trembling rather than shivering. Each time the hut creaked he fancied he heard the approach of the rat. His senses were so acute he could not possibly have fallen alseep. Would he be able to hear the approach of a creature as small and stealthy as a rat? Nate did not hear the rat coming . . . He smelled it. It was an ungodly odor, a stench so foul it almost sickened him. In the winking light of the dying coals in the fireplace he saw the bloated rat creeping toward him.

"It's here, Luke," he whispered. "Right by your right foot."

Instantly, Luke Sawyer stabbed the rat through its side and held the squealing, wriggling creature triumphantly aloft. Taking Nate's bayonet, he cut off its head, slit open its belly, cleaned out its entrails, skinned it and stirred up the fire. Then he stuck the rat on the end of a sharpened stick and began roasting it over the fire.

"I got a confession to make, Natey," he mumbled sheepishly, crouching in front of the fireplace. "When I pinched Cap'n Walker's poodle, I found a liter of rum in his tent. Now we'll really have a feast. Taste what's in my canteen, Natey, and you'll know what I mean."

Nate opened Luke's canteen and took a swig. His eyes sparkled. "Oh, boy! And you had this all this time without telling me, you selfish bastard? Some buddy."

"I . . . I only took a little at a time. I was goin' to give you your share when I got down to half."

"That's where it is now," Nate said maliciously. "So you can drink water."

"Aw, Natey," Luke muttered pleadingly, turning the rat to roast the other side. Then he looked up eagerly and said, "Let's make us some Salamanders."

"Good idea," Nate said, and poured rum into two cups. Taking a brand from the fire, he set the liquid afire, handing one of the flaming cups to Luke. Both men gulped their drinks down, fire and all, rubbing their bellies appreciatively. Nate quickly made two more Salamanders, and they downed those, too. Luke sighed in contentment and wiped his mouth with the back of his hand. He began to hum "The World Turned Upside Down." Soon he and Nate were singing it.

> When I was in my prime!
> The lasses took delight in me,
> I was so neat and fine.
> I roved from fair to fair,
> Likewise from town to town,
> Until I married me a wife
> And the world turned upside down.

They laughed after they finished and Luke withdrew the rat from the fire and cut it in two. They sat down to eat, washing the meat down with swigs of rum.

"Damn good!" Luke grunted. "Tastes just like chicken."

Nate nodded, and then he said, "Why is it when someone doesn't know what something tastes like, they always say it tastes just like chicken?"

Luke didn't answer and Nate kept on eating. Suddenly he began to feel nauseous. He remembered the foul stench of the creature he was eating and the sight of the two rats in the meat wagon gnawing on a dead man. He might as well be a cannibal! he thought in sickening dismay. The foul flesh in his mouth had once been human. With a cry of loathing, Nate sprang to his feet and ran for the door, yanking it open just as a stream of puke arched from his mouth.

"Aw, Natey," Luke Sawyer grumbled, reaching for Nate's unfinished portion, "you got a stomach like a spoiled little princess." He began to munch greedily. "I always did think yer pa brung you up too soft."

Chapter Twenty-Two

General George Washington was well aware of the wretched state of his troops. Day after day he sent off letters to Congress, pleading for food and fuel and clothing:

Unless some great and capital change takes place in these continued shortages, this Army must inevitably be reduced to one or the other of these three things. Starve, dissolve or disperse . . .

What, then, is to become of the Army this winter . . . ?

Few of the men have more than one shirt, most only one, some none at all . . .

By a field return this day there are no less than 2,898 men unfit for duty because they are barefoot and otherwise naked . . .

My men are not made of sticks and stones, but flesh and blood. They need food and shelter. Nor do they walk on paper, but on earth. They need shoes and stockings . . .

To all these entreaties, Congress, which had fled from Philadelphia to York, Pennsylvania, responded with silence. The winter worsened and so did the army. When the youthful Marquis de Lafayette arrived in camp to offer his services to Washington, he was dismayed to see officers walking around in what looked like hospital gowns and bed sheets. He was even more horrified to discover that they were. Again and again, Washington ordered out raiding parties to attack the British, only to be forced to cancel them because the men were either barefoot or too weak to march.

"By Jehovah, I cannot bear to review my troops," Washington said to Colonel Gill the day after Lafayette arrived. "It is too painful. I cannot believe that men can endure so much, or that their fellow citizens can do so little to relieve them. Do you know why the army is in such straits, Daniel? It isn't the winter so much. Actually, it was much colder in Morristown. It's the spirit of greed and profit that is destroying this army. Do you know why my men go hungry? Because the farmers around here prefer to sell to the British in Philadelphia for hard cash! Because New York's farmers prefer to sell to the British in New York City for the same reason. And why are my soldiers half-naked? Because the merchants in Boston refuse to move government clothing from their shelves for anything less than one thousand to eighteen hundred per cent profit!

"I tell you, Daniel, the true story of this war can never be written. Greed and profiteering everywhere. A profiteer meets a farmer on his way to market, buys his produce for a hundred dollars and then turns around to sell it to the army for a thousand!" Washington struck his hands together in a fury. "Would that I had the power to hang them! Hang them from a gibbet four times as high as Haman's! And the treachery! Howe has almost as many Tories under his command as I have Patriots! And the professional bounty-jumpers! A soldier enlists in this militia for thirty dollars, and deserts. Enlists in another for twenty-five, and deserts. Comes to me for fifty, and deserts. How can any historian ever say with accuracy how many men the United States of America actually had in the field?"

"And now," he snorted, picking up a letter from his desk, "here is the final piece in my crown of thorns. Congress has authorized me to commandeer my supplies! I am leading the fight to free my country from a tyrant's yoke, and my country tells me to adopt a tyrant's tactics to feed my army! *Take what I need. At the point of a bayonet!*"

Daniel Gill shook his head sympathetically. "It's terrible but true, Excellency, you become what you fight. If I may say so, sir, there doesn't seem to be any other way. If the local farmers had had the slightest spirit of patriotism, you wouldn't have to do it."

"I suppose you are right," Washington said with a sigh. "You had better begin drafting the order authorizing the requisition parties. But, remember, everything seized must be paid for."

In the morning, scores of forage wagons began rolling out of the Valley Forge encampment. Because of Luke Sawyer's knowledge of horses, he had been placed in charge of one of them. Nate Gill was his assistant.

"Remember these are our countrymen," Captain Walker warned the two soldiers. "You must be courteous. And you must pay for everything you take." He handed Luke a money bag. "There's three hundred dollars inside," he said. "You'd better count it to make sure." Luke counted it slowly, and nodded his head, and the captain said, "Get a receipt for everything you pay for." Luke nodded again and drove off.

"Continentals!" Luke snorted, once they were out of ear-shot. "Who's gonna sell us anything for Continentals? Legal robbery, that's all it is. They *have* to sell to us, whether they want to or not. And the money they get ain't worth the paper it's printed on." Luke grimaced. "I don't think I'm gonna like this duty, Natey."

They rode on in silence, until they saw a tiny farmhouse tucked away in a wood on the right side of the road. There was a path leading up to it, and they followed it. A barn came into view. An enormous fat woman with three chins and a fallen stomach was rolling a barrel from the barn toward the farmhouse. She was helped by a boy of about ten with a mop of unkempt blond hair and greenish freckles. Luke reined in the horse and the two soldiers jumped down. When the woman saw them, she straightened up and put her hands on her hips belligerently.

"Git off my farm, you dirty soldiers!" she yelled.

"Dirty soldiers!" Luke repeated in an aggrieved voice. "You ain't got no call to call us names, lady. My buddy an' me's been fightin' fer yer freedom fer nearly three years."

"Who asked you to?" the woman cried scornfully, her chins shaking in her agitation. "King George never done nothin' to me. It's troublemakers like you and that pack of stuck-up swells in Congress what got us into this mess. Now git off my farm!"

"What's in that barrel, lady?" Luke asked.

"None of your business!"

"Lady, Congress has authorized General Washington to commandeer all the supplies he needs. What's in that barrel?"

"Commandeer," she sneered, putting a protective hand on the little boy's shoulder. "A fancy word for stealin'. It's pickled beets, that's what it is."

"I'll give you five dollars for it," Luke said, reaching for the money bag.

"Five *dollars!* In Continentals? A Continental ain't worth a penny in hard money. That's no better than robbery. You people are just as bad as the Hessians. No, soldier boy, you ain't gettin' my beets. I'm not gonna starve just because that crowd of cowards in Congress says I have to." She sniffed. "What a bunch o' yellow-bellies. Ran away from Philadelphia with the British a good fifty miles away. They say John Adams got up on a horse for the first time in his life and fell on that little round behind of his. Too bad it wasn't his head."

"Did you say 'starve,' lady," Luke said with a grin, running a calculating eye over her huge body. "I think it would take you a little while to starve."

"Shut up or I'll sit on you!" she snapped, and Luke raised his hands defensively in mock horror, just as the little boy darted forward and kicked him viciously in the shins.

"Ow!" Luke yelled, reaching for the boy. But the youngster squirmed free. Luke shook his fist at him. "You try that again, younger, and I'll pull down yer pants an' paddle yer backside!"

"Good fer you, Abraham," the fat woman said, laughing so hard her chins shook like gelatin and her enormous breasts moved like sacks of flour. "Now, you clear out of here like I said."

"Lady," Luke said pleadingly, "I've got to have that barrel o' beets. It's my duty. I'll pay you ten dollars for it."

She shook her head stubbornly, uprighted the barrel and sat on it, panting from the effort. "You ain't gettin' it," she said, spreading her skirts around the barrel.

"Then I'm gonna have to take it," Luke said warningly. "I'm tryin' to be perlite, but if I have to, the general says I can use force." He pointed to the wagon. "We got loaded muskets and bayonets . . ."

Turning to the boy, the woman said, "Get me my pitchfork, Abraham." At once the little boy ran to the barn and returned with a glittering pitchfork. Luke and Nate could see the tines had been recently sharpened. The woman arose with the pitchfork held in front of her. She walked menacingly toward them.

"Git!" she growled. "Git off of my farm or I'll put so many holes in you you'll think yer a Swiss cheese."

Astonished, Luke and Nate began backing away. They clambered up on the wagon box, watching the fat woman warily. Nate reached for his musket.

"Shall I shoot over her head to scare her?" he whispered.

"Hell, no! She don't look like much of a scaredy-cat. And I ain't shootin' no woman. Let's git outta here." Luke flicked the horse's back lightly with the reins. "Giddap," he called, and the wagon began to move. Turning, he called to the fat woman. "Keep yer beets, fatso. Have 'em fer lunch. Then mebbe you kin eat a cow fer dinner." Chuckling, Luke drove back to the road and turned right.

They rode on in silence for about a half hour, when they came to another, larger farmhouse on the same side of the road. Luke turned up the path. A red-haired girl of about nineteen ran down the farmhouse steps to aim a musket at them. Flabbergasted, Luke and Nate threw up their hands. The girl hesitated, slowly lowering her weapon.

"Oh, you're Americans," she said. "I thought you were Hessians. They come out from Germantown to rape and rob the farm people." She stared at them sullenly, and Nate saw that she had eyes so blue they were almost purple. "What do you want?" she asked in a guarded voice.

"Food," Luke said. "Congress has given General Washington the power to seize all the supplies he needs. I'll pay you for it."

"I can't give you any. We don't have enough for ourselves."

Luke studied the neatly kept farmhouse behind her and the sturdy barn to her left and shook his head in disbelief. "Mind if I check the premises?" he asked.

"Yes, I do," she snapped, lifting the musket again.

"Don't do nothin' foolish, honey," Luke said, reaching for his musket. "We got guns, too, and I think we know how to use 'em better 'n you do. Where's yer pa? I can talk more reasonable with a man."

"Pa's dead," the red-haired girl said in a dull voice. "He was killed at the Brandywine."

"Yer pa was a sojer?"

"No. He was a farmer. He led Washington out of Howe's trap, but he was killed doing it. After Pa died, I moved up here with my sick aunt. That's why I can't give you any food. There's barely enough for the two of us."

Nate saw movement in the woods behind the barn. At first, he thought the black-and-white dappled animals were horses, but then he realized that they were cows.

"Are those your cattle in the woods?" he asked the girl.

"Don't you touch our cows!" the girl exclaimed. "That's all my aunt and I have to live on. We get our milk and butter and cheese from them. Leave them alone!"

"Butter, huh?" Luke grunted, jumping to the ground. "Most folks don't eat plain butter. They puts it on bread. Which means flour. Where you hidin' the flour, honey?" The girl bit her lip and said nothing. Luke tried to walk around her, but she interposed her body between him and the front steps.

"Don't you dare!" she cried fiercely, her blue eyes blazing. "You leave my poor aunt alone!"

"Hold it, Luke," Nate said, studying the aroused redhead with interest. "Don't do anything until I check those cows."

Nate trotted toward the woods. The March thaw was underway and his feet sank into the soft ground. He could hear gurgling water ahead of him and guessed that a brook ran through the woods. That was where he found the two cows, drinking from a shallow little stream. He stopped to study them, and felt a pair of soft hands cover his eyes and a shy voice behind him say:

"Guess who?"

Nate laughed. "What's who's name?"

"Winnie."

"I say it's Winnie," he said, and she dropped her hands. Nate turned to look into her purplish eyes.

"Please don't take our cows, soldier," Winnie murmured, dropping her eyes and then raising them invitingly. She came a half step toward him.

Nate put his arms around her and kissed her on the mouth. She stuck out her tongue. Nate slid his own tongue into her mouth and she darted hers in and out, still clinging to him.

Nate swung her into the air and carried her to a pile of leaves beneath a beech tree. He lay down beside her, caressing her passionately. She returned his ardor, breathing hard. Nate slid his hand beneath her petticoat and began undoing her knickers. She sat up. "Let me do it," Winnie said, panting. She slipped them off and lay down, her white legs spread and her red-haired crotch inviting him. Nate took off his breeches and knelt between her legs. He gasped in incredulous delight. She was so small and tight! Her organ seemed to possess the power of grasping. It seized and released . . . seized and released his penis during the rhythm of the act. Now he knew what Luke Sawyer meant when he talked about a "snapping pussy." Nate had never before experienced such sexual delectation and when he reached his climax he moaned so loud in ecstasy that the squirming girl beneath him put up her hand to cover his mouth.

A few moments later, Nate arose and put his breeches back on. Winnie slipped into her knickers. She stood up, blushing as she looked at Nate. He glanced at the brook and saw that the cows were gone.

"Looks like I can't find any cattle," he muttered, taking her hand. "But I've got to keep looking, you know. Do you mind if I come back every now and then to look for them?"

"Not if you don't find them," Winnie said, squeezing his hand.

Nate and Luke were disappointed in their first day of foraging. Riding down the road for another two hours they found most of the farmhouses deserted. Two of them were burned to the ground along with their barns. At one of them the embers were still smoking. They rode up to it, drawn by the unearthly buzzing noise of clouds of black flies. The bodies of an elderly man and woman lay on the ground. They had been shot and bayoneted. Swarms of greedy flies had formed cones above their wounds.

"Hessians, God damn their souls!" Luke swore. "That's why the farms are deserted. What the hell did they need to kill an old farmer and his wife for?"

"Shall we bury them?" Nate asked.

Luke glanced around him. "I don't see any shovels. They probably stole 'em."

"We can cover them with stones, then," Nate said. Luke

nodded and they began piling stones over the corpses, cursing and flailing their arms at the flies that flew into their eyes and mouths and ears. A half-hour later they remounted the box and started riding back the way they had come.

Near Winnie's farmhouse, Nate put a hand on Luke's wrist. "Hold it, Luke—I think I heard someone screaming." The horse stopped and the two soldiers cocked their heads toward the farm.

"You sure did!" Luke said. "C'mon, let's get up there fast."

Nate reached behind him to seize their muskets. Struggling to keep his balance in the swaying, clattering wagon, he made certain they were loaded and primed. He tested the bayonets to be sure they were in place. Coming in view of the farmhouse, they saw a cart piled high with food and household belongings. There was a mattress and a pair of brass candlesticks, an enameled clock, a fireplace bellows, two sacks of flour, smoked hams, kettles, pots and pans, jugs of cider, lanterns—in fact, most of the contents of Winnie's farmhouse. In front of the barn stood two horses with green saddlecloths and carbines stuck in holsters. From behind it, the screams became muffled.

Both men jumped down and sprinted for behind the barn. Nate was the first to get there. He saw Winnie sprawled on the ground with her skirt over her head and her legs thrown open. He could see her red-haired crotch. A grinning Hessian jaeger in a green coat held her down while a second green-coated cavalryman knelt between her legs unbuttoning his breeches. His erect penis came jackknifing out of his fly and he seized it in his hand and moved toward Winnie with a shout of anticipatory delight. He did not see Nate, but his comrade did.

Drawing his saber, the jaeger sprang to his feet and raised the blade over his head. Nate took aim and fired. The bullet struck the Hessian between the eyes, spinning him around. His saber flew into the air and Nate caught it as it came down. Wheeling, he confronted the rapist who was now on his feet. With a single swift slash, Nate cut off the man's penis. It fell to the ground, beginning to shrink. The emasculated man clutched his crotch in agony. Horror dilated his bright blue eyes. He opened his mouth to scream just as Luke Sawyer's bayonet plunged into it and came out the other side of his neck.

Ten silent, stunning seconds—and it was all over.

Nate knelt beside Winnie. She had sat up in time to see what happened to the jaeger who had tried to ravish her. She had covered her eyes and fainted. Nate pulled her skirt back to cover her nakedness. He arose and walked over to Luke, who had brutally kicked the rapist's penis into the bushes.

"Let the pigs eat it," Luke growled. "In fact, we oughta leave 'em both fer the pigs."

Nate shook his head. "I know they had it coming to them. But they are Christians, just like ourselves. I think we should bury them."

"Christians! That wasn't a very Christian thing you done to him with that saber, Natey. What's all this tender talk about buryin' 'em?"

Nate motioned toward the unconscious girl on the ground. "Do you want Winnie and her sick aunt to do it? We can't just leave them here."

"If you put it that way," Luke grumbled, walking toward the barn. "I'll get a couple shovels."

Winnie did not awake until after the two soldiers had dug a shallow grave and dragged the bodies into it. She came unsteadily to her feet and walked toward them, weeping softly. Nate put his arm around her, but she pushed him away. With reddened eyes she stared at the two dead Hessians lying in their graves.

"They . . . they look like sleeping babies," she whispered. She put her hand to her throat. "I know they were terrible men. Robbers and rapists . . . But they're . . . they're only boys. . . . Their mothers must have loved them. And now . . . so far away from home . . . they're dead . . ." Winnie gave a sob and turned away. Luke shoved his shovel into the pile of dirt beside the graves. Winnie turned back to him. "Haven't . . . haven't you got something to cover their faces with? I mean . . . you're not just going to throw dirt on their faces?"

Luke Sawyer shook his head, staring at the girl in astonishment. Winnie turned to Nate. "Let me have that sword." Astounded himself, Nate handed it to her. Winnie took it and walked to a tree. She stood behind it, sawing on her petticoat with the saber. She came back with two squares of white linen in her hand. Kneeling beside the dead Hessians, she tenderly covered their faces with the cloth.

"There," she said, getting to her feet, and Nate and Luke began shoveling dirt onto the bodies. Winnie watched them in silence. After they had finished, she handed Nate the saber.

"You didn't have to do what you did," she said to Nate. "I know you saved me from . . . from . . . Maybe even death besides . . . But you didn't have to do that. It was hideous. I saw it," she said, covering her eyes. She began to sob. "I'll always see it. I'll never forget it." She removed her hands and stared steadily at Nate. Her purplish eyes were cold, now. "You said you were coming back to see me. Please don't. I couldn't think of it. Not after what you did." She turned and walked slowly back to the farmhouse, her shoulders shaking with her sobs.

Nate watched her go with sad, moist eyes. "The better I get to know women," he muttered, "the more I realize I don't understand them."

Nate and Luke returned to their wagon. They passed the Hessian's cart. Luke put his hand on the sacks of flour and gazed inquiringly at Nate. Nate shook his head. Luke could see there were tears in his eyes.

"Awright, fergit it," Luke mumbled, remounting the box. "God damn it, Natey, I told you we wasn't gonna like this duty."

Chapter Twenty-Three

Although George Washington had developed a paternal affection for the young Marquis de Lafayette, the European volunteer whose services he prized most was Lieutenant General Baron Freidrich von Steuben. Steuben arrived in Valley Forge with the reputation of having been aide to King Frederick of Prussia. Actually, he had served only briefly in the Prussian Army, where his last rank had been that of captain. But Steuben was also a protégé of the Comte de Vergennes who, recognizing his ability and the fact that the Americans were impressed by titles, invested him with a counterfeit nobility and sent him to the United States on the ship bearing the first of Caron de Beaumarchais's shipments of munitions. Steuben made his way to Congress, where he received his lieutenant general's commission and thence to Valley Forge.

Washington's pale eyes shone with delight when Colonel Gill brought Steuben into his presence. "At last!" he exclaimed. "A real Prussian drillmaster! Next to long-term enlistments, General Steuben, an officer of your experience has been the desire closest to my heart."

"Dank you," Steuben said in his guttural broken English.

"Do you think you can make professionals of my soldiers?" Washington asked eagerly. "Have you seen them?"

Steuben's eyes gleamed. "Ach! I have seen dem. Dey have der spirit superb! No troops in Europe could ever endure what your soldiers are suffering in dis blace." Then he rolled his eyes and rubbed his big nose dubiously. "But dere discipline! Ach, dey are anarchy in motion. Every man guiding on himself. But I dink I can drain dem."

"Excellent."

"I gan't give dem der Europen drill, General. It iss too gomplicated. I vill draw up a drill more suited to der American demperament." Steuben's eyes twinkled. "I must make allowances for der famous American spirit of independence."

Washington scowled. "By Jehovah, that's the one thing I don't want encouraged. Some of my soldiers are too damned independent. Especially the backwoodsmen. They don't like to see their comrades locked in the guardhouse and sometimes they take steps to set them free. You won't have an easy task, General. Why, almost all of the state militia have different drills. If you can draw up a single, simple, uniform drill and train my army in it, you will have done as much for the cause of freedom as any man in America. I tell you," he said, reaching for a nut in the bowl on his desk and cracking it between his palms, "if I can command troops who can march and countermarch on the battlefield like Howe's regulars, I can finally seek decisive battle."

"Don't vorry, General," Steuben said, rising to his feet. "I vill giff you such an army." He turned to Colonel Gill. "Could you giff me one gompany each from three different states?"

Daniel nodded. "Of course. You can have Captain Walker's company and one each from the Delaware and Maryland lines."

"Goot," Steuben said. "I vill vait for dem on der parade ground."

Fifteen minutes later, the three companies came marching onto the parade ground, forming in front of the waiting drillmaster. In the front rank of Captain Walker's company, Nate Gill stared in curiosity at the general with the big nose and the uniform coat plastered with orders and decorations. Suddenly, Steuben straightened and roared an order. At once, Nate's company brought their muskets crashing down to order arms, the Delawares brought theirs up to right shoulder arms and the Marylanders slouched at ease. A roar of laughter rose from the assembled companies and Steuben shook his head in despair.

"Dumpkoffs!" he shouted, lapsing into the mixture of German, French and bastard English that soon became familiar to the troops at Valley Forge. "God damn de *gaucheries* of dese *badauds*. *Je ne puis plus*. Dake dem away, Captain Valkaire, *mon ami, mon bon ami. Sacre!* I gan gurse dem no more!"

Chuckling, the American troops shambled off in the loose,

free-swinging style that Washington detested so. But General
von Steuben had them back on the parade ground next day,
and day after day thereafter, standing in the mud or rain,
cursing them, waving his arms, howling tirelessly until at last
he had drilled some semblance of order and uniformity into
them. Steuben even compelled the American officers to drill
their men personally.

"But we don't do that, General," Captain Walker protested. "We let the sergeants do it."

"Ach, der sergeants, vhile der officers live in der fancy
houses far avay from der smelly huts of der men. Dis iss a
republican army? Iss it der sergeants who lead der men in
battle, or iss it der officers? *Viens,* Valkaire, *mon ami,* you
drill der men like I dell you to."

Shrugging, Captain Walker strode out in front of his company. "Commm—panee!" he called. "Tennn-shun!" Nate and
his comrades snapped smartly to attention. "Right shoul-
deh—ahms!" With a single brisk slapping sound, they shouldered their muskets. "Forrrward—march!" In a single
motion, Walker's soldiers stepped off on their left feet and
went marching smartly down the parade ground.

"Column right—march!" Nate swung sharply to his right,
marking time while the other ranks made the turn. Now Captain Walker was counting cadence. "Three, four, your left!
Your left, your left! Left oblique, march!" A solid unbroken
mass, the company angled a half-step to its left. "Right oblique,
march!" Still a solid phalanx, Walker's soldiers swerved
a half-step right. "Three, four, your left! Your left, your
left!" Nate Gill felt his heart swelling with pride. At last they
were marching like true soldiers! He felt his entire being
merging with the formation of marching men. His individual-
ity seemed to have been lost in that impersonal but purposeful
mass. "To the rear, march! To the rear, march!" Without
thinking, he about faced and about faced again. "Right flank,
march!" Again, the voice touched his brain and he turned immediately right, the entire company instantly changing direction with him. "Left flank, march! Column right, march! To
the rear, march! To the rear, march! Compannnee, halt!"
One, two—with a single clicking of heels, the company came
to an immediate halt.

General von Steuben was clapping his hands in delight. He
was surrounded by dozens of officers who had been drawn to

the parade ground by the spectacle of a company of American soldiers marching like British regulars.

"*Sacre*, Valkaire! *Dese badauds* are *dumpkoffs* no more. Dey are *soldiers!* I gongratulate you, gentlemen," he said, addressing the smiling officers around him. "Ve vill celebrate der birth of der American Army tonight at my quarters. Salamanders und firecake!" he cried, his eyes twinkling. "Moldy beef und old potatoes. Ve is druly a republican army and ve vill eat vat der men eat."

"Are we all invited, General?" Captain Walker asked.

"Everyvun! Everyvun who has der breeches mit der seat vorn out. Ve vill celebrate Valley Forge style and form der immortal Society of der *Sans Culottes*."

"I don't speak French, General," Walker said. "What does *sans culottes* mean?"

Baron von Steuben's eyes twinkled and he winked and smiled, and said:

"Mittout pants."

Chapter Twenty-Four

In the spring of 1778, General Sir William Howe was notified by Lord George Germain that the recall he sought so eagerly had been granted. Howe was still in Philadelphia, and he immediately sent for Sir Henry Clinton.

"I am returning to England," Sir William said after Clinton took his seat opposite him. "And I can tell you, my dear Henry, I shall be delighted to be relieved of this painful service. I only came here on the direct orders of the king. I should not have come for the War Office alone. My brother, Dick, and I have always been fond of the Americans. After our oldest brother, Gussie, was killed at Ticonderoga in fifty-eight, the Americans erected a statue to him in Westminster Abbey."

"I understand," Clinton said quietly, wondering if this might explain his chief's repeated failures to destroy Washington. "When are you leaving?"

"In May. The chief command will then fall to you. I recommended you to Germain in the highest terms."

"That was most kind of you," Clinton murmured, arising to make his departure.

Returning to his quarters, Clinton spoke to his aide, Captain John André. "Sir William is going home in May. I will be taking his place."

"Congratulations, Sir Henry!" the handsome young captain exclaimed.

"Yes. Things do seem to have turned out rather conveniently. It was all Sir William's doing. I say, André, let's give him a jolly good send-off."

"Of course! An extravaganza! A ball! A gala!"

"Quite. You handle it, André. Spare no expense. Sir William must be made to remember our gratitude."

"I will indeed, sir. Rely on it, it will not be ordinary—just another gala. We'll have something so special . . . unique, even . . . by George, I've got it! We'll call it the *Michianza.* That's the Italian word for medley. It will be a medley of themes, sir. Italian Rennaissance . . . the Middle Ages with jousting knights . . . and yes, by George, even a Turkish motif. . . . I'll get busy on it right away."

By May 18, 1778, the date set for the *Michianza,* Captain John André had pressed most of General Howe's army and half of Admiral Howe's navy into service for his grand fete. He had assembled an enormous regatta of three divisions. They were gathered at Knight's Wharf at the northern extremity of Philadelphia, and were to sail downriver to the splendid Wharton Mansion-house. In the lead were three large flatboats with a military band playing lively martial airs in each. Next was the galley of honor bearing Sir William Howe, Lord Richard Howe and Sir Henry Clinton, together with the officers of their suites and some ladies. Amanda Courtney was among the ladies. She did not attend Sir William, who was in full dress, because of the military nature of the *Michianza.* Joel was with her. He wore the uniform of a colonel of the Loyalist Queen's Rangers. Amanda had struggled hard to suppress a smile when she joined Joel in the drawing room of their home in Philadelphia. His short dark green jacket ended halfway down his huge paunch, making it seem as though he carried a pillow beneath it. Amanda herself was gorgeously dressed in a scarlet and white satin gown sewn all over with pearls. Around her neck were Jennifer's pearls. Joel had stared in mild surprise at the necklace. "Where'd you get those pearls?" he grunted.

"Silly, you gave them to me," Amanda lied.

"I did? That's strange. I don't remember buying anything that expensive. They must have cost me something, I can tell you." Amanda said nothing, relying on Joel's preoccupation with the coming feast to take his mind off the pearls.

Lord Cornwallis's galley, with his lordship, General Knyphausen and three British generals, their officers and ladies, brought up the rear. Around the entire concourse of gaily decorated ships rowed six barges of soldiers to keep off the civilian boats that swarmed on every side of the procession.

Meanwhile, transports from Lord Howe's fleet were anchored
in the river from end to end of the city. Far downriver near
the Wharton Mansion-house lay the admiral's flagship, *Roebuck*, with his flag fluttering from the fore-topmast head.

Suddenly, *Roebuck* fired a signal gun. At once the seamen
in the regatta stopped rowing and lay on their oars. The
bands began to play "God Save the King." With one gigantic
voice, the revelers aboard the boats of the regatta, the on-
lookers in the civilian boats and the multitudes lining both
shores began to sing. After they had finished, three thunderous
cheers burst from their lips.

"Hip, hip—hurray!"

"Hip, hip—hurray!"

"Hip, hip—hurray!"

Lord Howe's barge pushed out from the Wharton shore
and *Vigilant* boomed a seventeen-gun salute. The Howes and
Clinton stepped into the barge, followed by their entourage—and the *Michianza* had begun.

"Isn't it thrilling?" Amanda whispered to Joel, as they
disembarked. "Oh, see the triumphal arches! They're in my
Billy's honor."

"Yes, and your Billy is going home—curse the luck." Joel
stared morosely at the lines of grenadiers forming the avenue
through which they passed. Behind them were light horsemen
on mounts prancing gaily to the music, now provided by the
massed bands of the entire army. Joel looked eagerly toward
the huge park opening ahead of him, hoping to see sideboards loaded with food. But he saw only more troops and
two pavilions facing each other across a lawn evidently
prepared for a medieval tournament. In the front of each pavilion sat seven beautiful young ladies, all daughters of the
principal Tories of Philadelphia. They wore Turkish bloomers
of bright-colored silks and in their turbans were favors with
which they intended to reward the British officers who were
jousting in their honor. Joel and Amanda sat behind them in
the pavilion dedicated to the Knights of the Burning Mountain. Amanda peered eagerly below her at the maidens in
their Turkish habits.

"Oh, my goodness, I don't see the Shippen girls. Aren't
they coming?"

"No." Joel grunted, still searching the park for signs of

food. "Edward Shippen wouldn't let his daughters come. He didn't like the idea of their wearing Turkish bloomers."

"How mean! The old spoilsport. And Peggy is so beautiful. They say she's in love with Captain André. Oh, there he is!" Amanda cried, pointing to the Pavilion of the Blended Rose opposite them. "Isn't he *handsome?*"

John André was indeed a dashing figure in black lace and satin and orange velvet, seated astride a splendid sleek horse evidently trained in the intricate motions of the drill ring.

"My God, look at those costumes!" Joel grumbled. "They must have cost a fortune. I hear André spent twenty thousand dollars on the Turkish habits alone. It's a scandal the way the army throws the king's money around."

Seeing Captain André made Amanda think of Benjie. She wondered, now that General Howe was leaving, if General Clinton would terminate Dr. Gill's dangerous mission among the Yankees and allow him to return to British lines.

"What do you think of General Clinton?" she asked Joel.

"Seems to be an excellent soldier. Nothing like Howe, of course. Cold. Aloof and withdrawn. No chance of any relationship there."

"Oh, you! Don't you think of me as anything but a tool?"

"Clinton's taking the army back to New York," Joel continued with a scowl, ignoring Amanda's question. "Germain's orders. The War Office got word France is sending a big fleet to America. Germain's afraid the French could bottle up Lord Howe's ships in the Delaware and catch Clinton in between themselves and Washington. So he's going back to New York."

Amanda gasped in dismay. "But what's to become of us?"

"I'm to command a regiment on Long Island. Organize the Cowboys there."

"Cowboys?"

"Loyalists who steal cows from the Rebels and sell them to Clinton. The Rebels have raised a band of ruffians to oppose them. Call themselves the Skinners. There's also a prisoner-of-war camp in my command." His thick lips twisted in a greedy smile. "I'm to contract with the British army for the prison food. Piece of cake."

"How dull," Amanda said, pouting. "Philadelphia is such fun."

"Not without the British Army, it won't be."

From the opposite pavilion came the pealing of trumpets and a party of officers dressed as medieval knights in white and red silk mounted on gray horses caparisoned in the same colors came trotting into the arena. To either side of them walked their esquires bearing their lances and shields. The chief Knight of the Blended Rose was attended by two young black slaves with sashes and pantaloons of blue and white silk, their torsos bare and each with a large silver clasp around his neck. One by one the Blended Rose knights rode past their pavilion, each bowing to the young lady for whose favor they were entering the lists. Another blast of trumpets signaled the arrival of their herald, who rode into the center of the arena to shout:

"The Knights of the Blended Rose, by me, their herald, proclaim and assert that the Ladies of the Blended Rose excel in wit, beauty and every accomplishment those of the whole world. Should any knight or knights be so hardy as to dispute or deny it, they are ready to enter the list with them, and maintain their assertions by deeds of arms, according to the laws of ancient chivalry."

To fresh blasts of the trumpets, the challenge was repeated twice more, after which the Knights of the Burning Mountain made their entry in costumes of black and orange and issued their challenge. The chief of the Blended Rose threw down his gauntlet, the Burning Mountain chief picked it up, the opposing knights took their shields and lances from their esquires and galloped off to opposite ends of the lawn.

"Oh, I hope they don't hurt each other!" Amanda burst out anxiously. "Those lances look terribly sharp and they don't have any armor on."

"Rubbish!" Joel snorted. "The lances are paper toys and the shields are made of tinfoil."

Once again, the trumpets pealed and the knights came thundering down the lawn to shiver their lances against each other. They rode back, returned at a gallop and fired their pistols into the air. Charging a third time, they actually fought each other with their swords, the clanging of their steel echoing and reverberating around the park. At last they were separated and the tournament was over.

Now the knights dismounted. Preceded by their squires they passed through the first triumphal arch in Sir William's

honor and down an avenue a hundred yards long lined with
British soldiers and the colors of all of Howe's units planted
at regular intervals. Once more, the bands began to play. The
second triumphal arch opened on a garden, and a flight of
steps from the garden led into a spacious, carpeted hall. Joel
Courtney's eyes lighted up when he saw black slaves in blue-
and-white silk moving among the company with silver trays.
But once again he was disappointed.

"Lemonade!" he snorted. "Tea! When am I going to get
something to eat? I'm famished."

From the hall, the party moved up another flight of stairs
to an enormous ballroom decorated in blue and rose-pink,
the walls festooned with natural flowers. Scores upon scores
of gilded mirrors reflected the colors of the decorations and
the uniforms and dresses of the officers and their ladies.
Candles burned on dozens of branch candelabra. Amanda
was transported with delight. She turned to speak to Joel and
found that he had left her side. She saw him disappearing
into one of four drawing rooms opening off the ballroom and
guessed immediately that he had found the food. Amanda
was not disappointed at being left alone, because now the
dancing had begun and she had succeeded in attracting the
attention of Captain André. With a bow, he asked her to
dance, and they moved out onto the floor.

"Congratulations, John," Amanda murmured, "my husband was just telling me of your promotion."

"Yes, thank you, Mrs. Courtney, it will be Major André
from now on."

"You're so young to be the adjutant general of a British
army," Amanda said, drawing closer. "General Clinton must
think a lot of you."

"Really, that's very kind of you . . ."

"I do hope the general will do something about Dr. Benjamin Gill."

"Beg pardon?"

"He's been so long among the Yankees. Really, one won-
ders how much longer his luck can hold out."

"Indeed."

"Dr. Gill is so anxious to serve his majesty under his true
colors."

"Quite."

"I'm sure that just a word or two from you, John, on Dr. Gill's behalf—"

There was a thunderous explosion outside the mansion and the ballroom was illuminated by flashes of light. Amanda's eyes widened in fear, but André merely chuckled and took her by the hand.

"Don't be alarmed, Mrs. Courtney," he said, evidently relieved to change the subject, "it's the fireworks display. Allow me." Laying her hand on his wrist, Amanda permitted André to escort her to the windows thrown open for the exhibition.

Fiery rockets arched through the night, exploding with showers of stars. The sky was slashed and crisscrossed with streaks of yellow, red, blue and green. From the throngs gathered on both sides of the river rose choruses of "Oooh!" and "Ahhh!" Gradually the display rose in sound and fury until, at the conclusion of twenty different exhibitions, the heavens were alight and thundering with an uninterrupted stream of rockets, the interior of the triumphal arch was illuminated with exploding bombs, its wings spouted Chinese fountains and the figure of Fame appeared at the top blowing showers of sparks from her trumpet.

At midnight a trumpet blew and huge folding doors hitherto unnoticed were swung open revealing a magnificent saloon 240 feet by 40 and 22 feet high. Three alcoves on each side served as sideboards on which the food and wine for a sumptuous meal were heaped. Tables draped in white linen gleamed with the silver of fine flatware and 430 different covers and were riotous with the color of fine china for twelve hundred diners. There were one hundred silver candelabras of three lights each and three hundred wax tapers lighting the tables. Overhead hung eighteen lustres of twenty-four candles each, their flames making points on the cheekbones of twenty-four black slaves in oriental dresses with silver collars and bracelets, bending to the ground at the approach of General Howe and Admiral Howe.

"Now, this is something worth spending money for," Joel Courtney murmured as he took his seat next to Amanda and unfolded his napkin. Amanda did not hear him. Her eyes were on Sir William at the head of their table. Catching sight of her, the general bowed graciously and lifted his glass. Smiling happily, Amanda lifted her own and drank.

After supper, Sir William led Amanda back to the ballroom where dancing was resumed. Major André watched her with a mixture of pity and amusement in his eyes. "I feel sorry for the Sultana," he said to the young lady beside him. "After tomorrow, she's just plain Mrs. Joel Courtney again."

Chapter Twenty-Five

Major General Charles Lee had been exchanged. He returned to the American encampment full of his customary hauteur and disdain for American troops, and was immediately invited by Baron von Steuben to review the new army. Among the troops he chose for the march-past were those of Captain Arthur Walker's company.

Marching in matchless unison, their left arms swinging and their gleaming bayoneted muskets on their right shoulders, the American soldiers swung briskly past the two generals on the reviewing stand.

"Eyes right!" Captain Walker called.

In a single motion, the men of his company swiveled their heads in the direction of the stand. Luke Sawyer's eye fell on General Lee and he groaned under his breath.

"The king of the canines is back," he whispered to Nate Gill just as Captain Walker bellowed, "Eyes front!" and the heads swiveled back again.

After the review was over, Steuben glanced inquiringly at Lee, who was bending his riding crop. "Vell, Cheneral?"

"Oh, I don't doubt there's been some improvement," Lee said with a supercilious smile. "But you can't really expect these ragged fellows to compete with European troops."

"Compete mitt dem? Dey'll beat dem!"

"Rubbish, my dear Baron. Why, the light infantry would march circles around them."

Steuben smiled maliciously. "Dat's strange," he said musingly. "Only last veek Lafayette led der same troops in a reconnaissance-in-force around Philadelphia. Clinton tried to trap him mitt der light infantry and der liddle marquis made der monkey out of him."

"Rubbish!" Lee snapped again. "Pure, unadulterated rubbish. There aren't any troops in the world that can stand up to the light infantry."

General von Steuben rubbed his long nose with twinkling eyes. "Maybe you vould like it better yet if der men vas dogs already," he said, just as a courier mounted the stand, saluted and said, "General Washington desires you to report to his quarters immediately." At once, the two officers descended the steps, mounted their horses and rode off to the commander-in-chief's quarters. They found Washington in a council of war with Greene, Wayne and Stirling. Colonel Daniel Gill and the Marquis de Lafayette were also present. Washington nodded coolly as General Lee entered the room. He had not been overjoyed to see him back. Washington's informants in Philadelphia had told him that Lee had passed much of his time in captivity instructing his captors on how to defeat the Americans.

"Clinton is leaving Philadelphia for New York," he announced. "Today he put about three thousand Tories aboard Lord Howe's ships and sent them down the Delaware. He wants to get out of Philadelphia before Comte d'Estaing arrives with the French fleet. So he'll be leading most of his army across New Jersey tomorrow. Any suggestions, gentlemen?"

"Why not try to beat him to New York?" Lee asked.

Washington shook his head. "We don't have enough boats to get us across the Delaware as fast as Clinton can. Besides, Clinton is making for Sandy Hook where Howe's ships will lift him across the harbor to New York. We could never beat him marching overland." Washington's pale eyes shone with confidence as he studied the sober faces of his commanders. "It is my plan to pursue. Hang on Clinton's tail until the opportunity arises to strike his rear guard. He's bound to be strung out for miles before he reaches Sandy Hook. What do you say, gentlemen?"

Silently, with the exception of General Lee, who sat lounging in his chair with his thin legs crossed, the officers nodded in agreement.

On the morning of June 27, 1778, General Sir Henry Clinton crossed the Delaware and began marching for Sandy Hook. Washington followed him. That night, with his forces strung out for a dozen miles, Clinton stopped to bivouac at

Monmouth Court House. In the morning, he began marching again—leaving a covering force of between fifteen hundred and two thousand men behind him.

"Now is the time," Washington said to his generals gathered around him in a horseback council of war. "We can cut off Clinton's rear guard."

"I disagree," General Charles Lee declared vehemently. "Clinton will double back and smash us."

"Not before we have cut his line of march," Washington said quietly. He stared reflectively at Lee. He still distrusted him, but Lee was the second-ranking general in the army. It would be an insult to offer command of the operation to anyone else. "Please lead the advanced corps forward, General Lee. I will follow with the main body."

"I must decline the honor," Lee replied haughtily. He glanced disdainfully at what appeared to be a ridiculously small number of units forming the advanced corps. "After all, one does not ask one's second-ranking general to command a corporal's guard."

Washington flushed in momentary anger. He turned to Lafayette sitting his horse next to him. "Please take command of the advanced corps," he said to him, and Lafayette urged his mount forward. To Lee's surprise, more and more units marched up to follow the marquis. They stirred up choking, billowing clouds of dust. Eventually, about five thousand profusely sweating soldiers had assembled in Lafayette's corps. With a mumbled apology to Washington, General Charles Lee rode forward to supersede the young Frenchman.

Lee had no battle plan. He proposed merely to strike the British rear guard but he gave no instructions to his subordinates as to how it was to be done. Soon, the Americans moving east along the road became an uncoordinated mass. Some of them began sniping at scarlet coats visible through the trees. The British fired back. Then the sniping exchange spread and individual fights between units flared. Lee ordered Lafayette to attack the British left. Declaring that he was not yet in position to attack, the Frenchman began moving his troops to the right. The movement unmasked other divisions which began falling back. Lafayette also withdrew and Charles Lee gave the order for a general retreat.

"Kee—rist, I thought we come here to fight," Luke Sawyer

grumbled. He tied a handkerchief over his mouth and nostrils
to keep out the dust raised by the retiring soldiers. Suddenly,
he seized Nate Gill's arm and pointed down the road. "Oh,
oh, here comes trouble," he whispered.

Luke was pointing at the figure of George Washington
galloping down on General Charles Lee. Mounted on a beautiful great white horse given him only that day by Governor
Livingston of New Jersey, his face livid, trembling with anger, Washington drew rein beside Lee in a cloud of dust.

"You God damned poltroon!" Washington roared. "What's
the meaning of this retreat? Who gave the order?"

"I did," Lee replied coldly. "If I hadn't, Clinton would
have destroyed the advanced corps. Furthermore, I demand
an apology for your insulting language."

"I don't want a retreat, God damn you! I sent you here to
fight, not to run! Get to the rear! The only apology you'll
hear from me is to my country for trusting you too long."

Wheeling, Washington rode down the road toward the last
two American regiments. As he did, he saw dust clouds rising
into the sky behind the British and guessed that Clinton had
come to the rescue of his rear guard. Grinding his teeth,
Washington halted the retreating Americans and ordered
them to turn and hold the British while he re-formed his
army behind them.

Riding back to his main body, he selected high ground
near a ravine and put Stirling on the left, Greene on the right
and himself in the middle. Behind him holding a second line
was Lafayette, while Wayne held an outpost to Washington's
front.

Cheering, the British struck at the American left. The
battle raged for an hour, with as many men fainting from the
fatigue caused by the hundred-degree heat as fell from enemy fire. Sitting his horse like the splendid equestrian figure
he was, Washington watched the battle anxiously. The British
seemed to be penetrating. Washington swung his riding crop
in the signal for his reserve to strike the British right. Instantly, marching like veteran professionals, two regiments
wheeled into line under fire. They began working around the
British right, forcing them to withdraw.

Next, Clinton struck the American right. He sent his finest
troops against Greene's soldiers. Lord Cornwallis personally
led the assault. But volley after volley of American musketry

thickened by the shot of an artillery crossfire sprinkled the battlefield with crumpled redcoats and the British withdrew.

While Cornwallis was engaged, Clinton hurled his grenadiers against Wayne's frontal outpost. They were led by Lieutenant Colonel Henry Monckton.

"Forward to the charge, my brave grenadiers!" Monckton cried, waving his sword toward the Americans. At once, bugles blew and the grenadiers in their red coats and bearskins surged forward.

"Steady, men, steady!" General Wayne called. "Wait for the word, then pick out the king-birds."

At forty yards, Wayne shouted: "Fire!"

Smoke and flame crashed out from the American line. The grenadiers were scythed to the ground. But the survivors came on. Nate Gill felt his musket recoil into his shoulder and knelt to reload. Already, gunsmoke was drifting into his eyes. By the time he had reloaded, the charging redcoats were ten yards away. Nate fired again. Beside him Luke Sawyer fired. Colonel Monckton clutched his breast and fell, his head almost touching the American parapet. His battalion colors fluttered to the ground from the hand of a stricken grenadier. Luke Sawyer leaped over the parapet to seize the dying Monckton and drag him inside the American position. Nate followed to grab the British colors.

"Won't Jenny love it when she sees her new tablecloth?" Nate chortled, draping the huge flag around his body. Suddenly, the order came from General Wayne:

"Cease fire!"

Clinton was withdrawing all along the line, and the Battle of Monmouth, the last of the northern battles, was over.

Chapter Twenty-Six

After the British left Philadelphia and the Patriots returned, General Washington appointed General Benedict Arnold as military commander of the city. At first, Arnold was chagrined. His fiery, passionate nature aspired to field command only: to glory. But then, upon reflection, he saw in the command of America's largest, wealthiest city the opportunity to enrich himself. Moreover, the wound suffered at Saratoga had not healed properly and Arnold was compelled to hobble about on crutches. Field command was then an impossibility.

So he accepted, and rode through Philadelphia through tumultuously cheering crowds in a procession led by town notables and a regiment of militia.

It had been Arnold's plan to capitalize on the scarcity of European goods in America brought about by the British blockade. Philadelphia, however, because of the British occupation, was crammed with foreign luxuries. It occurred to Arnold that he could buy up these goods and sell them elsewhere in the country at enormous profits. To do so, he could use the smuggling ship *Charming Nancy*, in which he held a half-interest. When Arnold had been officer-of-the day at Valley Forge, he had given permission to its owner, Robert Shewell, to sail the ship from the Delaware to another port, where she could dock and unload. Arnold's action might have been illegal, or it might not, but it did result in his obtaining a half-interest in the *Charming Nancy*. Now, in Philadelphia, he resolved to use it, and he called for his aide, Major David Franks.

Franks was a young and wealthy Englishman who had embraced the cause of liberty and lent his money to the Americans. He had spoken to General Arnold of his intention to leave the army to recoup his fortune.

"You need not leave the service, David," Arnold said. "I want you to buy up as much European and East Indian goods as you can. The country is starving for them. I will provide the money."

"But, sir," Franks began, putting a hand to his heavily powdered hair, and Arnold waved a hand impatiently.

"It may be illegal, it may not be," he snapped. "But how do you think profiteers like Robert Morris have grown so rich? Why should the soldiers who fight the war have to live in poverty? If civilians can do it, so can we."

"I didn't mean that, sir," Franks said, proffering a paper he held in his hand. "I meant this. The Pennsylvania Council wants you to issue an order closing all the shops."

"Why?"

"So that the quartermaster, clothier and commissary generals can buy what goods they need for the army."

A scowl crossed Arnold's hawkish features. "That means speculation will be out," he grumbled. Then he smiled. "Don't worry, Franks. I think I can arrange things with the army clothier-general. James Mease is a sensible man. We'll just have him buy what we want. Ostensibly for the army, but actually for us. Just luxury goods. This is even better. We should make enormous profits."

Arnold and his associates did reap huge profits from this secret arrangement, and from other operations in New York City and Newport, Rhode Island. Soon, the general had moved into the Penn House, the most splendid mansion on fashionable Front Street and the one in which Sir William Howe had lived so extravagantly. Arnold bought a magnificent coach, and hired a coachman, footmen, a butler, valet and servants, all of whom he clothed in his own livery. He entertained lavishly, and a frequent guest at his epicurean table was Dr. Benjamin Gill.

"Really, Benedict, that dinner you gave last night was simply elegant," Dr. Gill murmured to Arnold one day. The two were in the general's chambers. Arnold sat behind his desk with his wounded leg propped up on a stool. The cane which he had exchanged for his crutches rested against the desk. "Such delightful company!" Dr. Gill continued. "Robert Morris . . . Edward Shippen . . . I must say Peggy Shippen is perhaps the most beautiful girl I've ever seen."

"She is indeed," Arnold murmured, his blue eyes softening.

"And the claret! Wherever did you get such glorious wine?"

"Thank you, Doctor. It is the best that can be bought in Bordeaux. From the famous Chateau Margaux. It should be tasty, Doctor—cost me five hundred pounds a cask."

Dr. Gill rolled his eyes in amazement. Then, leaning forward in his chair and lowering his voice, he said, "I have come to warn you. The British are planning to raid the smugglers' nest at Egg Harbor in New Jersey."

"Good God!" Arnold exclaimed, reaching for the bellpull behind him. "The *Charming Nancy*'s at Egg Harbor. Loaded to the gunwales with tea, sugar, linens, woolens and glass. I've got to salvage her cargo," he said, giving a vicious yank on the bellpull.

Major Franks came rushing into the room, nervously patting his powdered hair. "Franks, you must go at once to the army wagonmaster," Arnold said to him. "Tell him that I want to rent twelve teams of horses. Immediately!"

"But, sir, the Pennsylvania Council has just denounced the private use of public equipment. Specifically, army wagons."

"Rubbish! I'm in charge here, not the Council. Do as I say, Franks—and tell Colonel Mitchell to do as I say!"

Nodding, patting his hair again, Major Franks left the room. Arnold waited until he was out of earshot, before he turned his hard blue eyes toward Dr. Gill and asked, "How did you find this out?"

"I have friends on the other side of the river," Dr. Gill murmured with a mysterious air.

"You do, eh?" Arnold countered, his eyes hard and suspicious again. "All true lovers of liberty, I trust."

"It's getting so difficult to tell the difference these days," Dr. Gill said in a bored voice. "Really, the way places like New York and Philadelphia change hands. Scratch a Rebel and you're likely to find a Tory. And vice versa. Those men who were your guests last night—Morris, Shippen and the others—they're not exactly flaming Patriots. Yet, they can go as they please."

"That's because they have money," Arnold grunted.

"So did Joseph Galloway."

"Galloway was a fool!" Arnold exclaimed. "He changed sides just because Sir William Howe promised to make him his chief of police. And now he's a pauper on his way to some back-of-beyond crossroads in Canada and his poor wife is penniless. Morris and Shippen and the others were wiser. They kept their mouths shut."

"And they didn't go to the *Michianza*, either. That was even wiser. No blackball for them. I understand the dashing Major André was heartbroken when Peggy Shippen's father wouldn't let her go." Dr. Gill chuckled, pretending not to notice Arnold's quick flush. "Just imagine, a pair of bloomers breaking up a love affair. How the ladies cried when Sir William and André and the others left. And now they've dried their eyes and are going to the Patriot balls. Yes, my dear General, I do believe one's safest course these days is to carry two sets of flags. Do you agree?"

"No, I don't agree! There's only one flag for me: the stars and stripes. And one cause! Sacred liberty!"

"Indeed," Dr. Gill said suavely, rising to his feet. "I do hope you get your cargo out safely."

"I will," Arnold muttered, avoiding the doctor's eyes. "And I must tell you how grateful I am for your warning. If the British seized that cargo, I'd stand to lose about forty thousand dollars. Maybe a lot more, if they burned the ship. I tell you, I'm grateful to you, Doctor."

"Thank you, sir. Any time. I am always at your service, General Arnold."

General Benedict Arnold sat sunk in thought after Dr. Benjamin Gill departed. Two sets of flags, eh? Not for him, not for Benedict Arnold. One flag only for him. But how had the stars and stripes been treating him lately? Outrageously, Arnold thought, simply outrageously. Arnold still smarted from being passed over for promotion to major general. Five brigadiers junior to him had been promoted. Not one of them his equal in experience or ability! How he had seethed with fury and resentment at that insult. It had taken his repulse of the British at Danbury—where he'd had two horses shot from under him—to get Congress to make him a major general. Even then, they had withheld the seniority that was his by right over the other five. And then Saratoga, and Congress voting a gold medal to that fat-assed old woman of a Horatio Gates, when it was he, Benedict Arnold who had won the battle—as even General Washington knew. What about that rascal John Brown libeling him everywhere, calling him a thief and scattering his scurrilous handbills all over the country. Called me a criminal, said my only God was money and would sell out my country for it—and not a hand raised to stop the wretched liar's mouth. Only Washington believed in me. Washington knew I was being slandered and got others to believe in me, too. If it hadn't been for Washington, Congress would never have listened to my demand that they investigate my record and clear my character. And then what did they do? Began asking questions about Quebec! How should he know how the money for the expedition had been spent? The fools! A general doesn't go on a campaign with bags of money over his shoulders. What are staff officers for? Ask them, if they think there's money missing and stop the sly innuendos. Check *their* records. It was a pleasure to tell them that if they wanted to check mine they could dredge up my ship from the bottom of Lake Champlain. Valcour Island! Another victory I got no credit for. Well, at least Congress had declared that Brown had "cruelly and groundlessly" besmirched my character and conduct. But then they made a mockery of my service by granting me a horse in recognition of Danbury to replace the two shot from under me. A *horse!* A God damn horse, and still no seniority over the others! That was how he had been treated under the flag he loved so recklessly, for which he had bled and sacrificed and become a permanent cripple! Benedict Arnold was not a soft or self-pitying man, yet there were bitter tears in his eyes when he had finished his morose rumination and swung back to the paperwork on his desk.

Then his bleak eyes softened. He had caught sight of the picture of Peggy Shippen next to his sander. It was a pen-and-ink drawing done by John André. Benedict Arnold knew that André had been Peggy's beau. It caused him no jealousy because now *he* was Peggy's beau, and a suitor for her hand. He had been delighted when Peggy had given him the picture, her most cherished possession. It showed her with her powdered hair piled high on her head beneath a jeweled, beribboned hat which André had designed for her. The major was a fine artist, Arnold thought. He'd captured the glint of intelligence behind Peggy's beautiful wide gray eyes, the gaiety and vivacity of her nature in her smile. Suddenly, Arnold yanked the bellpull behind him. Major Franks came into the room.

"Major, Edward Shippen and his daughter, Miss Margaret Shippen, will be dining here tonight. It will be a private dinner. Just the four of us. Please be sure Holmes is notified."

Major Franks nodded, then seized his head in mortification when he caught sight of himself in a gilded oval mirror on the wall. "Oh, my Lord," he groaned, "my hair is a mess! It's not powdered evenly at all. How can I face the Shippens looking like this?"

Arnold grinned. His aide's preoccupation with his hair was a source of amusement to him. "Maybe you'd better go to a barber."

"I haven't time. I'm too busy." He brightened. "I'll have the barber come here." Rushing outside, Franks found a militia sergeant named William Matlack.

"Please go fetch the barber, Sergeant."

The soldier's face flushed sullenly. "Soldiers ain't servants or errand boys. I signed on to fight, not to run for the officers' barbers."

"You will do as I command," Major Franks said, adopting his chief's imperious manner.

"I ain't no lackey, I tell you. I tole you that before. I'm a free man."

"You are a soldier, and soldiers obey orders. Please go and fetch my barber."

"I'll go," Sergeant Matlack mumbled sulkily, "but I'm gonna complain to General Arnold."

His chin lifted haughtily, Major Franks watched the sergeant go slouching down the hall with deliberate slowness. Then he went searching for the butler to inform him of the general's distinguished dinner guests.

Benedict Arnold felt the poignant pangs of hopeless infatuation when he saw Peggy Shippen alight from her gleaming carriage on the hand of her father. She was dressed in white silk which made her seem in Arnold's eyes a radiant virgin. The gown was decorated with seed pearls and lined with scarlet, so that when she lifted her beautiful white hand the long hanging sleeve flashed red. Her soft blond hair glistened in the light of the coach lamps, which fell sparkling on the diamond comb in her hair. Peggy's father was dressed in sober gray with black shoes with silver buckles, while Arnold wore his general's uniform of blue and buff, heavy with gold braid.

The two men were a study in contrasts as they sat at the dinner table. Arnold, the ebullient, his eyes glittering brilliantly, pouncing on the subjects of conversation like a bird of prey, his whole being seeming to be inflamed by the presence of Peggy like the effect of fire on incense; Shippen, the reflective lawyer and judge, speaking in a low voice, pausing to think before replying, suffering Arnold's interruptions quietly, his fond eyes seldom straying from the face of his daughter.

Upon completion of the meal, Peggy arose to return to the drawing room for coffee, while her father and Arnold remained at the table for a glass of port. Major Franks, complaining of a headache, retired to his quarters. Alone with Shippen for the first time, Arnold swooped.

"Mr. Shippen, may I ask you for your daughter's hand?"

Shippen remained silent, gazing reflectively at Arnold. He did not appreciate the general's interest in his daughter. True, he was a major general and a national hero. But Edward Shippen, like most unviolent men who excel in council, distrusted the military and abhorred heroes. Moreover, Arnold was thirty-seven—nearly twice Peggy's age. He was a widower with three children. He was already in trouble with the Pennsylvania Council—they had charged him with eight counts of misconduct—and his style of life was so opulent and flamboyant that many Philadelphians were wondering aloud how Benedict Arnold spent more in a month than he made in a year. Yet, as Shippen knew, Peggy was madly in love with Arnold—and Edward Shippen seldom denied his headstrong daughter's wishes.

Benedict Arnold took Shippen's silence to be a sign of indecision and he rushed on eagerly.

"I know that I am much older than Peggy, but we both love each other dearly. My fortune is not large, but sufficient. I ask no dowry. I shall make any settlement on Peggy consistent with the duty I owe my three lovely children." Shippen still did not speak, and now Arnold showed signs of apprehension. "My public reputation is well known, sir," he said,

speaking rapidly. "My private one is, I hope, irreproachable."
Benedict Arnold paused to swallow. "Our difference in political sentiments, I hope, sir, will be no bar to my happiness."

Edward Shippen sipped his port slowly. Clearing his throat, he asked, "Has my daughter told you she will marry you, General Arnold?"

"Not yet. I haven't asked her, yet."

"Then I think you had better. I will abide by my daughter's decision."

Benedict Arnold pursued his courtship of Peggy Shippen throughout the remaining months of 1778 and into early 1779, seemingly unmoved by the storm of criticism raging around him. The father of Sergeant William Matlack—the militiaman who Major Franks had so peremptorily sent running for a barber—was a member of the Pennsylvania Council. Timothy Matlack was so enraged that his soldier son had been ordered to perform menial tasks that he made this one of the eight charges which the Council filed against Arnold. The pass for the *Charming Nancy* was also uncovered, together with Arnold's use of public wagons to move the ship's cargo, while his order closing the shops was construed as an abuse of his office from which he profited by privately buying up scarce goods. These were the four most serious of the eight charges leveled against him. Arnold laughed at them all, and when a committee formed by Congress to investigate them threw out all but the wagons and menial duty counts, he was jubilant—so exultant that he chose the occasion to ask Peggy to marry him.

"Yes," Peggy said, "yes, yes, yes! I will marry you, Benedict, and love you always!"

Arnold was transported with joy. Unfortunately, Congress chose to bury the committee's report and once more plunged into an acrimonious exchange with the Pennsylvania Council, which burned to see Arnold disgraced. The debate became so bitter that at one point Congress considered leaving Philadelphia while the Council threatened that if it did not leave, then it would withdraw to Lancaster itself. Eventually, Congress settled for a recommendation that the general should be tried by court-martial on four charges: the *Charming Nancy* pass, assigning menial duties to militia, closing the shops for personal speculation and misusing public wagons.

Peggy Shippen was shocked and distressed. "What will we do?" she wailed. "What will we do?"

"Have no fear, my dearest," Arnold said calmly. "Trust General Washington. He is my affectionate friend. I shall demand to be court-martialed immediately. And I shall resign my command here. It has been for me nothing but a source of irritation and frustration." Limping into his chambers on his cane and high-heeled shoe, Arnold sat down to notify Washington of his resignation and request for a quick trial. "If your Excellency thinks me guilty (he wrote), for heaven's sake let me be immediately tried and, if found guilty, executed. I ask only justice."

There was a glimmer of grim humor in Arnold's eyes when he wrote "executed." He knew that he was in no such danger, and he was confident that he would be cleared of the charges. He made certain of the *Charming Nancy* charge by meeting in private with Robert Shewell.

"I would be insane to talk," Shewell assured him. "Do I want a noose around my own neck?"

Clothier-General James Mease was blunt: "Nobody knows but you and me. You won't tell them and neither will I."

Arnold spoke also to Colonel John Mitchell, the army's wagonmaster. "I do not intend to testify for either side," Mitchell said grimly. "If compelled to, I will say I considered it my duty to do as you asked and emphasize the fact that it was not an order but a request."

Only the matter of the militiaman remained, and Arnold was confident that his commander-in-chief would uphold him there. There seemed no reason to delay the wedding, and on April 8, 1779, in the drawing room of Edward Shippen's house, Benedict Arnold married his idolized Peggy.

Peggy never looked lovelier in her gown of white satin. Pride shone in Arnold's hard blue eyes as he stood resplendent in his blue-and-buff uniform, leaning on the arm of Major Franks; but his eyes softened when he turned to kiss his bride. At the reception which followed, he sat on a sofa with his leg stretched out on a stool with Peggy beside him.

After the wedding he took Peggy to the new home he had purchased on the Schuykill River on the outskirts of Philadelphia. It was called Mount Pleasant, the most sumptuous home in Philadelphia and perhaps in all America. A magnificent house surrounded by gardens, lawns and orchards, with half a dozen smaller buildings for servants, horses and carriages, it was, in elegance and splendor, easily the superior of the Wharton Mansion-house.

"It's just like a *castle!*" Peggy exclaimed. She had never been so thrilled. "It *is* a castle. Oh, Benedict, how beautiful!"

"It's your wedding present, my dearest. Now let those Council wolves howl."

"Why do they hate you so much?" Peggy asked wistfully. "Why is Congress so mean to you? After all, you've done so much for your country."

"Jealousy," Arnold said, taking Peggy's hand and leading her back to his shining coach. A liveried footman helped them inside. The whip cracked and the carriage lurched gently forward. "Congress is nothing but a crowd of cowardly scribblers," Arnold continued bitterly. "They're jealous of our glory. They resent the fact that the Revolution can't be won without a war. They'd like to legislate it into being, but they know in their hearts it has to be fought for. Like all cowards, they hate heroes."

"Kings don't hate heroes," Peggy said, straining beside the window for a last glimpse of the magnificent estate of which she was to be mistress. Imagine! At nineteen! "No, kings don't hate heroes," she repeated, her gray eyes gleaming with interest in the turn the conversation had taken. "They reward them."

"That's true," Arnold said musingly, unaware that Peggy was watching him carefully. "Do you know, it just occurred to me: not one of the men who signed the Declaration of Independence is in uniform fighting for those ideals. Benjamin Franklin, Charles Carroll, the Lees of Virginia, the Rutledges of South Carolina, the Adamses—not one of them! And Thomas Jefferson who wrote it! He's safe and sound in his little snuggery in Williamsburg."

"King George wouldn't have treated you like this, Benedict," Peggy said softly. "It was such a terrible, terrible mistake for the colonists to have separated from the Crown. Oh, I know there were injustices. But to revolt against the *king!* Besides, he tried to patch things up. But Congress wouldn't listen. They sent the Carlyle Commission packing. King George was willing to let us have a confederation just so long as it was under the Crown."

"You might be right," Arnold said slowly. "I've been doing a lot of thinking about the Declaration of Independence lately. At the time, I was all for it. I thought it should have come sooner. I hated the king for all those taxes. The way customs could interfere with the way I ran my shipping fleet. Parliament in London taxing us without any of us represented in Parliament." The Arnolds were back in Philadelphia, now. The horses' hooves rang on the cobblestones. "Maybe I was too impulsive, then. It's been four years, nearly five, since the war began. Things aren't any better. They're worse. Taxes are even heavier now and trade regulations are abominable."

"The colonies *can't* win!" Peggy said fiercely, clutching a coach handle as the carriage lurched to avoid a platoon of militia scampering across its path. Arnold looked at them and grimaced. "Not with ragamuffins like that." But the wrinkles etched into Arnold's forehead did not all derive from his disgust with the militia. He was worried about his finances. He had borrowed heavily to buy Mount Pleasant—which was being rented—and was paying off a steep mortgage. Debts were piling up. Having resigned his command, he had no income; being under suspicion, he dared not enter any questionable financial schemes.

"They can't win!" Peggy repeated. "A nation so new and small and poor just can't stand up to the most powerful country in the world. The Rebels can't last. Even with France. And when they're defeated, the retribution will be terrible. There's been enough blood spilled already over their silly liberty, but wait until the king begins to scourge them." Peggy put her face in her hands, but her eyes were dry. "Oh, Benedict," she cried in a sobbing voice, "you could save them."

"I?"

"Yes, you. General Washington has always said that you are the most competent commander in the service. If you . . . if you could use your position to serve the British cause . . ." The coach stopped outside the Penn House and the doorman opened the door. Peggy motioned him to shut it again, and turned eagerly to her husband. "Do you remember General Monk?"

"George Monk? Cromwell's general who brought about the restoration of Charles II?"

"Yes, and King Charles made him a duke." Peggy's gray eyes were watchful of her husband again. She could see him frown and guess that the notion had taken root. "Do you know," she whispered, "I heard that the Carlyle Commission was going to offer Washington a title." Her cool hand sought Arnold's. "Just think: *Lord and Lady Arnold*." Arnold's tense and hawkish face relaxed, becoming dreamy. Peggy squeezed his hand. "Of course, you would never change sides just for a title."

"No, but I would certainly have reasons to after what I've suffered at the hands of my countrymen."

"But you are much too noble to do anything for spite. No, it would be to *save* your countrymen. You could be the one to end all this killing and maiming and misery. Look at how the country is torn by faction. Look at the levelers strutting in the street as though they were born of the royal blood! Quality just doesn't count in America anymore. But you could return our country to a firm class structure. The king is chastened, now, understands us better. You could bring us back to his wise and benevolent rule. America would be forever grateful to you, Benedict! Benedict Arnold, American savior!"

Arnold's hard blue eyes were gleaming, now. "Yes, yes," he murmured eagerly. "I have always felt this within me. This greatness. How else explain my rise to world fame in just a few short years? This . . . this might be the great mission for which I was born." His hand closed on the door handle. "But, who . . . ? How shall I get in touch with them?"

"There is always John André. He's adjutant general for the entire British Army, now," she said proudly. "They say he's Clinton's right-hand man."

Arnold closed his eyes. "But, still . . . We must have our own emissary. A go-between from this side . . ." He opened his eyes with a smile. "But, of course! Dr. Benjamin Gill . . ."

Major John André was pleased to see Dr. Benjamin Gill.

André was chief of British intelligence. Dr. Gill reported to him every month or so, usually bringing valuable information.

"I have great news for you, Major," Dr. Gill said, his dark eyes gleaming. "A high-ranking officer in the American Army wishes to offer his services to Sir Henry."

"Officer. What rank?"

"General."

André was startled. "What is this general's name?"

"I cannot tell you, sir. One condition of my service to this man is that I cannot reveal his name."

"But, this is rubbish, Dr. Gill. You are yourself an officer in my intelligence service. How can you withhold his name? What if I were to order you to reveal it?"

Dr. Gill hesitated, his saturnine features darkening in a scowl. "In that case, I . . . I would have to disclose it. But I do not think it would be in our interest to do so now. It might prejudice the affair before it gets started. As you know, sir, in war there is no such thing as a secret. Ultimately, everything comes out. If my man knew you knew who he was before we came to any agreement, it might scare him off."

André pursed his lips thoughtfully. "You might be right, Doctor. Does he have a pseudonym?"

"Yes. For the present, he wishes to be known as Monk."

André whistled. "Well, well, George Monk, eh? It seems your man knows British history. Monk changed sides against Charles II when it seemed the king was winning. Got a dukedom out of it. Does this Monk think we're going to win?"

"Yes."

"And what does he want for his treachery? Does this Monk expect a grateful king to bestow great gifts on him? What if we lose?"

"Win or lose, he would expect to be rewarded."

André was silent for a moment. "Is he offering to desert the American Army and serve with us?"

"He told me to tell you that he would do whatever you thought would be best for England."

Major André arose and reached for his hat. "Stay here a bit, Doctor. I must discuss this with Sir Henry."

General Clinton was sipping a glass of port when Major André entered his chambers. His full face was flushed.

Beneath the massive mahogany table that served him for a desk, André could see his fat little legs tucked under his chair. Clinton's small tight mouth curled in a smile of welcome when he saw André. He was fond of his handsome adjutant general, perhaps the only man in his army he did not hold off at arm's length.

"Well, John, you seem excited. You have good news?"

"I do, indeed, Excellency. There is a prominent general in the American Army who wishes to come over to us." Rapidly, André told Clinton what Dr. Gill had told him.

"Monk? Rubbish! It's Arnold. It has to be Arnold!"

André smiled ruefully. "Peggy Shippen's husband, eh? If I know that clever little lady at all, she's behind it. But why do you say Arnold, sir?"

"It's got to be he! He's in all sorts of trouble. Facing a court-martial. Your own spies have told us he's deep in debt. About to go under." Clinton pondered for a moment, pushing out his thin lips. "Let's not rush into anything, John. Arnold's a sly chap. He's pulled the wool over Washington's eyes again and again. Tell Dr. Gill to arrange a correspondence between you and Monk. Sign yourself . . . well, sign yourself Mr. Anderson."

"You sound as though you don't want him to come over to us, Excellency."

"Not unless he can bring an army or a priceless position with him. At the moment, he's more valuable providing information. What a pity he's resigned! You must try to persuade him to return to active service. Oh, and make your correspondence in code. Make the letters sound like business letters between merchants. You're an ingenious chap, John. You invent the code."

"I will do that, Excellency," Major John André said with a smile.

During the following three weeks André struck up his correspondence with Monk. He devised a simple code, although sometimes there were messages in invisible ink written between lines of innocuous missives. These were brought out by applying fire or acid to the paper. The letters were marked *F* or *A* for that purpose. Anyone opening the letters by accident would have found nothing more than an exchange of business correspondence between merchants living in New York and

Philadelphia. Peggy Arnold quickly guessed that her husband's correspondent was John André, and she wrote in one of the letters: "Madame Arnold presents her particular compliments."

Major André smiled when he read that. Dear Peggy: beautiful, clever and ambitious. Exactly the wrong kind of woman for a scoundrel like Arnold. André didn't doubt that Peggy had put her husband up to treachery. He also smiled at Arnold's protestations of nobility.

"He rants and he raves," André said to Clinton. "At one moment he's the savior of America, bringing the colonies back to peace and prosperity under the benign rule of a chastened king, at the next he's the mortal foe of France—the enemy of the Protestant religion. If the Rebels win with French help, he says, there will be the worst Inquisition in America."

"Poppycock, eh, John?"

"Pure and perfect! Him a patriot? All he wants is money—hard cash."

"Be careful in your dealing with him. He's a traitor. But we shall deal fairly with him and keep any bargain we make. But be cautious."

Gradually, it became clear to André that the big problem was how Monk was to be rewarded. Monk made it clear that he was prepared to risk anything, but he must be paid well. Mindful of Clinton's warning, André proceeded cautiously. He wanted information, he told Monk. He urged him to return to active service and a field command. If he could enable the British to defeat a large American force in a decisive battle, he would be rewarded beyond the dreams of avarice.

"What information?" Monk replied.

"We want to know the movements of Washington's units, the number and location of American troops, the location of magazines and how much ammunition they hold. Try to get other officers like yourself to desert. Try to get some of Burgoyne's captured officers returned to us."

Arnold's next letter contained some such information, but nothing of great value. Once again, André urged him to return to duty. Then he could allow himself to be surprised by the British and be forced to surrender. The surrender of five or six thousand American troops would be a splendid achievement and Arnold would be well paid for it.

In July of 1779 Dr. Benjamin Gill brought André a letter

signed Gustavus. In this, Arnold named his terms. He wanted ten thousand pounds, the equivalent of fifty thousand dollars in American money. But he wanted English currency, not the inflated American money.

"Ten thousand pounds!" Clinton exclaimed. "That's quite a sum! And for what? He hasn't given us much more information than you could get from your own spies, John. See if you can get him to come down."

André tried haggling with Arnold, but the American traitor stuck to his price.

"Let's test him," Clinton said to André after another Gustavus letter was received. "Ask him for an accurate map of West Point and a description of its fortifications."

"West Point?"

"Yes. It's the key to the Hudson. And, as you know, if we can control the Hudson we can split the colonies in two and probably win the war. I should like to have detailed information on West Point. The number of troops, their weapons, their officers . . . the number of gunboats . . . the strength of that chain they've stretched beneath the water from shore to shore to stop our ships . . . I might very well pay fifty thousand dollars for such detailed information. But I'd rather pay less."

André quickly forwarded Clinton's request to Arnold, but the American general replied that he didn't have a map of West Point and did not know how to obtain one. He added that he was to return to active service soon. No more letters arrived that summer. Nor in the fall and early winter.

"Do you think he's cooled?" General Clinton asked André.

"It seems so, sir. But I'll write to his wife just to keep the channels open."

"Very well," Clinton said musingly, pursing his prim lips. "But I'm beginning to think we shan't be needing him. The war's going rather well. I've always agreed with Germain that the south was the place to beat the Rebels. Now that we've taken Savannah, all of Georgia is falling over themselves to take the oath of allegiance. I rather think I'll try Charleston next. That will bring the Carolinas back to the Crown. And then Virginia. Yes, John, I do believe we can at least save the south for the king. We might have to give up on the north altogether, now that they've got a French army in Newport. I seriously doubt that the king can spare any more troops for America."

"Are you taking command yourself, Excellency?"

"Yes. With Cornwallis second. You'll be coming with us, of course, John. I hope to have Charleston in hand by early February."

Chapter Twenty-Seven

Although Benedict Arnold had demanded a speedy trial, his court-martial did not convene until December 23, 1779. It sat in Norris's Tavern in Morristown, where Washington had gone into winter quarters for a second time.

Bendedict Arnold was supremely confident that he would be acquitted. With Peggy on his arm, he limped into the courtroom on his cane and high-heeled shoe, moving so vigorously it was difficult to believe that one leg was shorter than the other. Arnold knew that his enemies had failed to unearth a shred of evidence supporting the most serious charges of the *Charming Nancy* pass and the closing of shops to buy goods. Of the others—making a militiaman perform menial chores, private use of public wagons—he was certain he could exonerate himself. After all, they were so trivial.

As he expected, the prosecution could make nothing of the fact that the owners of the *Charming Nancy* were "disaffected persons." The phrase was so vague and confusing the charge came to nothing. Ignorant of the secret agreement between Arnold and the clothier-general, the prosecution could only claim that the general had closed Philadelphia's shops so that Major Franks could make purchases with money given to him by his chief. But Franks testified that he had made no purchases. The menial chores issue was the result of Major Franks having ordered Sergeant Matlack to fetch a barber, a charge so trivial in an army that it was hardly pressed by the prosecutor. Actually, the trial focused on the use of the public wagons, and turned on whether Colonel Mitchell had done Arnold a favor—in which case the fault was Mitchell's—or had been obeying Arnold's orders.

"The general did not order the wagons," said Mitchell, who had decided to testify. "He requested them. I thought it was my duty to comply."

Benedict Arnold arose in his own defense. He went stumping around the courtroom for everyone to see how crippled he had become in the service of his country. He read aloud letters of praise from General Washington and resolutions from Congress extolling his achievements.

"I was one of the first to appear in the field," he thundered, his face flushed and his eyes glowing, "and never from that hour to this have I abandoned my duty. Is it probable that a man so honored by his commander-in-chief, by the Congress, should all at once sink into a course of conduct equally unworthy of the patriot and soldier? No! My conduct from the earliest period of the war has been steady and uniform. Here I stand, a hero charged with practices the soul abhors!"

Arnold's eloquence did not impress the officers of the court. On January 26, 1780, with Arnold sitting cockily before them and a smiling Peggy beside him, they found Arnold guilty of acting illegally and improperly in issuing the pass to the *Charming Nancy* and of acting improperly and imprudently in using the wagons.

"For these two offenses the court orders you to be publicly reprimanded by your commander-in-chief."

Peggy Arnold burst into tears and Arnold struggled erect, his face black with rage.

"*Reprimanded!*" he shouted, trembling with anger. "For what?"

At once, his weeping wife seized him by the shoulder and turned him toward the door. He had come limping in, but he went hobbling out.

"This is strange, Daniel," General Washington said, glancing up from a stack of letters. He removed his spectacles and reached for a nut from the bowl on his desk. "Here's a letter from Benedict Arnold. He wants a naval command. Of course, I know that he's an accomplished seaman. Valcour Island proved that. But his reputation was made on land. He says his leg isn't well enough to take the field, and that the doctors think life aboard ship would make him recover quicker. Odd. What do you make of it, Daniel?"

"Prizes," Colonel Gill grunted laconically. "A very clever way to recoup his fortune. As a privateer, he'll keep the ships he captures."

"Yes, I suppose you're right. I shall have to write the Admiralty Board to tell them I disapprove." Washington sighed and returned to his correspondence. This time he looked up with a smile. "You know how much I disapprove of dueling, Daniel."

"Indeed I do, Excellency," Daniel replied, flushing.

"Well, here is a duel," the general said, shaking a letter in his hand, his pale eyes twinkling, "of which I find it most difficult to disapprove. It's a letter from General Conway. He was badly wounded in a duel with General Cadwalader. Because he fears he is near death, he has written to me to apologize for all the trouble he has caused me. He says if he gets well, he will return to France."

"Good riddance," Colonel Gill said sharply. "I don't want him to leave the world, of course. Just leaving the country will suit me fine. So that's the end of the Conway Cabal, I guess. With General Lee cashiered, that should be the end of your troubles, sir."

"I think so," Washington said musingly. "I really never believed Horatio Gates was after my job. Conway and Lee were the real troublemakers. Well, Daniel, are you ready to sail?"

"Yes, sir. My wife arrived from Boston yesterday and we're sailing tomorrow on the tide."

Washington raised his eyebrows. "I wasn't aware that you were taking Barbara with you."

"Yes, Excellency," Daniel said, slightly embarrassed. "You see, I'm thinking of moving to South Carolina after the war."

"Indeed? And leave the Old Dominion? We'll miss you, Daniel."

"It's not that I don't like Virginia," Daniel went on hastily, still embarrassed. "It's just that I think rice is more profitable than tobacco."

"Until the rice birds get at it," Washington said with a wry smile. "Arthur Middleton told me those damn bobolinks eat a third of his crop every year."

"I never heard that before, sir," Daniel said slowly, his dark blue eyes unhappy. "Well, anyway, I thought this trip to Charleston was the chance to show Barbara the property I wanted to buy."

"I see. Well, give Barbara my best. And, remember, you must impress upon General Lincoln how vital Charleston is to the Revolution. The loss of Savannah was bad enough. But to lose Charleston, too, may be tantamount to losing the entire south."

"I've been thinking that's what Clinton is after, sir. With Spain joining France in the war against England, he probably won't get the forces to conquer all America. Maybe he figures he can at least save the south for the Crown."

"I believe you're right. Remember, now, Daniel, Benjamin Lincoln must be made to know that I expect him to hold Charleston at all costs."

The *Sea Nymph*, with Captain Francis Butler, was preparing to drop down the Delaware for the open sea. Daniel and Barbara Gill stood on deck in a fascination of delight, watching the seamen swarming nimbly over the masts and spars, listening to the stream of orders coming from the bridge.

"Loose the outer jib."

"Lay aloft, some of you, and loose the topsails."

"Up with that jib smartly, my lads."

"A hand after here at the wheel."

The three topsails were quickly set and the windlass manned. Within a quarter hour the *Sea Nymph* was under way, gliding silently down the vast river with the outgoing tide making wrinkles around her bows. Now Captain Butler called for extra canvas, hoping to make the open sea before nightfall. He set the fore and main top-gallant-sails and spanker. The yards were braced up sharply. The *Sea Nymph* strained forward, her great white sails floating above her like the puffs of white cloud in the blue sky.

"We're really flying, now," Daniel shouted exultantly. He squeezed Barbara's hand as the wind freshened and drove them forward into Delaware Bay. "Pretty big, huh?" Daniel called above the wind. He pointed ahead of him. "That's Cape May at the tip of New Jersey on the left."

"Port side, you landlubber," Barbara said, and Daniel laughed. Barbara frowned. They were nearing the open sea and she gazed at it apprehensively. "This . . . this is where my mother and father drowned," she muttered. "Off the Delaware Capes." She shuddered. "Strange. My father was a sea captain and they were shipbuilders on my mother's side. And I'm running a shipyard. Yet, I . . . I'm afraid of the sea."

"You'll get over it," Daniel said, putting his arm around her. Barbara nodded, putting up a hand to catch her black hair flying around her face. Now the helmsman put the *Sea Nymph* over to starboard and headed her south. The wind strengthened and the graceful ship lay over slightly on her starboard side. It was a glorious day. There were just enough puffs of white cloud in the sky to make the heavens seem bluer. The sun shone brilliantly, dancing and sparkling on the ship's brasswork as though it were burnished gold. Daniel and Barbara walked forward to gaze in delight at the emerald sea leaping about them in tiny, white-capped waves. Looking over the bows they could see the prow shredding white water and a curl of foam at its base.

"Know what sailors call that?" Daniel asked proudly.

"A bone in her teeth," Barbara said, laughing at his consternation. "You know, I do know something about the sea."

Daniel looked sharply aft, saw no one watching them, and quickly drew Barbara to him and kissed her. "There, that's for being so smart."

Barbara pushed him away in embarrassment. "What if someone had seen us?"

"Can't a man kiss his own wife?"

"Not in public in front of a bunch of sailors."

"All right, then, I'll kiss someone else's wife."

"You'd better not," Barbara said sharply. She walked upward toward the slightly higher port rail and leaned over the side, standing on tiptoe.

"What are you doing?" Daniel asked, joining her.

"I'm trying to see the bottom of the ship. I want to see if it's been scraped." She turned, her eyes shining with delight. "What a day! What a way to begin the honeymoon we never had. I honestly don't care if we never get to Charleston."

That night, after dining in Captain Butler's cabin, Daniel and Barbara retired to their own quarters. They began to undress for bed. Barbara pulled her dress of hunter-green velvet over her head and removed her petticoat. She heard Daniel swear.

"My God, Barbara, what on earth have you got strapped to your thigh?"

"A stiletto."

"A stiletto! My God, are you planning to turn pirate?"

"Don't be silly. Grandma Gill gave it to me. She always carried a weapon when she went traveling. She hated defenseless women. 'A woman's defenseless because she makes herself that way,' she'd say. 'If a man can carry a weapon while he's traveling, his wife can too. Supposing something happened to him? Then she might have to depend on someone who has a different set of values.' "

"All right, so there is some sense to that. But why a stiletto? Why not a pistol?"

"Grandma said pistols make noise and attract attention. Sometimes they don't go off. Anyway, a stiletto's quieter—just the thing for the kind of trouble a woman alone can get into."

Daniel had taken off all his clothes. He got into bed with a grin. "If I start making that kind of trouble, will you promise not to use the stiletto on me?"

The weather remained fine almost all the way to Charleston. About a day's sail above the city, with the approach of night, a mammoth calm overtook the ocean. The sea seemed to level off, gleaming faintly. It was as though the *Sea Nymph* were gliding slowly over a surface of obsidian. The calm was followed by a gigantic swell, which lifted and dropped the ship with such a sickening and terrifyingly prolonged rise and fall that Colonel Daniel Gill became alarmed and came on deck.

A mysterious silence seemed to reign upon the sea. It was now full night and an inky blackness engulfed the ship. The air was heavy, suffocating. Daniel gasped in the thickness of the atmosphere. He could hear sails flapping lazily overhead. Daniel sensed the approach of a violent storm and stood on the deck momentarily transfixed, his heart beating rapidly with awe and fear. Above him he heard the anxious voices of the sailors and guessed that they were furling all the lighter sails. But the great topsails still rattled ominously.

"I thought you had turned in, Colonel," a voice said out of the dark.

Daniel recognized Captain Butler's voice. In the faint light of the galley lantern he could see the dark bulk of his figure. "I was about to," Daniel said, "but the rise and fall of the ship worried me. Is there a storm approaching?"

"Looks like a hurricane," Butler muttered. "But I can't tell from what quarter." He put his finger in his mouth and held it up. "Son of a bitch!" he swore. "Not a breath of air stir-

ring. Avast there!" he shouted at his first mate. "Close reef
the mizzentop and get the mainsail furled."

The two men stood on the rolling and pitching vessel. The
heavy swell still rose and sank the *Sea Nymph,* washing her
sides almost to the height of her bulwarks.

"God *damn* that sea!" the helmsman swore, struggling with
his wheel. "It's making the rudder buck like it was alive."

"Reef the topsails!" Butler roared, his voice carrying eerily
in the stillness of the night.

At once there was a rush of feet on the deck and a medley
of curses from the sailors clambering aloft to obey the skip-
per's orders.

"They don't like it," Butler muttered. "It'd be easier reefing
the topsails in daylight with a hurricane blowing than in the
dark. Even with a calm like this."

It *was* calm. Extraordinarily so. The monstrous swell continued. Because it was so black, Daniel fancied that the ship
was rising high enough to touch the sky. The breathless air
was sinister and the close atmosphere oppressive. Now the
topsails were close-reefed and Butler called to his first mate:

"Are the decks clear?"

"All clear, sir."

"Fore topsails sheets?"

"Ready for running, sir."

Turning to the helmsman, he asked, "How's her head,
now?"

"Sou'west, half south."

Turning back to the first mate, he snapped: "Keep a brisk
lookout north'ard. Sing out if you see the sky clearing."

"Aye, aye, sir," the first mate said, moving away from
the helm to get a clearer view aft. Daniel Gill followed him.
He stiffened. He saw what he believed to be a ship's light
standing over the horizon left astern. Another light sprang up
above it. Another . . . another . . . Daniel's heart sank. He
thought it was the British fleet coming up on them. Because
of the atmosphere, the lights seemed red and Daniel took
them to be running lights. He was about to call out warningly
to Captain Butler, when he stiffened again. The lights were
stars!

"Stand by the starboard braces!" Butler roared.

At once, the crew came stumbling out on deck.

Below, the sky was clearing magically. The stars shone. But

then great flying wreaths of clouds rushed over them, obscuring most of them, but always leaving a few brightly burning in a foreground which seemed to be advancing upon the ship with frightful speed. Within a few moments Daniel heard the wild shrieking of the wind whirling down upon them. Yet, the sea around them was still dark and silent and unruffled, the air stagnant, and the great silent swell still heaving like the oily back of a whale.

Whoooosh!

With a dreadful, deafening peal the storm struck. Screeching and wailing, the wind stirred the sea into a boiling froth and hurled the spray into the faces of the *Sea Nymph*'s sailors. In an instant, every man was drenched. The decks were awash with water. The masts creaked and groaned fearfully and it seemed that every square of canvas was singing a mighty, dolorous dirge.

The *Sea Nymph* was staggered. She rolled and lurched, and then stood terrifyingly still while a monster swell gathered beneath her bow to tilt her astern into the teeth of the hurricane, hurling her aslant into the gale like a toy. A shudder ran down her frame aft and forward. Daniel Gill held his breath. Then, miraculously, eerily, with an unnatural suddenness, the swell subsided. The pressure of the wind flattened the sea so that now the *Sea Nymph* flew over a level surface of froth. Sometimes the capricious wind seized masses of crackling froth to hurl it against the ship's sides with the sound of cannon fire. A gust of water struck Daniel in the face with such scorching force he feared that he was blinded. He staggered about, his hand over his eyes, until he felt Butler's hand on his arm and his calm voice saying: "You'll be all right. I think we'll all be all right. It isn't quite a hurricane, yet. Lucky she struck us astern. If it had been forward, we'd never have righted."

Daniel opened his burning eyes. He squinted into the wind. He found it difficult to breathe, for the wind seemed to be blowing into his mouth and up his nostrils. Suddenly, he thought of Barbara and rushed below. He swung open their cabin hatch just as the ship rolled and threw him violently inside and against a bulkhead.

"Daniel, Daniel! Is it you?" Barbara's voice was anxious, but it seemed controlled.

Daniel stumbled toward the bunk in which she was lying.

He gathered her into his arms and held her close. The screeching of the wind was in both their ears. "My dearest, I should never have left you. But the storm hit so suddenly. It was terrible."

"Will it get worse? Will we be all right?"

"The captain seems confident. He says it won't reach hurricane force."

"Thank God."

A howl of wind struck the side of the *Sea Nymph* with the sound of a thunderclap and the ship yawed hideously. Daniel heard Barbara gasp and hugged her closer.

"Barbara?"

"Yes, Daniel?"

"Would you mind very much if I went back topside?"

There was a pause. "If you think you're needed."

"I'm not a sailor, of course, but I may be able to help in an emergency. I think I'd be of more use to you up there than down here."

There was another pause, more prolonged. "Of course, Daniel," Barbara said in a low voice. "Your place is with Captain Butler."

Daniel kissed her gently and left the cabin. He went lurching up the ladder and when he came on deck he was astonished to see the sea beginning to rise. In the growing light of dawn he could see it boiling in short waves which the wind shattered and blew flat. But larger and larger waves rose out of the ocean which the wind could not control. They struck at the *Sea Nymph* from every quarter setting her to rolling and pitching wildly. Now the wind was rising, too. For a moment, Daniel thought it would blow the *Sea Nymph* out of the water. Even though the ship was running before the wind, Daniel could see that the ship's sudden lurches to windward put too much pressure on the three topsails.

"All hands stand by!" Captain Butler roared through a speaking trumpet, his voice barely rising above the wail of the wind. "Clew up and furl the fore and mizzen topsails! Look lively, now!"

At once, the sailors went swarming up the masts. Daniel marveled that they could hold on, until he realized that they were skillfully using the wind to plaster their bodies tight against the masts. One of the sails was so taut it might have been made of metal.

"Spill the air out of her!" a sailor roared to the helmsman, who put the helm down hard. The ship came to and the sailors at once seized the shaking sail and began to furl it. Soon, the two topsails were furled, but the *Sea Numph* still flew over heavy seas furiously lashing her bows. Daniel thought she looked naked with only the close-reefed main topsail still flying canvas. Then there was a dreadful splintering sound and before Daniel's horrified eyes the mizzenmast buckled in two, the upper part coming crashing down on the deck; flinging sailors who had been sitting on her furled spars screaming into the raging sea.

One of the mast's spars pierced the deck and became wedged there, while another leaned over the rail and plunged into the ocean, acting like a giant rudder that began to turn the struggling ship directly into the devastating violence of the wind.

"Axes!" Captain Butler roared through the trumpet. "Free that spar!"

Daniel Gill saw at once that if the entire mast were not quickly freed and sent over the side, the spar-rudder would present the *Sea Nymph*'s bow to the wind, which would surely capsize her. Tearing off his uniform coat and shirt to expose his bulging biceps he ran to the cluster of seamen striking ringing but aimless blows at the lodged spar to seize an axe from one of them.

"Stand back!" he shouted, lifting the axe high over his head and bringing it down with all his enormous strength.

Crack!

The spar shivered, but remained firm.

Daniel swung again.

Crrrraaack!

The spar parted to the cheers of the sailors.

"Heave!" Daniel roared, stooping to seize the broken end of the mast. "Under and over!"

With one motion, the sailors joined him. Together they strained and strained until they had got the mast standing on its spar above the rail. But they could move it no farther. Gasping, Daniel backed off and charged the mast. He struck it full force with his shoulder with the sailors still straining to move it. It teetered for an instant, moved slowly toward the water and then went splashing into the sea.

Too weak to cheer again, the exhausted sailors sank down

on the deck of the plunging ship. They stared at Daniel in amazement and shook their heads wonderingly.

"Look lively there!" Butler bellowed at them. "Clear the deck!"

Wearily, they arose and began gathering the debris caused by the crashing mast and threw it over the side. It was a difficult task. Although the wind was abating, the sea was still wild and the *Sea Nymph* still pitched and rolled. Each time she did, the water on her deck rushed against her bulwarks where it met incoming waves from the sea to fall booming back upon the deck in high plumes of water. Gradually, the sea also began to subside. By noon, both wind and water had died down. The air was clear and invigorating and a bright sun beamed overhead. With the deck completely clear of debris, Captain Butler began issuing orders to spread canvas and Daniel was preparing to get into the galley to take some food to Barbara, when a lookout called down:

"Sail ho!"

Captain Butler rushed to the starboard rail and put his telescope to his eyes. His face blanched and he groaned aloud.

"What is it?" Daniel cried in alarm, rushing to his side.

"Pirates!" Butler replied. "If I'm not mistaken that's the Jolly Roger of Black Dick Doyle. Here," he said, handing the glass to Daniel, "what do you make of it?"

"A black flag," Daniel said, peering through the glass, "with a white skull and a bleached white thigh bone underneath it. On the right, a red heart dripping blood, and the left a red dagger also dripping."

"That's Black Dick, all right! Stede Bonnet's old rag. God help us!"

"But, Captain, we're bigger than they are. Can't we fight or outsail them?"

Butler shook his head morosely. "Not without our canvas spread. Look at him coming down on us. The bow's got a bone in her teeth. He'll be on us before we can crowd on all our canvas."

"My God, Captain Butler, then the least we can do is go down fighting! This won't be the first time I've manned a cannon. Let's man the g—"

"It's no use, Colonel," Butler said, his face now almost completely drained of color. "When the mast fell, it stove in the powder locker. All our powder's wet." He turned toward the first mate, standing among a crowd of sailors fearfully watching the approach of the pirate ship. "Run up the white flag," he called in a trembling voice.

"You're *surrendering?*" Daniel exclaimed aghast.

A puff of smoke burst from the side of the pirate ship and a few seconds later a spout of water rose into the air a hundred yards ahead of the *Sea Nymph*'s bow.

"Yes, I'm surrendering," Butler said, pointing to the geyser of water. "He's just playing with us now. Wiping our nose. But if I don't haul down my colors right away, he'll put us on the bottom in an hour." Butler glanced above him where the American flag came fluttering down the mast and the white flag of capitulation ran up it. A cheer came faintly on the wind from the pirate ship. Daniel could see a longboat swing out from it. Soon it came speeding toward them, the sun flashing on the oars of the rowers. Daniel thought of Barbara and his heart was wrung with anguish. Why did I *bring* her? he thought in despair. Why did I tell her how beautiful Charleston was and make her want to come? Daniel had brought a pair of pistols with him. A bullet apiece, he thought grimly. I'll never let them near her. He turned to go below to load the pistols, but he paused, startled, when he heard Butler mutter:

"It's all up with me."

"You? Why just you? What about the rest of us? I never heard anywhere that pirates had tender hearts."

"They don't. But they also have hard heads. You and your wife should bring them a handsome ransom, and I don't doubt that all of my men will sign on as pirates rather than walk the plank."

"They *really* do that?"

"Of course they do. And that's what I'll be doing in another half-hour." Captain Butler's voice broke. He was almost on the point of sniveling, so great was his fear of certain death. Daniel was amazed. The captain had been so brave and calm and competent during the storm. But, now . . .

"But, why just you?" Daniel persisted.

"Black Dick Doyle and I were partners once." The finger Butler raised to cover his trembling mouth was also shaking. "We had an argument . . . a duel. I won. And I marooned him on a desert island. He was pretty badly wounded. I . . . I thought he would die."

Daniel was astonished. "You were a *pirate?*"

Butler nodded, wiping his sweating forehead with a blue bandanna. "Who wasn't? Even John Paul Jones was on the account at one time." He walked to the rail to gaze at the approaching longboat. It was only a few hundred yards away. Captain Francis Butler rocked back slowly on his heels. His shoulders seemed to square and his spine straighten. He turned and came back to Daniel a changed man.

"I beg your pardon, Colonel Gill," he said with a bow. "I have been acting like a frightened puppy, and I apologize. You are a gallant man, sir, and I thank you for saving my ship. It was not your fault that you saved it for a scoundrel." Bowing again, he walked towards his cabin. Daniel followed at a distance. He heard the clink of glass and the popping of a cork, followed by the gurgle of liquid falling from a bottle. Captain Francis Butler sighed deeply before pouring another glass. Daniel Gill tensed, bracing for the report of a pistol shot.

When it came, he rushed below to Barbara.

Barbara was standing beside him when the pirates came aboard. She wore a short lavender jacket over a dress of violet silk. Although her features were calm, Daniel could feel her hand trembling in his.

"Don't worry," he said, squeezing her hand. "Captain Butler said that the worst we could expect would be to be held for ransom."

Barbara did not answer. Her dark eyes had widened in fear when she saw the pirates clambering over the rail. Daniel had never seen a more villainous looking crowd of men. They all had their long hair tucked up inside tricornes or bandannas of red and blue. All wore earrings. Some of them had their beards plaited and tied with little red ribbons. All carried cutlasses and had pistols thrust into wide sashes of yellow, red or blue. At their head was the man Daniel guessed was Black Dick Doyle. He was tall and strongly built, although not quite as big as Daniel. You'd need to be at least that strong to boss a crew of cutthroats like that, Daniel thought. Doyle also had a curling black mustache and his swarthy, hawkish complexion reminded Daniel of Benedict Arnold. He wore a long satin coat of red with a pistol stuck in a blue sash. His breeches were silver and there were silver buckles on his black shoes. A cutlass with a gleaming brass guard and hilt hung from his hip. Quite the swashbuckler, Daniel thought, watching through narrowed eyes when Captain Doyle's black eyes roved approvingly over Barbara. Daniel's buff-and-blue uniform also seemed to interest him. Doyle bowed low.

"My pleasure, sir. Your name, please."

"Colonel Daniel Gill. This is my wife, Barbara."

Again Doyle's eyes flicked toward Barbara. Then he frowned. "Gill? Colonel Gill? The name sounds fam—" He snapped his fingers and exclaimed, "Of course! You're General Washington's right-hand man."

Now a gleam of greed and cunning replaced the prurience in his eyes.

"I am the general's aide, yes," Daniel replied coldly.

"Of course. We shall discuss your value to him another time." Doyle leered again at Barbara, before glancing around him in mock dismay. "But where is my host? Where is dear Francis to welcome me aboard the ship he stole from me? Superfluous, is it not, my dear colonel, to capture one's own ship?" He glanced up at the jagged mizzenmast stump in dismay. "You'd think he'd have been more careful with it. Come, sir, where is Captain Butler?"

Daniel pointed to the captain's cabin. "In there."

Captain Doyle frowned. Drawing his pistol, he strode to the cabin and kicked the door open. He scowled. "You cowardly carrion!" He kicked the dead man in the face. He replaced his pistol, returning to the quarterdeck with his face contorted with fury. "Thinks he'll deny me my little fun, eh? The gutless snake! He must have known damn well I'd make someone else pay." Doyle's blazing eyes fell on the terrified crew of the *Sea Nymph* being herded aft by his pirates. He singled out the first mate with an evil smile. "Well, Harkins, we meet again. And wasn't it your idea to maroon me? And wasn't it you who rowed me ashore?"

"No!" the first mate screamed, falling to his knees and stretching out his arms piteously. "It wasn't me! It was *him!* It was Butler who made me!"

Black Dick Doyle began to chuckle hideously. "Seize him! Feed him to the fishes!" A cheer arose from the pirates. They yanked the sobbing man to his feet and rushed him to the rail while one of them ran to the carpenter's cabin to return with a wide plank. This they pushed over the rail while four of the strongest held it in place. Laughing horribly, the pirates seized the cowering, weeping Harkins and forced him out on the plank. The pitiful man threw himself down on it and clutched its sides desperately. His eyes were squeezed tight shut, but Daniel could see the tears leaking out their sides. One of the pirates drew his cutlass and made as though to force Harkins erect by pricking him with the point.

"Belay that!" Black Dick Doyle shouted. Still chuckling, he strode to the rail to stare quizzically over the side. "No welcoming committee in view yet," he muttered. "Well, let's whet their appetite." Turning, he yelled: "Get Butler's body."

Daniel heard Barbara gasp and felt her hand grow cold in his. He immediately lifted her in his arms and went below to their cabin, where he laid her gently on her bed. Her eyelids fluttered. She passed a hand over her forehead. "I . . . I can't believe what I've seen . . ."

Daniel kissed her tenderly on the cheek. "Stay here," he said. He went into the closet where he kept his pistols and stuck both into his trousers. Coming out, he saw Barbara lying on the bed with her eyes still closed, breathing deeply. "I'm going," he said. "Lock the door after I leave."

Daniel came on deck just as the pirates shoved Captain Butler's body over the rail. They had seen a dorsal fin sliding through the water and they dropped the corpse directly in the shark's path. There was a loud splash and then a sudden furious swirling movement in the water. Instantly, the water boiled white and frothy and then became red. The pirates laughed and cheered. Four or five more fins sped through the water drawn by the blood.

"Bye-bye, Francis," Doyle chuckled, unsheathing his cutlass. "You were the main dish. Here's the dessert." He turned to the babbling Hawkins still clinging to the plank and with two deliberate strokes of his blade cut the man's hands off at the wrists and sent him toppling with a shriek to the circling, swirling sharks below.

Colonel Daniel Gill watched the pirates' hideous sport trembling with rage and frustration. His fingers itched for the feel of the butts of the pistols stuck in his breeches. But he knew he was helpless. He might kill Doyle and another pirate, but that would mean the end of himself and Barbara. Captain Butler's crew would be absolutely useless in a pinch.

They stood cowed at the stern, and when Doyle ordered the plank placed over two powder kegs and sat behind it on another cask, they crowded forward eagerly to sign on as pirates. Ordering them aloft to spread the *Sea Nymph*'s canvas, he arose and strode towards Daniel.

"You did not find our little frolic amusing, Colonel?"

Daniel said nothing. Still, his dark blue eyes were like steel when they bored into Doyle's black ones.

"A pity," the pirate said, sighing. He reached a hand up to twirl the ends of his curling mustache. Then he drew his pistol and aimed it at Daniel and said, "Please take off your coat."

Daniel hesitated and Doyle's eyes narrowed. "Beggs," he called to a bearded pirate, "on the double." The pirate ran up to him and Doyle pointed with the pistol at Daniel. "Take off the colonel's coat." At once, the pirate ran behind Daniel to seize the lapels of his uniform coat from behind and pull them toward him. Daniel was pinioned. His pistols came into view.

"So foolish of you," Black Dick Doyle murmured, reaching forward to pull the pistols free and place them on the plank. "Let him go, now, Beggs." The man released Daniel who straightened his coat, his eyes still directly on Doyle's. "If you will, my dear Colonel, you may remove your coat yourself." His eyes now ablaze, Daniel took off his coat and handed it to Doyle. "All right, Beggs, take his two pistols and cover him while I see what," he said rummaging inside the garment, "see what I can find here." He pulled out an envelope with Washington's seal on it. It contained the general's written instructions to Lincoln. "Indeed!" Doyle exclaimed, beginning to read eagerly. Finishing, he glanced up at Daniel. "This is better than a chest of jewels, my dear Colonel. Just imagine what General Clinton will be willing to pay for such information. And for you! And your lovely lady! At first, I had thought of going to General Washington for your ransom. But the British are so close!" He turned to the west where the sun was setting in a round red ball. "Just over the horizon. Now, if you will, Colonel," he said, drawing his pistol again, "please lead me to your cabin."

Daniel hesitated, his eye on the pistol muzzle. It seemed to yawn as wide as a cannon's mouth. Without a word, he went down the ladder to his cabin. He knocked on the door.

"It's me, Barbara. Please open the door."

The door swung open. Barbara gasped when she saw Doyle behind her husband. The two men entered and Doyle kicked the door shut with a backward movement of his foot. He pointed to a closet fastened by two stout wooden bars. "Open it," he said to Daniel. "And don't get any ideas about those bars." Daniel walked to the door and lifted the bars from the angle irons that held them, putting them on the deck. "Open the door and go inside." Daniel entered the closet. "Now, you," Doyle said to Barbara, "put the bars back." She hesitated, and he lifted the pistol. She complied. Doyle motioned Barbara away from the door, walking to it but still keeping an eye on her. "You will remain there until I conclude my deal with General Clinton," he called through the door.

"What about my wife?" Daniel shouted, his voice muffled by the thick oak door.

"She will be well taken care of," Doyle replied, with a leer at Barbara. He motioned her toward the cabin door. She opened it and went out into the passageway. Doyle turned to study the closet door thoughtfully. "To be safe, I'd better put a guard in here," he muttered. Then he closed the door, walked to an adjoining cabin, opened the door and waved Barbara inside. She turned to face him, her breasts heaving. She saw his black eyes glittering with lust, and after he put his pistol outside the cabin, locked the door and put the key in his pocket she knew what to expect. He came toward her, breathing heavily. The volutes of his nostrils flared cruelly. She backed away in horror.

"There's no place for you to hide," he said, leering again. With a bound, he seized her in his arms and pressed his mouth on hers.

Barbara felt as though she were in the grasp of some foul creature. The touch of the hairs of his mustache filled her with revulsion. She struggled to free herself, clenching her fists as though to strike him. Suddenly, to Doyle's surprise, she relaxed and kissed him back. She pressed her body against his. He released her.

"What's this? What's this?" he sputtered, wiping his mouth with the back of his hand. He eyed her suspiciously. "You like me?" he asked dubiously. "You want to make love to Black Dick Doyle?"

"My grandmother was very practical," Barbara replied,

moving her right leg slightly to make sure the stiletto was in place. "She taught me that if rape is inevitable, you might as well relax and enjoy it."

Doyle chuckled, but he still watched her warily. "When the lady consents, it isn't rape. What are you after?" he asked in a guarded tone.

"My husband's safety. He could suffocate in that closet. Promise me you'll let him out . . . let him have the cabin to himself with a guard outside the door . . . however you arrange it . . . and I'll make love to you like you've never known it in any of your pirates' brothels."

Doyle drew in his breath. His black eyes were gleaming with lust again. He nodded his head slowly. "All right. I'll let him out . . . afterward . . ." His breath starting to come fast once more, he watched her while she removed her short jacket with a sensuous motion that delineated the arch of her full breast beneath the violet silk dress. She sat on the bed to remove her shoes, pulling the dress back to reveal her crossed white legs. She arose and began removing the dress. Now she stood before him bare-breasted, with only her petticoat and knickers on.

"Aren't you going to undress?" she inquired, moving slightly so that her breasts swung tantalizingly.

Black Dick Doyle could contain himself no longer. He threw his tricorne on the bed and struggled to tear his coat off. So great was his passion that his arms became temporarily stuck in the sleeves.

"Let me help you," Barbara Gill murmured, slipping around behind him, where she let her petticoat fall, seized the stiletto and plunged it up to the hilt in his heart.

Black Dick Doyle sank to the deck with a long trailing moan. He rolled over. Blood bubbled from his mouth. For an instant, his eyes still gleamed with lust. Then they faded and began to roll upward in their sockets.

Barbara watched him die, her hand to her mouth in horror. She swayed and stumbled to the bed to sit down on it. She sank back on the pillow. Her head reeled. The room spun and whirled around her. Gradually, she recovered her balance and clarity of mind. She arose and went to Doyle and took the key from his waistcoat. She opened the cabin door, locked it again and ran to the next cabin. Rushing up to the closet door she removed the bars and yanked it open.

Daniel was inside, sunk on the floor, breathing slowly. Fresh air flowing into the tiny enclosure revived him.

"Barbara!" he cried, his astonished eyes falling on her bare breasts. "Where's Doyle?"

"Dead. I killed him. Hurry!"

Barbara grabbed Daniel's hand and pulled him outside. She unlocked the door of the other cabin while Daniel stooped to seize Doyle's pistol lying outside of it.

Inside, Daniel knelt beside Doyle's body. He rolled it over and pulled out the stiletto, which he wiped off on the bed cover.

"He tried to rape me at first," Barbara explained. "I pretended to make love to him so that I could take off my clothes and get at the ... the stiletto ..."

A sob half broke from her lips, but she caught her breath and stifled it. When Daniel handed her the stiletto, she took it grim faced, and strapped it into place again. Immediately, Daniel began stripping the body of its clothes. He took off his own and put Doyle's on. He crammed Doyle's tricorne low on his head to hide his blond hair. He paused.

"Give me the stiletto," he said, and Barbara handed it back in surprise.

Grasping Doyle by the hair, Daniel cut off sections of it and stuffed them inside the tricorne.

"Turn around," he said to Barbara, and when she did he cut off the dead man's lips with their black mustaches and dried them on the bed cover. Barbara gasped when she saw what he had done. But Daniel shrugged. "I'll hold them to my mouth," he said. After Barbara had put her dress back on, he stuck the pistol into his breeches and led the way topside.

Stepping out of the hatch with Barbara behind him, Daniel saw with relief that the *Sea Nymph* was not yet underway. He held the mustaches to his lips while searching the ranks of the pirates for Doyle's lieutenant, Beggs. He saw him and motioned him to him. Beggs came trotting to his side, gasping when Daniel jammed his pistol into his ribs.

"Order a longboat lowered," Daniel growled. "Or you'll be joining Doyle in hell."

Beggs licked his lips, his terrified eyes shooting a question.

"Yes, he's dead," Daniel said softly, jabbing him again

with the pistol. "Now do as I say. Tell them I'm going ashore to parley with the British."

Wincing, the man cupped his hands to his lips and shouted: "Avast, there! Lower a boat away! Cap'n's goin' ashore to parley with the British."

Daniel watched while a boat was swung out and lowered out of sight. He prodded Beggs again. "I want them all up in the rigging when we leave. Order them up."

"All hands on deck!" Beggs bawled. "Clew up and furl the sails!"

Within a few minutes all the seamen aboard the *Sea Nymph*, including the pirates, were swarming aloft.

"Now, we'll go," Daniel said, putting the hand that held the pistol into his coat pocket. "One false move, and you're dead."

Trembling, Beggs led the way to the jacob's ladder. Barbara was the first to descend, then Beggs. When Beggs was halfway down, Daniel put the muzzle of the pistol between his teeth and began climbing down with his eye on Beggs. Once the three of them were in the boat, Daniel leveled the pistol at Beggs and said, "Start rowing."

Three hours later Daniel saw the bulk of Sullivan's Island rising above the horizon to his right. A few minutes later he saw the top of James Island to his left. Between the two islands was the mouth of Charleston Harbor. In dismay, he made out the Union Jack flying from the masts of the ships in the harbor.

"Oh, my God," he groaned aloud, "they must have gotten past Fort Moultrie." Glancing at Beggs, he said, "You can stop rowing, now." He pointed the pistol at him and snapped, "Over the side!"

Beggs's little eyes darted fearfully around him. "Not here," he pleaded. "These waters are full of sharks."

"Yes, I know," Daniel said mockingly. "Perhaps you'll run into some of the fellows you fed Harkins to." He cocked the pistol. "Over the side!"

Trembling, his face working, Beggs stood up and jumped into the water. He surfaced and began swimming toward Sullivan's Island, now only about a mile away. Daniel took his place at the oars and began rowing south.

"Where are we going?" Barbara asked.

"Kiawah Island. It's about twenty miles south of Charleston. It would be too dangerous to try to get into the city from the sea. I'll try a roundabout way from Kiawah. Raincloud, the chief of the Kiawah Indians, is my friend."

It was not until shortly before nightfall that Daniel made Kiawah's northern tip. Fortunately, it was high tide and Daniel was able to row the boat well up on the island's sand bar. Taking off his shoes and stockings, he stepped into the surf and dragged the boat to the edge of the beach. After putting his shoes and socks back on, he took Barbara by the hand.

"I think I can find the path to Raincloud's village," he said.

Barbara glanced with foreboding at the darkening swamp forest beyond the beach. It was a forbidding tangle of myrtle, palmettos, water oaks and huge, grotesque live oaks. She thought she saw a gleam of water within it. Then she saw a pair of baleful green eyes staring out of the dark at her and she shrank back in terror.

"What . . . what's that?" she asked Daniel.

"Looks like an alligator."

"How horrid! I thought it was a log at first, and then I saw the eyes." She shuddered. "Are they dangerous? I think I read somewhere that they eat people."

Daniel chuckled. "Not usually. They might eat a dog or a cat. Raincloud told me they don't attack humans. At least not on land." Daniel squeezed Barbara's hand and led her back to the beach. "But I'm taking no chances. We'll look for the path in the morning."

They sat down beside their beached boat, watching the light fade from the sky. A risen half moon silvered the waves. Soon the stars were shining overhead. Barbara put her head on Daniel's shoulder, listening dreamily to the murmur of Kiawah's gentle surf. She was enchanted.

"It is beautiful down here," she said. "Just like you said. Kind of ghostly." She thought again of the alligator and shivered. "Will . . . will we be safe here?"

"Of course," Daniel said, tightening his arm around her reassuringly. "If you're thinking of the alligators, don't worry. They never come on the beach. They don't like salt water."

Barbara relaxed. She lay on her back looking up at the stars. "How tiny and mean and miserable we are," she murmured. "If all those millions of stars are other worlds as the philosophers say, how miniscule we must be. How unimportant." Barbara closed her eyes. She reviewed the hours of fear and horror she had endured since the storm struck. Suddenly she was struck by the horrible emptiness and aimlessness of life. People robbing each other . . . killing each other . . . deceiving each other . . . struggling . . . posing . . . strutting . . . fretting . . . worrying . . . For what? A few baubles? A few hours of pleasure? Something to preoccupy the mind lest it meditate too deeply on death. What was it all about? Captain Butler dead . . . Black Dick Doyle dead . . . that poor first mate dead . . . Death, the end of it all. Barbara remembered Grandmother Gill lying on her deathbed. Was Grandma really in heaven with Jesus? She opened her eyes again. Did God really make this . . . this immense, endless, yes, infinite universe . . . just for *us* . . . ? Closing her eyes she looked down the years toward her own deathbed. There would be children and even grandchildren. There would have been laughter and tears . . . joy and anguish . . . defeats and victories . . . For everyone it would vary in duration and variety . . . but for everyone it would have the same end: death. Was death the end of life? Or was it the beginning of the new exalted life the parsons talked so knowingly about? Where did they get that knowledge, anyway? Why did parsons always talk as though they went to school with God? Barbara sighed. Suddenly she felt incredibly weary, and she rolled over on her side and fell asleep.

In the morning, Daniel found the path through the swamp. It was only a few feet wide, forcing them to follow it single file, but it was a good two or three feet above the level of the numerous ponds and lagoons it traversed. Barbara was thankful for that. She shuddered each time she saw an alligator sunning itself beside a lagoon, and she almost screamed when a water moccasin squirmed across the path in front of her. But it was also spring and wild azaleas were blooming everywhere in a riot of colors: red and pink, white and lavender. They gave a dainty and unearthly beauty to the ghostlike quality of the swamp forest: the great trees rising towering and forbidding from waters blackened by the acid issuing from the cypresses. It is pretty, Barbara thought to herself, and it is warm; but even if it is cold and stark back home we don't have any of these vile creatures snapping at our heels.

They came to a clearing formed by three hugh live oaks

growing in a triangle almost equidistant from each other. Beneath their gnarled boughs were about thirty wigwams. Daniel stopped and cupped his hands to his lips to give a bloodcurdling yell. Barbara gasped in alarm and Daniel chuckled.

"You keep forgetting I'm part Indian," he said.

From the village came answering war whoops and volleys of musket shots. Yelling braves, squaws and children poured from every teepee followed by packs of wildly barking dogs. A man dressed in buckskin came out of the largest wigwam. He was about Daniel's age, strongly built though half a head shorter.

"That's my friend, Chief Raincloud," Daniel said. He took Barbara's hand and led her toward the crowd of Indians peering curiously at him.

Raincloud smiled broadly when he saw Daniel.

"Welcome, my friend," he said, extending his hand. A murmur of approval arose from his fellow villagers, many of whom recognized Daniel.

"It's great to see you again, Raincloud," Daniel said. "This is my wife, Barbara."

The chief bowed low. When he lifted his head there was a twinkle in his eye. "When your husband hunted with me, Mrs. Gill, I always thought he was too choosy. But now I see that picking out the best is a virtue."

Barbara blushed and smiled. "Thank you, Raincloud," she said. To her surprise, the crowd of curious Indians which had surrounded them dispersed almost as quickly as it had gathered.

"They lose interest quickly if the visitor isn't a prisoner," Daniel explained. "When I yelled, I gave the scalp haloo and that made them think prisoners were arriving."

Raincloud nodded in confirmation. "But, why did you come, my friend?" Daniel told him of the storm and the pirates. Raincloud scowled. "It is good Doyle is dead," he said. "I knew him. He came here once for fresh water. But from the way he and his men looked at our squaws we knew what they really wanted. We drove them away. But you say you wish to get into Charleston?"

"I have to," Daniel said quietly. "I must see General Lincoln."

"It will not be easy," Raincloud said, shaking his head ruefully. "The British have the peninsula cut off by land and blockaded by water."

Daniel Gill was aghast. "Surrounded? But how did they get past Fort Moultrie? I thought it was impregnable."

"They sailed past it in a thunderstorm. Moultrie's batteries were useless. Clinton has been bombarding the city for weeks. He's already called on Lincoln to surrender."

Daniel groaned aloud. "By God, I have to get into Charleston before Lincoln pulls down his flag. That would be a disaster!"

Raincloud smiled and put his hand on Daniel's shoulder. "Don't worry, my friend. I'll get you into Charleston. We can paddle down the Kiawah River to Johns Island and then carry the canoe overland to the Stono. From there we can paddle to the Ashley and White Point, where the Ashley and the Cooper meet."

"Excellent!" Daniel cried. "But what about the British fleet?"

"Don't worry. If they hail us, I'll tell them I'm out to check my traps." He winked. "And I may sound a little drunk."

That night, under a starless sky, an hour after high tide so as to take advantage of the current of the ebb, with Barbara in the care of the chief's wife, Daniel and Raincloud put their canoe into the Kiawah River and began paddling downstream. An hour later they came to a beach on Johns Island. They dragged the canoe up it and carried it to the Stono River, again paddling downstream to the Ashley. There were no other vessels on the river, not a sound save the high keening cry of the night herons. But as they approached White Point they could make out the hulks of British warships. As they passed one of them, a sentry swung a lantern over the side and called out:

"Who's that down there?"

"Itsh Raincloud, chief of the Kiawahsh," Raincloud yelled in a thick, slurred voice.

"What are yez about?"

"Shetting my trapsh. You want some crabs?" Raincloud laughed and began to sing. "God shave our glacious queen."

"You mean king, you savage. Go along with you."

Still singing, Raincloud leaned into his paddle and sent the

canoe surging toward White Point. Dragging it up over the
sand bar, the two men plunged into a desolate swampy
morass of scrub oaks and palmettos. Suddenly, a voice called
out:

"Halt! Who goes there?"

"Colonel Daniel Gill. General Washington's aide-de-camp."

"Give the password."

"I don't know the password. I've just come from Kiawah
by canoe."

"Sorry, sir—you must advance with your hands up. Is anyone with you?"

"Yes, he'll hold up his hands, too," Daniel said. The two
men came toward the sentry with their hands held high, just
as the corporal of the guard rushed up with a lantern. He
held it in Daniel's face.

"I'm sorry, sir, but I must arrest you," the corporal said.
"You're not in uniform."

"That'll be fine," Daniel said. "Please arrest Chief Raincloud, too. Take me to your commanding officer at once.
Here," he said, pulling Black Dick Doyle's pistol from his
belt, "take this. You should have searched me, Corporal."

Even in the darkness, Daniel could sense the corporal's embarrassment. "L-let's g-get going," he stammered, and the two
men preceded him to the guardhouse. There, General Lincoln's intelligence officer was sent for. He recognized Daniel
at once and hurried him off to headquarters.

General Lincoln read Washington's letter by the light of a
sputtering candle stuck in an empty wine bottle. Daniel was
struck by the man's appearance. He was haggard and unshaved. The hands that held the letter trembled. After he had
finished the letter and glanced up, Daniel could see the defeat
lurking at the back of his lackluster eyes.

"It can't be done," Lincoln said, shaking his head, "I simply cannot hold out any longer."

"But, General, if Charleston falls, so will the south. You
must hold. General Washington was most adamant on this
point. Charleston must not fall."

"General Washington was unaware of my position when he
wrote these lines. I am surrounded. They have more men,
more guns and a fleet. With Arbuthnot's sailors, Clinton has
fourteen thousand men. I have fifty-five hundred." An explosion in the street made the building shake. Dust drifted

down on Lincoln's head. "Do you see? Their siege train gets closer every day."

"But, General, a peninsula like Charleston is made for a trap. Why didn't you abandon it and save your army?"

"The people wouldn't let me. They insisted on my defending the town. Why, do you know that God damned Governor's Council, when they heard I was thinking of withdrawing, some of them swore that if I tried it, they'd burn my boats, open the gates to the British and join them in attacking me!"

Daniel shook his head ruefully. "Soldiers shouldn't listen to civilians, sir. They have different values. Usually narrow and selfish. Have you no escape route at all, General?"

"I did have. I had a force of cavalry and militia about thirty miles up the Cooper. They were holding the pass open at Monck's Corner. But then that bloodthirsty bastard of a Banastre Tarleton hit them in a surprise night raid and drove them into the swamp. So now I'm trapped." Another shell exploded outside and the house shook once more. "I tell you, Colonel, it's hopeless. To fight on will only risk the lives of my men and those of the townspeople." He stared defiantly at Daniel out of beaten, sullen eyes. "I've already accepted their terms, Colonel. Tomorrow, May twelfth, we're surrendering." Daniel opened his mouth in horror, but Lincoln cut him off. "It's no use arguing. It's done. And my advice to you, Colonel, is to get back to Kiawah as soon as you can. If you're still here tomorrow, I'll have to surrender you, too."

Chapter Twenty-Eight

By the time Daniel and Barbara Gill returned to Washington's headquarters, making a wide swing to the west to avoid Clinton's troops and turning east again when they reached North Carolina, it appeared that the south had been lost. The disastrous fall of Charleston was followed in mid-August 1780 by another shocking battlefield defeat at Camden, South Carolina, after which Lord Cornwallis led his troops into North Carolina with the evident intent of detaching that state and Virginia from the Rebel cause.

Once again, Washington's own army had melted away, and was living on short rations hardly better than Valley Forge. Daniel Gill was dismayed to see that the hope that had shone so constantly in the eyes of his beloved chief had all but disappeared.

"We have hit bottom," he said to Daniel on his return. "There are so few horses and wagons available I cannot possibly go on the offensive. Congress is almost bankrupt. The people don't seem to care. I have been able to recruit only a thousand men since coming out of winter quarters. It looks like the end, Daniel. I have almost ceased to hope."

"But what about the French troops?" Daniel asked eagerly. "I heard they landed at Newport."

"Yes, five thousand of them under Count Rochambeau. That is one ray of hope. Perhaps the only one. But the British fleet has got them bottled up there and I won't be able to use them. Or five thousand more that the British have blockaded in Brest." The general sighed wearily. "I had hoped to use them in a summer campaign against Clinton in New York. But, now . . ."

"Clinton is back in New York, sir?"

"Yes, he left Cornwallis in charge in the south. I have an idea Clinton is thinking of trying the Hudson again. That is why I sent Arnold to West Point to strengthen the defenses there."

"General Arnold, sir? Has he returned to active service?"

"Yes. I wanted him to command the left flank of the Continental Army. The position of honor. I was surprised when he refused. He said his leg would not permit him to take the field. He seemed delighted with the West Point command. Strange, for a fighter like Benedict Arnold to want to sit in a backwater waiting for something to happen."

"It is odd, Excellency," Daniel Gill said musingly.

Benedict Arnold had revived his correspondence with General Sir Henry Clinton. The fall of Charleston had convinced him that the Revolution was doomed. He sent for Dr. Benjamin Gill. Dr. Gill was surprised to see that the general had moved out of the opulent Penn House and was living without servants in one of his father-in-law's rental properties. But Benjamin was delighted to learn that the general was writing to Clinton again. It could only mean that he had something to trade! Like Arnold, Dr. Gill was certain that the Revolution was dying. It's demise would make the doctor a wealthy man, and perhaps even a hero. The king might knight him. Imagine! Dr. Sir Benjamin Gill. And wouldn't Amanda love to be called "your Ladyship." If they could get fat old Joel off her neck! Overjoyed, Benjamin slipped into New York City and made straight for Clinton's headquarters and Major André.

"It's our old friend, sir," he said with a smile, handing André the coded letter. "This time he's calling himself Mr. Moore."

André took it and began to read. He gave a low whistle. "By Jove, this *is* interesting. I say, Doctor, would you write out your report like a good chap while I speak to Sir Henry about this." Dr. Gill nodded and André left the room.

"It's Arnold again, Excellency," André said to Clinton, unable to repress a grin of elation. "He wants to sell us West Point."

"Capital!" Clinton cried in a rare outburst of emotion. "But can he do it?"

"He's trying to persuade Washington to give it to him. He says he's gotten some influential members of Congress to intercede for him. He's confident he'll get it."

"When?"

"Before the end of the summer. Around August. But one thing, sir—he's upped his price."

Clinton looked up sourly. "How much?"

"Double. He wants a hundred thousand dollars for himself, protection for his family and property and a brigadier's commission."

"Haggles like a fishwife, doesn't he? Greedy beggar. Well, I agree. If he can give us West Point. It will win the war at a stroke. But I think we shall have to wait until he gets the command. Then, John, I think there should be a meeting between you. With so much at stake, we must nail it down. And that could only be done at a meeting between you. You don't mind, John?"

"Not at all, sir."

"Good. Then you arrange it."

Benedict Arnold took command at West Point on August 5, 1780. He chose to make his headquarters in a house across the river from the fort. It was owned by Colonel Beverly Robinson, a Loyalist serving in the British Army. The Robinson House was a large, cheerless rambling structure which did not impress Catherine Martin, Arnold's housekeeper.

"Gloomy, sir," she said to the general, shaking her head with the starched cap on it. "Not nearly as nice as the Penn House. The mistress won't like it nearly so much."

"Perhaps. But it's better than that wretched hovel we just left. We must make it as cheerful as we can for her. You had better get started cleaning, Catherine. You can hire servants in Buttermilk Falls." He turned to Major Franks, who had also accompanied him. "Major, I should like you to return to Philadelphia to bring Mrs. Arnold here."

Catherine Martin beamed. "Oh, sir, is she bringing the baby?"

"Of course."

"When is she coming?"

"In a few weeks. Now, Catherine, please be about your business." Still beaming, the housekeeper hurried off. Arnold swung back to Franks. "David, you must spare no pains to make Mrs. Arnold comfortable. I have provided for a coach and a wagon, the coach if it rains, the wagon if the sun's shining. Both are well upholstered. It will be quite a large

party. A noncom and a squad of infantrymen to act as
guards . . . Mrs. Arnold's maid . . . a nurse for the baby
. . . It should take about six days. I've arranged for you to
stop each night at a pleasant place. There will be hampers of
food and wine for the journey. Here is your itinerary."
Franks took the sheet of paper handed him by Arnold. The
general regarded him thoughtfully for a moment, before
asking, "Have you ever heard of a man named Joshua Hett
Smith? He lives in Haverstraw."

"As a matter of fact I have, sir. Colonel Lamb spoke to me
about him."

"John Lamb? He was with us at Quebec and Danbury. Is
he here?"

"Yes, sir. He recovered from his wound at Danbury and
now he's an artillery officer on the Hudson. He detests Smith,
sir. He says he acted as an American spy once. But Lamb
thinks he's really a British plant. A Tory at heart, Lamb says.
I wouldn't trust him, sir."

"Indeed. That's good to know. Thank you, David."

On the following day, General Benedict Arnold made a
trip to Haverstraw to visit Joshua Hett Smith.

"Hey, Natey—Natey, we're being transferred!"

"Where?"

"West Point. We're gonna do guard duty for General Arnold."

"What a break! Maybe we can get some decent food to eat
up there. Must be plenty of game in the woods. And from
what I heard of the brawls between the Cowboys and the
Skinners, the farms must be loaded with cows and chickens.
When do we leave?"

"End of the week. Our squad's gonna be the military escort
for Mrs. Arnold on her trip to the Point."

"By Jesus, our luck's finally changed. Can you imagine the
kind of food Arnold'll have for her?"

"Yeah, an' don't fergit all them pretty little Dutch gals."

In his visit with Joshua Hett Smith, Arnold had become
convinced that the fat pompous little man was a Loyalist at
heart and could be relied on to find a replacement for Dr.
Benjamin Gill as a courier. But days passed without a word
from Smith. Arnold became anxious, then pleased when his

secretary, Colonel Richard Varick, appeared on August 13. Arnold immediately set him to work making a thorough survey of West Point. Varick drew up lists of the three thousand men in Arnold's command, classifying them as gunners, sharpshooters or foragers. He made an inventory of all the post's supplies, paying especial attention to the amount of ammunition and the number of horses and mules. Varick also copied all the available maps of the West Point fortifications, and of the string of smaller forts in the surrounding hills. He examined the huge chain beneath the water across the Hudson designed to block British warships. He reported to Arnold that a few of the logs in the boom that supported it had sunk and that some of the links were twisted. General Arnold did not repair the chain, but he did include Varick's report in the massive fund of information he was gathering for General Clinton. At the bottom of it, he wrote: "A single heavy ship can break this chain." The survey was completed just when Smith visited Robinson House and told Arnold that a woman named Mrs. Mary McCarthy could serve him as a courier.

"She lives in Haverstraw and wants to visit New York with her children," Smith said. "If you give her a pass, Excellency, she can carry your letters into the city."

"Excellent!" Arnold exclaimed. He limped from his chambers into Colonel Varick's office. "Please write a pass for Mrs. Mary McCarthy and children of Haverstraw. She will deliver some letters I have written for Mr. John Anderson, a merchant in New York."

Varick was startled. "But Mrs. McCarthy is the wife of a British prisoner-of-war, sir."

"Quite. There is nothing of a military nature in my letters, Richard. It is strictly business correspondence."

"As you say, sir," Varick replied, and wrote out the pass. Later, he watched with unhappy eyes while a West Point barge rowed Mrs. McCarthy and her children down the Hudson. He spoke of his misgivings to Major Franks.

"I don't like this business of issuing passes to enemy relatives," he said. "It's a mistake to let them travel freely, just like Americans. And I don't like that fat little toady of a Joshua Hett Smith who's always tagging along after the general. I think he's a Tory."

"Rubbish, Richard! You're just letting the general's bad

mood get on your nerves. Wait until his wife gets here. Then
he'll be his old self again. Besides, who can advise Benedict
Arnold? I've been with him for five years and I've never seen
him listen to anyone yet. He's never wrong. You know that.
And don't criticize. If you do, you're his enemy."

"I suppose you're right," Varick said with a sigh, a frown
on his serious dark face. "But this Mr. Anderson business
bothers me. Now I must notify Major Tallmadge at North
Castle that if any letters from Mr. Anderson turn up, they
must be sent here at once. It's a strange business."

A few days later some letters from Mr. Anderson did ar-
rive. Benedict Arnold was elated. He had reached André!
Now he could plan the meeting between them that General
Clinton wanted.

On Thursday, September 14, 1780, Mrs. Peggy Arnold and
her entourage arrived at Haverstraw. Benedict Arnold had
himself rowed downriver in a barge replete with a band and
decorated with banners and flowers. He clambered stiffly onto
the landing, limping eagerly toward his waiting wife and embracing her tenderly. Then he took his infant son—Edward
Shippen Arnold—and kissed him softly on the cheek. Nate
Gill and Luke Sawyer watched curiously from the dock,
where their squad had been drawn up by Corporal James
Larvey.

"Oh, my Jesus, he sure is sweet on her," Luke whispered.

"Quiet!" Corporal Larvey hissed, and Sawyer fell silent, listening with the others to Arnold speaking to his wife.

"You look pale, my dear. Did you have a difficult trip?"

"Not at all. It was a very pleasant journey. David was
most attentive. But I am a little weary. Just before we got
here—down the road—there was a kind of battle. Just a skirmish, really. . . . Cowboys and Skinners, David said they
were."

"That's the local name for Tories and Rebels," Arnold said
grimly. "Nothing but young ruffians on both sides. I'll have to
patrol the roads more carefully. You're sure you're all right,
my dear?"

"Oh, yes. But I would like a cup of tea."

"Of course," Arnold said, leading her to the coach. "We're
stopping at the home of Joshua Hett Smith for the night.
We'll be there in a few minutes."

Helping Peggy inside the carriage, Arnold got in after her while Major Franks climbed up on the box beside the coachman. He flicked his whip and the coach rolled forward, the soldiers striding silently along beside it to form a guard. After the Arnolds entered Smith's home, Corporal Larvey spoke to his men.

"All right, fall out. We're spending the night in the tavern by the landing. And no hard drinkin', y' hear. In the mornin', we gotta fill a barge with Mrs. Arnold's possessions and row it up the river."

"Row!" Luke Sawyer exclaimed. "Hell, we ain't sailors."

"We are now," Larvey said grimly. "The general wants his barge manned round the clock. Two shifts. Twelve on and twelve off. That means us poor shitheads is the second shift. Eight men an' me for a coxswain. Only one who don't get this duty is you, Sawyer. They want you in the post smithy."

"Good-bye corn balls, hello horse balls," Luke muttered, and the soldiers around him laughed.

In the morning, they rowed their loaded barge upriver behind the general's barge carrying the Arnolds. Upon their arrival at the Robinson House, Nate and Luke gaped in incredulity. Colonel Varick stood on the dock flanked by four soldiers who bore on their shoulders a feather bed supported by long poles. They came toward the barge where General Arnold was assisting Peggy onto the dock. He stooped and gently swung her up onto the bed.

"There, my dearest. I couldn't bear the thought of your climbing all those dreadful steps." He stepped back and barked at the soldiers. "Look alive, lads—and be careful!" With Varick on one side and Arnold limping along on the other, the procession moved up to the Robinson House.

"I'll be go to hell!" Luke Sawyer swore. "He treats her like she was the Queen o' Sheba. I sure hope she don't feel no pea under that mattress, or else *he'll* burst out crying."

While Peggy rested, Benedict Arnold met once more with Joshua Hett Smith in his library.

"I need a boatman for the night of Wednesday, September 20, Mr. Smith," Arnold said. "I would like him to bring my business associate, Mr. Anderson, ashore at Teller's Point."

"No trouble, Excellency. I'll get the Cahoons. They have a boat. They're tenants of mine and they'll do as I ask."

"Excellent! When Mr. Anderson comes ashore, I would like you to take him to your home. He will stay there overnight and I will meet him Thursday morning."

"Of course. My wife and family will be away visiting in Fishkill."

"Then it is all settled," Arnold said eagerly, a look of immense relief coming over his face. "I will see you Thursday morning."

After Smith departed, Arnold sat at his desk to compose a letter in code to Major André. Colonel Varick came in without knocking.

"What's this, Richard?" Arnold asked in a sharp voice, looking up in irritation.

"A letter from General Washington, sir."

Arnold took it and tore it open. The commander-in-chief was going to Hartford to confer with Count Rochambeau. He would cross the Hudson at King's Ferry that night and spend the night at Peekskill. Because he was traveling without a guard, he asked Arnold to send fifty men to Peekskill.

Benedict Arnold's eyes gleamed. What an opportunity! At once, he drew another sheet of paper to him and began a letter to Sir Henry Clinton, informing him of Washington's plans. Then he finished the note to André. He was to board the British sloop, *Vulture*, on the night of Wednesday, September 20. A boat would bring Mr. Smith to the *Vulture*, who would take him ashore and put him up for the night. Arnold would meet him Thursday morning to complete the details of the betrayal, after which André would be rowed back to the *Vulture*. André must be disguised.

The following day, General Arnold and Major Franks rode to Peekskill to greet General Washington. Arnold was disappointed when he found the general safe and in good spirits. He hoped for great things from the French troops in Newport. Evidently, Arnold thought, Clinton hadn't had time to capture Washington. Or else he didn't get the letter. Which meant that maybe André didn't get his, either.

Benedict Arnold began to worry.

"I don't like this bit about your being in disguise, John," General Clinton said to Major André. "I don't want you to wear one."

"I won't, Excellency."

"If they caught you behind their lines in disguise, they could try you as a spy. You could be hung. And don't go behind their lines, either. At least not far. Just stay at the house where you're to meet Arnold."

"As you say, sir," André replied with his charming smile.

At seven o'clock Wednesday night, André boarded the *Vulture* off Teller's Point, fourteen miles below Arnold's headquarters. He waited until midnight for Arnold's emissary, and then until dawn. But no one came.

In the morning, Colonel Varick knocked on General Arnold's bedroom door to hand him a note from Joshua Hett Smith. Arnold read it with a sinking heart. The Cahoon brothers had refused to row their boat out to the *Vulture*. Smith had argued with them past midnight, but they had remained adamant. It was with difficulty that Smith had persuaded Samuel Cahoon to deliver this note.

Benedict Arnold threw on his clothes with his jaws working with rage. Alarmed, Peggy came to his side and read the note.

"Does this . . . does this mean the scheme has fallen through?" she asked anxiously.

"I don't think so," Arnold replied, his swarthy face black with fury. "I should never have relied on Smith. He's a fool! A pompous little ass and an idiot! I'm going down to Haverstraw immediately." Flinging himself outside the bedroom, he ran down the stairs shouting: "Richard! Richard! Order my barge at once!"

Arnold was almost running, his limp almost forgotten, when he came rushing down the steps to the landing. Fortunately, Corporal Larvey saw him coming and instantly ordered his men to their oars. Nate Gill leaned on his, watching the general enter the boat. *He seems terribly excited*, Nate thought.

"Shove off!" Larvey roared, and the oarsmen dug their blades into the water.

Just above Teller's Point, Arnold motioned to Larvey to cease rowing. Nate and the others lay on their oars, watching the general curiously. Arnold stood up in the barge and opened his telescope. He focused downriver. Yes, yes! The *Vulture* was still there! But was André still aboard her? He could not be sure. But he would have to act as though he were.

"Let us return to headquarters, Larvey," the general said.

Back at the Robinson House, Benedict Arnold received a strange letter from Colonel Varick. It was from Captain Andrew Sutherland of the *Vulture*. He was indignantly protesting the fact that American gunners had fired at his ship when it was under a flag of truce. It seemed a sincere routine protest, but Arnold's eyes gleamed when he saw that it was signed, "John Anderson, Secretary." André was still there! It was his handwriting. Unmistakably!

At once, he dismissed Varick and began gathering the lists and reports and maps assembled by the secretary. He folded them in a neat parcel and put them in his desk. Late that afternoon, he mounted his horse and set out for Haverstraw.

That night, General Arnold met Samuel Cahoon in an upper room of the Smith house. Smith was in the courtyard outside, talking to Samuel's brother, Joseph.

"Now, Samuel," Benedict Arnold said, "I want you and your brother to row Mr. Smith out to that ship tonight."

Samuel Cahoon shook his head stubbornly. He was a strongly built man with a low forehead and dull eyes. "No, your Excellency. We cain't do it. Joe 'n me's tired. We was up all night and I had to deliver that there note."

Benedict Arnold's eyes flashed imperiously. "You have no love for your country? This is a serious errand in the American cause. You're not a Loyalist, are you?"

"Hell, no!" The remark angered Samuel.

To placate him, Arnold spoke soothingly. "All you need to do is to row Mr. Smith to the *Vulture*. We have a business friend aboard her. I have provided the boat. You will row this friend to a point near Long Cove Mountain. It's only six—"

"Hell, no!" Samuel repeated, raising his voice this time and sputtering. "I ain't gettin' shot at by them British gunboats around the *Vulture*."

Arnold's eyes clouded in exasperation. He ground his teeth. Walking to the window, he saw Smith below with Joseph Cahoon and motioned to him to bring the man up. Arnold saw with dismay that Joseph was even slower witted than his brother, to whom he seemed to defer. He decided to continue to work on Samuel.

"Now I want you fellows to do as I ask without any ifs, ands or butts. If you don't, I will have you arrested as Tories. I am in command here, and my word is law. Do you hear?"

"Yep," Samuel said, shaking his head doggedly. "But we still ain't agoin' to do it."

Once again Arnold concealed his exasperation. "I'll give each of you fifty pounds of flour," he said coaxingly. "How long has it been since you've had even an ounce of good wheat flour?"

Both brothers licked their lips greedily. "A long time, I reckon. Mebbe since the war began. All our crops go to the army. Still, we ain't agoin' ter—"

"You will do as I say!" Arnold thundered, rising to his feet, his hawkish face terrible with rage. "Or I'll have you arrested and thrown into jail! This minute!"

Samuel and Joseph exchanged frightened glances, and Samuel mumbled sourly, "I reckon we'd better."

It was a beautiful clear autumn night, the mountain air fresh and invigorating with a slight chill hinting at the advent of winter. Benedict Arnold rode on horseback to the spot opposite the *Vulture* which he had selected for his meeting with André. Behind him came Smith's servant leading a third horse. Arnold dismounted and ordered the servant to move out of earshot. Benedict Arnold began to tremble with trepidation. Would André come? He studied the mighty river flowing black and tranquil, gleaming under the stars. It calmed him slightly. He peered into the darkness, stiffening when he heard a slight ripple of water. It was the boat, being rowed with oars muffled in sheepskins. It grated softly on the sandy beach. Joshua Hett Smith's portly little body was the first ashore, followed by a tall slender man wrapped in a greatcoat.

"Gustavus," Arnold murmured, stepping out of the shadows.

"Anderson," André replied in a soft voice.

They did not shake hands, immediately withdrawing into the darkness of a cluster of fir trees higher on the riverbank.

"General Clinton has agreed to my offer?" Arnold asked eagerly.

"Yes."

"When will I be paid?"

André's voice was slightly disdainful. "As soon as you deliver the fort.

"My family will be protected?"

"Of course."

"Good. Here is the information Sir Henry desires," Arnold said, handing André the packet. "It is complete. As he will see, the fortifications are in disrepair. I have not improved them. In fact, I have weakened the critical points by ordering their garrisons to the strong points. When you attack, I shall make a pretense of resistance, but then I shall surrender." André nodded in the dark and Arnold continued, "I will join your army after the surrender. I am sure my decision will bring many other ranking American officers to your colors."

The two men continued deep in conversation until the first faint roseate light of dawn crept over the eastern rim of the sky. Joshua Hett Smith came clambering up the riverbank. "It is four o'clock," he said. "You'd better be going back, Mr. Anderson."

They went back to the boat and the grumbling Cahoon brothers.

"Row Mr. Anderson back to the *Vulture*, Samuel," Arnold said.

"No, we won't!" Samuel replied, glaring up at Arnold defiantly. "We've had enough of this monkey business."

"You'll go, God damn your eyes, or you'll rot in jail!"

Both the Cahoons shook their heads. Open, sullen defiance glowed in their dull eyes. Benedict Arnold flew into a paroxysm of rage. *At the very last moment!* He swore and commanded and cajoled and threatened but the Cahoons sat unmoved in the boat.

"We'll row as far as Mr. Smith's landin', and no further," Samuel muttered.

"Wait a moment, Excellency," Smith said, putting a restraining hand on the livid Arnold's wrist. "You've got an extra horse. It was intended for me. Let Mr. Anderson ride it and I'll go back to my house in the boat. Mr. Anderson can stay the night."

Arnold glanced at André. "What do you think, Mr. Anderson?"

André glanced anxiously around him. "Am I behind American lines?"

"Yes."

"Then I think we'd better get to Mr. Smith's house as soon as we can. I'll wait until dark, and go back in darkness as I came."

He swung aboard the horse held by Smith's servant and fell in beside Arnold. They rode off in silence, glancing anxiously upward at the brightening sky. It was full daylight when they reached Smith's house.

"That will be all," Arnold said curtly to the servant, and led André inside. André threw off his greatcoat, standing before Arnold in his brilliant scarlet uniform and gleaming boots.

"You're not disguised," Arnold cried in dismay.

"No. Sir Henry was dead against it. I am not a spy, Général Arnold," André said coldly.

From downriver came the dull sound of an explosion.

"Artillery!" Arnold shouted, seizing his telescope and rushing to the window. "Some of our people are bombarding the *Vulture!*"

"Oh, my God!" André groaned.

"It's not by my orders, Major. It's not my gunners. It must be an outpost. No more than a round or two. It can't last."

André sank into a chair, relieved, until Joshua Hett Smith came panting up the steps from the river and burst inside his house.

"They're bombarding the *Vulture!*" he gasped. "She's upped anchor and she's dropping downstream." Smith gaped when he saw André's uniform. He looked at Arnold wonderingly. Major André's inquiring eyes were also on the general.

"How shall I get back to the *Vulture?*" he asked. "Can you find a set of more obliging oarsmen?"

It was Smith who replied. "You must go by the roads. I'll go with you. We'll take the ferry across the river and ride south."

"Isn't that rather dangerous, Mr. Smith?"

"Mr. Smith has passes signed by me," Arnold said. "I'll write one for you, too." Arnold looked at the parcel in André's hand. "You'd better divide that packet and put those documents in your stockings."

"My stockings?" André repeated, startled.

"Yes, and put on some civilian clothes. You can't possibly hope to escape detection in that uniform. Mr. Smith, what can you lend him?"

"I've got a beaver hat that'll fit you," Smith said to André. "And a handsome purple greatcoat trimmed in gold lace."

Purple! André thought in dismay. Good God! "Well," he said aloud with a wry grimace, "I suppose a man in my situation can't be too choosy."

Upon his return to the Robinson House, Arnold went at once to his wife. Jubilant, he told her that the scheme had succeeded. They embraced. Arnold went next to Colonel Varick, who reported that General Washington had sent word he would be stopping at Arnold's home that Saturday on the way back from Hartford.

"Excellent, Richard," Arnold said, smiling to himself. By Saturday, Major André would be safely back in New York.

Major John André and Joshua Hett Smith left Haverstraw late Friday afternoon. At about dusk they clattered onto the ferry to cross the river. Around nine o'clock they were halted by an American militia sentry who demanded to see their passes.

"Joshua Hett Smith and Mr. Anderson, merchant, eh? Signed by General Arnold. All right. Where are you headed?"

"White Plains. What's the best way?"

"North Castle, usually. But don't try it tonight. Them God damn Cowboys is out and you might run into trouble. If I was you, I'd stay at a farmhouse till mornin'."

Thanking him, they rode off. Smith pointed to a farmhouse beside the road and turned his horse into the path leading up to it. André was dismayed.

"You're not taking the sentry's advice?"

"Of course, sir. It's a warning, actually. If we ignore it, he might report us as suspicious."

They slept that night at the farmhouse of Andreas Miller. Early Saturday morning they were on their way again. Smith was amazed by the growing gaiety of his companion, who had seemed so apprehensive the night before. He became loquacious. His body, once tense and rigid in the saddle, now swayed to the rhythm of his discourses. John André spoke of British history, of the American war, of his hopes for an early peace. He recited verse in a low, moving voice. He regaled Smith with appreciations of music and painting. Reaching high ground to see the broad blue Hudson flowing majestically through the autumnal hills of orange and gold, he spoke with emotion of the magnificence of this great country which soon (because of the documents beneath his feet) would be returned to its allegiance to the Crown. John André was the essence of the cultivated young British officer and gentleman whose name (again because of those papers and his own constancy) would shine upon the pages of that history he loved so deeply.

They were nearing Pine Bridge across the Croton River. Fifteen miles away was the British outpost at White Plains. At Pine Bridge, the Rebel patrols ended. But before they reached Pine Bridge, to John André's consternation, Joshua Hett Smith halted his horse and said: "This is as far as I'm going. You'll have to go the rest of the way yourself."

"Alone!" André exclaimed indignantly. "My good man, I'm a stranger here! I might as well be on the moon, for all I know of this place. My God, Mr. Smith, don't you understand? You promised to lead me to safety. General Arnold expects you to."

"There's too many of those damn Cowboys across the river," Smith said. His was the unruffled calm of the man whose personal survival takes precedence over all other considerations. "You'll be all right, Major. The Cowboys are Loyalists. They wouldn't harm you, a British officer. But they might be rough on me."

Major André sighed wearily. His apprehensive air returned. Evidently, he thought glumly, what begins bad, ends worse. "I have no money," he said. "Can you lend me some? I might find occasion to need it."

"Certainly, sir. Here's fifty Continental dollars."

"Thank you," André said, taking his gold watch from his pocket. "And here is my watch for security."

"Nonsense, Major. I trust you completely. Well, I must be on my way."

Turning his horse, Joshua Hett Smith rode back the way he had come.

• • •

Not only the Cowboys were out. So were the Skinners. Like their Loyalist enemies, with whom they sometimes cooperated in looting the region, these ruffianly Rebels were in search of plunder. They plodded along the Tarrytown Pike in ragged bands. One trio included John Paulding, David Williams and Isaac van Wart. Paulding was the leader, both because of his great size and because he could read.

"Pretty slim pickin's nowadays," Paulding grumbled, waving a hand at the deserted farmhouses to either side of the road. "Listen at them wasps," he said, pointing to an orchard. "Eatin' all the fruit with nobody to shoo 'em off. Looks like everybody's done skedaddled."

"Mebbe we can ambush some Cowboys," Williams mumbled.

"What makes you think they'll have any better luck 'n us?"

"I dunno," Williams said, as they approached a bridge. "Mebbe we can ambush a swell. Or a farmer . . ."

"Good idea," Paulding said with sudden enthusiasm. "C'mon, let's hide here under the bridge."

The thunder of his horse's hooves on Pine Bridge restored Major John André's earlier confidence. It seemed to him that his mission was completed. To either side of him he saw the desolation caused by the depredation of the Cowboys and the Skinners. At last, he thought, the agony convulsing this unhappy land would end. Again because of the papers beneath his feet, the war would soon be over. His Loyalist friends would recover their confiscated estates on the banks of the Hudson. Dr. Benjamin Gill and Joel Courtney would return to Boston wealthy men. Well-bred Christian men of substance would recover their authority, and the peasant rabble that once had mocked them would return to their proper place as hewers of wood and drawers of water. The king would undoubtedly create an aristocracy which would rule in his name, and civilized nations would cease to shudder at the bloody and unwashed menace which had threatened to destroy all that was of value in the world. Major John André was wondering if the king would hang Washington and the others when he came to another bridge and heard a wild shout and three evil-looking ruffians jumped across his path with leveled muskets. One of them grabbed his horse's bit.

Momentarily startled, André quickly recovered his com-

posure. "Gentlemen," he said with a light laugh, trying not to
wince at the word. "I hope you belong to our party."

"What party?" Paulding growled.

"The lower party."

Paulding nodded. Taking heart, André raced on: "I am
glad to see you. I am an officer in the British service. I have
been in the country on business. I hope you will not detain
me. To prove to you that I am a gentlemen, I show you this,"
he said, taking out his gold watch and dangling it.

Paulding seemed unimpressed. "Get down!" he growled.

"You are Cowboys, aren't you?"

"We're Skinners."

"Skinners?" André repeated, puzzled.

"Patriots."

"Of course!" André cried, masking the sickening dread
that overtook him. "So am I! I am Mr. John Anderson, a
Patriot merchant of New York. I have just done business
with General Arnold at West Point. He has given me a pass.
Here it is."

Paulding took it, scowling. He read it slowly, his lips moving painfully. "Damn Arnold and his pass! You said you was
a British officer. Where's yer money? An' get down, like I
said!"

Still dangling his watch, André dismounted with a feigned
air of jauntiness. "I only said that, gentlemen, because I
thought you were Cowboys. But I am a true Pat—"

"Hey!" Williams shouted. "Look at his watch! It's got a
crest on it. Like the Britishers have!"

"You're right!" the giant Paulding cried. "Let's search him,
mates! Here, you," he said roughly to André, "squeeze
through that gate in the fence there."

André obeyed and was led into a thicket.

"Take off your clothes!" Paulding commanded.

One by one—Smith's beaver hat, his hideous purple coat,
his nankeen breeches, André's own underclothes—the gar-
ments were removed and handed to Paulding who searched
them thoroughly.

"Well, at least we got his money and the watch," he muttered, scratching his head. He stared suspiciously at André,
standing nude but with his boots and stockings still on.

"Are you convinced, gentlemen?" André asked.

"Like hell we are!" Paulding snarled with sudden fury. "Take off them boots!"

André removed his boots and nonchalantly handed them to Paulding, who held them upside down and shook them. Then he felt inside of them. His eyes glinted.

"Now the stockings!"

André hesitated.

"Off with 'em!"

In silent despair, Major John André removed his stockings so that the documents that were to end the war and save the civilized world fell plainly into view. Paulding seized them, broke the seal and studied them.

"He's a spy!" Paulding yelled. "A British spy! He's stolen the maps o' West Point!"

"Absurd!" André murmured. "Absurd! I tell you, gentlemen, I must get to New York." André paused, his throat dry. "What's your price?"

"Your horse," Paulding replied. "Saddle, bridle and all."

"And five hundred dollars each," Williams said.

"Done. Take me to Kingsbridge and you shall have your money."

"Yes, and when we get there, you'll have us arrested," Williams sneered.

"All right, then, two of you guard me while a third goes to the British lines. I will give you a note to procure three thousand . . . yes, five thousand dollars."

The eyes of the three Skinners shone with greed, until Paulding clapped his forehead as though remembering something. "Don't listen to him, mates! He's a spy! The law says when you capture a spy you get to keep all he owns. So don't let him trick you with his big talk about five thousand dollars. Even if we got it, they'd probably send out a company of soldiers to arrest us. Be content with what we got—horse, saddle, bridle, watch and money. Maybe even a reward."

"I tell you, I am a Patriot," André insisted.

"Mebbe so," Paulding said, pointing to André's clothing on the ground. "But we're still taking you to Major Tallmadge at North Castle. So get your clothes on, Mr. Patriot."

Chapter Twenty-Nine

General George Washington did not arrive at the Robinson House that Saturday. He sent word that he had been detained in Hartford and would not be there until Monday. Benedict Arnold was glad that he had not come. He could think of nothing but André's safety. When Joshua Hett Smith and his wife arrived for dinner, he took Smith into the library and asked him if André had arrived safely in White Plains.

"I think so, Excellency."

"*Think* so!" Arnold repeated, his face darkening. "Didn't you escort him there?"

"No, sir. I left him at Pine Bridge. I was afraid of the Cowboys across the river."

"You fool!" Arnold hissed. "You utter, idiotic, imbecilic fool."

At dinner that evening, an argument broke out between Smith and Colonel Varick. Smith spoke slightingly of the American currency.

"Mr. Smith," Varick said, laying down his fork, "you sneer at everything American. I resent it!"

"So do I!" said Major Franks.

"Gentlemen, you are too sensitive," Smith said. "Perhaps it is my language that offends you. I am not a scholar."

"The question is, Mr. Smith," Varick said coldly, "are you an American?"

Smith's wife struggled to her feet, wailing, "He's insulted us, Joshua. We've been insulted."

Mrs. Arnold hastened to change the subject. "Let us talk of other things," she said soothingly. The dinner continued in a strained silence. Arnold was furious, but because he wished to do nothing to alarm his aides, he said nothing to them publicly. In private, he asked Varick to apologize to Smith. Varick refused.

Sunday was an even more trying day. It rained constantly.
Arnold could think of nothing but the possible capture of
Major André. That fat, cowardly fool of a Joshua Hett
Smith! Why had he trusted such a jellyfish? Arnold limped
painfully around the library. Clammy weather always affected
his wounded leg. Paggy was also ill and had taken to her bed.
And little Edward had the colic. Arnold could hear him
wailing in his crib. When would Washington arrive? Arnold
never felt less like entertaining. Probably, the general would
be attended by his staff: General Knox, General Lafayette,
Colonel Alexander Hamilton and Colonel Daniel Gill. Franks
had told him that the *Vulture* had moved upriver again and
once more was again anchored off Teller's Point. *Why?* Was
André safe in New York?

Major Tallmadge was not at North Castle when the Skinners arrived with their prisoner. Lieutenant Colonel John
Jameson, a less than shrewd field officer with no experience
in intelligence, was in charge. He listened in bewilderment to
Paulding's story, glancing from time to time at "Mr. Anderson," who seemed bored by the entire proceeding. Jameson
also studied the packet of papers, instantly recognizing the
handwriting as Arnold's.

Jameson was mystified. He remembered that General Arnold had sent letters to a "Mr. Anderson," and had issued instructions that if he were to appear at North Castle he was to
be sent on to West Point at once. But Mr. Anderson had
been captured going in the wrong direction. The papers in his
possession could be very dangerous to the Patriot cause. Yet,
some of them were written in Arnold's hand, the same hand
that wrote the prisoner's pass. It was preposterous to think
that the hero of so many battles could be a traitor. It would
be even worse, for Jameson's career, if he were to cast doubt
mistakenly on the reputation of such an illustrious officer.
The last consideration decided him.

"I'll keep these papers for Major Tallmadge to see," he
said, "before I send them on to General Washington. In the
meantime, I'm sending you to General Arnold."

André bowed graciously, hope gleaming once again in his
dark eyes. He waited while Jameson wrote a note to Arnold,
explaining that he was sending Anderson to him and that he
was sending the captured papers to Washington. The note

was given to Lieutenant Solomon Allen, who drew his sword and pointed to the door. André went outside, nonchalantly ignoring the sword. Allen ordered four soldiers to tie André's hands behind his back. With a soldier on all sides, with Allen in the saddle waving his sword and threatening to run André through with it, the party set off for West Point.

They had not been gone an hour when Major Tallmadge returned to North Castle. Jameson told him what had happened and showed him the captured documents.

Tallmadge was thunderstruck. "You didn't hold him? He's a *spy!*" He tapped the documents he had read. "With this information, the British can destroy us!"

"But, Major, much of it is in Arnold's handwriting. You're not suggesting that—"

"I certainly am! If Benedict Arnold wrote any of this, he's a traitor! If he did, he's preparing to surrender West Point! Colonel, I beseech you, allow me to send these papers on to General Washington. And please, if you will, send out a party to bring Anderson back here."

Reddening at having to submit to the will of a subordinate, Jameson nevertheless did as he was asked. A courier pounded off in the darkness to intercept Washington at Danbury, while another galloped down the road taken by Lieutenant Solomon Allen and André.

The first messenger failed to find Washington, who spent the night in Fishkill. The second overtook Allen and Anderson at Peekskill.

"We're turning back," Allen announced, sending John André into despair once more. "I'm continuing on to West Point with a note for General Arnold. You men," he said to his soldiers, "are to take Mr. Anderson back to South Salem."

Trudging back to South Salem, a post chosen because it was farther away from the British than North Castle, John André's head was bowed in thought. The situation was hopeless. Once Washington saw those papers, he would move swiftly against Arnold. The plot had failed. And now, far more horrible for a man of André's noble character, his honor was in peril.

André did not doubt that his imposture would soon be discovered, and that he would be treated as a spy. The more he pretended to be Mr. Anderson, the more likely the Rebels would be to brand him with that detestable epithet. Slowly but surely, John André was making up his mind to confess. Upon his arrival in South Salem, he was placed in custody of Lieutenant Joshua King.

"My clothes are filthy, sir," he said to King, glancing in loathing at his soiled purple coat. "I haven't shaved for days. Would you be good enough to provide me with clean clothes and a bath?"

"Of course, sir," King replied.

After bathing and changing clothes, André walked with King in a spacious yard surrounded by guards. His head was again lowered in thought. Suddenly he turned on King and said:

"Lieutenant, I am not John Anderson. I am Major John André, Adjutant General of the British Army." Lieutenant King was astounded. "I beg of you, sir," André continued, "to provide me with pen and paper that I may write to General Washington."

King obliged him, and André sat down to reveal the entire plot to Washington, omitting only the name of the general with whom he had corresponded. He wrote with passion, for the entire purpose of the letter was to escape the opprobrium of being held as a spy.

"I came ashore in my own regimentals," he wrote. "I was forced behind American lines against my will by my correspondent. I was therefore a prisoner of war. A prisoner of war has the right to attempt to escape in civilian clothes."

By this tenuous argument, John André hoped to escape the ignominious noose of the hangman.

On Monday morning, September 25, 1780, General Benedict Arnold sat alone at the breakfast table, awaiting the arrival of General Washington and his staff. It was very early. Peggy was still in bed. Arnold was sunk in worry. He drummed his fingers on the table, starting nervously when two young officers came into the room. He recognized them as Majors Samuel Shaw and James McHenry, aides to Washington.

"General Washington will be here shortly," Major Shaw said.

"Good," said Arnold, motioning to them to sit down. "Have you breakfasted?"

"No, sir. The general told us to ride at dawn."

"I'll have some food sent in to you," Arnold said, rising and limping into the buttery. There he was accosted by a lieutenant in an extremely dusty uniform. It was Solomon Allen. He handed Arnold two notes from Jameson. He opened it casually, and read:

"I have sent Lieutenant Allen with a certain John Anderson taken going into New York. He had a passport signed in your name. He had a parcel of papers taken from his stockings, which I think of a very dangerous tendency. The papers I have sent to General Washington."

Benedict Arnold swayed, leaning heavily on his cane. But then he looked eagerly at Allen, and asked: "Is Mr. Anderson here?" Allen pointed silently at the second message, which explained that Anderson had been taken back to South Salem.

Momentarily, a gulf seemed to yawn beneath the feet of Benedict Arnold. It was as though he were plunging down, down, down into disgrace and defeat. Catching himself, with a curt, "Wait for my reply," he limped hurriedly into the stable yard.

"Saddle my horse immediately!" he shouted at a stable hand, and then, to a passing servant, "Go at once to the landing with my orders to have my barge stand by!" Whirling, he went limping rapidly upstairs to his bedroom.

Peggy was still in bed. She was in high spirits.

"I've just sent some young officers to the orchard for fresh peaches," she exclaimed happily.

Arnold's face cracked in an agony of grief. He rushed to Peggy's side and embraced her with tearstained cheeks. "All is lost! André has been taken prisoner! The parcel of papers has been sent to Washington! He will be here any minute! I must fly, my dearest. Immediately! I may never see you again!" Arnold bent to kiss her once more, but Peggy Arnold had fallen back on her pillow in a swoon. Pausing to fondle little Edward in his crib, he rushed to the door, nearly bowling over Major Franks coming in.

"His Excellency is almost here," Franks reported, but Arnold bolted past him, shouting over his shoulder that he was on his way to West Point to prepare a reception for the general.

In the stable yard, Arnold sighed with relief to see his horse saddled and waiting. He swung aboard and rounded the corner of the barn. Four of Washington's light horsemen barred his way. His hand dropped to his saddle pistols, but the men saluted in respect and parted ranks. Arnold galloped through down to the landing and the waiting barge.

Nate Gill saw him come plunging down the steep slope. Arnold sprang from his horse and turned to hurry to the barge. Then he paused. He was going over to the British penniless and without a horse. He had not delivered West Point and could expect little. Even nothing . . . At the most critical moment of his life, he paused to unbuckle his saddle and drag it—pistols and all—to the barge and throw it in.

"Row at once to Stony Point, Larvey!" he gasped, lowering himself into the craft. "As fast as you can!"

Arnold gasped again. A boat was approaching from West Point.

"There's breakfast waiting at the house, lads," he called. "Tell General Washington I'll be back for dinner."

As he rowed, Nate Gill stared curiously at General Arnold. He had never seen an officer of such rank so agitated. His hard blue eyes darted about like a hawk's. The hand that gripped the gunwale was white. So was his face, and he was sweating profusely. Suddenly, Arnold stood up and tied a white handkerchief to the mast.

"What's that for, sir?" Larvey asked.

"A flag of truce. I'm going to parley with the British on that sloop," he said, pointing downstream to the *Vulture*.

Larvey nodded and steered the barge alongside the ship. Arnold climbed aboard, followed by his eight oarsmen and Larvey. Captain Sutherland was on deck. Arnold introduced himself.

"But where is John Anderson?" Sutherland asked anxiously.

"Captured," Arnold said laconically. "The Rebels have him prisoner."

Sutherland stared at Arnold in horror. "Oh, my God, Sir Henry will be beside himself." His expression of dismay changed to one of faint contempt. Arnold was stung. Aware that his first impression had not been a good one, he determined to impress his new comrades with the power of his personality. He strode determinedly toward his bargemen chatting with a group of British tars.

"I have left the Rebel cause," he announced to them. "It is

an evil one. I have returned to my true sovereign. I am now a general in the British Army empowered to raise a Loyalist brigade. If you will join me my lads, I will make sergeants and corporals of you all. For you, James," he said to Larvey, "I will do something more."

Corporal Larvey spat on the deck in contempt. "No, sir! One coat is enough for me to wear at a time."

Arnold flushed. He felt the blazing black eyes of a mere private boring into his.

"You are scum!" Nate Gill said quietly. "You are everything that begins with *S-C*. Scum, scurvy, scab, scrofula, screwworm, scorpion—and may God lead you to your final *S-C*—the scaffold!"

A lusty cheer broke from the throats of the nine scornful Patriots. Even some of the British sailors grinned in delight. His face reddening, Benedict Arnold turned to roar at Captain Sutherland: "Make these men prisoners! Throw them in the hold!"

"May God will it that you will one day be our prisoner!" Nate Gill shouted, struggling between two sailors who had seized him. "Then we'll cut off that left leg of yours with its honorable wounds and bury it with full military honors. But the rest of your rotten carcass—your traitor's soul and your pirate's heart—we'll swing on high for the birds to peck out the swinish, lying eyes that turned away from free—"

"Put that man in irons!" Benedict Arnold roared in a ghastly voice, swaying on his cane. "And if he says another word, pull his impudent tongue out of his head!"

General Washington and his staff were welcomed to the Robinson House by Major David Franks.

"General Arnold has gone to West Point to prepare a reception for you, Excellency." Washington smiled in pleasure, and Franks continued in an anxious voice, "We are in some confusion here. Mrs. Arnold is not well and Colonel Varick is in bed with the ague."

"Do not distress yourself, Major," Washington said with another smile. "We'll have our breakfast alone and then go over to West Point to see General Arnold."

After breakfast, leaving Hamilton with Major Franks, the general and his party were rowed across the river to the fort. Although there was a powder shortage, Washington half expected a formal gun salute. He was surprised and mildly disappointed when none came. Nor was anyone on the landing to welcome him, except the customary sentries who sprang to attention with surprise on their reddening faces. Colonel John Lamb came hurrying down the hillside with a startled look on his seamed face.

"Excellency, my apologies! I had no idea you were coming. I would have prepared a reception for you."

"Didn't General Arnold tell you I was here?"

"No, sir. I haven't seen General Arnold all day."

Washington exchanged glances with Colonel Gill. "Let us proceed," he said to Lamb, and led his staff in an inspection of the fort's defenses. What he saw appalled him and his staff, especially Knox the artillerist.

"General Arnold has been here for seven weeks and he seems to have done very little," he said to Lamb.

"He's done nothing!" Lamb burst out with his customary bluntness. "If anything, we're worse off than we were before. Frankly, Excellency, I don't think we could stop them if they attacked now."

His eyes grave and thoughtful, Washington returned to his barge. Across the river, Colonel Hamilton was waiting on the landing.

"Messages from Tallmadge at North Castle, sir," he said, handing him a parcel. "A packet of documents taken from a spy, and a letter to you from the spy himself. You should have had them yesterday, but Tallmadge's courier missed us on the road from Hartford."

Washington took them. The word "spy" had caused him to look up in dread. "Has General Arnold returned?"

"No. I've been told he was seen going down the river toward a British ship anchored off Teller's Point. That was a few hours ago—"

"Great God!" Washington cried in a voice of thunder. "After him, Hamilton! He must be stopped! Ride south! Stop him!"

Together with Major McHenry, Hamilton went galloping south. Washington continued on into the library accompanied by Colonel Gill. He sat at the library to read the papers in his hand. His hands trembled.

"Treason!" he cried in a loud voice. "He has betrayed us!"

"Not . . . not Arnold, sir?" Colonel Gill exclaimed.

"Yes, Arnold." Washington's eyes were full of an ineffable sadness. *"Whom can we trust now?"*

When Peggy Arnold recovered consciousness, she began to realize with growing dread that even if her husband successfully escaped to the British, she, personally, might be reviled and perhaps even arrested as his accomplice by the enraged Patriots. She resolved to create sympathy for herself. Jumping from her bed she ran to her bureau and examined herself in the mirror. Seizing her blond hair, she disarranged it so that it hung wildly over her eyes. She opened her negligee to expose the tops of her breasts. Stooping to take little Edward in her arms, she opened her bedroom door slightly and gave a loud, piercing shriek.

Colonel Richard Varick heard the shriek and sprang from his sickbed to struggle into his bathrobe and go racing upstairs to the Arnolds' bedroom. Bursting inside, he saw the disheveled Peggy standing there with the baby looking wildly around her and babbling incoherently. Varick glanced quickly away in embarrassment when one of her breasts swung into view. Seeing him, Peggy gave another shriek and ran up to him to seize his hand.

"Why have you ordered my little baby to be killed?" she screamed.

Varick was horrified. "Madam, I've done no such thing."

"You have! You have! You know you have!"

"But, Madam," Varick pleaded, backing away, "this is madness! You must be ill. Come, let me help you back into bed."

"Don't touch me!" Peggy shrieked, shrinking away. Then she returned her baby to its crib and fell on her knees before Varick. "Please! Please, don't kill my baby!" Suddenly, she collapsed in a faint. Varick bent over her intending to lift her and carry her to her bed. But he had been so weakened by fever he was unable to move her. To his relief, Major Franks and a physician burst into the room. Between them, they carried Peggy to her bed. A few minutes later she opened her eyes and began to sob.

"Oh, how I am persecuted!" she wailed. "I have no friends in this house! I am alone! All alone!"

"Please don't say that, Mrs. Arnold," Franks said, leaning over her consolingly. "You have many friends. Varick and I—"

"Colonel Varick wants to kill my baby!"

"General Arnold will be home soon," Franks said soothingly.

"My husband has gone! He has deserted me!"

"Oh, no! General Arnold is at the fort."

"General Arnold has gone *forever!* I shall never see him again!"

Frank and Varick exchanged glances and said nothing, watching in dismay while Peggy dissolved into tears.

"I must see General Washington," she burst out suddenly. "There is a hot iron on my head and only he can take it off."

The general was brought to her bedside and took her hand gently in his. Peggy began to wail again.

"You are not General Washington!"

"Mrs. Arnold, surely you know me."

"You are not General Washington. You are the man who is going to help Colonel Varick kill my baby." Weeping, she clung to Washington's hand. "Where is my husband? You have taken him from me. You have accused him of some foul deed, and I shall be made to suffer for it."

"Oh, no, Mrs. Arnold. You will not suffer. I would never make the innocent suffer for the guilty."

Peggy Arnold seemed to relax. Her sobs subsided. She had shrewdly sensed that everyone in the room—the commander-in-chief, Varick, Franks, the doctor—had the deepest sympathy for her. She was safe.

Major John André had been moved from South Salem to Tappan, not far from Washington's headquarters. His "prison" was a comfortable apartment above Mabie's Tavern. He had a bedroom and a large living room. Through its windows he could see a little Dutch church and neat rows of gambrel rooves reminding him of towns he had seen in Holland.

John André impressed his captors with his beautiful manners and calm composure. He was delighted when Washington permitted him to send for his servant to bring him clean linen and his British uniform. Flinging aside Joshua Hett Smith's detestable purple coat, he clothed himself in his own scarlet coat, his sashes and his splendid gold-hilted sword. He was ready for trial.

Whether or not he would live or die turned on whether or

not he was a spy. In his letter to Washington, André had insisted that he was forced behind American lines against his will and was therefore technically a prisoner of war. Unknown to him, however, Colonel Beverly Robinson, owner of the Robinson House, had also written to Washington claiming that André had come ashore under a flag of truce.

These were the considerations before the board of generals which tried André in the little Dutch church. They did not take André's rather naive defense seriously, being more concerned about the flag of truce. Both Sir Henry Clinton and Benedict Arnold contended that he had had one. Arnold even wrote to André's judges to say that he had sent him one. He wrote to Washington threatening the most fearful consequences if André were not released:

"I call Heaven and earth to witness that your Excellency will be justly answerable for the torrent of blood that may be spilled in consequence."

Still, John André was ignorant of this defense, when he was asked directly:

"Did you come ashore under a flag of truce?"

"No," André replied. "Certainly, if I had come ashore under a flag of truce, I might have returned under it."

With this answer, John André sealed his own conviction as a spy. The judges' decision was read to him:

"Major André, Adjutant General of the British Army, ought to be considered a spy from the enemy, and that, agreeable to the law and usage of nations, it is their opinion he ought to suffer death."

As a convicted spy, André would hang—an ignominious death which he strove fervently to avoid. He sought, instead, the mode of death suitable to "an officer and a gentleman"—execution by a firing squad. He wrote to Washington: "Sympathy toward a soldier will surely induce Your Excellency and a military tribunal to adapt the mode of my death to the feelings of a man of honor."

Sir Henry Clinton also tried to persuade Washington to change the mode of execution, and there was widespread sympathy for André among members of the general's staff.

"Wouldn't it be possible to shoot him, Excellency?" Colonel Daniel Gill asked upon his return from a visit with André. "He is such an honorable man. He is everything that Arnold is not. He told me to thank his judges for their generous treatment of him. To thank you for the same. He even said that he has changed his mind about Americans and now thinks them among the fairest people on earth." Daniel shuddered. "The gibbet for such a man . . . It just seems . . ."

"I understand, Daniel," Washington said quietly. "Colonel Hamilton feels the same way. But, you see, I have no choice. If he is to be executed at all, it is as a spy—and the prescribed mode of death for a spy is hanging. If I were to change it, I would cast doubt upon his conviction, and give the enemy the chance to make propaganda of it." There was anguish in the general's pale eyes as he spoke. "We have given André every consideration. We did not try him on a drumhead and string him up without benefit of clergy as Howe did to Nathan Hale. And yet, I would release him, if Clinton would trade Arnold for him."

"You would?" Daniel asked in surprise.

"Yes, but Clinton has already rejected that suggestion. He said, 'A deserter is never given up,' and he's right. There is nothing to be done. The hanging will have to go forward as scheduled."

On the morning of October 2, 1780, Major John André prepared for his execution. He spoke cheerfully to his guards, some of whom had tears in their eyes. He rebuked his servant who had begun to weep after he had shaved him for the last time. "Leave me, until you can show yourself more manly!" André ate breakfast and then sat before the mirror to do a self-portrait of himself in pencil. Finally he put on his coat and hat heavy with gold braid. From outside came the sound of fifes and drums and the steady tread of marching feet. André put himself between his two officer guards and went out the door.

"I am very much surprised," he said in a clear voice, "to find your troops under such good discipline. And your music is excellent."

The band struck up the death march. André strode in step to it along a country road and up a hill to a field crowded with spectators. His judges mounted on horseback rose above the throng. André bowed to each of them and they returned the courtesy. Seated on Liberty next to Washington, Colonel Gill had tears in his eyes. He caught André's eye and tried to smile. The doomed man smiled cheerfully and strode on, bowing again when Colonel Alexander Scammell, who was in charge of the execution, approached him. Catching sight of the gallows, André halted in dismay.

"Must I then die in this manner?"

"It is unavoidable, Major André," Scammell replied.

"I am reconciled to my fate," André went on, raising his voice, "but not to the mode."

He strode calmly on to the cart standing beneath the gallows. He climbed up on it. He looked up, and shrank back momentarily. Instantly straightening, he murmured: "It will be but a momentary pang." Then he took off his hat and handed it to his weeping servant. He put his hands on his hips and walked back and forth on the cart, glancing at the horses that were to pull it away, or staring upward at the gallows.

Colonel Scammell read the death sentence, and then turned to him and said, "Major André, if you have anything to say, you can speak, for you have but a short time to live."

"I have nothing to say, gentlemen, but this: you all bear me witness that I meet my fate as a brave man."

A wailing cry rose from the crowd surging closer.

The hangman leaped up on the cart. He was a filthy contrast to the immaculate man he was going to kill. He was unshaved and his face was covered with soot. André at once snatched the rope from the man's dirty hands. He took off his neckcloth and put it in his pocket, turning down the collar of his shirt. Opening the noose, he put it over his head and pulled the knot tight under his right ear. Still calm, he drew a white handkerchief from his pocket and tied it over his eyes.

"His hands must be tied," Scammell shouted.

André drew down the handkerchief and extracted another from his pocket, handing it to the hangman before he rebandaged his eyes. The hangman tied André's arms behind his back, just below the elbow. Then he shinnied up the gallows post to fasten the rope to the gibbet. He slid down and jumped back into the cart.

The crowd began to yell and wail. André stood motionless. The hangman cracked his whip, the horses lurched forward and eternity opened up beneath the feet of Major John André.

Chapter Thirty

Because of the insults he had showered upon the head of Benedict Arnold, Nate Gill was kept separate from the other imprisoned oarsmen. The sailors who rushed him below pushed him into a space in the *Vulture*'s prow hardly larger than a big coffin. The air was close and Nate had difficulty breathing. He wondered if he would suffocate, and was relieved when he heard the rattle of the anchor chain coming up the hawse pipe and felt the prow rise and fall with the motion of the ship. Soon he fell asleep.

He was awakened by the feel of hands grabbing him roughly and dragging him out of his tiny prison. His captors pulled him up on deck. It was daylight. Squinting in the bright sun, Nate realized that he was in New York harbor. Then he saw General Arnold and Captain Sutherland standing by the mainmast. Next to them was a bos'n's mate holding a cat-o'-nine-tails in his hand. Seeing Nate, he grinned cruelly and shook the nine-tailed whip menacingly.

"Strip the foul-mouthed Rebel swine and tie him to the mast!" Captain Sutherland roared. "By rights, I ought to keelhaul the beggar!"

"Ah, yes," Arnold said, "but this way you can listen to the music."

The ungentle hands seized Nate again and tore off his coat and shirt, hustling him to the mast where they wound his arms around it and tied his wrists together. The rough tarry surface of the pine mast scratched Nate's stomach.

"Commence!" Sutherland bellowed.

Nate braced for the first blow, contracting the muscles of his back. It came.

Swish, craaack!

The leather bit deep into Nate's back with a hot, stinging flash of pain. But he did not cry out.

"One!" the bos'n counted grimly.
Swish, craaack!
"Two!"
Still, Nate remained silent.
Swish, craaack!
"Three!"
Swish, craack!
"Four!"

Nathaniel Gill sank his teeth into his lips to keep from crying out. He could feel the blood beginning to trickle down his back. The bos'n and Arnold and Sutherland waited confidently for their victim to scream. At the tenth stroke, when the bos'n began the overlay, Nate seemed to cringe visibly. With each successive stroke, he slid lower on the mast until he was almost on his knees. But he still did not scream. His lips were a pulp of flesh and blood and his back was a skinned red mass, but he still gave Arnold and Sutherland no satisfaction. At the twenty-ninth lash he slipped mercifully into unconsciousness, and at the thirty-ninth the flogging stopped and he was cut down and carried below and thrown into a tiny cell.

Benedict Arnold was disappointed. "I don't wish to seem blasphemous, Sutherland," he murmured. "But I do think Moses was far too lenient with his thirty-nine lashes."

"The law of the sea, General," Sutherland grunted.

"More's the pity. In the British Army they give out stripes by the thousand."

While Nate was unconscious, a naval physician visited him to spread unguents on his wounds. Nevertheless, when Nate awoke two days later it was to pain so excruciating that his little cell swam before his eyes and he finally did begin to scream. His cries brought a guard rushing to his cell.

"Singing at last, eh, you Yankee bastard?" he cried gleefully. "Keep it up, lad, it's music to me ears."

At once, Nate regained control of himself. He sank down on his haunches. He remained that way for days, subsisting on the pint of water and four moldy biscuits a day that the guard brought him each morning. At first, his lips were so tender he could not bear to bite the biscuits. Instead, he broke them into the water and made a paste of it. And it was a week before he could bear the pressure of his shirt against his wounds.

Two weeks after the flogging, he was ordered to put on his uniform and hustled back on deck again.

"Take him to Sugar Loaf with the others," the bos'n growled, and Nate was shoved down the gangplank to a waiting horse cart filled with other American prisoners. He climbed up on it, wincing in pain. One of the prisoners stared at the thick scabs on both his lips.

"What in tarnation happened to you?"

"Flogging," Nate grunted, speaking with an effort. "I bit my lips to keep from hollering."

"Did you?"

"I don't think so. I passed out before it was over."

"Good for you," the man said admiringly. "What's your name?"

"Nate Gill."

"Nate Gill!" the man exclaimed incredulously, "Why, the whole army knows about you. You're the one who cussed out that traitorous skunk of a Benedict Arnold." He put out his hand proudly. "Shake, Nate—my name's Hallam. Will Hallam."

They shook hands just as the cart lurched forward. It turned up Broad Street. It was noon and the street was thronged with soldiers in Loyalist uniforms or Tories in civilian clothes. They thronged around the cart jeering, pelting the cringing prisoners with stones or horse dung. The guards walking behind the cart laughed and cheered them on. By the time the cart reached Sugar Loaf, there was hardly a prisoner who was not bleeding from a stone or smeared with dung.

Once again, Nate was separated from the others and thrown into a bare stone dungeon. Even the floor was of stone and the walls ran water. There was no light. When Nate tried to stand erect he hit his head on the ceiling. It was now late fall, but Nate was given neither a blanket to cover him nor a board nor straw to lay on. He sat chattering on the stone floor or walked crouching around the cell, waving his arms to keep his blood circulating.

On the following day, the iron door clanged open. A guard with a lantern followed by a Loyalist lieutenant entered the dungeon. The guard put the lantern on the floor and went outside.

"Are you hungry?" the lieutenant asked.

"Yes, sir. I haven't eaten in two days."

"You'll eat after you enlist in His Majesty's forces," the lieutenant said, his voice turning imperious.

"Never!" Nate yelled fiercely.

"Then starve!" the lieutenant yelled back, and picked up the lantern and strode outside. The door clanged shut. Next day the lieutenant was back.

"If you enlist, you'll get a bounty of a hundred dollars."

"Only a hundred?" Nate sneered. "Is that all that's left after you paid Judas?"

"Judas?"

"Yes, Benedict Arnold."

"God damn your insolence!" the lieutenant cried, slapping Nate hard across the mouth. "Now you will starve to death!" He went outside again. His blow had knocked the scabs off Nate's lips. They began to bleed again and he sank to the floor on the brink of despair. He heard a rustling beside him and felt a rat nibbling on his shoe. He jumped up in horror, kicking his feet. His head hit the stone ceiling. He reeled, clutching his head in agony. Crouching, Nate Gill walked around and around in his dungeon, around and around, fearful of standing still to be attacked by rats. At last, the dungeon door clanged open again. This time it was just the guard with a lantern.

"Look alive, you," he said, swinging the light. "You're ticketed for a prison ship."

Nate was delighted to see Will Hallam among the prisoners in the crowded longboat being rowed out to the prison ship. The two embraced like old friends, although they had known each other for hardly more than an hour. When they reached the ship, the rowers lay on their oars. The boat wallowed gently in the swells. It was directly opposite one of the ship's lower portholes, from which a foul stench issued.

It was a mixture of urine and excrement and human sweat and the odor of diseased flesh so loathsome that everyone in the boat—even the oarsmen—groaned and clutched their noses. From the porthole came a deathlike voice.

"We ain't so dainty, are we, lads? Give yourselves a week, an' you'll stink the same. Death has sucked us dry, lads, and don't want us no more. He likes to feast on fit newcomers, like yerselves." The voice gave a ghastly chuckle, and Nate Gill and Will Hallam exchanged horrified glances. They scrambled up the accommodation ladder with fear and foreboding, barely protesting when their Scottish guards jostled them roughly up the gangway onto an upper deck. Passing through a barricade, they came to a desk where each man gave his name and rank to a captain, who entered them in a book and directed a corporal to hand each prisoner a canteen and a wooden bowl.

"You'll be issued your food every morning," he growled. "Do as your told, and you'll have no trouble. If you try to escape, you'll be flogged and put in solitary confinement on bread and water for a month."

Going down a ladder, the prisoners came to the main hatch where the guards pulled aside the grating over it. Nate and Will crept slowly down into a black, airless, stifling hold where the same reek struck them like a blow in the face.

"Oh, my God, how can anyone live in this?" Nate gasped. He felt something wriggle beneath his foot and an irritated voice snapped: "Fer Christ's sake, get yer God damn foot off my hand. An' keep movin' to the end of the hold where you belong, newy. This place near the grate is fer us oldtimers."

Still gasping, Nate and Will Hallam stumbled towards the end of the hold, helped along by the pushes and curses of groaning men who resented their intrusion. At length, Nate bumped into a bulkhead and slid down into a sitting position on the deck. He was still gasping. So was Hallam.

"I . . . I can't breathe," Hallam said in a choking voice.

"Neither can I," Nate said. "Maybe if we try to breathe slower . . . Otherwise, I think we'll just suffocate."

The two soldiers sat there with the other newcomers, their heads in their hands, gasping, their stomachs turning with the nauseating stench, their ears full of the lamentations of the diseased and broken-spirited men around them. As his eyes became accustomed to the darkness, Nate perceived a glimmer of light coming through the grate over the hatch. Air! he thought. Maybe I can squirm up there and get a breath of fresh air! He began crawling across the deck, over the bodies of prostrate prisoners. Almost immediately, he aroused an angry chorus of curses and imprecations.

"Where the hell you think yer goin', you cheeky bastard? Get the hell back where you belong!"

"The nerve of the newy son of a bitch. He ain't been here two hours and he wants the same place I've been waiting seven months for."

Unnerved, Nate crawled back to the bulkhead beside Will Hallam. "Did you hear that?" he groaned.

"Seven months!" Will muttered in dismay. "I hope I'm dead before then." Suddenly he broke wind. "Sorry, Nate," he mumbled.

"Forget it. Maybe it'll make this hellhole smell sweeter."

Will chuckled, and then he mumbled, "I gotta take an awful crap." He raised his voice and shouted into the dark hold. "Where's the necessary house?"

A yell of derision rose from the veteran prisoners. "You mean head, newy?" a voice cried. "It's topside."

"How do you get to it?"

"You cain't. Not until morning when they let us up there so's we can use it."

"What do you do until then?"

Another shout of laughter went reverberating around the hold, and the same voice answered, "You shit on it."

In the morning, one of the Scots guards pulled back the hatch grate and shouted down into the hold, "All right, you shower of shit—look alive." At once, there was a great bustle and stirring among the prisoners. They began climbing the ladder, causing Nate to grasp instantly the worth of seniority among the imprisoned. Those with the most time were nearest the grate and climbed almost immediately into the sunlight and fresh air. But it was a half hour before Nate and the other "newies" came up on deck. Since they would also be the first to descend, that meant another half hour of respite for the "oldies"—a total of one additional hour of basking in the blessed sun and sucking in the precious uncontaminated air.

On deck, most of the men hurried toward the wooden shanties serving as heads. Long lines formed. Again, seniority was accorded the privilege of place. Will Hallam, who had spent the night groaning with stomach pains, saw with relief that many of the prisoners ignored the heads and rushed to the rail, either urinating over the side or dropping their pants to hoist themselves onto the rail and empty their bowels into the water. Will and Nate both rushed to follow suit.

"Mebbe we can shit on a passing Tory," Will chortled gleefully.

"Yeah, but it's kind of tough trying to take aim with your behind," Nate said.

A sharp-faced oldtimer beside him chuckled. "Take a tip from me, newy. Don't try this in winter. Them Scotch bastards like nothin' better 'n to knock you over the side so's you kin freeze to death."

"Why do they hate us so much?"

"I dunno, but they do. They're the worst. Even worse than the Hessians."

Nate and Will jumped down, stooping to recover the canteens and bowls they had left on the deck. They got on the end of a long line of prisoners passing through the open-air galley to receive their food ration. Nate studied the men whose company he had joined. He was appalled. They were walking skeletons. Their tattered uniforms hung on them in filthy folds. All of them were bearded and some had matted, tangled masses of hair reaching below their chests. Their eyes were sunk deep in their sockets and their flesh pallid. Nate wondered how their shrunken necks could support their heads, the size of which was magnified by the thinness of their shoulders and limbs. Of course, they all stank, and as they stood in line they were scratching furiously at body lice roused by the warmth of the sun.

"That's what we'll be like in a couple of months," Nate murmured. Will nodded, and then gasped when he saw the guards emerging from the hatch, two-by-two, swinging the naked bodies of corpses between them. They ran to the rail and flung them over it. Nate shuddered when he heard the loud splash of their bodies hitting the water.

"Them's the lucky ones what died durin' the night," the sharp-faced man explained. "Not too bad today. On'y five. That's how you gets yer seniority, newy," he said with a ghoulish chuckle. "On'y other way out 'v this floating hell is to 'list for the king."

"Never!" Nate cried fiercely.

"That's the spirit, lad!" the sharp-faced man said, clapping Nate on the back. "Wisht t'Gawd them gutless turncoats had it," he went on, pointing to a group of about twenty prisoners being marched down the gangway. "An' some o' them's on'y been here a few months."

Nate scowled, but said nothing. He had come opposite a guard standing in front of a scuttlebutt. Nate handed him his canteen and he filled it. Nate moved on to another guard ladling out dried peas from a pot. He dropped about four ounces of them into Nate's bowl. The next guard put in about the same measure of rancid uncooked pork from a fly-covered mound in front of him. Nate brushed away the flies lighting on his food and asked:

"How do I cook the meat?"

"Aye, lad, y' dinna," the guard said in a thick Scots burr, grinning maliciously. " 'Tis juicier raw."

Nate glanced down in disgust at his bowl. For a moment he felt like hurling it at the guard's jeering face. But he had not eaten in four days and he took his meager ration down into the stinking, suffocating hold where he gulped it down with relish.

Like all the other Americans aboard the prison ship, Nate Gill and Will Hallam could think or talk of only two things: to be exchanged for British prisoners, or to die quickly. They never spoke of escape, if only because winter had come and no man could live long in the freezing waters of the Hudson. Frequently, the two soldiers talked of the Revolution. When Nate had been imprisoned, the Rebel cause had been at its blackest. South Carolina and Georgia had been conquered and it appeared that North Carolina and Virginia would also fall. But then a new batch of prisoners told them of the American victory over the Loyalists at King's Mountain. There was much laughter and even some singing in the prison hold that night. During the succeeding months, each new batch of prisoners was eagerly pumped for news of the war. One day in February, 1781, a band of new arrivals proudly brought the intoxicating news of the defeat of Banastre Tarleton and his Highlanders and Tory horsemen at the Battle of Cowpens.

"We slaughtered 'em," one of the newcomers cried exultantly. "Tarleton had about eleven hundred men and we must've killed or captured a thousand of 'em. We made shit of his Highlanders. They were on foot and couldn't get away like the Tories, and we just mowed 'em down."

Nate Gill was electrified. "It's the turn of the tide!" he said to Will Hallam squatting beside him in the dark. "We've won the last two battles, and I've just got a feeling the British are getting sick of the war."

That night there was even more laughter in the hold and the singing grew in volume. When they came to "Yankee Doodle," every prisoner was on his feet bellowing:

> Yankee Doodle came to town
> A'riding on a pony,
> Stuck a feather in his cap
> And called it macoroni.

The jubilation of the American prisoners infuriated the Scots guards, who had also heard of the slaughter of their countrymen at Cowpens. They ran to the grate and struck at it with the blunt edges of their cutlassess, trying to drown out the singing with the clangor they raised. But the voices rose higher.

"Quiet, you Yankee scum!" one of the guards shouted. "Or we'll give you some Cowpens of your own."

"Hey, Jock," Nate Gill bellowed, "now we know what a Scotchman wears under his kilt," and the jeering hold responded in a single thunderous voice:

"A wang! A wang!"

"We cut them all off at the Cowpens, Jock," Nate yelled again, and the hold reverberated once more with the derisive shout:

"They're gang! They're gang!"

From above came the ominous rasp of the grate being pulled free. Dozens of lanterns came into view bobbing down the ladder. A sinister silence fell upon the hold.

"Made shit of us, did ye?" one of the descending guards yelled in a furious voice. Now the light of the lanterns gleamed off a dozen bare cutlasses, and the terrified prisoners shrank back against the bulkheads. "Cut off the Heeland peckers, did ye? Well, hold on to yer own little daubers, Yankee swine—because now we're going to make capons out of you."

Uttering fierce wild Highland yells, the Scots guards fell upon the helpless Americans with swinging blades. The hold ┐hoed to the screams and shrieks of stricken men. A ┐d with a swinging lantern and upraised cutlass charged ┐ill. Nate seized his canteen and hurled it at him. It struck the guard full in the mouth. His blade fell clattering on the deck. Nate stooped and grasped it and swung it savagely upward beneath the arm that held the lantern. The guard screamed and fell, dropping his lantern. Now Nate was invisible in the dark. But the guards were marked out by their lanterns. One by one, Nate slipped up on them unseen and struck them dying to the deck. Now it was Scots' screams that rolled around the hold. Soon, one of the guards realized the peril.

"Topside, lads!" he yelled. "There's a Yank on the loose with a blade!"

"Outen the lanterns!" another guard cried. "Then he won't know who we are."

"You bloody fool!" the other cried. "We'll be lost in the dark! Topside!"

Swinging their cutlasses whistling around their heads, holding their lanterns in front of them, the guards ran for the ladder, clambering up it and dousing their lights once they reached the hatch. With a screech of steel on steel, they replaced the grate.

Gradually, like the clucking and lowing that slowly returns to a frightened farmyard, human voices were heard once more in the darkened hold. Nate ground his teeth at the groaning and whimpering of the wounded. Twice, he heard the dreadful cackle of the death rattle.

"Will," he shouted into the blackness. "Will Hallam. Where are you, Will?"

A loud groan came from his right. He hurried toward it on hands and knees, stopping when he came to a body. He put out his hand and felt the man's neck. It was wet with blood.

"Is it you, Will?" he asked in anguish.

"It's me, Nate. I . . . I'm goin', Nate," Will gasped. "I . . . I don't want to go . . ."

Nate found Will's hand and squeezed it. "You'll be all right, Will. You'll get better."

"No . . . Nate . . . I can . . . feel it . . . goin' out of me . . ." The dying youth gasped. He began to choke. His body shook in convulsions. Nate felt a tiny pressure from his hand. "Nate?"

"Yes, Will?"

"If . . . you live . . . tell . . . my ma . . . I loved her . . ." There was another choking pause. Nate felt the

pressure again. "It was good knowin' you, Nate. . . . You're
the bravest soldier . . . I ever . . ." Will Hallam uttered another loud groan and died. Nate felt the lifeless hand relax in
his and tears came to his eyes. A black rage seized him and
he felt for his cutlass beside him—until he became aware of
an unfamiliar warmth in the hold and heard a crackling overhead. Looking up at the grate he saw yellow flames leaping
into the night sky.

"Fire!" someone shouted. "The ship's on fire!"

"The filthy bastards! They set it on fire a' purpose to hide
their murders!"

"They're gonna burn us all!"

Cries of alarm and panic rose all around Nate. There was
a wild scurrying in the dark. Every prisoner who could move
was running toward the foot of the ladder, where they piled
up and began struggling with each other for possession of the
lower rungs. Nate rushed over and began beating them on the
back with the flat of his cutlass.

"Get back!" he roared. "Get back or we'll all die!"

They paid no attention to him. Within a few minutes the
space around the ladder was a surging, screaming, tangled
mass of terrified human beings—until there was a loud
screech overhead and the grate was drawn back to reveal a
night sky illuminated by orange flame.

"Stand back from that ladder!" a voice of a Scots officer
roared. "Come up here, one by one."

The mob sobered. Now Nate discreetly dropped his cutlass
and began pulling men off each other's backs. No one protested. The appearance of hope had calmed them, and they
began scrambling quickly up toward the hatch—ignoring the
pitiful entreaties of the wounded.

Nate cupped his hands to his lips and shouted up to the officer at the hatch. "What about the wounded?"

"What wounded? There are no wounded! You keep babbling about wounded and I'll slam the hatch shut!"

With a single helpless backward glance, Nate bowed his
head and climbed slowly upward. On deck he heard a thunderous crackling and roaring. Flames ran like fiery snakes up
the ship's masts and out onto the furled sails on the spars. All
of the ship's superstructure was ablaze. In the light of the fire,
Nate could see the battery on the New York shore. Troops of
redcoats were drawn up as though apparently on the chance

that the burning ship might be an American ruse. Crowds of civilian spectators thronged the waterfront. Longboats were beng rowed out to the ship.

From the hatch to the gangplank stood a double row of guards with fixed bayonets. From the scowls on their dour faces and the hatred blazing sullenly in their eyes, Nate realized that they were anxious to use their blades. He walked quietly between them, down the gangplank and accommodation ladder into the waiting-boats.

Halfway to the battery, Nate saw a blinding flash obliterate the ship and heard a monstrous explosion. Shock waves came rolling over the glittering black water. A mountain of debris seemed to sail into the air, but before it fell back tinkling and splashing into the water, darkness reclaimed the river.

Chapter Thirty-One

Jennifer Gill learned of Nate's imprisonment in a letter from Luke Sawyer. Reading it, she burst into tears.

"That horrible Benedict Arnold!" she cried when she broke the news to Barbara that night. "He had them row him out to the British ship and then he had them imprisoned." Although there were tears in her eyes, Jennifer's chin lifted proudly. "Luke said a deserter from the British ship told them what Nate said to the dirty traitor. Listen," she said, quoting from the letter.

Tears of pride came to Barbara's eyes. "Spoken like a true Gill," she murmured. "How Grandpa would have loved to have been there."

"But what am I going to do?" Jennifer wailed. "Luke says he heard the prisoners were being shipped to Canada."

"Why not go there?" Barbara said simply.

"Would you . . . would you . . . ?"

"Of course I would. Mrs. Wilmot can take care of Mark. He's almost five, now, and won't be any trouble. Don't worry about the tavern. I'll find someone to run it while you're gone."

"I'll go, then," Jenny said, hope gleaming in her eyes. "If I find him, I'll stay as close to him as I can so I can bring him food and things. I've heard British prison camps are dreadful."

"I'll write to Dan to see if he can do something about getting Nate exchanged."

"Oh, that would be wonderful!"

For comfort that night, Jenny took Mark into her own bed. She lay with her hands under the covers, one of them grasping Mark's warm little hand, while the tears rolled silently down her cheeks. Mark reached up with his other hand and felt her wet cheeks.

"Why are you crying, Ma?"

"Because your pa's a prisoner "

"What's a prisoner?"

"The British captured him. They have him in a jail."

"I hate the British. I hope Pa kills lots more of them."

"Shhh, Mark! Don't be so bloodthirsty."

To the boy's surprise, his mother kissed him and hugged him and burst into tears.

In the morning, Jennifer prepared for her trip to Canada, and she left on the following day. She had no trouble crossing the border. When she reached it and explained her mission to the officer in charge at the crossing point, he wrote her a pass. For weeks, Jenny haunted the prison camps around Montreal and Quebec. Night after night, she cried herself to sleep; although sometimes she went to bed in the belief that she had at last found the camp in which Nate was imprisoned, only to come to another disillusioning and heartbreaking dead end the next day. Finally, in deep dejection, Jennifer returned to Boston for Christmas. There she found another letter from Luke Sawyer in which he said that Nate was believed to be aboard a prison ship in New York harbor.

"Prison ship!" Jenny exclaimed in dismay. "They say they're even more horrid than the camps." A thoughtful look came into her soft brown eyes. "But maybe it'll be easier to find him on a ship."

"They'd never let you visit him," Barbara said.

"I know. But at least I'd know where he was."

"You're going to New York?"

"Of course. Why not?"

"New York is full of Tories, Jenny. A lot of them from Boston. You might be recognized."

"I'm not going to go as Jenny Gill, the wife of a Rebel soldier. I'll be Jennifer Courtney, the daughter of a Tory officer. And I'll wear real high heels and a wig." Jenny laughed. "I'll get one of Amanda's. Amanda loved wigs, the silly goose. With her beautiful blond hair, she still loved to wear a wig to a fancy ball."

"When are you leaving?"

"After New Year's. I think I'll get a job as a barmaid at a waterfront tavern. That's what I meant when I said it should be easier with a ship. There'll be lots of British sailors there, and they'll talk."

"Be careful, Jenny," Barbara said warningly. "And remember what I said about traveling armed."

Jenny smiled and lifted her petticoat to reveal a pistol strapped to her thigh. "It's loaded," she said proudly. "You see, Barbara, I'm a genuine Gill."

Before she left Boston, Jennifer went to her father's house and made straight for her stepmother's bedroom. To her delight, she found a black wig with long curls. She put it on and examined herself in the mirror. With the unusually high heels she was wearing and her sober dress of Quaker gray trimmed in black, she seemed a stranger to herself. Jenny next went to her father's chambers hoping to find some of his stationery. Jenny was expert in forging Joel Courtney's hand, having done it frequently as a schoolgirl to write sick notes for the days she had played truant from Miss Marlboro's School. It had occurred to Jenny that she might find occasion to cloak herself in her father's authority, and she was pleased to find the stack of embossed letterheads lying on the desk where Dr. Benjamin Gill had dropped them. She stuffed half of them into her pocketbook and went downstairs to her carriage.

Jennifer had no fear of traveling alone. Seven or eight years ago, such conduct might have been considered outrageous or even immoral, but the war had so uprooted American society that unescorted women were a common sight on the roads. Jenny was neither molested or even noticed on her five-day trip to New York. When she arrived, she immediately made the rounds of the taverns on the battery and was finally hired at The Rogue's Roost.

"You'll do, lass," grunted Big Tawm Toolan, the proprietor, running an appreciative eye over Jenny's figure. "Room and board and two dollars a week, plus tips." He smiled leeringly. "Five cents for you each time they buy you a drink. Second door on the right," he said, pointing to the stairs. Jenny moved gracefully away, carrying her pocketbook and bag. Big Tawm watched her go, stroking his bald head approvingly. They'll be standing in line to stand that one a drink, he thought.

That night, Jenny had been relieved behind the bar to take her supper in the kitchen when she heard a British sailor in the taproom shouting: "Fire! There's a prison ship on fire out in the 'arbor, mytes! Cor, is she burnin'!"

Jenny rose and rushed outside with the others. She joined the crowd at the water's edge staring in fascination at the blazing ship. She felt a hand on her waist and pushed it away angrily, but then, seeing that it was the sailor who gave the alarm, she smiled coquettishly at him. He might be able to tell me things, Jennifer thought.

"Is it really a prison ship?" she asked.

"Bleddy well roight she is."

Jennifer's hand flew to her mouth in terror. She prayed that Nate was not aboard it. "Will they . . . will they save the prisoners?"

"Coo! D' y' think we're a bunch o' bleddy Yankee savages? Of course they'll save 'em. There," he said, pointing to the glittering surface of the harbor, "there's a boatload of 'em pullin' away roight now."

Jennifer watched the approaching longboat with her finger-tips again at her lips. Other boats were following. Then the ship blew up. A roar of delight rose from the crowd. It was as though they were at a fireworks display and this was the grande finale.

"Oooh!" they cried in childlike ecstasy, and then the darkness descended on the river and part of the crowd drifted back to the taverns. But Jennifer did not move. She made her way to the wharf where blazing pitch torches illuminated the ranks of British redcoats drawn up with fixed bayonets. The sailor followed her. Jennifer started. She had seen a fat lieutenant colonel in the green uniform of the Queen's Rangers seated on a huge gray horse. It was her father! He was even heavier than when she had last seen him on that hideous night of the bombardment nearly five years ago. He needs a horse that size, she thought. I wonder what he's doing here?

"That's Colonel Courtney," the cockney sailor volunteered, following Jenny's eyes. "Fat, ayn't 'e? Cor, they oughta give 'is bloomin' 'orse a medal."

Jennifer said nothing. Her eyes had shifted from her father to the prisoners arriving on the wharf. The redcoats had formed a double row facing each other. The prisoners were being forced to run between them to a line of waiting wagons. Jennifer was horrified. She felt like weeping. The poor Americans were emaciated scarecrows! Their flesh was as

white as death and their filthy, ragged uniforms hung on
them in folds. From the way they scratched themselves waiting their turn to run she realized they were covered with ver-
min. Jennifer Gill's heart seemed to stop. *Oh, no! But it was!
It was Nate!* She had never seen him so thin. But he still had
that proud carriage as he strolled nonchalantly between the
lines of redcoats. He wouldn't run, Jenny thought proudly,
not my Nate! She fought back the tears. Momentarily, she
thought of crying out to him, of waving her hand; but the
gesture would be useless and would only give herself away.

"You there!" a voice roared, and Jenny recognized it as
her father's. "Goddamn you, I know you, Nathaniel Gill, you
filthy cutthroat of a Rebel. Run! Run, like the rest of the
swine." Nate gave his father-in-law a glance of distilled contempt and continued his nonchalant stroll. "Run I say!" Joel
Courtney spluttered. He spurred his horse forward and struck
Nate across the face with his riding crop. A bloody welt six
inches long like a red snake instantly appeared on Nate's
cheek. The crowd roared angrily. They began to hiss and
jeer. Even the cockney sailor joined in. So did Jenny, hissing
so vehemently that she felt spittle trickle down on her chin.
Her father glanced at the crowd with surprised apprehension.
Nate Gill stopped. He put his finger to the wound and then
to his mouth, before spitting straight into Courtney's face.
The crowd roared its approval. Courtney raised his crop as
though to strike again, but stopped when the roaring, furious
crowd surged toward him. Instead, he dropped his hand and
rode back to the wagons.

"And 'im a colonel in the king's army," the sailor sneered
contemptuously.

"Why do you think he's here?" Jenny asked, watching as
her husband slowly climbed into a wagon.

"To tyke the prisoners, I guess. 'E's commander of the
prison mine on Long Island."

Tears of joy came to Jennifer Gill's eyes. She had found
him! He was in the power of her father whom she now hated
with a patricidal fury, but Jenny knew how to counterfeit
that authority. She had not only found him, she was going to
set him free!

When Nate and the other shivering prisoners arrived at the

mine, they were taken from the wagons to the guardroom. A lieutenant there took their names and rank.

"There'll be no trouble if you don't make trouble," he said. "You'll be brought up every other day. Your meals will be lowered to you." He pointed to a trapdoor and ordered a sentry to open it.

Nate went down first. After about a dozen feet he came to a little sentry room. Two soldiers were playing cards at a little table with a lantern standing on it. One of the guards arose, picked up the lantern and opened another trap door. He held the lantern out over it. Nate felt dizzy. Way, way down he could see men lying on a patch of sand. He thought he detected a gleam of water. It must be sixty feet deep, Nate thought in despair. No chance of escape.

"All right, get going," the sentry said, waving the lantern back and forth. The men below yelled when they saw the light.

"Company's coming," the sentry shouted derisively, and gave Nate a little shove that almost sent him tumbling to his death. Steadying himself, Nate began climbing cautiously down a slimy iron ladder. It took him ten harrowing minutes. One by one, the others climbed down. But the last one slipped on the ladder and fell fifty feet screaming hideously all the way down. The men below scattered and the screeching prisoner struck the sand with a horrible, squashing thump.

"Is he dead?" the guard called down, his voice echoing hollowly in the cavern.

"Are you joking?" a bearded sergeant shouted.

"Oh, God damn it! Now we've gotta haul him up." He slammed the trapdoor shut in exasperation.

A vast silence encompassed the cavern. Nate was surprised to see shadows flickering on its oozing walls. "Where does the light come from?" he asked the sergeant.

"The charcoal braziers," the sergeant replied, pointing to a pair of braziers. "If we don't burn charcoal, we suffocate."

Nate nodded. He was surprised that he and the other new arrivals had stopped shivering. "How come it's not so cold down here?"

"You won't ask that in the summer. You'll be shivering, then. It's seventy feet down. More than enough to reach the

subterranean temperature. Fifty-four or fifty-five. It stays that
way all year round."

"Seventy feet," Nate muttered in dismay. His despairing
eyes followed the charcoal smoke drifting up to the ceiling,
where it eddied for a moment before drifting down to glide
along the surface of what appeared to be an underground
pond. "No way out?"

"None. They've got iron bars over the top. If you try to
follow the water out, you'll come to an iron grill at the end
of the mine shaft." He shook his head emphatically. "No
chance of escape." He pointed to the braziers. "Usually, the
newcomers tend the braziers. But don't fall asleep while
you're doing it. If you do, and the fire goes out, you'll get
thrown in the pond. Take you a week to dry out."

"How come you do that?"

"Simple. If the fire goes out, we have to dicker with the
guards for flint and spunk and kindling to get it started again.
They may hold back half of our food for a week so's they
can sell it outside."

"They're all scum. How long have you been here?"

"Two years."

Nate wagged his head despairingly. "Two years!" He
studied the bearded sergeant. "But you really don't look bad."

"No. The food isn't bad. Peas and biscuits and baked
bread. Sometimes even pork."

"Cooked?"

"Yep. Another good thing. No lice."

"How come?"

"I dunno. Maybe it's the temperature."

The sergeant walked away and lay down among perhaps
forty veteran prisoners lying silently on the sand. Nate
studied them. They had the look of beaten men. Most of
them had their eyes closed. Others lay with their hands
beneath their heads listlessly watching the charcoal smoke
curling upward. Despair clutching at his heart like a cold
hand, Nate Gill joined them.

Jennifer Gill rode slowly in a gig back from the shore of
the Long Island Sound toward the prison mine. Jennifer had
bought a rowboat which she had pulled up on the beach at
Herod Point and hidden it in a thicket. In her pocketbook
was her letter of introduction from her father together with a

note she had written for Nate. She felt the pistol bound securely to her thigh and the little bag of bullets and powder just below it.

It was a cold day, and Jennifer wore a plain black coat over her dress of Quaker gray and had a bonnet of the same color on her head. The road she took was deserted until, a few miles from the prison, she saw a carriage approaching also driven by a woman. Jenny gasped. It was Amanda! There was no mistaking that beautiful blond hair tucked up under a red velvet hat with a long gray feather. Amanda also wore a coat of a glistening black fur that Jenny thought might be Russian sable. *How she spends Pa's money!* Jenny thought, and then started when the carriage jolted over a rut in the road, throwing the coat open at the neck to reveal Jenny's pearl necklace.

At once Jenny reined in her horse and drew her gig across the road to block Amanda's path. Amanda quickly stopped her own horse and stood up with her whip in her hand, her face white with fury.

"What do you mean by this?" she shouted angrily, snapping the whip. "Who do you think you are?"

"I'll show you who I am," Jenny said, sweeping her wig off her head and stepping out of her high heels. She shook her head to loosen her soft brown hair.

Amanda was aghast. "Jennifer! What are you doing on Long Island? Why, you could be arrested and put in jail!"

Jenny pointed to Amanda's throat. "Where did you get those pearls?"

Amanda's hand strayed nervously to her throat. She swallowed. "None of your business."

"I know where you got them. From Nate's cousin! Ben Gill!"

"What if I did?"

"Those are *my* pearls! Ben stole them when he broke into the Concord farmhouse and took all the Gill family jewels."

"That's a lie!"

"It is not. Give me those pearls, Amanda."

"I'll do no such thing, you . . . you little fly-by-night . . ."

Jennifer lifted her skirt and unfastened the pistol. She grasped it and leveled it at the astonished Amanda. She held out her hand.

"Give me that necklace, Amanda," Jenny said in a grim voice.

Amanda shrank back in terror, her hand again going to the pearls. Suddenly she became aware of the whip in her hand and snapped it viciously at Jenny. It struck her on the shoulder but the movement caused Amanda to lose her balance. She flailed the air wildly with her arms. But she could not recover, and she toppled off the box onto Jenny. The collision made Jenny's finger tighten on the trigger and the pistol fired. Amanda Courtney sank wordlessly to the ground with a bullet through her heart.

Jennifer knelt beside her, sobbing. "Amanda! Amanda! Speak to me, Amanda!" When there was no answer, Jenny threw herself across her stepmother's body, weeping piteously. "I didn't mean it! I didn't mean it!" she sobbed. "It went off by accident." Jennifer cried for perhaps ten minutes, before she realized that it was dangerous for her to risk being found beside the dead woman. She arose. Then she knelt beside Amanda and gently removed the pearl necklace. She put it in her pocketbook. Then she drew the bag of powder and ball from beneath her skirt and reloaded the pistol, restrapping both to her thigh. Getting to her feet, she unharnessed Amanda's horse and slapped it on the rump, sending it galloping into the woods. Replacing her wig, stepping back into her high heels, she remounted the box of her gig and rode rapidly toward the prison.

When she came to the gate, the sentry challenged her. She showed him the forged letter of introduction from her father. The sentry stepped back and saluted.

"You'll find Lieutenant Bain in the guardroom, ma'am," he said, and Jennifer drove on into a courtyard, getting down and walking to the guardroom. Inside, she presented her letter of introduction.

"Of course, Miss Courtney," the lieutenant said. "I recognize your father's handwriting. What can I do for you?"

"My father has a message for a prisoner named Nathaniel Gill. It's very personal. About his family back in Boston. We . . . we knew each other in those days."

"I understand, ma'am," the lieutenant said. He opened the trapdoor in the floor and called down, "Send Nathaniel Gill up here," turning back to Jenny with a smile.

● ● ●

On his third day in the mine, Nate was surprised to hear the trapdoor open and see the lantern swinging and hear the guard's voice calling: "Gill. Private Nathaniel Gill. Get yer ass up here."

Nate arose wonderingly. What did they want him for? Because of his despairing state of mind, he guessed that his father-in-law was up to some deviltry. Nate began to climb the ladder with slow care, remembering the man who slipped and fell to his death. Maybe his father-in-law was going to have him beaten, Nate thought glumly. Beaten for breakfast. He'd like that, the fat slob. It would make his food taste better if he could see his son-in-law beaten while he was eating.

"C'mon, get a move on!" the guard called, and Nate quickened his pace. Inside the sentry room, he climbed the other ladder to the guardroom. The lieutenant who had signed them in was there, talking to a tall, pretty woman with black hair.

Oh, my God! Nate thought, his eyes widening. It *can't* be. Jenny frowned a warning, and he lowered his eyes.

"This is Miss Jennifer Courtney, daughter of the commanding officer," the officer said to Nate. "She has brought you a message from the commandant. You may read it, but you may not keep it."

Nate bowed stiffly to Jennifer and silently took the note she handed him. He read:

Dearest Natey,
    It's me! Jenny! I have a loaded pistol and a bag of powder and ball tied to my right thigh. I am going to pretend to faint. When I do, you tell the officer to get me some rum. When he does, you take them.

While Nate read, Jenny began to sway back and forth. She put her hand to her heart and closed her eyes. The officer stared at her in concern, and Jenny crumpled to the floor.

"Oh, my God, she's having one of her fits!" Nate cried.

"You know her?" the lieutenant asked in alarm.

"Yes. She's been having fits since she was a little girl. Please, sir—would you fetch her some rum? That's the only thing that helps her."

Without a word, the lieutenant rushed outside and began bellowing for the sergeant-major. Nate rushed to the prostrate

Jenny's side, slid his hand under her skirt and drew forth the pistol. He ran behind the door. When the officer returned and ran to kneel beside Jenny, Nate strode up behind him and put the pistol muzzle at the base of his neck.

"One false move, and you're dead."

The lieutenant stiffened.

"Stand up."

He obeyed.

"Lock the door and give me the key."

The lieutenant obeyed once more.

"Now take off your clothes."

With an embarrassed glance at Jennifer who had risen to her feet, the lieutenant began undressing until he was down to his underclothes. Nate handed the pistol to Jenny who covered the red-faced lieutenant while Nate undressed. Then Nate put on the officer's clothes and Jenny handed him back the pistol. Nate unlocked the door and motioned Jenny to step outside.

"Turn around," Nate ordered the lieutenant. The man hesitated, fear dilating his blue eyes. "Do as I say!" Nate barked. The man swung reluctantly around. Nate seized the pistol by the muzzle and brought it savagely around against the man's temple.

Spaaat!

With a low groan, the lieutenant sank to the ground. Nate dragged his body over the trapdoor to isolate the sentries below. Then he went outside, locked the door and walked nonchalantly toward Jenny waiting nervously in the gig. He got in beside her, seizing the reins and flicking them on the horse's back. The vehicle lurched forward and they drove slowly out of the prison camp. At the gate, a guard snapped to attention and saluted. They drove on.

Both of them gave deep sighs of relief. Jenny put a hand on Nate's thigh and squeezed it. "I'm so proud of you, Natey. You're the bravest man in the world. I saw what Pa did to you at the battery."

"You did? You were in New York?"

"Yes. I came to look for you. I took a job in a tavern as a barmaid. I was on the battery when your prison ship blew up. Oh, Nate—I'm so proud of you. Everyone knows what you said to Benedict Arnold. General Washington had it read out to the whole army."

Nate flushed with pleasure and pride. Then he stiffened. A detail of Queen's Rangers was trotting toward them, led by a sergeant. At once, Nate stopped the gig and seized Jenny, kissing her hungrily on the mouth. With loud chuckles, the Rangers clattered past. Relieved, Nate picked up the reins and started the horse moving again.

"I like playing tricks like that," he said with a laugh.

"I don't think you should ride much farther with me," Jenny said, frowning. "I think you'd better strike out overland. I have a rowboat hidden in a thicket at Herod's Point." She described the area to him, and Nate nodded his head.

"I'll get down as soon as we go around that curve ahead," he said.

Beyond the bend was Amanda's horseless carriage. Jenny drew in her breath. Quickly, she told Nate about the accidental death of her stepmother. Nate stopped the horse. He began to get down, but paused. Both of them had heard the unusual sound of a man weeping. Jenny stood up in the box. She gasped and sat down quickly.

"It's Cousin Ben!"

"Ben! So the dirty liar and thief and all those other things Dan called him is a traitor besides! What's he wearing?"

"Civilian clothes."

"Behind enemy lines! That tears it!"

"Maybe he's a spy for us."

"Ben? Risk the noose for *anything*? *Anybody*? Besides, Dan is in charge of our intelligence. I can't think of him trusting Ben to spy for us. No, Jenny, it's the other way around."

"I guess so," Jenny said in a sorrowing voice. "He's . . . he's just lying there with his arms around her sobbing like a baby. It's . . . it's pitiful . . . even if it is Ben. I guess Amanda knew that Pa was going away somewhere and she arranged a rendezvous."

"You mean tryst," Nate said scornfully. "Now that I think of it, I'll bet it was Ben who told General Gage where we hid our supplies back in seventy-five. Didn't he give your stepmother a beautiful pendant right about the time of Concord and Lexington?" Jenny nodded, just as a horse whinnied. Nate looked quickly to his left and saw a saddled bay mare nosing among a patch of myrtle. "Must be Ben's," he muttered. He got down. "I'm going to grab her. You just drive the gig nonchalantly past Ben. He won't recognize you in your wig. As you pass, and distract him, I'll mount her and ride off." Jenny nodded, tears moisting her eyes. She leaned down to his upturned face and kissed him fondly.

"Back to the war, Natey?" she asked ruefully.

"Yes," he said fiercely, "back to the war. The war we're going to win!"

Jennifer smiled sadly and flicked the reins on the horse's back. She looked straight ahead as she passed Amanda's horseless carriage, pretending not to see Dr. Gill sprawled across her stepmother's body. Benjamin glanced up with reddened misery-filled eyes when he heard the sound of the carriage wheels. He stared dully at the tall, black-haired girl in the box, starting at the sound of his horse whinnying and the thud of galloping hooves.

In an agony of grief and rage, Dr. Benjamin Gill sprang to his feet to put both hands to his coat and tear it from his body.

Chapter Thirty-Two

"I tell you, it was Ben, Cousin Dan! Both Jenny and I saw him. In civilian clothes!"

Colonel Daniel Gill sat behind his field desk, gazing thoughtfully at his fiery young cousin. "You're sure, Nate?"

"Sure as my name's Nathaniel Gill. You didn't send him behind their lines in civilian clothes to spy for you, did you?"

"Ben? I'd sooner trust Benedict Arnold. All right, Nate, I'm going to General Washington with this. We've got Ben at last. Maybe, when we search his quarters, we might find the jewels. That was strange . . . Jenny running into Amanda like that. . . . I wonder if she'll ever wear that necklace, now that her stepmother's blood is on it."

"Jenny's not that squeamish. She's sorry it happened, but she knows it wasn't her fault."

"That's good. Give me strong women like Jenny and Barbara any day. All right, Nate, I'll keep you informed."

Nate turned to go, but spun back around with an eager glint in his eye. "Is it true we're going to attack New York, Dan?"

"That's really not the sort of thing I can talk to you about, Nate," Daniel said gently. "Where'd you hear that?"

"The whole army's talking about it. They're saying while General Greene keeps Lord Cornwallis busy in Virginia, General Washington and Count Rochambeau are going to hit Clinton in New York."

"Well, there was an armed reconnaissance while you were in prison. But I honestly can't tell you the result."

"I understand, Cousin Dan," Nate said, trying to conceal his disappointment. "I'll be waiting to hear from you about Ben."

After Nate had departed, Colonel Gill arose to go into

General Washington's quarters to speak to him about Captain Benjamin Gill. Washington listened quietly to his report.

"Shall I have him arrested, Excellency?" Daniel asked.

"Not immediately," Washington said thoughtfully. Seeing the surprise on his aide's bronzed face, he went on, "He might be more useful to us alive and free. I'm anxious to have Clinton think we're coming at New York."

"I thought you had changed your mind about that, sir."

"I have. The reconnaissance convinced me that Clinton is far too strong for us. Even with Rochambeau's troops, we have only ten thousand. Clinton has fourteen thousand and a fleet. And he has the advantage of the defensive. But I'd like him to think we're coming there. Actually, we may move south. Against Cornwallis in Virginia. He's moved into Yorktown. Lafayette is watching him there." Washington smiled. "We may be onto something big, Daniel. Rochambeau has advised me that Admiral de Grasse is available with the French West Indian Fleet. He's in Haiti, now. If Rochambeau and I can get down to Yorktown without Clinton's knowledge . . . if de Grasse can get into the Chesapeake . . . we'd have Cornwallis bottled up by land and sea."

Colonel Gill's blue eyes glowed. "You'd have him like a pudding in a bag!"

"We would, indeed, Daniel. That's why it's so important to misinform Clinton. That's why this blackguard of a cousin of yours may be an instrument sent from heaven." Washington leaned forward to take a walnut from the bowl on his desk. He cracked it between his palms, his pale eyes calculating. "I have ordered Staten Island to be made into a staging area as though I intended to cross to New York from there. Bake ovens are being built in nearby Chatham, New Jersey, as though for a siege. This, of course, is to deceive Clinton. Actually, I'm going to leave three thousand men above New York. The other two thousand will cross into Jersey and Rochambeau's five thousand will follow. We will pretend to be making a leisurely march to Chatham. Actually, we will head south—at a much faster pace."

"Excellent!" Daniel exclaimed eagerly. "And you want me to make sure my cousin learns of all these plans for New York."

"I do. Get him out to Staten Island and Chatham on some pretext. Make sure he sees the road crews improving the roads to both places. Find a way of getting copies of the correspondence between Rochambeau and me on the New York campaign into his hands."

"I will, Excellency," Daniel said with a grin, rubbing his hands. "I will, in—"

There was a knock on the door and a courier entered, handing Washington a letter. "From Count Rochambeau, Excellency."

Washington eagerly broke the seal and opened the letter, putting on his spectacles. As he read, his eyes shone with excitement.

"De Grasse has left Haiti and is making for the Chesapeake!" he cried in delight. "Twenty-eight big ships and three thousand men! Daniel, we can end the war!"

Because of his experience with Benedict Arnold, Sir Henry Clinton had become wary of American traitors. Clinton had come close to hating Arnold. He suspected that André had lost his life because Arnold had been too careful of his own. He had been sorely tempted to trade Arnold for André, but had not because he wished to encourage American desertions. Unfortunately, the stream of ranking American officers following Arnold into the British camp had not materialized, as Arnold had boasted it would. Only his wife came to his side, exiled from Philadelphia by a Council outraged by Arnold's boasting. Soured by such reverses, Sir Henry Clinton was not especially pleased when Dr. Benjamin Gill came into his presence.

There was no enthusiasm in his voice when he asked, "You have some information for me, Dr. Gill?"

"Yes, Excellency. Very *important* information."

"Yes?" The voice was still tired and unimpressed.

"Washington is going to strike New York!" Benjamin replied eagerly. "Staten Island is being made into a staging area. They're building bake ovens in Chatham, New Jersey, about thirty miles from the Staten Island crossing. All the roads are being improved, Excellency. Washington is going to leave three thousand men above New York, and then he'll march with two thousand and Rochambeau's five thousand for Chatham." Sir Henry Clinton had come forward attentively, a glimmer of interest in his cold eyes. Dr. Gill drew a sheaf of papers from his pocket. "Here, Excellency," he said

with a triumphant air, "are copies of the correspondence between Washington and Rochambeau. All indicate that New
York is their objective."

Now Sir Henry Clinton was impressed. He put on his spectacles to read two of the letters. "Hmmnn," he murmured, removing his glasses and leaning back in his chair. "This seems
quite conclusive." He thought of Cornwallis on the Yorktown
peninsula between the James and York rivers. Quite safe,
Clinton thought. With the Americans and French coming at
New York, Cornwallis was in no danger. If menaced from
the land, the British fleet could still supply or reinforce
him—even evacuate him, if need be. British control of Chesapeake Bay meant easy access to Yorktown by water. Of
course, there was a report that Admiral de Grasse had left
Haiti for the Chesapeake. But Admiral Sir Samuel Hood had
been sent from the West Indies to intercept him. Cornwallis's
position at Yorktown still seemed secure. In fact, Sir Henry
Clinton thought, he might be able to spare some troops for
me.

"I am much obliged to you for this information, Dr. Gill,"
Clinton said. "I shall not neglect to mention it in my report
to Lord George Germain. Your service to the Crown has
been outstanding, sir. You shall be rewarded for it. Your
claims on the Boston properties shall take precedence over all
others, and I am now relieving you of your painful and dangerous mission among the Rebels."

Dr. Gill bowed graciously. "I am most grateful to you, Excellency."

"I have just one more request to make of you. I should like
you to sail to Yorktown to give Lord Cornwallis the same information you have given me. And I should also like you to
convey my request to send three thousand of his troops to me
here in New York. There is a fast frigate leaving on the tide
this afternoon."

Dr. Gill bowed again. "I shall be aboard it, Excellency."

Admiral Sir Samuel Hood arrived at the Chesapeake three
days ahead of Admiral de Grasse. Finding no enemy inside
the bay, Hood withdrew and made for New York, where he
joined the fleet of Admiral Samuel Graves. There were now
nineteen ships of the line in the British fleet. Graves, the sen-

ior officer, took chief command. On August 31, Graves sailed for the Chesapeake. To his horror, he found de Grasse inside.

The Fenchman at once slipped his cables and stood seaward for battle—parading his ships with slow majesty to impress the indecisive Graves with his superior strength. Graves was aware that his nineteen sail and fourteen hundred guns were no match for the Frenchman's twenty-four ships and seventeen hundred guns. Nevertheless, because he held the advantage of being to windward of his enemy, he gave battle.

De Grasse quickly brought his superior firepower to bear. His guns mauled five British ships so badly that Graves broke off the action and withdrew. De Grasse deliberately remained at sea five more days to keep the mouth of the Chesapeake open for the arrival of a French squadron under Admiral de Barras carrying Rochambeau's artillery. After de Barras slipped inside, de Grasse joined him and Graves sailed back to New York.

That was the news contained in the correspondence a hard-riding courier handed to General George Washington as he came hurrying south toward Williamsburg. Washington took the letters with a mixture of hope and trepidation. All the way down from Chatham he had been asking himself a single, fateful question: Where is de Grasse? All the way down he had heard not a single word from the French admiral, on whose appearance off Yorktown the entire war depended. Quietly, Washington broke the letter's seals. He read. He turned with shining eyes to Colonel Gill riding beside him.

"De Grasse is here! He's driven the British off! He's in the Chesapeake with twenty-eight ships and three thousand men! De Barras is here, too! With Rochambeau's guns and my provisions. At last! At last!"

"Hurrah!" Daniel shouted, turning Liberty to ride quickly back to spread the word. Cries of "Hurrah! Hurrah! We've got him! We've got him!" followed his progress to the rear of the column. Soon the American column was singing as it marched into Williamsburg on the James. A few days later Washington and Colonel Gill rode to the landing to greet Rochambeau's soldiers arriving by boat. When Washington saw the French general and his elegant aides approaching, he waved his hat in elation. Rochambeau stepped ashore and the tall American commander ran up to him and embraced him.

"De Grasse is here! And de Barras."

Now French hats went sailing into the air. Rochambeau beamed. "Surely it is the end, *mon Général.*"

"Not quite, my dear Count. But at least it is the beginning of it."

Lord Charles Cornwallis was caught, and he knew it. The realization rubbed him raw when he opened the letter from Sir Henry Clinton brought him by Dr. Gill and read its contents.

"Three thousand men!" he exploded. "Is he daft? He needs them to protect *New York?* From Washington and Rochambeau? Fancy! He must have written this standing on his head." Glancing up at Dr. Gill, he recovered his composure. "That will be all, Doctor. And thank you. I should like you to report to the surgeon-general. I suspect that we shall be needing physicians."

Concealing his dismay, Dr. Gill bowed and departed.

Cornwallis quickly drew a sheet of parchment to him and began writing furiously. It was he who needed reinforcements, he wrote to Sir Henry Clinton, and ships to break the French blockade. So far from sending any troops north, he was concentrating his own forces. He had seven thousand men against a Franco-American force of ten thousand and a powerful fleet. To concentrate, while awaiting reinforcements, he was abandoning his outer redoubts.

General Washington was delighted to find the British outer redoubts empty and he ordered them occupied immediately. On October 6, 1781, the French and the Americans began digging trenches which would enable them to bring their artillery closer to Cornwallis's lines. On October 9 the French on the left opened up. On the right, George Washington approached a loaded cannon with a slow match in his hand. He applied it to the touchhole.

Ba—loom!

With a shriek the American ball sped toward a British frigate on the York River. It sent a geyser of water into the air near its bow. Other shots followed raising more spouts. The frigate upped anchor and took shelter on the Gloucester shore. On the next night, two bigger batteries began roaring. The French set another frigate hopelessly afire and sank two transports. Soon, fifty-two big guns were battering the town. Buildings collapsed . . . soldiers were killed and maimed. Cornwallis was beginning to lose men at the rate of six an hour. He wrote ominously to Clinton, pleading for speedy relief. ". . . against so powerful an attack we cannot hope to make a very long resistance."

But Clinton, astounded when he learned that Washington and Rochambeau were at Yorktown, had only belatedly begun putting a relief force together. The work of refitting the ships proceeded with agonizing slowness. They would not be ready until October 5 . . . then October 8 . . . then 12 . . . On October 17, seven thousand troops were embarked and the troops began dropping down Sandy Hook—only to be forced to wait another two days for favorable tides and winds.

Meanwhile, a Franco-American force now swelled to sixteen thousand men drew closer to Cornwallis's besieged seven thousand. General von Steuben and his engineers opened another parallel only three hundred yards away from Yorktown. As the trench approached the river edge, the Americans toiling in it were raked by fire from two British redoubts close to the water. Washington ordered them stormed in a night attack.

The French were to strike the redoubt on the left while the Americans assaulted the one on the right. Colonel Alexander Hamilton commanded the Americans. He appeared before them at sunset with a bayonet fixed on a stave. Nate Gill and Luke Sawyer noticed that Captain Arthur Walker carried the same weapon. So did many of the other officers.

"Don't load your muskets, men," Hamilton cried. "We're going after them with the bayonet. Remember how the British sneered at the rabble in arms six years ago? Yankee Doodle didn't like to dance to British steel, they said. Well, tonight, we'll give them some cold American steel and see how they like it."

The men cheered. Darkness fell. Sappers and miners carrying axes slipped forward in the darkness. They were to cut through the abatis protecting the redoubts. These were the tops of big trees pointing outward with sharpened limbs. Nate and Luke lay down in the darkness waiting for the signal to move out. It came. Three shells.

"Up, up and out," Captain Walker called softly.

His soldiers stole forward silently. They heard the ringing

of the sappers' axes. When they reached the abatis they found a passage cleared through it—just as the British opened fire.

"Forward, men!" Alexander Hamilton shouted, swinging his makeshift bayonet.

Nate Gill ran forward. Shells exploded around him. He heard men screaming. Oddly, men began disappearing as though yanked from the earth. Nate wondered why, until his feet flew out from under him and he fell into a deep pit. He lay there momentarily, the wind knocked out of him. Suddenly he realized that they were attacking through a field gouged by huge American shells. More enemy shells howled overhead, but Nate arose and climbed out of the shellhole. A British ball went shrieking over his head not six inches above it. Nate could see it, a red blob in the black. British musketry twinkled ahead of him like fireflies in the night. He came to the parapet and threw himself over it. A kneeling grenadier fired at him but missed. He jumped to his feet and charged with his bayonet. Nate struck downward with his own blade, deflecting it, then upward into the man's neck. The grenadier sank to the ground both hands clutching at his torn throat. Suddenly, as though in a single miraculously instant, a marvelous silence squelched all the screeching, banging, booming, yelling, hideous din of battle. The redoubt had surrendered. A few seconds later on the left, French voices were raised in triumph.

"*Vive le Roi!*" they cried. "*Vive le Général Washington!*"

Cheers rose from the Americans. Nathaniel Gill groped through the dark until he found Luke Sawyer. He embraced him.

"We've won!" We've won!" Nate cried, tears of joy springing to his eyes. "Luke! Luke! It's all over! We've fought our last battle."

Dr. Benjamin Gill glanced up from his desk in the infirmary. The appearance of an ample figure in the open doorway had blocked out the light by which he had been reading a medical report.

"Joel, what brings you here? Good Lord, man, you look terrible."

"I feel terrible," Joel Courtney said, sinking wheezing into a chair opposite Benjamin. Courtney's misery was reflected in his face, not his still obese body. His eyes were unhappy, there were new lines to either side of his nose, his cheeks hung in dewlaps and his thick lips were cracked. "I just wanted to say good-bye. I'm going to London."

"London! Good God, man, have you lost your mind? Cornwallis is going to surrender in a few days. He has to. That breakout attempt last night was the last straw. Clutching at a straw, that's what it was. Cross the river and break through the Yankees and the French at Gloucester, then make New York by forced marches. Out of his mind. Thank God the storm broke it up."

"But I am going to London, Ben. I resigned my commission two months ago. I'm a civilian, now."

"You're a Tory. Cornwallis will have to give up his Tories."

"What about yourself. If they find you here . . ."

"They won't," Dr. Gill said grimly. "My dear cousins would like nothing better than to put my neck in a noose. Rebel slime! They'd never have made it without the help of France."

"Well, they did," Joel said with a helpless gesture. "And I'm a ruined man. My fortune and my wife are gone. I'm a pauper and a widower. And when I arrive in London I'll be just another petitioner asking the king to reward my loyalty."

"You keep talking about London," Benjamin said irritably. "You've got to know there's a French fleet out there."

"I've made a deal with a blockade-runner. He took my last shilling, the scoundrel. He says he had no trouble running the British blockade and the French should be no problem."

"Very interesting. Where is this invaluable gentleman?"

"His sloop is tied up at the Gill Plantation on the James. I suppose that would be your cousin."

"Yes. Dear, dear Cousin Daniel," Benjamin sneered, opening a desk drawer and extracting a sheaf of letters. He handed one to Joel. "You may find this interesting."

Joel Courtney's face blanched as he read. "You blackguard!" he cried, his jowls trembling. He made as though to tear the letter in pieces.

"Go ahead, Joel," Benjamin said, holding up the thick sheaf with a malicious smile. "Sam Adams was quite a letter writer. Another one more or less won't make much difference."

"You thief! Where did you get them?"

"From your desk. I couldn't believe that you would leave such damning documents lying around."

"Confound it! I told Amanda to bring them. We were at sea before she remembered she'd forgotten."

"Serves you right for trusting Amanda with anything important. Poor dear scatterbrain. Her head was full of cotton, hay and rags."

"Give me those letters!" Joel demanded.

"I will indeed. In exchange for your berth on the blockade-runner."

"Never! By God, you won't stop at anything, will you? First you're a thief, and now you're a blackmailer!"

"I must admit it's an unfamiliar profession," Benjamin said with a suave smile. "But I shall try to do my utmost in it. Now, if you will, Joel, your passage . . ." Joel hesitated, his hand straying to his coat pocket. "If the king were to read these," Benjamin said, tapping the letters against his hand, "he might not think too highly of your loyalty. He might even be inclined to . . . ah . . ." Joel Courtney's fat hand went to his thick neck. He withdrew it and dug it into the pocket, bringing out a written agreement between himself and the blockade-runner. He handed it to Benjamin.

"The letters," he said in a croaking voice.

Benjamin handed them to him. Joel stuffed them into his pocket, breathing heavily. He started to rise, but sank back into his chair, perspiring freely. With an effort, he struggled to his feet, swaying. He clutched his heart. With a loud groan he toppled over on his face. Dr. Gill knelt beside him to open his shirt and place a hand on his heart. He arose, shrugging.

"I always told him he ate too much," he murmured aloud. Then he stepped over Joel's prostrate body to go outside to his horse, thinking: Wouldn't it be fun to burn Cousin Danny's fine house down to the ground?

Colonel Daniel Gill was alarmed. His head slave had located him and told him that an American gentleman had appeared at the Gill Plantation and gone aboard the sloop docked there. The slave had brought lunch aboard the ship as its captain had paid him to do and he had heard the gentleman bragging about his plans to set fire to the mansion.

"He say he your cousin, Massa," the slave said.

"He is," Daniel said grimly, and immediately requested

permission from General Washington to ride to the plantation.

"It sounds risky, Daniel," the general said.

"Not at all, Excellency. I'll take a path I'm sure the British don't know about. It's a shortcut through a swamp full of snakes. The British don't like snakes." He laughed. "My grandfather always said there are no snakes in Ireland because St. Patrick drove them all over to England."

Washington smiled. "All right, Daniel—but hurry back. Tomorrow we apply the crusher."

Before riding off, Daniel borrowed a cavalry saber from a brother staff officer. "Much better than a sword when there's snakes around," he explained. Mounting Liberty, he rode off toward the James. Soon he was trotting through the swamp. A murky light filtered down through the tangle of trees overhead. Daniel could hear bobwhites singing. Suddenly, Liberty shied—and Daniel saw a water moccasin alongside with raised head. His mouth was open, a sign that he was disturbed. Daniel could see the cottony white insides of it. He swung his saber viciously and cut the serpent in two.

Outside the swamp Daniel sighed with relief when he saw the chimneys of his mansion rising above the gleaming surface of the river. He urged Liberty forward. Cantering up the broad lawn he saw the "gentleman" with a gang of slaves piling wood against the building. Daniel Gill smiled.

"Cousin Ben!" he shouted, drawing his saber. "I've come for you! You thief!" he yelled, laughing wildly and slashing the air with his blade. "You murderer!" *Slash.* "You liar!" *Slash.* "You filthy fratricide!" *Slash.*

At once, Benjamin mounted his horse and drew his sword. "But, my dear Cousin," he cried as Daniel approached, "you forgot to mention arson." He bowed mockingly and pointed to the pile of wood against the mansion. "I shall burn your dear, dear carcass in the ruins of your lovely home."

With the same feigned indifference which he had assumed in their first duel, Benjamin rode slowly toward Daniel with lowered blade. Daniel struck at it lightly. The clang made Liberty prick up his ears. There was another clash of steel. Liberty tossed his head. He seemed to be enjoying the duel. Suddenly Daniel realized that Major Pitcairn's horse probably had been trained in the movements of the Spanish drill ring.

He could give his horse his head, freeing him to concentrate on fighting.

Benjamin thrust quickly at Daniel. Liberty backed off and Daniel easily struck the blade down with his saber. He swung hard at Benjamin. Dr. Gill deflected the saber upward, thrusting again. But he was too far away. At once Daniel brought his saber down on Benjamin's sword. Benjamin winced. Daniel laughed.

"Not the same on horseback, is it Cousin Ben? Those clever feet of yours are useless now." He swung viciously in a whistling stroke at Dr. Gill's sword. It struck with a ringing clangor. Benjamin winced once more. His face whitened. Again and again, Daniel aimed powerful blows at Benjamin's blade. He made no attack on his cousin's body, seeking only to break his sword in two. Benjamin's face turned whiter and whiter. He was breathing hard. At last, he turned his horse and attempted to flee to the river. Liberty overtook him easily, and now Daniel Gill rose high in the saddle to bring his saber down with a mighty slash at the point where Benjamin's neck joined his shoulder. With a hideous scream, Dr. Benjamin Gill fell from his horse.

Daniel reined in Liberty and dismounted. He cautiously approached the dying man, his saber still in his hand. He had no pity.

"Where are the jewels?" he asked.

Benjamin's eyes were rolling upward, but they moved involuntarily toward his horse. Daniel's followed them and saw a square bulge in the saddle bag. He walked toward it, undid the bag and withdrew the teakwood box. He opened it, examined the contents briefly and then closed the lid and put it under his arm.

"Good-bye, Cousin Ben," he said softly, standing over Dr. Gill's shuddering body. "Say hello to the devil for me."

On the morning of October 17, 1781, the day the ships of Clinton's relief force began to drop down Sandy Hook, General Washington's allied artillery battered Yorktown with a fearsome bombardment. One by one the British works collapsed. There was no answering fire because the British had no more ammunition. Nate Gill and Luke Sawyer watched the dreadful cannonade with awe in their eyes.

"Thank God it's them and not us," Nate shouted above the uproar. Suddenly he saw a red-coated British drummer boy stride out on the parapet beating a parley.

"This is it, Luke!" Nate yelled exultantly, pounding his friend on the back. "It's all over!"

At sight of the drummer, the allied guns fell silent. A British officer advanced to be blindfolded and taken to General Washington.

"His Lordship asks for a truce of twenty-four hours," he said.

"I shall grant him two," Washington replied coldly. "After which, I shall resume the bombardment."

The officer bowed and withdrew. He returned with Cornwallis's surrender terms, including the condition that his army be returned to Britain on parole. Washington refused, and Cornwallis agreed to surrender his soldiers as prisoners of war.

Two days later the gay music of the French sang out and the vivacious French soldiery went into line for the last time on American soil. Opposite them, moving to the Celtic lilt of fifes and rums, tall Americans in hunting shirts and uniforms of buff and blue came into position. Nate Gill and Luke Sawyer stood proudly in the front rank of Captain Walker's company. They saw General Washington ride up on a great bay horse and halt to their right. Nate's eyes filled with proud tears when he saw Colonel Daniel Gill ride past on Liberty, the crest of the Gill family prominently displayed on his green-and-gold saddlecloth. It made Nate think of home. Of his valiant grandfather, Jedediah Gill, and the fighting family he had founded . . . of his brave father and uncle . . . of Barbara who had made the saddlecloth for Cousin Dan . . . but most of all of Jenny. Jenny! Jenny! Jenny! Nate's head turned slightly north toward her, and now the full thick tears flowing down his cheeks were of love as well as pride. Jenny and Mark! Mark, another Gill to serve the beloved country being born before his eyes. And Mark's cousin: George Washington Half Moon Gill. He, too, would bring more honor to the family name. No more Cousin Bens! No more Judases! Only honor! Honor and glory!

On the French side, General Rochambeau and Admiral de Barras sat their horses. To their right Yorktown's main sally ports were flung open. Faint on the wind came the squeal of

fifes and rattle of drums. Out rode Brigadier General Charles
O'Hara. No Cornwallis? Nate asked himself indignantly. Too
much a blueblood to surrender to "Mr." Washington? What
else could you expect of a spoiled baby of a British lord?

O'Hara rode toward Rochambeau, but the count graciously
inclined his head toward Washington. Flustered, O'Hara approached Washington. The tall Virginian indicated General
Benjamin Lincoln. Deputy must surrender to deputy. O'Hara
handed him Cornwallis's sword, and Lincoln promptly returned it.

Now the enemy soldiery came out. First, the Hessians, brilliant in blue and green, striding briskly to stack their arms,
mercenary troops uncaring of the disgrace of defeat. Then
the British, moving slowly, their faces sullen, some of them
weeping. Down went their weapons in a disorderly crash.
Drummer boys kicked holes in their drums. Red-coated soldiers smashed their musket butts and stomped on their cartridges. Pouting officers with boyish faces avoided the eyes of
their captors. Suddenly the British bands began to play.

Nathaniel Gill listened to the tune. A grin game over his
face and his eyes danced. It was his and Luke's favorite song.
It made Nate think of the wine cellar they broke into and the
night they ate their shoes. Beside him, Luke Sawyer began to
hum it and then sing it softly. Nate joined him. Soon, to the
astonishment of Captain Arthur Walker, his entire company
was singing.

> I roved from fair to fair
> Likewise from town to town
> And then I married me a wife
> And the world turned upside down.

Actual Historical Characters

Adams, John; signer of the Declaration of Independence and second President of the United States

Adams, Samuel; signer of the Declaration of Independence

André, John; British major executed as a spy

Allen, Solomon; American lieutenant who guarded André

Arnold, Benedict; American general and traitor

Arnold, Edward Shippen; son of above

Barras, Comte de; French admiral

Barrett, James; American militia colonel

Beaumarchais, Pierre Augustin Caron de; French playwright who supplied Americans

Brown, Timothy; American militia captain

Burgoyne, John; British general

Cadwalader, George; American general

Cahoon, Joseph; farmer who refused to row André to safety

Cahoon, Samuel; brother of above

Carroll, Charles; signer of the Declaration of Independence

Clinton, Sir Henry; British general

Conway, Thomas; American general

Cornwallis, Sir Charles; British general

Davis, Issac; American militia captain killed at Concord

Dawes, William; American courier who rode with Paul Revere

Dearborn, Henry; American militia captain

Erskine, Sir William; British general

Franklin, Benjamin; signer of the Declaration of Independence

Franks, David; American major and aide to Benedict Arnold

Fraser, Simon; British general killed at Saratoga

Gage, Thomas; British general

Galloway, Joseph; signer of the Declaration of Independence who later joined the British

Gates, Horatio; American general

Gerrish, Samuel; American colonel
Gerry, Elbridge; signer of the Declaration of Independence
Grasse, Comte de; French admiral
Greene, Nathaniel; American general
Glover, John; American colonel
Gridley, Richard; American colonel
Hamilton, Alexander; American officer and first Secretary of the Treasury
Hancock, John; president of the Continental Congress
Harcourt, William; British colonel
Harrison, Benjamin; signer of the Declaration of Independence
Heister, Philip de; Hessian general
Hosmer, Abner; American drummer killed at Concord
Hood, Samuel; British admiral
Howe, Lord Richard; British admiral
Howe, Sir William; British commander
Hunt, Abraham; Tory merchant in Trenton
Jameson, John; American lieutenant colonel
Jasper, Sergeant; American soldier who rescued the flag at Charleston
Jefferson, Thomas; author of the Declaration of Independence and third President of the United States
King, Joshua; American lieutenant to whom André confessed
Knox, Henry; American artillery general
Lafayette, Marquis de; French noble who served as an American general
Lamb, John; American colonel at West Point
Larvey, James; American corporal who rowed Arnold to safety
Laurie, Captain; British officer
Lee, Charles; American general
Lincoln, Benjamin; American general
Louis XVI; King of France
Martin, Catherine; Benedict Arnold's housekeeper
Matlack, Timothy; member of the Pennsylvania Council
Matlack, William; American sergeant
Mawhood, Charles; British lieutenant colonel
McCarthy, Mary; wife of British prisoner who helped Arnold
McHenry, James; American major and aide to Washington
Mease, James; American clothier-general
Mercer, Hugh; American general
Miller, Andreas; owner of farmhouse where André slept
Mitchell, John; American wagon-master
Moncton, Henry; British lieutenant colonel killed at Monmouth

Morgan, Daniel; American commander of sharpshooters
Morris, Robert; Philadelphia financier
Moultrie, William; American colonel
Murphy, Timothy; American sharpshooter
O'Hara, Charles; British general
Parker, Sir Peter; British admiral
Parker, Jonas; American militia captain killed at Lexington
Paulding, John; American who helped capture André
Percy, Earl; British general
Piel, Jacob; Hessian lieutenant
Pigot, Sir Robert; British general
Pitcairn, John; British major killed at Bunker Hill
Pollard, Asa; American soldier killed at Bunker Hill
Prescott, William; American colonel
Putnam, Israel; American general
Rall, Johann; Hessian colonel
Revere, Paul; American courier
Robinson, Beverly; Tory colonel
Rochambeau, Comte de; French troop commander
Rodney, Caesar; signer of the Declaration of Independence
Scammel, Alexander; American colonel in charge of André's
   execution
Shaw, Samuel; American major and aide to Washington
Shewell, Robert; accomplice of Benedict Arnold
Shippen, Edward; Philadelphia lawyer and judge
Shippen, Peggy; daughter of above, wife of Benedict Arnold
Smith, Francis; British lieutenant colonel
Smith, Joshua Hett; accomplice of Benedict Arnold
Stirling, Lord; American general
Stark, John; American colonel
Steuben, Friedrich von; Washington's drillmaster
Sullivan, John; American general
Sutherland, Andrew; British naval captain
Tallmadge, Major; American intelligence officer
Tarleton, Banastre; British cavalry leader
Varick, Richard; American colonel, secretary to Benedict
   Arnold
Vergennes, Comte de; French foreign minister
Ward, Artemas; American general
Warren, Dr. Joseph; chairman of the Committee of Public
   Safety
Washington, George; American commander-in-chief and first
   President of the United States

About the Author

Born in 1920, Robert Leckie grew up in Rutherford, N.J., where at sixteen he began working as a sportswriter for *The Record* of Bergen County. Mr. Leckie joined the Marines on Pearl Harbor Day, 1941, and served nearly three years in the Pacific as a machine gunner and scout for the First Marine Division, being both wounded and decorated. From that experience came *Helmet for My Pillow*, a personal narrative of the war which he wrote while pursuing his postwar career as a newspaperman and newsreel editor. With its publication in 1957, Mr. Leckie devoted himself full time to writing and has since had more than thirty books published, most of them on military history, as well as short stories and articles.

Mr. Leckie, who attended New York University and Fordham, is married to the former Vera Keller. They have three grown children and live in Byram Township, New Jersey.

Mr. Leckie is the author of *The Bloodborn*, the first novel in Signet's Americans at War Series, and is currently at work on volume three.